C0-AUF-821

The Anarchist

Also by Daniel A. Coleman

Ecopolitics: Building a Green Society

The Anarchist

A Novel

by

Daniel A. Coleman

Willowbrook Press

Chapel Hill, North Carolina

This is a work of fiction. All the characters and events portrayed in this novel are either fictitious or are used fictitiously.

The Anarchist
copyright 2001 by Daniel A. Coleman
all rights reserved

Published by Willowbrook Press
P.O. Box 17211
Chapel Hill, NC 27516

Publisher's Cataloging-in-Publication
(Provided by Quality Books, Inc.)

Coleman, Daniel A.
    The anarchist : a novel / by Daniel A. Coleman. --
1st ed.
    p. cm.
    LCCN 2001089488
    ISBN 0-9709781-0-3

    1. Anarchism--Fiction. 2. Presidents--United States
--Assassination--Fiction. 3. Criminal psychology--
Fiction. 4. Historical Fiction. I. Title

PS3553.O47388A53 2001   813'.6
                                     QBI01-700477

To Micah Asher Jules Coleman

The dawning day still found me pacing my cell, Leon's beautiful face, pale and haunted, before me.

Emma Goldman, *Living My Life*

Preface

~

Tuesday, October 29, 1901

I did not want to be there, not for a minute. But Dr. Gerin had insisted it was part of my training and he and I had been the first to arrive. Empty, the room had seemed a grim place, with a palpable presence of death. That feeling was now masked by the slight activity of the couple dozen men who had filled it. Jonesy stood stoically by my side, his light-hearted persona for the moment obscured. Nearby, a man fiddled with his watch, taking it out of the pocket of his waistcoat, giving it a slight twirl, and putting it back. Closer to the door, another played with the thick curve of his waxed moustache. By the far wall, two men spoke in hushed tones. The last to enter had been the chaplain whose ministries had been repeatedly rejected over the preceding weeks. Even so, his faith insisted on the value of his silent prayers. Only Dr. Gerin, my mentor, seemed fully engaged in the event at hand. He stood poised by the door in anticipation.

Jones placed a hand reassuringly on my shoulder.

"Parker, you're trembling," he whispered.

I mustered a grim smile across my clenched teeth and nodded in agreement.

A moment later, the steel door swung open and Warden Mead walked quickly in followed by Collins, the Superintendent of Prisons. Collins surveyed the room, gauging the mood of those present. He instructed us to stay in our places and trust everything to the hands of the officials. Around the chamber, heads bobbed uneasily in assent.

Collins turned back to the open doorway and beckoned to those waiting unseen in the long, dimly-lit corridor beyond. Two guards entered, tough old Tupper, the Principal Keeper, and a younger man whom I didn't recognize. Between them, they half led, half dragged Leon into the room. Two more guards followed behind. They pushed the prisoner roughly into the waiting chair, his head thrown against the seat back with an audible thud.

Leon's gaze scanned the room, sad and defiant as if attempting to register his presence in the minds of the strangers who had been called together as his final witnesses. Finally, his eyes found my own and locked onto them as if they were the one island in a perilous sea. The look could not have held for more than a moment, but it spoke loudly, as if to say "remember me and the deed I have done." I could feel the perspiration beading up on my forehead, the tension churning in my stomach. Meanwhile, the guards methodically tightened the thick, leather straps around his arms, legs, and chest as if he were little more than a parcel being secured for transport. The rubbing of the leather against the wooden chair and the clink of the metal clasps as they were firmly fastened echoed loudly in the surrounding silence. My pulse pounded in my ears. My vision blurred, only to be pulled back into focus as the Superintendent finally approached the prisoner.

Chapter One

~

Saturday, September 7, 1901

Few of us see our lives as a part of history. For most,
history is something we were forced to study in school in a bleary-
eyed recitation of dates, names, and places. Some say they are
"bored to death" by it, ironically failing to recognize that it is
usually only in dying that one can transcend the study of history
and become a part of its content. A few were, and remain,
enthralled by its twists and turns, its powers and personalities, and
its seemingly endless depth of detail. We are taught that history
happened long ago, probably before we were born, and that it
happened to someone else. It is a foreign land, the home of heroes,
the abode of an Alexander, a Caesar, a Lincoln. Ordinary people
are rarely the subject of history and thus we give little thought to
how it carries along and shapes our own lives. Even less do we
comprehend how our own actions, however insignificant they may
seem, are shaping the course of historic events. It is as if we were
on a different plane, witnessing history's unfolding but with no
recourse to the provinces of the great. Still, some come to see
themselves and history differently. A McKinley or a Roosevelt
perhaps views history as a mountain to be climbed, much like
Teddy's own fabled charge up San Juan Hill. They seek above all
else to erect a monument on that mountain top where future
generations will see their mark. And then there is Leon. Did he
assert himself onto a field for which he was never born, or did he
stumble, madly perhaps, into infamy? Certainly, a place in history
was never his conscious goal. As for myself, I know all too well how
history lifted me up for that brief, private moment, shook me
firmly, and set me down a new man.

~

September 7, 1901, was one of those bleak days I grew to expect in Auburn--overcast and dreary. I almost wished it would rain just to break the monotony. The low cloud cover obscured the otherwise bright, lush hills, and the sweet, clear streams that ran down to the shores of Lake Owasco. In upstate New York, the first week of September holds many a magnificent day. This was not among them.

Like the day, I brooded. All morning I'd sat silently and stared out the window of the room our landlady, Mrs. Thomas, had agreed would serve as a study when Jones and I each rented a bedroom for the semester. The gray clouds exhausted my attention much as they seemed to drain the color from the green leaves and late summer flowers. The psychology text I'd opened dutifully at dawn, now, at mid-morning, rested ponderously on my lap, little more than a prop in a tableau of tedium, its pages curling in the late summer humidity. William James' *Principles of Psychology* (even this abridged version we called the "Jimmy" as contrasted with the truly massive "James") was a volume of great weight, in both senses of the word. My eyes had glazed over and I had lost my focus midway through James' discussion of will:"If we believe that the end is in our power, we *will* that the desired feeling, having or doing shall be real, and real it presently becomes."

Even my usually coveted cup of morning coffee sat on the small wooden table by my side half empty, a swirl of brown coagulation forming across the top. My thoughts were too unfocused, too dim and diffuse, to leave any lasting impression. For the past few months I had felt like someone waking from a long, unplanned nap. Previously, I had sailed through college and the first few years of medical school, happy to hold to the course my father had set for me. Now, with another graduation looming ahead the coming spring, the question was taking shape as to just what my life would ultimately be about. It was a question I was not quite ready to ask and certainly not prepared to answer. Perhaps, as the eminent psychologist maintained, it was a matter of gathering my will to break loose from this sluggish stream of consciousness.

My reverie was jarred a bit by the sight of Ezzie coming into view. She slunk low along the fence, stalking some unseen prey. I could spend hours watching Mrs. T's cat, self-declared mistress of the household. A cuddly if demanding purr-pillow when indoors, she transformed herself into a fierce huntress once outside. It was the outdoor beast that most entranced me--the infinite patience, the perfect concentration, her full being gathered for a single strike and, often failing in the attempt, her contentment at beginning all over again. I envied those few people whom I imagined might share those qualities, ones I saw dismally lacking in myself. In my more philosophical moments I compared Ezzie's twin abilities to relax and focus with my inability to attain either state in the last year of medical school. A tense malaise had definitely been my lot during the past months.

Ezzie now zeroed in on her target. She crouched low on her haunches mapping her strike. Somehow feeding on her liveliness, my tired brain perked up a notch and I picked up the nearby cup, oblivious to its now somewhat disagreeable contents, and slowly lifted it toward my lips. At that moment, Ezzie leaped forward with a shrill feline war-cry, the study door burst open without warning, and I, turning one way and then the other, wound up with tepid coffee covering my shirt and dripping down onto the textbook.

"Oh dear," said a flustered Mrs. Thomas. She pulled the ever-present rag from her apron waist band and began to wiping up the coffee. "Mr. Parker, I'm so sorry. I wanted to make sure you'd heard the news."

I rubbed my sleeve hard against the wet pages hoping to prevent a stain from marring the book. "As far as I'm concerned, the big news here is that I'm soaking wet."

"It's the President. He's been shot."

I was speechless for a moment while it sunk in.

"President McKinley?" This news was unbelievable. "Who would do such a thing? McKinley's been in Buffalo, hasn't he? At the Exposition?"

"He was in Buffalo, but that's all I know. Mrs. Casey who told me didn't know any details. That's why I thought you might run downtown and bring back some news."

"What about Jones? Is he still here?"

"No, your friend went out around an hour ago. I was straightening up his room when Mrs. Casey came by."

I was more than ready to go out in search of the latest information. I grabbed the textbook under my arm and ran up the stairs two at a time to my room. My head spun with wild speculation over Mrs. T's news. Who could have done such a deed? Was McKinley still alive? If not, what kind of president would Roosevelt make? What if a foreign power was behind the assassination? Could it mean another war? My excitement was boosted by the relief of leaving my studies behind. The spell cast by the gloomy weather was broken, and, after setting the "Jimmy" out to dry and putting on a clean shirt, I left the boarding house and walked at a brisk pace down North Street toward town.

As I turned up Genesee Street, I saw the familiar lanky form of Jones up ahead. "Jonesy!" I called out. "Wait for me."

He turned and, seeing me down the street, stopped to wait. I quickened my pace. A newspaper boy hawking the latest edition called out for my attention.

"President shot in Buffalo! Read all about it!"

I was about to stop to purchase a copy, but Jones waved his arms to show me that he already held a paper in his hands. A moment later I was at his side.

"I see you've heard about the assassination," I said. Before my friend could reply, I grabbed the paper from his hands. In the largest typeface I'd ever seen, the headline blared out, "McKinley Twice Shot By Assassin." The subhead read, "Dastardly Attempt on Life of the President at Buffalo."

"This is incredible," I said, momentarily mesmerized by the headlines. I started to skim through the lead article. Jones interrupted before I could get far.

"Come on, there'll be time for that. Let's go over to O'Malley's and see if anyone's heard more since the paper came out."

"Just a moment..." I'd reached the section discussing the would-be assassin and had to know something about the man who could do such a deed. "My God, it's an anarchist! Another Bresci."

"So they say. I'd hoped regicide was one fashion that we'd leave to the Europeans."

In the couple of minutes it took to reach the saloon, Jonesy began to fill me in on the few details he'd learned. The President had been shot late in the afternoon the previous day. He was shot twice and rushed away for treatment. Not much was known yet about his condition, but there was hope that he would survive. The assassin, a solitary gunman, had been immediately apprehended and was in the Buffalo jail. Vice-president Roosevelt was returning from a hunting trip in the Adirondacks.

"Do you think he's sane?" Jonesy asked after he'd laid out what he knew.

"Who, TR?" I grinned.

"Not Roosevelt!" Jones punched my arm. "The assassin."

"Would-be assassin, you mean. Don't really have anything to go on, of course. Maybe he is. Maybe not. If you'd let me finish the article, I might have something on which to base an opinion. Have you heard anything besides what's in the paper?"

"No, that's it. But there's got to be more news since it rolled off the press. If only we were back in New York. Then we'd get all the news right away." O'Malley's appeared just ahead, it's familiar wooden sign swinging in the breeze.

O'Malley's saloon was a discovery I had shared with Jones shortly after we arrived to begin our internship. In our first weeks in Auburn, we'd learned that it was a place where we could count on finding a diverse cross-section of townsfolk congregating. Cheap food and liquor as well as Dan O'Malley's own gregarious nature encouraged the patrons to freely discuss, debate, shout, lampoon, and generally debauch. No topic was too sacred or too profane for the crowd at O'Malley's. At first, this all-purpose bar-restaurant-gathering place had been a shock to my citified sensibilities. I was accustomed to restaurants where you could dine comfortably while the hum of neighboring conversation stayed politely in the background, and to taverns which, if noisy, nonetheless maintained a certain decorum. There was no lack of these more sedate establishments in Auburn, notably the dining rooms at the Osborne House and the Empire State Hotel. Not that there weren't quiet times at O'Malley's--if you wanted to eat at 2 or 3 in the afternoon, that is.

But the first time I had encountered O'Malley's, only two weeks earlier, it was just about high noon. After less than a week in Auburn, I was already tired of Mrs. T's bland cooking. Despite the fact that her meals were prepaid for the semester, I found myself desperate to vary my diet. I told her I was going for a mid-day jaunt through town and wondered where I might get a bite to eat. Mrs. Thomas looked up from her mending.

"Why don't I pack a sandwich for you?" Her reply was less a question than a proclamation. For her, frugality was the highest virtue.

"Thanks, but I think I'd like to eat out today. Part of exploring a new place is sampling the local cuisine."

"Well, you know I don't get out much, what with cooking every day for my boarders." Mrs T sighed, resigning herself to my intentions. "On your budget you might try O'Malley's. I know his wife who says he serves a nice, hot meal. You'd better stay away from the liquor though."

She laughed when I asked for directions. "You're not in New York anymore. This is Auburn, son. Just walk down Genesee Street. You can't miss it."

She was right. I strolled past the compact group of shops that occupied the ground floors of the two and three-story brick buildings that defined downtown Auburn. Scanning the brightly striped awnings and storefronts for my destination, I soon spied a lightly-stained wooden shingle swinging in the breeze with "Tavern" painted on it. Curving across the window in ornate etched letters was the single word "O'Malley's."

An envelope of noise surrounded the small clapboard building, emerging through the broken screen door that stood propped open in front. I stepped just across the threshold and struggled to orient myself. The scene was like a bizarre cross between a family reunion and an open-air market. I stood by the door for a minute trying to get a sense of the layout of the establishment and the decorum of its patrons. Laughter and conversation flew back and forth across the room. An old fellow at one end of the bar thought nothing of raising his voice to be heard by a man seated at the far corner table. Getting my bearings at last, I wove my way through a maze of ragtag tables and chairs to find an open space at the bar.

The beefy, powerfully-built, be-jowled fellow behind the bar, Dan O'Malley himself I soon learned, caught my eye. He looked like he'd been eating too much of his own cooking. "What'll it be, son?"

"What are the choices?" I replied warily.

"Food or drink?" O'Malley wiped his thick hands on a stained white apron.

"I'm hoping for lunch."

"Today I've got a thick beef stew with lots of potatoes. The bread is fresh yesterday. Guaranteed to fill you up and get you through the day." O'Malley spoke with just a hint of a soft brogue that indicated that his parents were probably Irish immigrants. A middle-aged man, a couple of decades in Auburn had made him sound like one of those second-generation Americans, their voices like old seashells, eroded practically smooth, with only a hint of contour and texture remaining to indicate the nature of the creature that had cast it off. That his proffered fare would fill me up, I could believe.

A savory aroma of stew wafted through the room. "All right," I said.

O'Malley served up a big bowl of stew and a thick piece of brown bread. "Two bits," he announced, handing me a spoon. I gave him a quarter and headed to an empty table near the fireplace at the far side of the bar. My lips puckered in enjoyment of the pungent stew, a nice change of pace from to Mrs. T's usually dull fare. The bread, a bit hard around the edges, succumbed readily to the hot broth of the stew.

I ate quickly, all the while fidgeting in my chair, my social discomfort translated into a physical unease. The chair itself, a well-worn straight-back, was fine. Given the saloon's evident lack of social boundaries, I could not help listening in on the conversation. Someone had recently returned from the Pan-American Exposition in Buffalo, and the bar-room discussion revolved around that prominent event.

"The kids just loved it," he was saying, "The boat ride through the canals was great fun. Tom and Bobby were crazy for the Trip to the Moon. Oh, and the African Village. What an elaborate affair that is. They've got nearly 100 natives from a dozen tribes. They do all their dances and show off their crafts. They were weaving cloth and carving ivory. The boys really liked seeing the weapons--spears, axes, swords--and the musical instruments, all kinds of whistles, horns, and bells. They got a real kick out of some of the tribal names, Bojokwe, Baluba, real strange sounding names. They'd like nothing better than to go back for another visit."

"The Exposition's been great for me, too, " called out a thin man at the bar. "My boys are working extra hard getting the apples in. I told them if we had a big enough harvest, we could go to Buffalo. Can't really afford it, of course, but it's not the kind of

event that's likely to come our way again any time soon.
Something to tell the grandchildren about."

"Well you'd better not wait too long," the first fellow said.
"The whole business is scheduled to shut down November 2nd, and,
I'll tell you, some of those big, fancy, make-shift buildings look like
they're about to blow away any day now."

I sat in my corner with my meal, not saying anything, not
feeling ready or able to break into the camaraderie. The discussion
of the tribal displays struck me as somewhat sordid. I'd read the
debates surrounding Rudyard Kipling's poem, *The White Man's
Burden*, and agreed with those who thought it reflected an attitude
comparable to that of the defenders of slavery a half century
earlier. Much as I believed in the progress represented by European
and American civilization, there seemed to be a fine line separating
paternalistic good will from an overweening arrogance. Too many
slipped all too easily across that line.

"And the lights!" the speaker continued. "You wouldn't
believe all the lights." The Exposition was, if nothing else, a
celebration of the work of Thomas Edison. It blazed at night with
electric bulbs that covered most buildings from foundation to
rooftop. It was an awesome sight to these country folk. As the fair's
designers intended, they saw in the brilliant display the bright
promise of the dawning twentieth century. It was all of a piece: the
genius of Edison, the greatness of the U.S. of A., and the hope for a
prosperous future.

"I don't know," O'Malley chimed in. "They're pretty but
these gas lights still serve us fine."

An older man, seated at the end of the bar, looking as if he
might have long ago retired permanently to his stool, called out
"What about the newcomer? You been to Buffalo?"

I realized he meant me and, choking down a mouthful of
stew, answered "No, I'm too busy with school. Couldn't really
afford the trip right now anyway."

"School?" came the incredulous answer, "what kind of
school is there for a man your age in these parts?"

"Medical school," I replied. "The school is in New York.
I'm just here for the fall, studying with Doctor Gerin at the prison."

"You'll find plenty of rot to examine there. You studying to
be a prison doc?"

"No, actually, an alienist."

"Hah!" he laughed. "If it's crazy folks that interest you, then you'd best do your studying right here at O'Malley's!"

And indeed I did. I soon became a regular member of the boisterous crowd that somewhat affectionately, I suppose, had christened me "Doc." In the few weeks since that day, I'd come to know them well.

~

As Jones and I walked into the saloon, a few of the regulars looked up and smiled or waved. The booming voice of Joe Whelan held the floor.

"It's just a matter of the chickens coming home to roost. Think of the strikers who've been gunned down. The workers beaten and overworked, impoverished." Whelan was a short man, built thick and strong, a strength honed in his demanding work assembling farm equipment at D.M. Osborne and Company. In the days since I'd first encountered him here at the saloon, I'd been impressed with the vehemence of his political opinions as well as with his ability to articulate them.

"But Joe," interrupted Jed Grant, the man who'd given me my nickname, "this is murder, pure and simple. The motive seems to be political, but it could just be the act of a mad man."

"That's something I've been wondering about," O'Malley's voice, as always, held sway in his own establishment. "What kind of a man walks calmly up and shoots another in a crowded building with no concern for his own escape or safety. That sounds pretty crazy to me. I'd like to hear what the young alienist thinks." All eyes turned in my direction.

"Well, I can't think anything until I know the details. Jonesy wouldn't even let me finish the paper he was in such a hurry to get down here. Someone fill me in."

"We don't know much." O'Malley held the floor. "Seems that the President held a receiving line yesterday afternoon in the Temple of Music at the Exposition. A young man, some foreign name no one can seem to pronounce, something like Ksollgawz, came up with his hand wrapped in a handkerchief, like it was injured, but really hiding a gun, and shot McKinley twice at point blank range. The police wrestled this fellow Ksollgawz to the ground. He's in custody. The President's in critical condition, but the doctors are optimistic."

"I guess that's pretty much what the morning paper said," I replied. "Let me see how that name is spelled." Jones handed me back the paper. "I'm pretty sure that C-z-o-l-g-o-s-z'would be pronounced Chollgosh. I've been exposed to enough Polish names in New York to know that the 'cz' is pronounced as 'ch' and the 'sz' as 'sh.' What else do we know about him?"

"Not much. As far as we've heard, he hasn't said much. Like you say, he's a Polack. Twenty-eight. Pretty nervous, according to the papers. But who wouldn't be? They found an article about Emma Goldman, the anarchist, in his pocket. Maybe she's linked to the crime. Some kind of conspiracy, maybe. But no one really knows. There was a fellow ahead of him in the receiving line who created a disturbance. An Italian. Might be an accomplice. Some think it makes sense given that Bresci was Italian, but so is my neighbor, Mike Anton. The assassin claims he acted alone. So, what do you think?"

I paused for a moment to ponder this question, well aware of the absurdity of their expecting some worthwhile opinion on the basis of such scant information. The others waited in anticipation, a rare moment of silence overtaking O'Malley's. I decided that only the broadest of comments would be appropriate and finally replied, "These are questions that alienists, and ethicists, continue to grapple with. Can a murderer ever be sane? Is it a form of insanity to believe in anarchy?"

"Just a minute." It was Whelan again. "The anarchists want to build a new society, one without bosses or governments, without injustice. You can't call that crazy."

"Well, Joe, many people do call them that. Remember that insanity is not a term with a scientifically precise definition. Legally, it means little more than unsoundness of mind. As far as the purported goals of the anarchists are concerned, idealism is not necessarily inconsistent with delusion. But, more importantly, what of their methods? It is certainly diabolical, if not outright insane, to advocate murder as a political tactic."

Jones piped in, "But what was the Spanish-American War if not the practice of murder as a political tactic."

"Why Jonesy, you're sounding like a socialist." I smiled, knowing he was playing devil's advocate.

"He sure is," said O'Malley whose nephew was a war veteran. "McKinley won that war for the American people and to free the people of Cuba and the Philippines from Spanish domination. We ought not to malign the President's work while he's lying in Buffalo, maybe on his death bed."

"Okay," I nodded in acknowledgment of O'Malley's patriotism. "So, the anarchists want to put an end to government. Let's set aside for the moment the question of whether or not that idea, in and of itself, constitutes insanity. Their method, or at least one of their methods, I don't know too much about them myself, is to kill heads of state, like Bresci's assassination of King Humbert over in Italy. If this Czolgosz is just a foot soldier following the program, you can't say on that basis alone that he's insane. You would need more information. Of course, you can't necessarily say he's sane either."

"But, Doc," Mike Johnson, an O'Malley's regular entered the discussion, "you work with murderers every day in the prison. Do you think they're all insane?"

"Don't forget that this is only my second week working with Dr. Gerin. And, giving someone a medical exam is not the same as giving him a psychiatric evaluation. But there are different kinds of murderers with different motives, different personalities, and different circumstances. The law considers most of them sane. A crime of passion is considered to be a momentary lapse for an otherwise sane individual."

"Kind of like the day I slipped up and ate some of O'Malley's cooking," Jed Grant suggested with a loud guffaw.

Jones rolled his eyes in amusement. "That would be a lapse in judgment," I corrected. "As well as he feeds us, I haven't witnessed much passion for O'Malley's cuisine. Anyway, as I was saying, a deranged criminal who murders as a result of his psychosis is considered insane and not responsible for his act. And then there's the cold, methodical murderer, the hired gun, someone whose crime is part of the functional adaptation of his life. This is where the question of ethics comes in. The law considers crime to fall on an ethical spectrum of good and evil. The sanity of the perpetrator comes into play only in extreme cases in which it can be demonstrated that the criminal did not know right from wrong.

Some of the states broaden the definition to include cases in which
the impulse to commit the crime is beyond the control of the
perpetrator, even though he knows it is wrong. We don't know yet
whether the assassin committed a crime of passion, if he is
deranged, or if he is a cold-blooded killer. Yet one has to wonder
about a society that can consider any murder to be the act of a
sane man."

The crowd seemed satisfied with this analysis and turned
its attention to some other item in the newspaper. I felt pleased
with myself and with my performance. Smiling with satisfaction, I
ordered a beer from O'Malley, which I proceeded to sip slowly,
leaving the discussion of the assassination to others. For the first
time I realized that I was saddened by the possibility of McKinley's
death. I had tremendous respect for this national leader who had
spurred on the great engine of progress and made the United
States a world power. His initial presidential campaign, back in my
college days, had offered me a first serious exposure to American
politics. Although few of my classmates at Cornell had attained
voting age, political debates had raged across campus in '96. Most
of the students were, like their parents, staunch McKinley
supporters. Few had encountered the kind of life experiences or
influences that might have altered their views. McKinley's call for
"peace, progress, patriotism, and prosperity" struck them as plainly
sensible.

The handful of William Jennings Bryan fans were
enthusiastic and boisterous. They had picked up the populist
rhetoric that surrounded Bryan and worked hard toward his
election. They spoke eloquently on behalf of a Common Man
whom none of them had likely met. Although I myself preferred
McKinley, I could not deny that there was a certain common sense
to Bryan's call for reform. Surely a great democracy like the United
States should seek to ensure a fair livelihood for the agrarian
yeoman and the industrial laborer, lifting the hardworking masses
out of poverty. But Bryan's public image both attracted and
repelled me. His legendary rhetorical skills were fascinating, but I
was put off by the common portrayal of his following as an unruly
and uneducated rabble.

Students had packed the auditorium in Sage Chapel for
the great face-off between our two debating society champions,
Calvin Simmons, representing McKinley, and William Dawson for

Bryan. Bryan supporters cheered loudly, believing they had won
the day, as Dawson closed with the Democrat's celebrated
declamation "you shall not crucify mankind upon a cross of gold."
But Simmons proved himself a superior orator to even McKinley,
replying smoothly "and you, my sanctimonious adversary, shall not
crucify him upon a cross of grime!" I joined the rest of the
Republican camp in a roar of triumph at this zinger, approving of
Simmons' ad hominem reference to Bryan's lower class supporters.
Among Cornell students, at least, McKinley was still the
frontrunner.

Two years later, like most of my classmates, I was caught
up in the call for Cuban independence. A few diehard socialists
claimed that the United States was only concerned with expanding
its economic sphere of influence, but their voices were drowned
out by those who saw our nation as the bastion and sustainer of
expanding global democracy. When spring classes ended, I
watched with envy those fellows who forsook their summer holiday
to enlist for the great escapade in Cuba. But they were not among
those fated to return with tales of adventure at El Canay, Santiago,
or San Juan Hill. Most of these late recruits, gentlemen
adventurers as they were, achieved only the dubious heroics of
marching around a muddy field in Virginia for a few weeks before
they were discharged and sent home. In mid-July, the Spanish
government was already petitioning for peace.

McKinley had made the United States a world power and
Theodore Roosevelt had fashioned himself into a national model
of rugged American manhood and patriotism. I basked in the pride
of my country, my era, and my generation. In 1900, I held my head
high as I marched to the polling place to cast my very first vote for
the McKinley-Roosevelt ticket. A few of my fellow students were
involved in the recently formed Anti-Imperialist League, railing
against militarism and conquest, but I had no patience for them.
The demands of medical school left little time for the great
political questions of the day. "Politics" was not a term found in
the index of Gray's Anatomy.

~

Back at the boarding house that evening, I reflected on the turn the discussion at O'Malley's had taken. I enjoyed the aura of authority that the barroom crowd invested in me. Medical school was characterized by an overwhelming sense of how little you knew, how much there was to learn. The physicians who served as our instructors were formidable in their command of medicine and intimidating in their demeanor. I looked forward to graduation when I could formally claim to have joined their ranks. For now, my occasional pronouncements at O'Malley's must suffice as my meager reward. Only Jonesy's mocking smile insistently reminded me that my expertise extended only as far as the saloon's front door.

The questions raised about McKinley's assassin and about the relationship of insanity to criminality were the very ones that had been on my mind in recent months, and which led me to seek out an internship at Auburn State Prison. Much as I thrilled to serve as expert to the barroom crowd, I felt frustrated, unable to meet my own standards for a satisfactory understanding. And I was not at all convinced that the answers would ultimately be found in texts like the Jimmy that lay waiting for me nearby, an indifferent Ezzie-cat napping contentedly upon its coffee-stained pages. Psychiatry treated each individual as if the dimensions of sanity and madness were totally encapsulated in one's own personality, revealed in one's upbringing and life experiences, if not in one's physiognomy. Emil Kraepelin's acclaimed taxonomy of psychiatric disease patterns was entirely individualistic. Whether a patient was diagnosed with catatonia or febrile deliria, hebephrenia or general paresis was based almost exclusively on the physician's observations at the bedside.

Yet the thought gnawed at me that society itself might exist in a range of, if not psychological, at least ethical or moral health, and that our actions might in the final analysis be properly evaluated only within that framework. Were we not all positioned somewhere on a continuum of mental fitness, our sanity judged in the context of our social conditions and in our response to the expectations of others? What really separated the criminal from the criminally insane, the troubled man whose knife was grasped only by his imagination from the murderer who struck in earnest? That night, such questions still danced in my head as I lay in bed drifting off to sleep; McKinley and his assailant, this Czolgosz, slowly receded from my consciousness.

Chapter Two

~

Monday, September 16, 1901

.

My habit, on returning home to the boarding house, was to turn my attention to the small table Mrs. Thomas kept in the foyer by the front door and look for any mail that might be waiting for me. A picture of Mrs. T's long-deceased husband stared across the entryway, one of several around the house. None of the photographs included the wife. It was as if she wanted to remember the man but to forget the young woman who had fallen in love with him. Mr. Thomas was a solid-looking, clean-shaven fellow who appeared less than comfortable in his ill-fitting suit. Unlike some widows who could chatter on endlessly about their lost husbands, she never spoke of him.

It had been a tiring day at the prison, and dinner with Dr. Gerin and his family was scheduled for the evening. It was a relief to have some time to relax, and I was pleased to find a letter addressed to me in the easily-recognizable, rounded hand-writing of Abby Tolson. I had heard from Abby only once in the weeks I'd been in Auburn and I'd written to her once in return.

It was during our third-year hospital rotations that Jones and I first met the nurses Abigail Tolson and her sister Judith. Jones, typically, had discovered them--Judith actually, with whom he quickly formed a romantic liaison and friendship. Since there was a sister, it was inevitable that I was included. As we made their acquaintance, Jonesy dubbed them the "Tolson twins." A year apart in age, they did look enough alike to pass as twins. Although they were a few years older than us, the Tolsons had the fresh complexions of teenagers and a playfulness that would seem youthful at any age. We had become quite the foursome. The sisters' shared apartment was the site of our frequent dinner parties at which plenty of wine was followed by song and dance. After an evening out, they often invited us for a nightcap or an intimate soiree. Judith was the more rambunctious of the two and kept things lively with Jones her ready accomplice. Abby was quieter and more my sort of girl. Although Jones, true to his character, embraced their friendship eagerly, I was less certain, never easily justifying any time spent away from my medical books.

Picking up the envelope, I walked into the study and eased into one of the soft leather chairs. I opened the letter and eagerly started to read. "Dear Jon," it began, "I hope you are well and enjoying your internship. Judy and I have had a pleasant summer. The hospital is keeping us very busy. I am writing because I think that it is proper that I let you know that a gentleman of my acquaintance has expressed an interest in courting me. Some, of course, would say that I am already getting old for marriage but, as you know, I am not quite that old-fashioned. Still, a girl must take advantage of such opportunities as present themselves. Although I have not given him an answer, I expect that before too long I will have to make my reply. In any case, I will look forward to seeing you on your return from Auburn... Sincerely yours, Abby."

I was stunned by this news. Abby's message was unequivocal: I still had a chance with her, but I would have to act quickly. To act--when it came to women, that indeed had been my stumbling block. When would I outgrow the numbing paralysis that overtook me whenever intimacy was at hand? I liked Abby very much and had missed her gentle laughter and warm caress since arriving in Auburn. Yet my ambivalence was undeniable. What a delight it was to kiss her sweet lips and lose myself in the scent of her hair. Often, we would linger on the divan late into the night, nestled in each other's arms. But, I know that I forestalled our lovemaking long before she would have, leaving her with a regular disappointment that, given her good nature, she would not express. I had told myself that I was practicing some latter-day chivalrous code. Saving myself for marriage, as it were. But I could not help suspect, with the budding introspection of the aspiring alienist, that with Abby, as with others before her, I had held up an invisible barrier between myself and the closeness I claimed to long for. Even when I had believed that I was wooing a woman in earnest, at a certain point my ardor would leave me and I would find myself bored, distracted, and ready to move on to other pursuits. At times, I would continue to go through the motions of courtship long after losing interest. I can still see the face of

Eleanor Martin, a college sweetheart, as she struggled to hold back her tears as she told me "Jon, I just don't think you like me very much." My protests to the contrary rang hollow to my own ears, as well as to hers.

"Mr. Parker, is something wrong? You look so sad. Not bad news, I hope?"

I looked up to see Mrs. T standing in the doorway. "Bad news of a sort, I suppose. Nothing I won't get over."

"I trust that everything is all right with your father."

"Yes, I'm sure it is. It's my lady friend. She's written to inform me that some other fellow is interested in marrying her."

"Oh dear. And will she marry him?"

"Unless I marry her first."

Mrs. T walked into the study and sat down in the chair beside mine. She gazed at me for a moment, her brow wrinkled in worry. "Mr. Parker," she said, "it just doesn't seem to me that you are ready for marriage. I hope you don't mind my saying so. I know it's very forward of me, hardly knowing you, after all."

"That's all right," I said with a half-hearted smile. "I need all the help I can get. Anyway, you're probably right. I'm never really sure how I feel. Even now, I hate to let Abby go, but I don't feel the fervor that might propel me to chase after her, to intercede and demand her hand. It's just so frustrating." I crumpled Abby's letter in my hand and tossed it across the room.

"Now, now. You may want that letter later on. Please don't despair." She took my right hand between hers and looked earnestly into my eyes. "I'm sure it's been hard on you, growing up without a mother to guide you in the more delicate areas of life. And you're still so young. All you need is to meet the right girl. Someone who will understand you. Someone with the patience you need to blossom into love."

I looked at her for a moment and, as Mrs. T awkwardly withdrew her hands, I realized that I was scowling. With this news from Abby, it was hard to imagine myself "blossoming" into anything.

"Thank you for your concern," I said, again attempting to smile. "I think I'll go upstairs and lie down for a while. I need to relax and try to gather my thoughts. I'll be fine, really." I picked up the letter from where it lay on the floor and trudged off to my

room. But, rather than relax, I proceeded to pace back and forth
in agitated thought.

It was not too long before there was a knock on my door.
It was Jones.

"I hear you've had some bad news, a bit of a set back," he
said, waltzing in before I could answer his knock.

"Here, read this." I handed him Abby's letter .

"That's tough, pal," he said as he finished the short note.
"I don't suppose you'll be rushing down to New York to claim her
hand."

"You're right about that. The difficulty is that I really like
her. I just wish I had more time."

"Time for what? To fall in love? To marry? If that was
where things were heading you'd know it by now. You wouldn't be
standing around moping in your room. You'd be leaping into
action."

"I guess you're right," I said without much conviction.

"Anyway, there's lots of fish in the sea. Why even tonight
you'll have the opportunity to meet Dr. Gerin's lovely daughter
Lucy. She's a real beauty, a veritable Gibson girl." His half smile
could not conceal the sarcasm in his voice. My friend was not
attracted to Lucy Gerin, whom he had met when he himself had
dined with our mentor's family the week before. It was a tradition
for newly arriving interns.

"Well, then, I suppose you'll be pursuing her yourself?" I
replied. Playing dumb was a favorite ploy when faced with Jones'
mocking irony.

"No, she's not my type. Much too clever." Jones was
nothing if not honest. "You might like her, though."

"Jonesy," I sighed, "I don't know how you expect me to
think about another woman right on the heels of Abby's letter."

"You know my philosophy--love is the best cure for
heartache."

"And, besides, I don't see how you can think about
romance with all the work we have to do."

"Hey, all work and no play makes Jon a dull boy." He
slapped me on the back as if he might jostle me free from my
disconsolate inertia and resistance. "I consider affairs of the heart,
or at least, of the flesh, to be an essential salve to our otherwise
dull existence in medical school. Live a little."

"Sorry, Jonesy, when I get through these last two semesters, I may have time to think about a social life."

"Wait 'til you see the young Miss Gerin. You may change your tune. She puts the Tolson twins to shame, although she may not be as ready and willing as Abby. Or at least as Abby was before Mr. Right came along." My response to this was to stick out my tongue in mute protest. Jones nearly collapsed with laughter at my childish behavior.

Under the circumstances, I could not believe that Gerin's daughter would move me any more than Abby Tolson had. Abby's letter was like a fist in my gut. As far as romance was concerned, the wind was knocked out of me. The last thing I could imagine was forming an interest in another girl. But that evening, as I prepared for the dinner party, I found myself stropping my razor extra sharp and paying a little more attention to the pomade applied to my thin moustache, to the lines of my collar and coat, and to the luster of my shoes. I must make my best impression on Gerin and his family to ensure a good review, I told myself.

It was a pleasant evening for the short walk around the block to North Street and the Gerin home. As I strolled along, I wondered whether the death of McKinley would cast a shadow over this evening's sociability. Like most Americans, I had eagerly awaited the daily news reports, which grew increasingly optimistic as the President's health improved steadily during the first week after the shooting. The news that McKinley had fed himself eggs and toast one day for breakfast held out a particularly palpable hope for most people. Unfortunately, his health took a sudden downturn and, eight days after the shots were fired, he passed away.

That was three days ago. On Saturday, there had been a funeral procession in Buffalo. Yesterday, a train loaded with dignitaries, Mrs. McKinley, and the coffin had departed for Washington. This morning, a formal state funeral had been held in the Rotunda of the Capitol, and on Wednesday the funeral train would arrive in Canton, Ohio, McKinley's final resting place. I had followed the news of the President's last days, understanding it for the important historical moment that it was; but, I was not obsessed with it the way most people seemed to be. Perhaps the awareness of life's many tragedies that comes with working daily at the prison lessened the impact of the assassination. Perhaps it was the way the long shifts behind the gloomy prison walls wore me down emotionally. Although I fully enjoyed the daily discussion of the latest news, at heart, I just didn't seem to care that much.

It was only a few minutes before the Gerin home came into view. While I had never been inside, it was a familiar sight since I passed by whenever heading downtown. The house was a modest-sized brick structure in the Italianate style that was popular at the time. The high-arching windows that looked out from both floors were surrounded in limestone. The same grayish-white stone also highlighted the corners, making a striking contrast with the red brick. A few well-manicured shrubs were placed along the front and sides of the house. A charming gazebo jutted out from the back corner. The convenient location gave Dr. Gerin an easy walk to the prison and all the family a short jaunt downtown.

I knocked on the door and was greeted by a somewhat stout, attractive, middle-aged woman.

"Ah, Doctor Parker. Welcome. Please come in. I'm Dorothy Gerin."

"Pleased to meet you," I replied, "but I'm not a doctor yet."

Mrs. Gerin led me into the entryway. She took my coat and hat with a cheerful smile as if she would thereby unburden me of all of my cares. "It's been so humid," she said. "You must be overheated under such a heavy coat." Mrs. Gerin had that sweet assertiveness, possessed by some women of her age, that could lead a fully grown man to surrender to cookies, warm milk, and a nap at her encouragement. I don't know if her husband's interns brought it out in her, but she seemed ready to take me in and provide not just the physical nourishment of a meal but the emotional sustenance that a young man far from home might unknowingly elicit. Her warmth and graciousness were matched by her diaphanous attire, a simple dress of crepe de chin which seemed both casual and elegant. Mrs. Gerin, her home, and her clothing all exuded an atmosphere of simple comfort.

As we entered the foyer, I heard Dr. Gerin's deep voice call out, "Jonathan! Welcome!" I looked to my left and saw my mentor rise from a stuffed leather chair in the parlor and stride toward me. He extended his hand with a controlled enthusiasm. I shook it vigorously. His hearty greeting belied the fact that we'd parted after our day's work at the prison a mere two hours earlier. "So, how's dinner coming?" he asked his wife.

"Sadie should be checking the turkey as we speak."

"Well, let's get to it. I'm famished. Where's that daughter of ours?"

As if on cue, a young woman appeared at the top of the stairs. "Here I am, Papa."

"Right on schedule," Gerin replied. "Hasn't your mother taught you that a proper young lady keeps the men waiting a few minutes?"

"Now father, you know I'm not one for such games." She skipped down the stairs in a display of childlike energy. "And this must be Dr. Parker. I'm Lucy Gerin." She arrived at the bottom and, assuming a more seemly air, offered me her hand

"Actually, I'm not yet a doctor. Still studying to become one." I repeated my oft-used refrain. Lucy's handshake was firm like her father's. Her smile was friendly, yet tinged with an air of youthful mischievousness. Jones was right about her looks. At first glance, Lucy could have indeed been a model for one of Charles Dana Gibson's celebrated ink drawings of the ideal American girl. All she was missing was the practiced, haughty air that typified women aspiring to Gibson's standard.

"Mr. Parker it is, then," she replied. As she smiled up at me, I saw that her beauty was marred by the fact that her mouth was a bit askew, the right corner of her smile angling slightly up, the left slightly down. The small gap between her two front teeth was not in itself unattractive. Perhaps this is what put Jones off, seeker of unblemished beauty that he was. But the mouth is at most half of the smile, the other half being the eyes and Lucy's were most arresting--a deep brown color under thick, dark brows, which, rather than unfeminine, made her all the more beautiful and even somewhat exotic.

"Are we ready to sit down?" Lucy asked her mother.

Mrs. Gerin nodded in assent and Lucy offered her arm to me.

"Allow me to show you to the dining room, Mr. Parker. This way, please." As I walked beside the Gerins' daughter, a sweet aroma drew my attention toward her. A hint of auburn glistened from the French twist into which her predominantly brown hair was carefully gathered. The tendrils that curled down toward her cheeks highlighted a round face with smooth skin. Lucy wore a princess gown of green chiffon and velvet that seemed sculpted to accentuate the curvaceous contrast between bodice and waistline. Lucy Gerin was headed toward her mother's luxuriant womanhood rather than her father's angular stolidity.

We walked into the next room, where a golden oak table was set for four. A steaming turkey awaited carving at one end. Two additional chairs had been pulled back to the sides of the room. On one wall stood an ornate sideboard with a display of china and cut glass. Above, there hung a matching oval mirror with a carved eagle perched atop. I was seated opposite Lucy with the Gerins at either head of the table. Mrs. Gerin rang a silver bell while, without ceremony, Dr. Gerin began to cut thick slices from the turkey. The maid responded promptly to the summons, entering from what I assumed was the kitchen, and offered side dishes to each of us in turn. A tantalizing aroma of cinnamon and nutmeg accompanied her from the kitchen. Sadie, the Gerin's housemaid, looked to be about the same age as the Gerins but, having fallen into the tough, constrained maturity of her class, could just as easily have been ten years younger or older than her employers. She was cut out of a familiar Irish mold: pale skin with faint freckles high on the cheeks and forehead, thin black hair tied up on her head, her body thickened from neck to calf from years of labor, and a no-nonsense demeanor that brooked little interference with her assigned tasks, not even from their assigners. Several of my childhood pals had tip-toed in fear around the harsh discipline of such servants.

"So, Jon," Mrs. Gerin was the first to speak, "tell us something about yourself. Where are you from? What does your father do? How did you come to study medicine?"

I broke in, "Perhaps I can start with one question at a time. I was born and raised in Brooklyn, a neighborhood called Lefferts Manor. It's in Flatbush near Prospect Park, Brooklyn's answer to Central Park."

"I understand that Brooklyn is quite a large city in its own right." Mrs. Gerin replied.

"It is, and getting bigger all the time. My father says that the real turning point came with the opening of the Brooklyn Bridge around twenty years ago. It allowed people to live close to downtown Manhattan without so much crowding. Now there's another bridge in the works. Things are getting pretty built up, but toward the eastern end of the borough there is still plenty of open space and farm land."

"Did you go to college in New York City as well?" Mrs. Gerin continued.

"No, I attended Cornell, over in Ithaca. I never spent much time in Manhattan until medical school. You asked about my father. He is also a physician, a pediatrician actually, with a small but busy practice at home."

"Does your mother help out in the practice?"

"Unfortunately, my mother is no longer with us. We lost her when I was a child." These misleading phrases that I'd used for years slid easily and unselfconsciously off my tongue.

"Oh, I'm sorry to hear that." Mrs. Gerin smiled sympathetically and, to my relief, tactfully changed the subject. "Do you plan to work with children, like your father?"

"And his father before him," I added. "No, I intend to be an alienist."

Lucy spoke up with a twinkle in her eyes, "Is it true what they say that people who become alienists are all kind of crazy themselves?"

"Lucy!" Her mother stared at her in shock. Dr. Gerin wiped his mouth with his napkin as if preparing to speak. I myself was surprised and a bit put off by the sarcastic nature of this question. I began to see that there might have been more than Lucy's smile that had bothered Jones.

"Actually," I said, pushing aside my discomfort, "it's a good question. After all, what does the adage 'physician, heal thyself' mean when applied to an alienist? Most people don't really think about questions of mental health, their own or others, unless confronted by outright lunacy. I think it's a fair question to ask what drives someone to enter a field that deals directly with the human condition. Not just that of psychiatry, but philosophy or religion as well."

"Well," Lucy was undeterred by her mother's reprimand, "what drives you, Mr. Parker?"

"It's hard to say exactly. I do have my share of lofty ideas of the sort that one associates with such callings. Can I develop some knowledge or theory that will improve human well-being? Can I come to an understanding of the nature of human psychology that might help people to lead happier lives? And so on. My father, and yours for that matter, thinks that I'm impractical. Too idealistic. People say that such idealism is a quality of youth that erodes with age. I hope not. After all, shouldn't a new century be launched with new ideals and dreams for the human race?"

"But, Mr. Parker, that's all so abstract. Surely you have some personal feeling toward your chosen profession."

"I suppose there is a personal factor, for me, in being an only child and having spent a lot of time by myself. Plenty of time for contemplation. But then you too are an only child. Do you share my madness?"

She laughed at the suggestion. "Let's just say I'm not crazy enough to go to medical school."

"Lucy is currently employed as a typewriter," her mother explained. "Downtown at the Auburn Savings Bank. That's the building with the clock tower right in the heart of town. But, tell me, is your work at the prison in psychiatry or is it general medicine?"

Before I could speak, Dr. Gerin replied, "Well, Dottie, I'm certainly not qualified to train an alienist. Mr. Parker is here for a general internship. At the same time, he is rather interested in the psychological condition of the inmates and feels he can glean some insight from his internship here in Auburn. He hopes to interview some of the prisoners to that end. I do see the practical side to his idealism and hope that, under my influence, that might come more to the fore." He looked intently at me with a hint of a smile playing along his lips. I didn't know if I'd ever seen Dr. Gerin fully smile. I'd surely never heard him laugh. "It's unfortunate," he went on, "that, when the women's prison was opened back in '93, the criminally insane were transferred to Matteawan, although I think we've still got plenty of fine cases for the young intern's casual study."

"As a matter of fact, I am particularly interested in those who are not conventionally considered to be insane," I added. "My view is that a major task for psychiatry is to get out of the asylums and look at the psychological factors in all forms of aberrant behavior. The question I've posed for myself is whether criminal behavior can be understood psychologically and mitigated by the intervention of alienists. There are really two sides to my pursuit. First, can a better understanding of the development of the criminal mind provide a means to identify those headed down the path to crime and thus allow positive intervention? Second, how can an understanding of criminal psychology help with the rehabilitation of felons into useful, law-abiding members of society?"

"So," Lucy stayed with her previous theme, "rather than join the madmen like most alienists and confine yourself to an asylum, you see yourself as more suited to the company of pickpockets?" Her mother frowned.

"And murderers," I added, attempting a fiendish leer.

"Of course." She laughed and seemed pleased that I did not withdraw from her challenge.

Mrs. Gerin, eager to change the subject, asked how I liked Auburn. She clearly was not happy with her daughter's quick tongue and ready wit, qualities not usually associated with the behavior of well-bred young ladies. She probably worried that Lucy's attitude would scare off potential suitors. And a reasonable fear it was. Most men might be expected, like my friend Jones, to recoil at such abrasiveness.

We chatted a while about the town of Auburn, the various sights and attractions, history and geography. Mrs. Gerin, it turned out, was a third generation Auburnite, well-versed in the town's lore. She had a dim childhood memory of the erecting of the Victory Arch across Genesee Street celebrating the end of the Civil War. Her husband had arrived as a young man to take his position in the prison and subsequently settled down. Theirs did seem to be a most settled existence. They expressed a warm affection for small town life, but, at the same time, envied my living in the great cosmopolitan city. That medical school left little time for museums or theater or even a nice meal out was somehow beside the point. Mrs. Gerin asked how I liked the accommodations at Mrs. Thomas' boarding house. "Nettie," as she called Mrs. T, apparently had a reputation for running one of the better boarding houses in town.

As the conversation was now divided more evenly around the table, I had some time to enjoy a very fine meal. The turkey was delicious, not too dry, and topped with a savory brown gravy. The side dishes of potatoes and green beans made the occasion seem much like Thanksgiving, the warm family atmosphere contributing to that sense. Lucy, apart from an occasional barbed repartee, seemed to get along quite well with her parents. She joined enthusiastically in the discussion of the high and low-points of Auburn life. I learned that she had been away the past four years at college and gleaned that there was some tension surrounding her now living at home and on the subject of her future. My sense was that her parents had not expected her to finish school without a marriage on the horizon.

I had to take care not to let my gaze rest too long on Lucy, especially while others were speaking. I did not want to offend her or her parents. But, this was no easy task. Something about both her looks and her personality drew my attention. My eyes wanted to linger over her slightest gestures. Again and again I was distracted by her repeated, if unconscious, efforts to discipline a stray curl of hair to stay off the side of her face. I would begin to lose myself in the dark pools of her eyes when she spoke, only to catch myself when someone else took up the thread of conversation. I was fascinated by the movements of her mouth as the strange angle of her lips occasionally gave her a somewhat zany look that her words steadfastly belied. Jones' admonitions to the contrary, I was intrigued by Lucy's oddly attractive appearance.

As the maid, Sadie, began to clear away the dinner plates, Gerin changed the subject again. "Well," he said with a sigh, "it really is too bad about McKinley." The news of the President's death had been foremost in people's minds and much discussed over the weekend, and I was surprised that it had not been a topic of our dinner conversation earlier. I surmised that the Gerins had intentionally maintained a lighter atmosphere while we ate.

"Yes," his wife replied, "and so unexpected. All the earlier reports were hopeful that he would survive, in quite good health even. What do you suppose went awry?"

Gerin replied "I've been in touch with Doctor Parmenter at Buffalo Medical School. As you know, for the first few days after surgery, the President seemed to be improving. Reports are that he ate, exhibited little pain, and conversed freely. Unfortunately, the bullet had pierced through the stomach. Although the wound was repaired, it became gangrenous. The pancreas was also grazed by the bullet and infection was found there as well. It was the infection plus the overall shock to his system that did him in. It's such a great loss."

"'Ask not for whom the bell tolls,'" offered Lucy. I braced at this glib remark. How rude and improper it was to take such a moment lightly. I could sense the tension rising in her father.

"This is no joking matter," Her father said in a low tone, restraining his anger.

"I mean it most seriously," she returned. "After all, he was the President for all of us." I could see by her expression that she was sincere. She went on. "You know I don't believe in killing anyone. It is a senseless act, whether you call it assassination or murder. And McKinley was very popular with the people, as those who wage and win wars usually are. The nation by and large is greatly aggrieved. Of course, I don't believe in the killing of Philippine nationalists either."

"Lucy!" her mother was adamant. "This is not appropriate. We have a guest."

Lucy looked my way, gauging whether I was averse to a little political debate at a time of national mourning. Her father, clearly biting his tongue, looked ready to explode.

"It's okay," I replied. I hoped I could find the fine line that would offend neither daughter nor parents. Part of me would be glad when the evening was over and Lucy Gerin's provocative smile and sharp tongue would be no more than a memory. "Although I think that this is primarily an occasion for mourning, it seems that we do no dishonor to the President's memory with a serious reflection on his political life. No man can rise to the heights of a William McKinley without stirring up a little controversy along the way. The Roosevelt Presidency will certainly have its share of contentiousness."

"Many people question whether the nation is ready for a reformer in the White House." Lucy said. "You were in New York when Teddy was Police Commissioner. What did you think of him then?" Lucy's eyes looked, smiling, encouragingly into mine. I felt suddenly at ease, as if she and I were alone in the room.

"I was pretty young then... and naive politically. Not to say that I'm not now. But he was quite the sensation, getting all the headlines. That's about all he's done as Vice President as well, grab headlines for himself, not that Vice Presidents are particularly known for their accomplishments in office."

"It makes me wonder," Lucy said, "just how serious he might be about reform. Or, to put it another way, whether a serious reformer can really act freely on the national political stage. Will Roosevelt be any less beholden to Mark Hanna and his ilk than McKinley was?"

"I believe you're wrong there, Lucy." Her father finally entered the fray. "Senator Hanna and McKinley were longtime friends from decades of political association in the Ohio Republican Party. It is only natural that Hanna would help McKinley in his campaigns. I consider Hanna to be a great national servant."

"And I think he's earned the moniker Dollar Mark," Lucy replied, referring to the familiar caricature of Hanna in the Hearst papers. "If Roosevelt wants to be re-elected, given today's political climate, he's going to need a lot of money. Mark Hanna will be the key to getting it."

"Well, Lucy," her father assumed his familiar air of authority, "as you know, I agree with our founding father John Jay's assertion that 'those who own the country ought to govern it.' The country owes a debt of gratitude to citizens like Mark Hanna who understand that wealth brings a special responsibility of stewardship for our society. Hanna did not make McKinley, but was a major factor in helping him reach his full potential as leader of the nation. Today, as we mourn the President, we should do so with respect not only to him but to his friends and supporters."

Lucy was ready to change the subject but not to abandon the topic of the assassination altogether. "All right," she said slowly,"but how about that anarchist? I guess he'll get what's coming to him."

Her father answered curtly, "If the court in Buffalo finds him guilty of murder then an execution is what will be coming to him, and I say he'll deserve it, along with the rest of his kind."

"Now, Daddy, you wouldn't condemn an entire group of people based on the actions of a single man?"

"As you well know," her father replied, "there have been many other anarchist assassins before Czolgosz. Since Russia's Alexander II twenty years ago, the list of its victims has grown. McKinley, the Prince of Wales, the King of Greece, the President of France. And we don't yet know if there will be others implicated in this Czolgosz' crime. They are holding that Goldman woman in Chicago. Many people are convinced that she had a hand in it, either her or that gang of cut-throats in New Jersey."

I was somewhat discomfited to hear Dr. Gerin express such strong political views despite the fact that they were not too far from my own. Up until this moment I had seen him only as a commanding figure within the small world of the Auburn Prison hospital, absorbed in his administrative duties and in the practice of medicine. I had viewed him more in the category of physician much like my previous mentors at the New York hospitals, mostly men of compassion, rather than in the category of prison administrator, a group that could be expected to come down hard on any threats to the established order. Now I understood that the prison environment molds even doctors with its inexorable fixation on discipline and the rule of law.

"Even if they found evidence against Emma Goldman, they could not legally extradite her nor could they charge her with any crime." Lucy thrust her chin out and wrinkled her brow. She looked around the table as if she had thrown down her gauntlet and dared any of us to pick it up.

"What do you mean?" I found myself taking Gerin's side, shocked at Lucy's assertion. "Surely, conspiracy to murder is a punishable offense, one allowing for extradition."

"Well, Jon, like my father, you haven't read the statutes carefully enough. A woman cannot be a citizen of the United States unless she is married to a citizen. Thus, Goldman is protected from federal laws. In addition, the State of New York defines its citizens as male persons and all of its laws are written with the masculine pronouns he, his, and him. There is no court that could properly claim jurisdiction to try her. Furthermore, there is no crime with which she could be charged other than those explicitly assigned to women such as sexual misdemeanors or abortion. They would have a tough time claiming that McKinley was aborted!"

Dr. Gerin glared at his daughter. "Lucy, you know very well that our prison contains several hundred women, all duly convicted by the State of New York for violation of its laws."

"Duly convicted," she replied, "but perhaps not according to the letter of the law. It seems to me, as well as to many prominent leaders of the woman rights movement, that women cannot fairly be subject to the restrictions of the criminal statutes without also enjoying all of the privileges that come with citizenship."

Her father sighed. "Lucy, sometimes you make me regret that I ever sent you to college."

Lucy ignored her father's tone of finality and was about to reply when Sadie appeared carrying steaming dishes of apple pie to the table. Mrs. Gerin happily took the opportunity to turn the conversation to the many varieties of local apples available this fall and which ones were whose favorites and so on. As she rambled on, the rising tension between father and daughter eased considerably but never quite left the room.

After dinner, we retired to the parlor. I was directed to one of a pair of cracked, over-stuffed leather chairs, while Dr. and Mrs. Gerin shared a divan that was upholstered in green plush. Nearby was a marble-topped table, home to an ornately bound photograph album. A thick flower print carpet covered the floor. Lucy went directly to the piano where she entertained us with lively renditions of popular songs, starting with *The Bird in the Gilded Cage*. She continued on with *The Sidewalks of New York*, which was all the rage during my high school days and which never fails to evoke feelings of nostalgia. *Shine on Harvest Moon* seemed to be a particular favorite with her parents, as Dr. Gerin exhibited a strong baritone.

While we sang, I took note of the ceiling-high bookshelves, sign of a cultured household. They were full of great works of fiction, from Hawthorne and Dickens to recent novels by James and Tarkington. I noted with a sense of irony a copy of Edward Bellamy's *Looking Backward* shelved between the two volumes of a thick history of Great Britain, the future somehow tucked away amidst the past. I wondered how many of these works Lucy had read, remembering how I had eagerly plundered my father's not dissimilar bookshelves in my boyhood.

A fat, old dachshund waddled into the room and lay down by Dr. Gerin's feet. The doctor obligingly scratched its belly with his foot as he sang. My attention was drawn back to the music as Lucy launched into a spirited performance of Scott Joplin's *Maple Leaf Rag*. I noticed her parents frown at one another, disapproving of the playing of the controversial, if popular, "Negro" music in their home. This, not surprisingly, turned out to be the final number in Lucy's performance. As I got up to take my leave, I thanked Mrs. Gerin for a delightful evening and a fine meal. Before

she could reply, Lucy answered for her, "Yes, Dr. Parker, it has
been delightful. I do hope you will come again." And with that, I
said good night.

Chapter Three

~

Wednesday, September 25, 1901

Wednesday was my day to work late with Dr. Gerin. Jones had gone on his merry way at our usual quitting time around four o'clock. Those last two hours until 6 pm were the longest and most tiring of the week. My sigh of relief may have been audible when Gerin at last informed me that we had come to the day's last patient. It was Fred Krist, the Waverley Murderer, up from death row. His execution was as yet unscheduled although it was expected to be set for early November. As was the standard procedure with felons awaiting execution, Krist was brought up to the clinic under heavy guard. The convict had a bland expression, his face puffy and pale, the skin pock-marked beneath a sparse, new beard. He was missing a few teeth and the rest were brown or black with decay. Several scars of varying lengths marred his arms and torso, souvenirs of some ignominious past activity. I cringed involuntarily at the sight of him, grateful for the presence of the extra guards.

The murderer must have sensed my fear. At one point, when Gerin was turned away, Krist caught my eye, his face suddenly coming alive as he wrinkled his brow into a maniacal glare and contorted his cheeks and jaw into a horrific snarl. He then began to laugh, a slow, uneven chortle which quickly broke up into a rasping cough. One of the guards grabbed him roughly. Gerin turned quickly around and motioned the guard away. His brow furrowed as he listened intently to the cough.

"What do you think of that cough?" he asked, ever cognizant of his didactic responsibilities.

"Could be a mild case of pneumonia," I replied after a moment's consideration.

"Or perhaps even an early stage of tuberculosis," my mentor added. "How would you treat it?"

"In either case, especially given that he may not outlive his illness, I'd prescribe rest, warmth, and plenty of liquids."

"Exactly right." And, as if following my directions, Gerin instructed the guards to provide Krist with some extra blankets, to make sure he stayed wrapped in them, and to give him plenty of hot water to drink, tea if possible. As Krist was led back to his cell, the doctor dismissed me for the day. I was tired from the long hours and pleased to finally be done with the workday.

I ignored a gnawing hunger that prodded me to head home for Mrs. T's waiting dinner and at dusk arrived at O'Malley's. The familiar aroma of tobacco and beer welcomed me into the tavern. Jones was ensconced at the far end of the bar, a fat cigar between his fingers. He smiled and blew a smoke ring in my direction, a reprise of our old college salute. I smiled and waved in reply. A group of men, mostly regulars, were gathered tightly near the center of the bar, engaged in an animated discussion. I drew closer to see what the commotion might be. As I expected, news of the trial had come out in the afternoon Auburn Bulletin. It was Bob Daugherty who held the paper.

"Listen to this," he exclaimed. "Czolgosz was really intent on his crime. Here's how this fellow Bull, the Buffalo police chief, says it went, 'Czolgosz said that he followed McKinley to the exposition grounds the day before the assassination and stood near the stand on the Esplanade. No favorable opportunity presented itself so he followed the President to Niagara Falls and then back to Buffalo. The next day, he got in line while the reception was in progress and when he reached the President he fired the fateful shots.'" One of the men whistled appreciatively at this account of the assassin's perseverance. "The patience of a tiger stalking its prey," commented another.

"And how does Bull know this?" asked Joe Whelan.

"Why, the prisoner told him, I suppose."

"'You s'pose!'" Whelan mocked. "Or maybe Bull made it up. Or maybe he got it part right. In any event, without an official confession or corroborating witnesses it's all hearsay. Did anyone see Czolgosz at the exposition grounds? And if they did, did they have any direct knowledge of his intent to assassinate McKinley? If not, then it's all pretty irrelevant to the trial."

"Well," Daugherty replied, "it does paint a pretty grim picture."

"But pictures, grim or otherwise, don't determine guilt or innocence."

"Oh ease up, Joe." Mike Johnson spoke up. "Everyone knows he did it. There were dozens of witnesses including police and various officials. They saw Czolgosz with the gun. They saw him take those two shots."

Whelan shook his head. "It's just that I don't like the way this trial has been conducted. Why the whole affair lasted only eight hours. The defense didn't call a single witness, barely made a rebuttal as far as the newspapers tell us. That trial was just a formality, with the guilty verdict a foregone conclusion. Any competent defense would have entered a plea for temporary insanity and likely made it stick. Instead, the defense calls in this hotshot alienist, McLane Hamilton, whose great grandfather palled around with Presidents. You expect this guy to do anything to help Czolgosz? I don't think so. No more than his renowned ancestor did to help Aaron Burr." I remembered the story from history class of Alexander Hamilton's efforts to sway the presidential election of 1800 toward Thomas Jefferson and away from Burr. But century-old history was hardly relevant to the qualifications of a well-respected alienist, one who might serve as a fine model for my own career.

"Dr. Gerin at the prison has met Dr. Hamilton," I said. "He told me that Hamilton is a fair-minded and highly competent alienist."

"And so he would. I expect those folks to stick together just as you yourself are being well-trained to defend your fellow physicians and the wealthy citizens who can afford your services. What does Gerin know of class conflict and of the likelihood that Hamilton would put his class interest before the interest of justice? A fellow of Hamilton's pedigree wouldn't have to think twice. For him, choosing sides is just a matter of following a path he was set on at birth."

"Now just a minute, Whelan. I'm hardly in the same class as McLane Hamilton." I was taken aback by this direct, personal rebuke, the first I had received at O'Malley's.

"Yet you're quick enough to come to his defense. I wonder why that is?" Whelan folded his thick arms across his chest, smirking, as he awaited my reply. I was suddenly at the center of attention.

Words eluded me. I stood at the bar, hang-jawed, my face turning red.

O'Malley came to my rescue. "Take it easy, Joe. I don't think Parker's ready for your revolutionary doctrine yet. Maybe after a few more beers." The men around the bar laughed at this suggestion. The tension eased.

"That may be so," Whelan replied. "But stick around, Doc. We'll help you see that medicine's only half the education they're giving you, The other half is all about how to fit in to your place in society and serve the interests of your betters, lessons you seem to be learning pretty well."

I was still fuming, embarrassed and speechless but, before I could reply to Whelan, O'Malley spoke up again.

"Maybe Parker's learned enough medicine to resolve our earlier debate about the missing bullet and McKinley's infection." For some reason, I, rather than Jones, was the resident medical expert. Jones tended to make light of his status as an up and coming physician. Therefore others did as well. I, on the other hand, took myself all too seriously.

"What are you referring to?" I asked, still glaring at Whelan. "I just got off work and haven't seen the paper or heard any news yet."

"Hand me that paper, Bob," O'Malley said. He walked around the bar and stood between Daugherty and myself. O'Malley took the paper in his beefy hands. He turned back to the front page, and scanned the lead article. "Here. Listen to this. 'Dr. Herman Mynter followed and his testimony was of importance in as much as it brought out the fact that the reason why the fatal bullet had not been located at the autopsy was because of the unwillingness of the President's relatives to have the body further mutilated by their instruments. Dr. Mynter and Dr. Mann, who followed him, both testified that the primal cause of death was the gunshot wound in the stomach. One effect of this wound was, they said, to cause the gangrene to form in the pancreas, and the spot of poisoned tissue was as large as a silver dollar.' Now, Whelan here says that if they can't find the bullet, they can't really prove that that's what killed him and that it shouldn't be a murder trial at all. What can you tell us, Parker, about gangrene and bullet wounds?"

"I believe Joe is mistaken." I thought I was on pretty solid ground offering an opinion here and pleased to gain the upper hand on Whelan. "We have to ask ourselves what facts have been established. We know that Czolgosz shot the President. The doctors could see the wound and knew that the bullet passed through both walls of the stomach, entering in the vicinity of the pancreas where the gangrene was later found. Now gangrene doesn't typically appear internally without some precipitating event. The connection to the missing bullet is pretty clear." I looked over to see Jonesy smiling at me in amusement. He got quite a kick out of watching me play medical expert to the barroom crowd.

"But, what you're overlooking, Doc," Whelan quickly replied, "is that these same good doctors were messing around in McKinley's guts themselves. They had their fingers and various instruments in there, poking at his organs, digging around looking for the bullet. They could easily have caused the infection themselves."

"You've got a point," I conceded.

"And," he continued "if the bullet wound is not necessarily the cause of death then Czolgosz is not necessarily a murderer and should be tried at the worst for attempted murder. Now, if a working bloke like myself can think of that, then why can't the esteemed Judges Titus and Lewis who have so nobly and reluctantly agreed to serve as defense attorneys? That's why I think the whole trial is a sham! That Dr. Mann, by the way, is a gynecologist, not exactly the kind of doctor you'd think McKinley was looking for under the circumstances."

What could I say? Whelan's argument had merit. I just hung my head, smiling grimly, embarrassed to be upstaged in my own field by a common working man.

"Let me have the paper back. I saw something else that looked interesting." It was Daugherty's turn to interrupt. He grabbed the newspaper back from O'Malley's hands, folded it over and pointed at a headline at the far right column. "Look at this. Some fellow named Ed Sastig in Saint Louis says he helped Czolgosz. It says he met with Czolgosz and Emma Goldman, the high priestess of the anarchists herself, and some guy from Philadelphia and that he was in Buffalo at the time of the assassination. He even confesses to tying the handkerchief around Czolgosz' hand."

A chorus of murmurs and exclamations followed this revelation as the paper was passed from hand to hand and the men read the short, three paragraph article. Those who could not read just passed it on.

"I guess that Goldman's goose is cooked," said Johnson.

But Joe Whelan only snorted with amusement when he finished the article.

"What a crock!" he said. "They'll do anything to paint a conspiracy and come up with more reasons to go after Emma Goldman and all the other known anarchists. Remember, in the first days after the shooting, they were rounding up anarchists all over the country and charging them with conspiracy without the least bit of evidence. There was that tailor in San Francisco who Senator Ellsworth said was part of a previous plot to kill McKinley. He was released for lack of evidence. If you remember that story, Ellsworth tried to link this tailor to Goldman and to the Paterson, New Jersey, anarchists who were connected with Bresci. Now, no one's ever proved that the Paterson anarchists had anything to do with Bresci's assassination of King Humbert. It's just a ridiculous lie to think of the three anarchists who you've heard of and accuse them of conspiracy. But it's so typical. Remember what they did to Johann Most? More of the same."

"Who's Most?" asked a middle-aged man whom I hadn't seen before. I whispered to O'Malley, asking him who this fellow was. Jake Kennedy, a farmer, he replied.

"You haven't heard of Johann Most?" Whelan threw his arms up, incredulous. "After Emma Goldman, he's got to be the best known anarchist in New York and the most influential. He's written some important political books and publishes the newspaper *Freiheit*. It's got a reputation for first-rate political analysis. Most really speaks out for the interests of the working man. The New York police arrested him because he reprinted a fifty year-old article that advocated assassination. This despite the fact that the paper was published the very day of Czolgosz' deed and there was no way Most could have either influenced him or been responding to the assassination attempt. If you'd been here a couple of weeks ago, Jake, you would have heard me railing about the headline that referred to him as 'Herr Most', as if emphasizing his foreign birth would somehow increase his guilt. Of course, they're going after Czolgosz for being a Polack despite the fact that he's as American as any of us, and even though we praise other Poles, Kosciusko and Pulaski, as great heros in the struggle for liberty. Let me tell you, those of you with Anglo-Saxon sounding names should count your blessings if you ever run afoul of the law."

"But they're holding Red Emma in Chicago," Kennedy pressed his point.

"And on what grounds?" Whelan countered. "None, you'll find. At least none that are legitimate. Remember that it was Goldman who said she would nurse McKinley back to health if given the chance. She holds no ill will toward individuals, only toward the system that enslaves and exploits working men. Sure, they'd like to shut her up but they won't find an excuse in this Czolgosz business, not if they follow their own rules of law, that is. If you look in today's paper you'll see that they've already released nine other Chicago anarchists who were arrested with Goldman. I imagine she'll be freed in a day or two as well. And this Sastig business will turn out to be just another fabrication."

"Why do you think people are making all of this up, Joe?" I asked. "It doesn't make any sense to me."

"That's because you're not a capitalist or ruler, Doc, even though you're being trained to think like one." The gleam in Whelan's eyes conveyed his pleasure at continuing to get his digs in. "They don't like the ideas that anarchists are spreading. Really, they don't care for anyone who speaks up for the working man. But it's the anarchists who've really put the fear of God in them." Whelan's shirt sleeves were rolled up, revealing powerfully muscled fore-arms. His forceful gestures added to the strength of his words. "The anarchist criticism has struck too close to home. They've shown that the emperors of big business and big government have no clothes. And our lords and masters don't much like being seen with their pants down. So they're using the newspapers to get people worked up over the McKinley shooting and against the anarchists. That way they'll have a free hand to set the police and the courts after them. That article the other day about the Marquette Club was a good example of the kind of measures you can expect."

"What's the Marquette Club?" It was Kennedy again who spoke. Later I learned that he was an O'Malley's regular but rarely got into town during spring sowing or fall harvest season. He'd missed much of the exciting news of recent weeks.

"They're some group of muckety-mucks. In Chicago, I think. There was a story about them in last Saturday's paper. It described their plans to press Congress to pass laws against the anarchists, outlawing their meetings, and banning their publications. Roosevelt's been taking the same line. All the politicians are lining up to take potshots at the anarchists these days. The Filipinos must be breathing a sigh of relief to have America's righteous furor turned on someone else for a while. But if that article's any indication, there are a lot of people in high places these days who don't think much of the U.S. Constitution, the First Amendment in particular."

"Now wait a minute, Whelan," Kennedy replied, "Are you saying that people like Czolgosz or Goldman who want to eliminate our form of government ought to share in its protections?"

"I'm just saying that if the law's not going to become a mess of contradictions and a complete sham then it has to apply equally to all citizens. It's one thing to outlaw assassination or armed rebellion or the destruction of property, all of which are in fact already against the law, but to ban meetings or free expression of political views is a clear violation of the Constitution. And, make no mistake about it, we'll be in big trouble if we let the government start deciding who the law applies to and who it doesn't. It's likely many of us would wind up on the short end of that stick."

O'Malley raised his beefy right arm and patted Whelan on the back. "Joe, how did you get so smart?" he asked. It was a question on my mind as well. Whelan's obvious intelligence and articulation were an affront to my college-educated sensibilities, to my sense of my own intellectual privileges and prerogatives. Who was he to speak so strongly and so well on matters of national import? Surely he was parroting some party line passed down from someone more educated than himself.

Whelan smiled. "Well, you know they've got those fancy schools for the capitalists and the privileged few. Doc here and Jones have been to them and could tell you all about it. But us working folks need to educate ourselves. Now I did my time at the Grover Street School and, while I never did make it to high school, I learned my ABCs well enough. Us working folk need to read as much as we can, newspapers and books on politics and high finance. We've got to get together and debate ideas, talk about the problems in society and how we can work together to make things better. The bosses own the daily papers like the one we're all crowded around today. And we're just mesmerized by it. But we've got our voices and our minds and we'd better learn how to use them if we want to be free men."

"I think we can all drink to that," O'Malley replied, his Irish brogue taking on a thicker cast. The men did not need any further encouragement and turned to the bar so that he could refill their glasses.

I sidled down toward the end of the bar and climbed onto the high, backless stool alongside Jones.

"So, buddy," I said with a grin, "it appears that we're on our way to becoming enemies of the people."

"Yup," he replied, "that windbag Whelan really seems to have it in for us."

"I sure don't appreciate being denigrated in front of a crowd." Whelan's chiding had ruffled my feathers, but something about his easy-going demeanor made it hard to take too personally. "I don't know that he means us ill by it. I get the feeling that he's more goading us, trying to get us to think about our assumptions and prejudices."

"Well, I've been enjoying my prejudice for this fine cigar." Jones took another long drag on the cigar and let the smoke drift slowly back out of his mouth. "Want one?"

"No thanks. Who needs tobacco with all this stimulating conversation? Another time, perhaps."

Jones and I sat slowly sipping our beers. I could hear that, across the bar, the discussion had broken down and moved on to a variety of other matters. A couple of men were discussing reports of the various yachts arriving for the International Cup races which had been postponed because of the assassination. The competition was scheduled to begin the next morning. Most Americans were convinced that Thomas Lipton's boat, the Shamrock II, was invincible but the latest news was that English bettors considered the Shamrock's chances slim. There was a good bit of national pride at stake in the outcome. It struck me that this topic was far afield from the discussion of working class politics that had prevailed only moments before.

A few other men were rehashing a news account of the illness of Old George who, it seemed, was Auburn's most venerable fire horse. Johnson, who had been a fireman for a while, was particularly concerned. The report, however, was favorable, indicating that the "faithful old equine" had a mild case of epizootic and that it was not serious. This apparently was the beast's first illness. I was amused to see these rough-looking men raise their glasses in salute to an old horse. As much as we tried to fit in at O'Malley's, Jones and I could never get over our education and upbringing enough to avoid some occasional disdain at the provincial interests of our bar-mates.

Nonetheless, our companions at the saloon managed to serve as unwitting ushers into the affairs of adulthood. Schoolboys, even when in the guise of adult medical students, take much for granted. The smooth functioning of society, the provision of roads and meals, of clothing, stores and entertainments, appear before youth independent of his own effort. But the working men who frequented O'Malley's were quite concerned with the many tasks required to keep up the economic, the political, and even the physical foundations of the town of Auburn. There I learned that a road might not be improved without fierce debate over who would pay the price and who would receive the contract. I came to understand that beyond consideration of the great deal to be had on shirts that week at the Big Store was worry over how great a loss its owners, well-known to my companions as fine local stock, were taking on an unwise and excessive purchase of goods.

It was at O'Malley's as well that I came to know Auburn as a community. In the saloon, it was clear that a certain pride cut across divisions of class or vocation. All spoke highly of their "ideal" geographic location, its unsurpassed natural beauty, its abundance of hydro power, its ready contact via two major rail lines to the world. And all, even those whom I later learned had reputations as agitators, were proud of Auburn's great industry, its several hundred manufacturing plants, and the hard work and acumen of laborer and industrialist alike. That fall, I came to understand that the rich detail of a town like Auburn, from the provincially opulent Burtis Opera House to the recently constructed Seymour Library to the stone walls of the Armory, can, in its way, rival the better-known magnificence of a great metropolis.

As various conversations swirled around us, Jones and I chatted about the day's unpleasantries at the prison. This was a familiar topic, one that always seemed to degrade into an exchange of complaints. Much of the past few weeks had been spent second-guessing ourselves as to our choice of internships. Jones sounded off about the great demands placed on the small medical staff responsible for hundreds of prisoners. The clinic was crowded and the practices were primitive compared to the city hospital at which we'd worked over the summer. I agreed, and added that the convicts were not exactly paragons of healthful living. Jones had a sarcastic comment on just about every patient. He never failed to remind me that I was the one who had thought it would be interesting to work with prisoners or, as he put it, that I was the one who'd "gotten him into this." He had gone along mostly through lack of any initiative of his own. We tried to reassure ourselves by saying that it was good experience and that we'd be better doctors for it. But this seemed a hollow consolation. I was rehashing my bone-chilling encounter with Fred Krist when Joe Whelan walked over to us.

"You know, don't you, that he'll be coming here after sentencing?" Whelan bent his head close between ours as if we were discussing some grave conspiracy.

"Who will?" I was nonplused by this intrusion.

"Why, Leon Czolgosz, of course. As a convicted murderer without extenuating circumstances he'll be sentenced to death, and the only working electric chair in New York is right here in Auburn. The chair at Sing-Sing is not currently in service."

"Well," Jones replied, "that should finally put Auburn on the map."

"And you two might get a little brush with history, working right there in the prison every day. The law requires a minimum of several weeks, a month maybe, between sentencing and execution. You may get your chance to hobnob with the world's most notorious criminal. Think about it. The prison will be surrounded by reporters. Each day, as you emerge through the gate at the end of your shift, they'll be there waiting, hungry for information. Did you see him? What did he say? What did he eat? What color is his piss? You could be famous. Who knows," Whelan placed a heavy hand on each of our shoulders, "you might even get to witness the execution."

Jones grimaced as Whelan turned and walked away. I just stared at Whelan's back, my mouth hanging open, dumbfounded. Perhaps we had chosen the right internship after all.

Chapter Four

~

Friday, September 27, 1901

"Parker, wake up."

"Huh. What?"

"Wake up!" Rough hands shook my shoulders. I groaned in protest and peered through uncooperative eyelids to see Jones standing in the darkness at my bedside. His long nose was strangely exaggerated in the dim moonlight.

"Christ, Jones!" I muttered. "What time is it?"

"It's about 1:30. Come on, get up. He's coming tonight."

I struggled to open my eyes fully . "Who is?"

"Czolgosz. He's on a train from Buffalo due in around 2 o'clock. There's already a crowd at the station. We don't want to miss it."

"And I don't want to miss my sleep. They've been expecting him on every train from the west for the past two days."

"But this time some of the keepers over at the prison say it's the real thing. They've snuck him out of Buffalo and he's on his way here."

"Jonesy," I said wearily, "even if he is on a train tonight, you and I don't need to meet it. We'll probably see him close up at the prison in the morning." Much as I might normally share Jones' excitement about the arrival of the assassin, I was too heavy a sleeper to be roused even for such a momentous occasion.

"Parker, you old stick-in-the-mud. Come on. This will be fun. It's a big event. A historic moment."

"Not for me. You go on if you like. You can tell me all about it later. I'm going back to sleep." I rolled over, closed my eyes, and tried to relax. After a moment, my senses perked up as I realized that Jones had not left the room. Suddenly, I flinched as a tremor ran from the sole of my right foot up my leg. Jones had reached under the blanket to tickle my foot.

"All right! Cut it out. I'm coming." I sat up and could vaguely make out Jones smirking by the end of the bed.

"Get dressed," he said as he turned toward the door. "I'll wait for you downstairs. Be sure to dress so we can go straight to work if need be."

I walked over to the washbowl on my dresser and splashed some cold water on my face. I was irked by the lengths to which Jones had gone to rouse me. It was not the first time he had shown persistence in an effort to include me in some bold undertaking that did not really appeal to me. In some ways, I served as his tether, he as my goad. For over a year, he had been trying to convince me to join him in a trip to an opium den in New York's Chinatown. To Jones, it was a fascinating prospect with Mott Street beckoning as a highway to adventure. I saw it as an experiment fraught with danger and best avoided. Perhaps hoping to wear down my resistance, perhaps somewhat sharing my concern, he had not yet gone without me.

Jones and I had been the best of friends since early freshman year. Despite the apparent differences between us, we really complemented each other well. For me college came after the socially dispiriting experience of high school. I had kept up with my group of grade school chums all along but, as we grew older, the relations failed to mature. By my teenage years, the same old games of football and jokes about the girls and teachers failed to sustain my interest. Despite being surrounded by my lifelong pals, I felt socially isolated, unable to reach out for new friends. It was as if, without the anchor of my mother's affections, I floated aimlessly through the sea of my school days. Despite an active life that was full of social intercourse, I felt a gnawing loneliness.

Jones seemed to sense this when we met at Barnes Hall on an October day freshman year. He made friends easily and was already in great demand, yet he pursued my companionship, seemingly attracted to and challenged by my inaccessibility. As we came to know one another better, he would brace at my persistent questioning of his brazen ways. Underneath his bravado, however, he appreciated the suggestion of limits and valued a friend who was not bowled over by his acerbic assertiveness.

The contrasts in our personalities were evident from our earliest encounters. Before our friendship had jelled, we would occasionally find ourselves competing in a dormitory poker game.

Jones' boisterous facade gave him a formidable poker face. "Oh, Johnny," he would taunt when I stayed with a hand despite his continuing to raise the pot, "you're going to rue the day you sat down at the card table with me." I did not deign to reply, maintaining a stony stoical expression throughout. One particular deal left him and me as the sole remaining players facing off across a large pot. I followed his raise with one of my own. "There's that nervous twitch again," he exclaimed. "A practiced eye can read your cards in your cheek muscles!" But he could not disrupt my composure. I replied in an even tone, "and your uncertainty can be heard in your absurd and exaggerated efforts to unnerve a superior opponent." I won the pot, his admiration, and his friendship.

~

I walked gingerly down the stairs so as not to disturb Mrs. T's slumber. In the foyer, Jones stood tapping his foot, my overcoat draped over his arm. I managed a weak smile as a I donned my hat and coat and we were soon headed down Seminary Street and across North Street toward the station.

A small crowd, a couple hundred people or so, filled the platform and overflowed onto the street. Men and women of all ages and appearances clung together in small groups, speaking in hushed tones. An air of tense anticipation seemed to hang over the gathering. Looking around, I recognized the faces of some of those who had been milling around the station the previous afternoon when I got off work. These were the handful who were so intent on catching a glimpse of Czolgosz that they were practically camped out at the station regardless of whether or not a train was due. Although few of those present had direct knowledge of the assassin's scheduled arrival that night, the presence of reporters and police tipped them off to the fact that something important was expected.

"There were even bigger crowds here for the evening train," Jones said. I just nodded silently, still uncomfortable with my presence in such an unseemly gathering.

Jones and I squeezed onto the platform and talked idly for fifteen or twenty minutes. Then, from the hum of conversation around us, a man's voice bellowed.

"Listen," he called out, "Jack Cavanaugh and I've been talking and we think maybe they're going to sneak him in over at the Lehigh Valley Station. That's where we're heading, if anyone cares to join us."

"You're nuts," someone called back. "Why would they use any station other than the one right across the street from the prison?" Through the crowd, I could not identify either speaker.

"That's right," replied the first man, "and what better way to throw us off if they know that's what we'll be thinking."

"Aw, go on then. Leave more room for the rest of us."

I shifted position and craned my neck and could see two men hop off the platform and head in the direction of the Lehigh Valley Station across town. A half-dozen or so stragglers soon hurried after them.

Jones shook his head. "They're making a mistake," he said.

About 15 minutes later, just after 2 o'clock, the crowd perked up at the sound of an approaching train, an arrival unprecedented at this late hour. Voices grew louder, a woman's shrill voice shouted "Here it comes," and the crowd pushed toward the tracks as a four-car passenger train pulled slowly into the station. The last car lurched slowly into view with only a faint glow of light penetrating its windows. The shades were pulled down and paper had been placed over the windows to prevent anyone from peering in. Recognizing this as the special car prepared for the assassin, the crowd, roaring with anticipation, surged toward it, following until it came to rest at the Chapel Street end of the platform. As the mob drew away from me, I saw a bench a few feet away and climbed atop for a better view.

The rear door of the car was thrown open and a dozen or more police officers were poised to disembark.

A deep voice shouted from the train, "Stand back. We will brook no interference and do not wish to hurt anyone." No one moved. Those toward the rear of the crowd saw no need to and those in the front were hemmed in. I turned to comment to Jones and realized that he had left my side. I quickly scanned the crowd but could not locate him.

The officers stepped down onto the platform. The throng hardly budged, compelling them to press forward forcibly. One of the officers drew his gun and those near him pulled back. I heard the same deep voice call out in a commanding tone "Don't shoot, men. Use your clubs." At these words some of the crowd pulled back, but others only rushed forward to take their place. Following the officers, a number of prison guards appeared by the train door. They surrounded several men in civilian garb and one man with head downcast who, undeniably from his demeanor, could be recognized as Leon Czolgosz.

Another roar went up from the crowd at the sight of him.

"Let us at him," one shouted.

"I've got my rope," called another, and I could see a noose held up above the mob.

The officers and keepers were well-disciplined and paid these challenges no mind. Within moments, they had descended from the train car and began to push their way through the crowd. Although they were mostly lost to sight, I could somewhat see, and more often hear, their efforts to clear the way. But, try as they would, they could not hold back the crowd. I could hear the angry shouts. "Let us have him!" "We'll give him his due!" The officers, with Czolgosz presumably dragged along somewhere in their midst, forced their way through the jam by sheer effort of strength and will. Those on the outskirts of the crowd continued to push forward in hopes of glimpsing the assassin even as those toward the center were pushed back by his guards.

From my vantage point on the bench, I watched the party fight their way across State Street. Soon they reached the far sidewalk and the big iron prison gate swung open. Guards, prisoner, and officials disappeared within. The crowd pressed against the gates as the keepers struggled to close them.

I looked around and saw there were only a few people left on the platform.

"Was that really the assassin?" one woman asked another.

"Who else could it be with all this commotion?" her companion replied, drawing her shawl tight against the cool night air.

An old man shuffled near to them and spit a glob of tobacco juice on to the platform. The women pulled back from him in disgust. Oblivious of their reaction, he leaned toward them and spoke.

"I spied one pasty-faced fellow with a top-hat and a sour complexion. I'm sure that was Leon Czolgosz." Later, I determined

that he had actually glimpsed the reporter from the New York
World.

Jones was nowhere in sight. I walked along the outskirts of
the crowd which showed no sign of breaking up but could not find
him. Finally, I shrugged my shoulders and turned to walk back
across the tracks toward the boarding house.

Arriving there, I went up to my room and saw that it was
only 3 am. What had seemed like hours had been a mere 90
minutes. The night's excitement ebbed before the beckoning
pillows and, shucking off my jacket and shoes, I lay down in my
bed and was soon asleep.

It seemed as if only minutes had passed when I sat up,
suddenly awake. I almost expected Jones to be there again but the
room was empty. It was nearly pitch dark with only a glimmer of
moonlight passing through the trees into my second story window
and casting a dappled pattern upon the floor. On the easy chair in
the corner, Ezzie was perfectly still. If she slept with one eye open, I
could not detect it in the dim moonlight. I reached over for the
watch resting on the night table and could barely make out the
time, 5:30. I'd slept for less than three hours. I wiped a thin band of
perspiration from my brow and tried to remember the dream that
had interrupted my sleep. I could remember standing on Brooklyn's
7th Avenue late at night. My mother approached with a shuffling
gait. "Mother!" I called. But she looked blankly past me without
recognition, much as she had when I'd last seen her. Suddenly,
Archie "Black-eye" Johnson loomed out of the darkness. Dr. Gerin
and I had examined Johnson the previous day, cleaning and
applying salve to a nasty assortment of bedsores. Johnson was small
and wiry, but with a hapless expression that belied the danger
conveyed by his nickname. It was not certain if his moniker came
from giving or receiving black eyes. I could only presume it was the
former. He was in for bank robbery, a repeat offender. In my
dream, Johnson now menaced my mother. He moved in on her, his
muscular arms and thin fingers extended to grasp her. Mother
retreated into the night through a thick fog down some
unidentifiable Brooklyn street. She called out to me in a panic
"Johnny! Johnny!" I stood as if frozen, unable to move, and could
only watch desperately as the fog and Johnson simultaneously
closed in on her. It was at that fearful moment that I woke up with

a start. As I mulled over the dream, I had the odd realization that the voice in the fog sounded more like Abby Tolson than my mother.

There was no point in trying to get back to sleep since I was due at the prison at 7. I stretched and groaned, clambered out of bed and fell into the armchair by the window. The second-floor room faced the front of the house and afforded a view across Seminary Street to the north. Bright moonlight revealed a faint outline of trees in the yard casting a dapple of shadow and light across the lawn. Auburn seemed to be at rest except for the distant rumble of some sort of heavy equipment moving around the yard of one of the city's many factories. If there was still any commotion in front of the prison, its sound did not penetrate the still night air. Even the crickets were asleep; the morning songbirds not yet awake.

Returning to bed, I lit the gas lamp on the night stand and picked up the thick novel I had been working my way through since arriving in Auburn. It was discouraging to see that I had found time to read only a couple hundred pages over the past six weeks. If only I had more than an occasional few minutes for light reading. Jones had loaned me his copy of Theodore Dreiser's *Sister Carrie* with a strong recommendation. He insisted I would enjoy its unorthodox realism as well as its frank discussion of sexuality. It is the latter, given that the heroine is what is generally viewed as a wayward woman, that had earned the novel its reputation for immorality and led to the sale of only a few hundred copies.

Jones was drawn to the scandalous as far as art and entertainment were concerned. The year before, the Tolson Twins and I had been his guests at a performance of the play *Sapho*. Abby Tolson poked me in the ribs and whispered "don't get any ideas, buster," when Fanny, the unmarried heroine, seems pleased to be carried up the stairs by a male acquaintance. This was the suggestive scene that had so offended Anthony Comstock and the other self-appointed guardians of public morality. Although Jones and the Tolsons went too far in praising the show's straightforward portrayal of the bawdy seductress, it certainly did not deserve to be censored. Fortunately, the actress Olga Nethersole was quickly cleared of public decency charges. When loaning me his copy of *Sister Carrie*, Jones said I should feel privileged that he would entrust me with such a rarity, boasting that he would some day be the owner of a valuable first edition of a literary classic. I had enjoyed Stephen Crane's *Maggie* a couple of years earlier, and was ready for another look at life in America's less genteel sectors.

At 6:15, Carrie having completed her first awkward performance on stage, I put the book aside. After some stretching and a few push-ups, I headed down the hall to the bathroom to shave and wash up. It was with some interest that I found it unoccupied. Jones, who was usually just finishing up as I arrived, apparently had not returned home from his over-night activities. Most mornings he was up before dawn for an early breakfast so he could enjoy a brisk constitutional around town before heading over to the prison. He swore by it as a key to health. The daily walks did seem to keep him vigorous.

Feeling clean and somewhat refreshed, I finished dressing, trying to smooth over the wrinkles in the pants and shirt I'd slept in, and went down for Mrs. T's usual breakfast of fried eggs, bacon, warmed bread, and coffee. The hot coffee was especially welcome this morning. As always, Mrs. Thomas wore a shapeless, cotton house-dress, protected by a frilly white apron. It was a uniform of her kind, ensuring that her womanhood would be clearly recognized as the matronly variety. She bustled around the kitchen, busy with her morning chores. We exchanged a few words on the weather, and she informed me she had a prospective tenant for the empty room on the third floor. Apparently, droves of reporters were already arriving in town in anticipation of the Czolgosz incarceration and execution. While many, particularly those with large expense accounts, would be rooming at the downtown hotels, others would seek the homey comfort and lower cost of Auburn's boarding houses.

Despite my night-time activities, I now felt rejuvenated and was ready to face the day. The dawning sun, just above the horizon, cast a long shadow before me as I walked down Seminary Street toward the prison. I remembered, as a child, feeling an odd sort of power in my ability to direct my shadow over certain flora or fauna, an errant insect perhaps, thereby depriving it of the sun's sustenance. Or sneaking up on a friend, watching to see when he would notice my shadow's gradual appearance in his path. How rarely we recognize the shadows that blend in with the contours of the landscape. And how easily shadows can reach out from the dark corners of our own lives to overtake us.

But in the morning light, the prison cast its shadow away from me. It seemed less imposing, as if the bright sunshine somehow penetrated its thick, brick walls if not quite banishing the darkness, at least diminishing its force. As the main gate loomed ahead, I was surprised to see a large assemblage of men and women and even a few children still gathered out front on State Street. With the assassin now ensconced safely within the prison walls, it was hard to imagine what they hoped to witness. The crowd was more pliable than it had been at 2 a.m., and with little effort I pushed my way through. Just within the gate, Jonesy stood among a group of men. I recognized Keeper John Martin, front-gate Keeper James Griffin, and Frank Winegar, the prison clerk.

"He really put on some act," Martin was saying as I walked up behind Jones. "I think he was shamming but Tupper is convinced he's crazy."

"Are you talking about Czolgosz?" I interrupted, pretty sure that I knew the answer to my own question. "What's been going on?"

"What happened to you?" Jones asked in return, turning to face me. "You missed all the excitement."

For the first time I noticed a bright red bruise on Jones' forehead.

"My god, Jonesy! How'd you get that welt?"

Martin laughed. "Your pal got a little too close to the wrong end of a billy club. One of the guards from Buffalo whacked him one as we were fighting our way across State Street."

I shook my head. "That's one bit of excitement I'm not sorry to have missed."

"Oh it's not so bad," Jonesy replied. "I was actually trying to help hold the crowd back but I guess to that fellow I looked like part of the mob. Anyway, Martin here had the privilege of serving on the welcoming committee and was just filling us in."

Keeper Martin doffed his cap at the acknowledgment of his important role.

"What I'd like to know," I said, "is how so many people knew to meet that particular train."

"Actually," Martin replied, "only reporters from the Auburn papers, the Bulletin and the Advertiser, were officially informed, but as usual the others seemed to find out. Of course, the police and keepers knew. There were a bunch of onlookers who somehow got word, including your pal Jones here. Most unseemly for a man of his stature." He frowned in mock reproval at Jones who laughed at the mild reprimand. "He claims you were out and about as well but no one else saw hide nor hair of you."

"I was there but I stayed well behind the crowd. I thought your job was tough enough without me joining the mob."

"And a mob it was," Martin continued, "Mostly it was the same crowd who've been out there the last two days every time a train comes in from the west, just hoping to catch a glimpse of the assassin. Hundreds of 'em, I suppose. They got all worked up when the train rolled into the station. I'd been on the train since Rochester and had the distinction of being cuffed to the prisoner."

"Who was that fellow who pulled the gun?' I asked. "That was scary."

"Yeah, I'd say that was a mistake," Martin replied. "Not necessary at all. He was one of the deputies from Buffalo, a fellow named Metzler. I think he just got a little over-excited as we exited from the train into the midst of the crowd. The people were pressing around and were pretty boisterous. Only a few were violent, but enough to give us a dickens of a time. Who knows what might have happened if they'd gotten their hands on the prisoner."

"Especially that one fellow who was shouting to kill him and throw rocks at him," Jones added. "He was just a few feet away from me. What a nasty expression on his face!"

I turned to Keeper Griffin. "It looked like you had a tough time with the gate."

"I've never witnessed anything like it in all my years at the prison," he replied. "We got the gate open all right but were barely able to get it closed. Try as we might, a couple of them slipped in. We had to round 'em up and throw them back out again. Almost threw Jones out with them." Jonesy's participation in the mob's activities had clearly marked him as a target for some friendly derision.

"So, what happened when you got him inside?" I asked.

Keeper Martin replied, "Well he was pretty scared. He was whimpering and hiding his head as we worked our way through the crowd. Just the kind of cowardly behavior you often see in these supposedly cold-blooded killers. And then, here's the real kicker, when we got him inside the Warden's office and sat him down on a bench, he starts twitching like he's going into convulsions and kind of passes out. And all the while he's still handcuffed to my left arm. Then, as soon as Doc Gerin shows up and starts to look him over, the prisoner perks right up. So we take him down to the condemned cells where he undresses as polite as could be and goes straight to bed. Later, Gerin said he thought Czolgosz was shamming illness but he won't know for sure until after the admitting exam later this morning. I assume you boys will be helping with that."

"We usually do," I said. I was beginning to look forward to that event and was pleased to have my upcoming role in the day's excitement acknowledged. The behavior that Keeper Martin was describing lent the assassin an air of mystery: one moment apparently overwrought, the next seemingly calm and controlled. We had some pretty strange characters in Auburn Prison, but this one might take the cake. It was encouraging to note that Gerin would be evaluating the prisoner's behavior during our morning examination. I was confident that I would form some opinions of my own, although it was unlikely that I would be bold enough to express them to my mentor.

"That's right," Jones added. "Gerin wouldn't know what to do without Parker and me there to sharpen his pencil." The men laughed.

"So Martin," I ventured, "what about on the train? Did Czolgosz talk much? Did you learn anything? Tell us, what's your impression of him?"

Martin cut off my inquisition. "You sure do have a lot of questions. But I can tell you, the prisoner had plenty to say, all right. And the guys from Buffalo said he was pretty talkative there too. Actually they said he ran hot and cold. One day he'd be all quiet and morose and wouldn't even answer a direct question about his own needs. The next day he's jabbering it up about politics and complaining about the dirt in his cell and when's he gonna get a change of clothing and whatnot. On the train, we asked him all the usual questions. Did he have any accomplices? What about that guy in St. Louis? Did he have help tying the handkerchief around his hand? He answered just like the papers said he would that he acted alone. He denied he knew those New

Jersey anarchists. Wouldn't say nothing about anyone else. He said he was sorry for Mrs. McKinley and, believe it or not, said he thought his trial was fair. That really threw me. Here's a fellow who'd like to overturn our whole system of government, if you believe that anarchist claptrap, and he thinks he's getting a fair trial. Pretty strange."

"Did he show any evidence of sickness on the train?" I asked, trying not to sound too much like the physician in training.

"Are you kidding? He was in great spirits. Ate a couple of sandwiches. Smoked a cigar. Maybe it's the cigar that made him ill." Martin gave out a guffaw at his own joke. "Well, you fellows may not know it but I've been working all night and I think I'll head home for some shut eye. You can read the rest in the papers." The men laughed again, knowing that Keeper Martin would be the last person to talk to a reporter. The keepers liked to poke fun at the newspapers for their exaggerations and sensationalizing about the notorious inmates of Auburn State Prison.

"Let me walk you out," Griffin suggested to Martin. "I'll help keep those reporters off your back."

The two keepers headed out the gate, each holding up a hand and shaking his head to caution the onlookers not to bother them. Heedless of the warning, several men, most likely reporters, approached them. A thin man with a pinched face and an ingratiating smile seemed about to speak when Griffin grabbed him roughly by the coat lapel and pushed him forcefully back. The man tripped over his own feet as he stumbled backward. He stood up and gave a meek smile of acquiescence, brushing the street dust off his pants. The other reporters retreated a few steps and the crowd drew back to allow Griffin and Martin to continue unmolested. The prison guards clearly had had enough. They would brook no more interference from Czolgosz' welcoming committee.

"I sure wouldn't want to get on Griffin's bad side," Jones said as he and I turned to enter the prison. We were definitely late for work, but this was a morning in which no one would notice.

~

A couple of hours later, the moment we had been waiting for since the end of the trial finally arrived. Flanked by prison keepers, Leon Czolgosz was ushered into the examining room. He wore the prison standard horizontal striped vest and pants over a white shirt. The flat-topped, brimmed cap sat uneasily atop his head. My first impression of him as he was seated on the examining table was of a quite ordinary man. The prison garb tends to make everyone look somewhat alike, but Czolgosz seemed fairly average in both stature and demeanor. I had assisted Dr. Gerin in enough of his systematic examinations of newly arrived prisoners that I was getting accustomed to viewing the inmates along anatomical and medical lines. With Czolgosz, the feature that drew my immediate attention were the nearly healed bruise marks around his jaw and eyes. Someone, whether his captors at the Exposition or his keepers in the Buffalo jail, had treated him roughly. One fresh welt swelled on his left cheek, a sure sign that a member of the early morning mob had landed a shot. At first, the prisoner appeared somewhat dim-witted, staring straight ahead with a dull look in his eyes. As the exam progressed, he looked around the room with apparent curiosity but little evidence of emotion. Only for a brief moment did I catch his eyes studying my face with what I took to be a look of intelligence and interest. When our eyes met, he held my gaze for the briefest moment before reverting quickly to his previous demeanor, offering no acknowledgment that there had been any contact between us.

Dr. Gerin began his examination, listening to the prisoner's heart, looking into his mouth and ears and feeling for his internal organs. Jones served as assistant, providing instruments as needed. It was my job to record Czolgosz' physical characteristics, which I did as follows: Height, 5 feet 7 ½ inches. Weight, 141 pounds. Several scars on each hand. Several moles on front and back of neck. Head circumference, 22.2 inches. Body, neither lean nor plump. Skin healthy. Musculature, minimal as of a person used to some leisure. Head, well-modeled, oval and symmetrical, the forehead a trifle narrow but fairly high. Hair, light brown and curly. The nose, straight and well proportioned, ears symmetrical. Blue eyes somewhat wide apart and deeply set. His upper lids seem heavy, giving the eyes a dreamy look. The left lid is a little more elevated. His chin, while not square, is well shaped and firm. Full lips. The finely chiseled upper lip lends a certain attractiveness to the face. The mouth is well proportioned and kept firmly closed. Normal teeth, but in poor condition. His expression is not unpleasant but leaves an impression of introspection and perhaps cynicism. His features convey little emotion or reaction except for his eyes, which rove constantly around the room, at times seeking to hold the gaze of others.

While making these observations, I was surprised by the prisoner's attitude in replying to Gerin's occasional questions. Many of the men we see are slow-witted, answering clumsily and with some difficulty, if at all. Others are sharper, responding more quickly and displaying attitudes that range from mocking to hostile to matter-of-fact. Only a few seemed at all thoughtful. These were rarely the career criminals but were more often found among the men who had lived conventional lives, perhaps convicted of crimes of passion. By contrast, Czolgosz seemed to ponder each question with some gravity, pausing as if to consider his answer, and only then appearing to self-consciously shape his reply, even if only a simple yes or no. He struck me as a man who took life very seriously--a man perhaps given to more contemplative moods. If so, he was a rarity among the inmates and not at all the sort of brutish rogue I had imagined the assassin to be.

Later, the examination completed and Dr. Gerin gone to report to the warden, I turned to Jones.

"So, buddy, what do you think?"

"He's certainly healthy enough. I guess they feed their assassins pretty well over in the Buffalo jail. No sign of any ill-effects from last night's journey. If he suffered from some extreme of nervousness, it seems to have passed."

"But weren't you surprised? I was expecting someone much more sinister, like our other murderers but even worse. Czolgosz seemed kind of shy, like a wall flower."

"Watch out for the shy ones, I always say. They are the ones who'll get you in the end." Jones had an answer for everything.

"Didn't he impress you as more thoughtful, yet, at the same time, more reserved than the usual prisoner?"

"Yeah. So what? Do you want to invite him to join the book club? Or bring him down to O'Malley's for a beer?" Jones walked over to the supply cabinet and picked up a roll of cotton which he began to toss idly in the air.

"No, not that," I answered slowly. "I'm thinking more along the lines of research. Do you remember about my idea about interviewing prisoners and learning about their upbringing and early life experiences? Trying to understand the forces that molded them toward their criminal purposes?"

"I do. And you'll remember my idea about learning medicine and making a buck at it."

"Right, and I'm sure you will. But listen. Czolgosz could be just the kind of subject I've been looking for. He could have the patience for that kind of interview, maybe even an interest in it. I might not have to pry everything out of him."

"I don't know, from what Keeper Martin and others have said, he keeps his own counsel. Talks when he feels like it and chooses his own subjects."

"That's my point." I hoisted myself up to sit on the examining table and leaned forward on my knees. "He does seem different from the common criminals we deal with every day, even the murderers. If he really is an anarchist then he's got a whole philosophy of life behind his actions. And, he could be a lot smarter than we're used to seeing."

"I don't know about that. The reports in the papers paint him as pretty dull. It's hard to think of him as much of a philosopher. It's more likely that he's the dupe of some pretty crafty people, a heartless thug eager to obey orders for some vainglorious cause."

"I'm not saying it will be easy, just that it could be an opportunity, an exceptional opportunity. Do you think it's possible?"

Jones thought for a moment. He dropped the cotton roll, walked over to my side, and, smiling broadly, slapped me on the back. "Parker, you may be right. This could be just the kind of criminal mind you'd been hoping for, someone a bit more complex than that old degenerate Krist. A case that will pave your way into the Philadelphia Medical Journal." Jones knew that I aspired to write and had set my sights on prestigious publications.

"Seriously, do you think so?"

"I can see you mean business here. If you're asking if I think Doc Gerin will go along, well, I kind of doubt it. And, if the warden has to be involved, you don't have a chance. This is a pretty high profile prisoner you're wanting to mess around with here. But, you know, my mother always told me that it never hurts to ask. She says the worst that can happen is that they say no, but I

say the worst that can happen is that you make a fool of yourself.
Of course, Gerin already looks askance on psychiatry as a career
choice. So, what do you have to lose?"
"My thinking exactly. I'll broach it with Gerin this
afternoon. That will give me a few hours to get my courage up and
figure out just how to put it."

~

        The rest of the workday primarily afforded me with plenty
of time to feel nervous. Although the thought of working with the
assassin was an exciting one, I dreaded bringing this idea to Gerin
and several times almost convinced myself to abandon it. But the
prospect of interviewing Czolgosz began to take on larger
proportions. Here at last was a way to prove the serious nature of
my interest in psychiatry to my father, to Dr. Gerin, and to myself.
Impatient with the day to day realities of life in medical school and
with my work in the prison, I yearned for some way to impart a
sense of grander purpose to my chosen profession. To work directly
with a prisoner of Czolgosz' notoriety was a once in a lifetime
opportunity to start my career with the kind of prominent
encounter that ordinarily was available only to the most renowned
alienists. I was already imagining the coup of publishing an
important journal article before even receiving my degree. Of
course, this could also be a once in a lifetime chance to incur the
wrath of my mentor and convince him that I was a complete fool.
The dread of being shamed, which had been my constant
adolescent companion, reared up again and again. Each time I
faced it down, but in the end could only hold my fear at bay. Thus
it was with a stormy mixture of excitement and trepidation that
the awaited hour approached.
        Finally, 4:00 pm rolled around. This was the time when
Dr. Gerin would be finishing up paperwork in his office and when
he was available to Jones and myself. I felt certain that, even
having been on the job since 3 a.m., Gerin would keep to his
schedule with his usual, nearly Prussian punctuality. My
confidence was not misplaced.
        "Parker, how nice to see you." Gerin looked up from a file.
He sat in his big, brown leather chair and leaned over his broad,
dark-stained desk. His framed medical degree, embodying as it did

my own holy grail, seemed to mock me from its perch on the wall behind him over a bank of file cabinets. Several landscape paintings adorned the side walls, Gerin's effort at overcoming the dull atmosphere of the windowless room. "I was just reviewing your notes on the assassin. Very thorough, although a bit of subjectivity seems to have slipped in."

"Sorry about that," I replied. "I guess it was the alienist in me overpowering the mere medical assistant."

"That's all right. It's nonetheless a good report. Have a seat and tell me what's on your mind this afternoon."

I sat down in one of the overstuffed chairs across the desk from Gerin. I leaned forward in tense excitement. "Actually, it's about Czolgosz, sir. I'd like to interview him. He seems like a potentially excellent subject." I'd decided that a short, direct statement would best serve my ends.

"Interview him? You can't be serious?"

"I am. You remember, on my application, my interest in identifying some prisoners whom I could study as part of my exploration of criminal psychology. I haven't really followed up on that so far. Partly out of my own inertia, and partly because none of the prisoners I've encountered have seemed like good subjects. But Czolgosz could be just right. He struck me as unusually thoughtful, the way he took his time answering your questions. I'd like to give it a shot."

Gerin sat for a moment in thought, tapping his pencil on the blotter. "This is a highly unusual request. I am certainly aware of your interests. Even if it were possible, are you sure this is the right inmate?"

"I do, sir. I've assisted dozens of examinations and Czolgosz is the first I've seen who has struck me as a likely subject, strange as that may be."

"Strange is a good word for it." Dr. Gerin gazed at one of his wall paintings as if he might peer through its two dimensions to a distant land. "The paternal part of me wants to protect you from his influence, perhaps from your own misguided inclinations as well. After all, who knows what kind of ideas he might infect you with. But, I must treat you as a young physician. I see that, at least for the present, you are dead set on this exploration of criminal psychiatry. But Czolgosz! It's outrageous." He paused again. I sat silently, knowing my best course of action was to let him think this through. I could imagine the struggle playing out in Gerin's mind. On the one hand, his conservative nature and studied formality would warn him against my project. But other forces would be pulling in my favor. I felt sure I had piqued his curiosity with my interest in criminal psychology. On some level, he too might view my study of Czolgosz as a refreshing change of pace from the routine of prison medicine.

"Warden Mead won't like it," Gerin said, as if talking to himself. "But then, he does not necessarily need to know. I'll tell you what, Parker." The shadow passed from his face and he came as close as ever to an actual smile. "It's not unheard of for condemned men to get more regular medical treatment, our scant efforts with Mr. Krist the other day notwithstanding. I'll schedule a weekly check-up for Czolgosz and try to keep him a little longer for your purposes. That is, assuming he's cooperative. Which is a big assumption."

"Thank you, sir. I promise you I will do everything I can to live up to the confidence you are placing in me." I started to get up.

"One more thing." Gerin now spoke forcefully. "You must not tell anyone about this. Jones will know, but I assume you can trust him to keep quiet. But if the warden finds out he'll put a stop to it in a moment. The guards will be a problem. I'll see what I can do to keep them at a distance. Really, I am taking a bit of a risk for you here. Don't be surprised if I change my mind over the weekend."

Somehow, I did not think he would. I got up and we exchanged "good nights." Already my mind was racing, nervous and hopeful, beginning to plot the strategy for the first session.

Chapter Five

~

Tuesday, October 1, 1901

"We'll holler if there's any trouble," Dr. Gerin reassured the keepers. He asked them to wait in the main room of the clinic and led Czolgosz and me into the auxiliary examining room. This smaller chamber had the same drab olive paint, little in the way of equipment, and a gray buffed-metal examining table. Of course, there were two of the cane-backed chairs, manufactured by the inmates in their workshop, that were ubiquitous in the prison. The wooden door swung with a slight creek on unoiled hinges. A small pane of glass two-thirds of the way up afforded a view into the outer room.

It had been late Monday afternoon when Dr. Gerin finally informed me that the first session with Czolgosz was scheduled for 11 a.m. the next day. Gerin expected that, barring a variety of potential obstacles, a session could be arranged for each of the next four weeks at this time. The fifth Tuesday, October 29, was the likely date of the execution. Four sessions! So few for such a daunting project. Each moment would be invaluable. At times, it was almost overwhelming to contemplate the task I had set for myself. After all, I could not escape the fact that I was very much the novice.

Despite having some familiarity with the theory and practice of psychiatry as developed by the great alienists--Jean Charcot and Pierre Janet of France, Josef Breuer and Sigmund Freud of Austria--I was well aware that book knowledge and a handful of lectures were a long way from practical training and experience. Many of these psychiatrists used hypnotism as a therapeutic device. In my psychiatry class the previous semester, there had been a lecture on the pioneering use of hypnosis by the French alienists Charcot and Bernheim. I had read William James' description of a variety of methods for inducing hypnosis--the use of pressure on certain body parts, staring into a patient's eyes, or encouraging concentration on a ticking watch--but, even if I were trained in such a method, it was hard to imagine that Czolgosz would submit to it. Under the circumstances, he could not possibly have the level of trust necessary to be brought successfully under a hypnotist's power.

I had kept up my German language skills and last summer had succeeded in working my way through Breuer and Freud's _Studien über Hysterie-_'studies in hysteria' it would be in English. In it, Freud advocated a method of analysis that does not rely entirely on hypnosis. This approach involves following a train of thought with the patient until encountering a level of resistance that indicates the presence of a pathogenic blockage. By continually probing along new threads, the alienist is eventually able to penetrate this nucleus, bringing to light the hitherto concealed unconscious motivations. Although Freud's technique was geared to the cure of hysteria, I believed that it could be applied more generally to exploring the psychological makeup of a given subject. I was eager to bring this methodology to bear on the assassin. My only concern was in Freud's caveat that success requires the full consent and confidence of the patient. And what a patient! Whether reluctant, willing, or even enthusiastic, he was in every sense an unknown quantity.

Monday night I had attempted a systematic review of what I knew about the prisoner, which was precious little, it turned out. I understood his physical condition, description, and health, but beyond that had only the vague impressions I had formed during his examination. Newspaper reports described him as taciturn, with little to say to the authorities, refusing to participate in his own defense, and making barely audible replies to the judge's questions. These could be signs of depression or just the smug determination of a committed fanatic. Czolgosz gave a simple account of the motivation for his deed–"I killed President McKinley because I done my duty." Reports were that he had planned and executed the assassination with painstaking deliberation, displaying no passion during or after the event. He was apparently not a reluctant killer, no Hamlet complaining of his crime, "O cursed spite, that ever I was born to set it right!"

And what of the anarchist philosophy which he claimed informed and inspired his act? As repellent as that doctrine was, I could not believe that holding to a political philosophy, no matter how extreme, was in and of itself delusional. The alienists who had examined Czolgosz in Buffalo had clearly agreed, finding him free of insane delusion, hallucinations, or paranoia. Having determined him sane by legal standards, their inquiry did not proceed to the thornier questions of what psychological conditions had turned this working man into an anarchist, this anarchist into a killer. I was convinced the answers could be found if only I could uncover those areas of his life with strong emotional associations, in particular his experience with authority figures--whether parents, bosses, or politicians. "If only," I reminded myself, trying to balance my tendency toward cocksureness with a healthy measure of reality. This feeling of apprehension was complicated by my understanding that Dr. Gerin also knew I was working in what, for me, was uncharted territory. Failure would be a betrayal of his confidence. Given our brief association and my status as a neophyte in the world of medicine, I was not sure why he would trust me enough to go along with this project in the first place. That uncertainty made me feel all the more beholden to him. Yet mixed with the tension and the doubt was a heady blend of excitement and anticipation. Here at last was the springboard that would set me on my own course, freed from my father's insistent footsteps, freed from my professors' bland counsel, freed from Jonesy's smirks and gibes, and freed, I could only hope, from my own listless inertia.

     With all this on my mind, I slept little, and awoke well before sunrise. The morning progressed at a snail's pace, time moving about as fast as the thick molasses that Mrs. T had poured over my breakfast pancakes. At the prison, work seemed to drag on endlessly, and I checked the time repeatedly on the large clock by the clinic door. Jones, so far in the dark as to my undertaking, asked at one point if I had a train to catch. At a quarter to eleven, Gerin sent Jones to check on some prisoners in their cells. Finally, the appointed hour arrived. The keepers, ever punctual, showed up right on schedule, bringing Czolgosz along between them. Dr. Gerin informed them that we would be conducting a special health assessment of the prisoner in the adjoining room. They seemed a bit pleased to have him out of their hair for the moment and looked on indifferently as we left the main examining room.

Czolgosz' attitude was passive: his face blank and non-expressive. If he wondered what was transpiring, he allowed no hint of such thoughts to show themselves on his countenance. Gerin directed the prisoner to sit in one of the cane-backed chairs. "This is Mr. Parker, whom you may remember from your admitting exam." Czolgosz nodded. "Mr. Parker is a medical student on assignment with me. He is studying to be an alienist with a special interest in criminal psychology. He believes that it would be advantageous for him to interview you."

"They examined me in Buffalo and said I ain't crazy," the assassin protested sullenly. He mumbled his words in a low tone, as if unconcerned as to whether they would eventually reach our ears.

"That's correct," Gerin continued, "and no one's saying that you are. Parker is interested in understanding the makeup of the mind of the sane person who commits a serious crime. It is for this reason that you are of particular interest to him."

Czolgosz stroked his stubbly chin. "How do I know you're not in league with the police, that this isn't another plot to try and trick me into identifying accomplices? If that's the case then you're wasting your time. They tried that in Buffalo with that copper pretending to be a plumber and getting all chummy with me. It's like I've always said, I did it on my own, start to finish, and you won't get me to say otherwise." The assassin gave Dr. Gerin a hard stare and folded his arms across his chest.

Gerin was ready for this resistance. "Frankly, you have every right to be suspicious. I understand that in your position it would be difficult to trust anyone in authority. But I'm sure you will agree that Mr. Parker does not look much like a police detective. In any case, your participation is strictly up to you. You are free to place any topic off limits and to end the session at any time."

Czolgosz looked me over, as if sizing me up and evaluating the reliability of Gerin's characterization. His indifferent expression gave no clue as to his thoughts.

"So, let's say I agree to this." He spoke slowly as if he had all the time in the world. "What's in it for me?"

Once more, Gerin was prepared. He had planned well for this discussion, anticipating each of the assassin's objections.

"A great deal or nothing at all," the doctor replied. "It depends on how you look at it. You'll get a break from your routine once a week, a chance to get away from the condemned cells, and some time conversing with a very bright young man." I could not suppress a slight smile at this unexpected praise. Gerin waited while the prisoner seemed to mull over these dubious if relatively substantial benefits.

Czolgosz let out a short, high-pitched, nervous sounding laugh. Whether it was the result of stress, madness, or dissembling, I could not be sure. "Okay," he said at last. "I guess I'm willing to give it a go. After all, what have I got to lose?" Many men would have chuckled or at least smiled at this ironic conclusion. Czolgosz remained stoical.

"Fine then, it's settled. I will leave you in Mr. Parker's hands while I excuse myself to continue with my duties. You are, of course, expected to be on your best behavior. The keepers will be waiting in the next room should they be needed."

With that, Gerin exited the room. The swinging door slowly oscillated back to rest behind him. I sat in the chair opposite Czolgosz, adjusting its position so I faced him at a slight angle. I took a deep breath, hoping not to reveal my nervousness, and gathered my thoughts.

"Let me tell you a bit about myself and about the direction I'd like our discussion to take." I spoke now for the first time. I felt it was important to reveal a bit of myself to the prisoner to gain his confidence, but I was also aware every second that I talked rather than listened was a moment of lost opportunity. "As Dr. Gerin indicated, I am a fourth-year medical student studying to be an alienist. I am here for the semester as an intern with Dr. Gerin. In the prison, we practice general medicine, not psychiatry. My interest is in the study of psychological factors contributing to criminal behavior, and Dr. Gerin has agreed to allow me to pursue this interest while I am here. Is that clear so far?" Czolgosz nodded and I continued, "It will be useful for me to learn about your family background, your life experiences, your education, your work, and your political thinking. There is not necessarily any need to discuss matters directly involving the assassination. Are you comfortable proceeding on that basis?"

Czolgosz looked at me for a moment in silence. "Well, I don't know." He paused again, staring now down at the floor. "I can't really see how my family or my life would be so interesting to anyone. Not much to either of 'em."

I was not particularly surprised by this reply. From what I'd read and heard of Czolgosz' behavior in the Buffalo jail, he was reluctant to discuss personal matters, but talked freely on a variety of other subjects. Of course, most men are reticent about their private lives. I was ready to back away from this initial sign of resistance in the hope of getting him talking.

"A lot of people feel that way," I replied. "But, I am also interested in your political views and especially in the experiences that helped you to form those views. How would that be for a starting point?"

"I do like to talk politics," he said, looking up at me again. He stretched his arms far out on either side and stifled a yawn. "Sure, that'll be all right." Czolgosz' gestures seemed to convey a lack of involvement. But, I was suspicious. Just as at his initial interview, I thought that I could perceive a sharp intelligence behind his vacant stare. I felt certain that he was more interested in this discussion than he was willing to let on.

"All right," I agreed. "Let's talk politics. Why don't you tell me how you first came to be a critic of the political system."

"That's an easy one." For the first time, his lips curled up into a slight smile. "And, I guess I don't mind telling you. It was the strike in '94 and all the lay-offs that first changed my thinking. Up until then, I'd pretty much taken it as it came, not thought much about exploitation or the war of the classes."

The assassin paused, his eyes half shut. I suppressed an urge to ask another question and waited quietly. After a moment, he spoke again, "I'd heard about socialism and strikes and all but had pretty much figured that was somebody else's business. The '94 strike is when I saw first hand how the bosses had the power and didn't give a damn about the workers. It really got me to thinking. For those capitalists it meant nothing to throw a lot of men off the job, men who'd worked pretty hard to make them rich too."

"Where was the strike? I mean, where were you working at the time?"

"It was at the Newburgh Wire Mill, in Cleveland. I'd been there just a couple of years. There was trouble in the economy at that time and they decided to cut our wages. We wouldn't have none of that. Walked right out on 'em. But they just laughed at us and hired themselves a fresh lot of workers. Scabs. That strike was a complete bust. The workers never got nothin'." I made a mental

note of Czolgosz' attitude toward the mill bosses: evidence of a
possible resentment of authority.

"Did you return to work at the mill?"

"Yeah, they hired a new foreman and a bunch of us got our
jobs back using false names. That's when I picked up the moniker
of Fred C. Nieman that maybe you've heard about. Fred's from my
middle initial. I never had a middle name, just the initial. For some
reason, my brothers took to calling me 'Fred' when we were kids.
Nieman is for my mom, my real mom that is. I stayed on until I'd
had enough and finally quit working back in '97."

I considered following this early opening to ask about his
mother or brothers, but it seemed too soon, given his reservations
of only a few moments earlier. I didn't want to scare him off just
when we were starting to make some progress. Any pretense of
reluctance on his part had been, for the moment, dropped.

"Do you like to be called Fred, or Leon?"

"Oh, Fred's all right back home on the farm. Otherwise,
it'll be Leon if you want to get familiar." His lips curled into a
definite smirk. I knew better than to accept this offer of ersatz
intimacy. I didn't need to be on a first-name basis with the assassin.

"What was the work like at the mill?" I asked.

Czolgosz grimaced as he thought back to his days in the
wire mill. "It was long, hard work and I was pretty beat by the end
of the day. That was dangerous work too. I always tried to work
steady and careful. Most of the men got a lot of fines but not me.
No sense in it really. I was a wire-winder and you never knew when
the wire might cut loose and grab you. A lot of men got cut bad.
But I knew to take it slow and keep an eye to safety. Got cut just
this one time, over here." He pointed to the small scar on his
cheek. "That wire snapped right back at me. It might have taken
my eye out if I'd been less careful, or less lucky."

"You said the strike changed your thinking. Could you tell
me more about that?"

"I s'pose I could." He leaned forward now, resting his
elbows on his thighs. I stifled a smile, hoping to appear as stoic and
detached as the assassin. I did not want to reveal how pleased I was
with Czolgosz' responsiveness. My initial gambit was working. "The
first thing is that I heard from some pretty smart fellows. Union
organizers. They had an idea of what was what and didn't mind
saying so right out. I learned a lot from them. And they got me

reading, union pamphlets at first, but then anything I could get my hands on. I'd only had a few years of common school but I read well enough. At first some of those books were a struggle, I'll tell ya."

"What sorts of things were you reading?"

"Books and pamphlets on socialism mostly. That seemed to be where people were writing about change. Talked a lot with my brother Waldek too. He's a few years older and had been around a bit. But don't start thinking he had something to do with Buffalo, 'cause he didn't, didn't know nuthin about it." He glared at me for just a moment, placing a thick exclamation point on this assertion. It occurred to me that Czolgosz must have been through quite an interrogation in Buffalo. He was looking for a trap at every turn.

"No. I don't think anyone's ever suggested he did. But what kinds of things did you and Waldek talk about?"

"The Bible, for one thing. You know I was more than twenty years old and never had read a word of it. Just took it all from the priests just like they told us. We believed that if we got into any trouble or need and prayed over it, the prayers would be answered. So when we were out of work, we prayed real hard like we were supposed to, prayed God would help us along but it didn't do no good. Then we went to the priests and said we wanted proof that what they'd been telling us was the truth but they just said to keep on praying. So we went and got ourselves a Polish Bible and, Waldek and me, we read it four or five times over. Learned that those priests told it their own way and kept back most of what was in the book. We figured out that the priest's trade was the same as the shoemaker's or any other. But I guess an educated man like yourself knows all about that." It seemed that a tiny smile ran along the edge of his lips. Was he taunting me? If so, better not take the bait. It was more important to follow up on this first evidence that the assassin did indeed possess a critical mind.

"Yes, you are correct. We did talk a lot about religion in college, among other subjects." I was surprised to learn that uneducated men would have taken this kind of initiative. It ran contrary to the common image of the ignorant masses following the most beguiling leader. "Tell me though, what else did you study, either with Waldek or on your own?"

"Lots of things really. There's all sorts of political pamphlets people were handing out around town. The Socialist Labor Party put out a bunch of them. I read one recently called *Echoes of the Working Men*, all about Poles in Philadelphia and New Jersey and how tough their lives are in the factories and their strikes and all. In one place, it takes apart the speech of some priest. I enjoyed that." Again, a slight suggestion of a smile played across his lips. "I read a lot of books too."

"Tell me about some of them."

"One of my favorites is called *Sweet and Holy*. I don't remember the name of the fellow who wrote it. It's about the lives of important socialists. Another book I've been reading is called *In the Name of God* by Stefam Czarniecki. All about a fellow name of Blanka who fought in the revolution of 1848 and winds up in prison for 17 years. They all called him 'The Revolutioner.' The guy fought with a plow in one hand. What an image! I'll tell you. Then there's this book by a guy named Lasalle. I forget what it's called. It's more complicated, all about economy and politics. He's against religion, government, and taxes--all the oppressions."

"What book was your favorite?" I asked. "Is there one that really stands out in terms of how it affected you?" Czolgosz was clearly enjoying this literary discussion. Continuing on this course seemed to be as good a line as any for getting him to agree to come back next week.

"I guess it would have to be that book by Edward Bellamy, *Looking Backward*. I suppose you've heard about it. I hung on to that one for years. I think Waldek's got my copy now. Or Bandowski."

"Bandowski?"

"Oh, he's the fellow that married my sister, Celia. A real smart guy. I kind of look up to him, I guess. He was secretary of the Polish Socialist Society for a while, before they broke up."

"I've read *Looking Backward*," I offered, "It's a powerful and visionary work." Although I could have predicted the novel's appearance on the Gerins' book shelf, until this moment I hadn't known that those with so little schooling read such books. "Tell me what you liked most about it."

"I like that the hero could go to sleep and wake up in a socialist society. That would suit me fine." Here, he smiled in earnest. A small smile, but nonetheless a genuine one. "It seems that anyone who's ever read a book at all has read *Looking Backward*. I even heard that at one time there were clubs all across the country to talk about it. Have you ever heard of that?"

"I have," I answered, "We learned about them in school. They were called Nationalist Clubs because of Bellamy's idea that the nation ought to own all of industry. I think the last one shut down several years ago."

"Yeah, well, think about it, people getting together just to talk about a book, a story, wanting to make its ideas come true. You've got to ask yourself how that could be. I say that folks know that things just ain't right, not the way it's set up today with some having so much service and others with nothing. They'd like to live in a world like in that book, where everyone gets an equal share and you can quit working when you turn forty-five. I know I would. Not that there aren't any problems with Bellamy's thinking, mind you." His eyes lit up now with the smug satisfaction of one who is holding rare and important information.

"Well, I haven't thought too much about it myself. I've heard *Looking Backward* criticized for being too socialist. Some even saw it as un-American. You must have different problems with it than those."

"I sure do. Mostly, it's all that nationalism business. I thought that it was fine at first but, since I've been talking to the anarchists this past year or so, I've realized that ain't the way to go. Really it's just about the opposite of how things ought to be. If you've got a few people making all the decisions then most people will never see their fair share, all Bellamy's fancy story-telling to the contrary."

I was poised to launch a line of inquiry into the anarchist philosophy but, just then, the door swung open and Dr. Gerin entered.

"Our time is up for today," he announced. "The keepers will take you back to your cell now. Do you wish to return on another occasion?"

Czolgosz nodded, any prior animation gone instantly from his expression. "S'pose so. Like I said, I don't have nuthin to lose."

"All right then," Gerin replied. "But, mind you, such treatment is very rare for a condemned man. You must not say a word about these meetings to anyone. Otherwise, we may not be able to continue." He looked sternly for a moment at Czolgosz, making sure that these words had sunk in. Then, he turned back to the door and called to the keepers. As they entered, Tupper glanced at me suspiciously as if wondering what business I could have had for so long with his charge. Czolgosz stood up, eyelids drooping heavily as if he was ready for a nap, and, without even a glance in my direction, he was led out of the clinic by the two guards. Though of average size, he looked small between the hefty keepers in their dark uniforms. They seemed to pull him along, impatient with his shuffling gait. When they were gone, Gerin turned toward me.

"So? How did you make out?"

"Very well, I think, for a first session. I'm glad I'll have a few days to think it over and plan out where to go from here. My strategy was to not press him on anything personal but to stick to the level of ideas. I did learn something of his work history and his readings. He says he'd like to retire at age forty-five." Gerin managed a slight smirk at the sad absurdity of this notion. "He's read a good deal. I was really surprised by it. He's quite the critic in fact."

"That sounds like excellent progress. I'm sorry I had to cut things off, but the keepers were getting a bit impatient. It's likely that it was good to keep the first session short. It doesn't hurt that I interrupted at a point when he seemed to have been engaged in the discussion. That should leave him thirsty for more. It sounds like you're off to a good start."

"I think I am. Really, it's about as good as I could have expected. And thanks for your help. I don't know if I could have handled all of his initial objections myself." Dr. Gerin's commitment to the success of my undertaking was a surprising and helpful development. It was as if, having made the difficult decision to allow the project to go forward, he was now invested in its success.

"Not at all," he replied. "If we're going to do this, we ought to do it right." I was pleased to note his use of the plural pronoun. "Anyway, isn't it time you were off to lunch?"

Agreeing gladly, I excused myself and headed out of the prison into a warm October day. The trees were mostly turned, their bright leaves giving Auburn a festive appearance. I practically skipped down the street toward the boarding house. I was elated, pleased with my performance, gratified by Dr. Gerin's attitude, and confident that I was on the right track. I was sure that I had succeeded, for the moment, in winning Czolgosz over. He was self-disclosing, at least on certain areas and as long as I didn't push things too far or too fast. Czolgosz seemed interested in eliciting my thinking as well. There was a clear basis for building rapport. That alone was a major accomplishment for an initial interview. But, could I get as far as I needed in the four weeks available? And, as the date of execution approached, could I be confident that he would remain a willing and interested participant? In the next Tuesday session it was imperative that I guide the conversation away from more abstract influences like books, and toward the actual experiences that had shaped his life.

I pondered what I had learned so far. Here was a man who, seven years ago, had concluded that his employers were not to be trusted. A few years later, he decided that the Catholic priests had deceived him as well. Then, he apparently hooked up with the anarchists and learned that government and rulers were no good either. Now, he had murdered the President, the greatest symbol of power in America, an action he'd defended to the authorities in Buffalo as "his duty." Clearly there was a pattern here. Yet, it didn't seem that the experience of a single strike or even several could account for this trajectory. Lots of men lost their jobs to scabs and didn't become anarchists or assassins. Czolgosz had developed a definite distrust and hostility toward authority figures. I must root out the source of that antipathy. But, even then, was that enough to make him kill? Surely thousands of men shared Czolgosz' background but were content to assuage their bitterness on a bar stool, through long hours of labor, or in gripe sessions with their fellows. Perhaps in our next session I could begin to understand the dynamic underlying his fierce resentment of authority. But, subsequently, I would have to turn my attention to those factors that had turned him into a killer.

Chapter Six

~

Friday, October 4, 1901

After a long morning with difficult patients, it was a relief when lunch break finally arrived and I could get away from the prison for a while. The combination of the stark, sterile atmosphere of the clinic and the ill-health and gruff demeanor of the inmates had put me in a pretty grim mood. Now, free from appointment, errand, or obligation, I was content to wander aimlessly along Genesee Street. A bright blue sky with only a few wisps of white cloud and a pleasantly cool autumn temperature eased my mid-day fatigue. Just stretching my legs and breathing the fresh air was an invigorating change of pace from the cramped and bleak environment of the prison.

In the window of the Model Clothing Company, a sign announced fall derbies for 69 cents. I was in the market for a new hat. It was, after all, time to put away my summer straw in favor of something appropriate for cooler weather. And this was as fair a price as I had seen. I entered the store and scanned the crowded racks and tables in search of the hat display. The Model Clothing Company's cramped quarters was a sharp contrast to the bountiful spaciousness of R.H. Macy's, where I usually shopped in New York. As I made my way to the derby display near the front window, a clerk intercepted me. He was a stout, pink-faced man with red hair and bright, curly sideburns. He quickly located a short, brown style in my size. I donned the hat and regarded myself in a small mirror that stood on a stand before the window. I tilted the derby this way and that on my head, checking whether it would convey just the right jaunty image. I was so absorbed by this activity that it was a few moments before I realized that there was a familiar face smiling whimsically at me through the window. It was Lucy Gerin standing in the shade of the store's blue and white-striped awning.

I had not seen her since that dinner at her parents' house two weeks earlier and hadn't particularly thought of her either. When I'd returned from the Gerins that night, I'd found Jonesy ensconced in the study, eager for a report on my evening. He seemed to have Lucy foremost on his mind.

"So, confess," he'd challenged me, "are you smitten?"

"With Lucy?" I'd answered as I took my usual chair, the memory of her capricious smile forming in my mind. "No, I don't think so. And, no, she hasn't driven all thought of Abby Tolson from my mind. She's certainly attractive enough, in an odd sort of way. You were on the money there. But she's so annoying, interrupting all the time, and with her contrary attitudes. Didn't you find her kind of forward?"

"Annoying, I'll grant you, but she wasn't forward with me. Maybe that's how she shows affection. Parker, I think she likes you." Jones smiled at my discomfort. He knew my resistance to any suggestion of interest in the opposite sex and relished the opportunity for a well-placed dig.

"I don't see any sign of that. You're the one who's preoccupied with her, despite all your protests to the contrary. It's those irresistible physical-chemical forces again. You just can't fight them." One of our on-going jokes centered around the theory of the German physiologist Du Bois-Reymond, who held that 'no forces other than common physical-chemical ones are active within the organism,' a notion we found to be both obvious and absurd. I pressed on with my offensive. "Really, Jones, it seems that you're protesting just a bit too much here."

"Ha! The last thing I want is a college girl. I'm interested in women whose education has been in the field of man-pleasing."

"I don't know. First, you go on about what a knockout Lucy is. Then, you're convinced on scant evidence that she's interested in me. I think you'd better reexamine your feelings here. As for myself, I'm sure that, if I settle down some day, I'll enjoy the company of an educated woman, but hopefully someone a little more restrained."

"C'mon, Parker. You know you're over due for some tender loving care from a nice young woman, especially now that Abby's doting attentions are lost to you. You need someone to soothe your aching heart. Lucy's just the girl to look after you." From Jones' perspective, I was unable to manage my relations with

women without his personal intervention. "Anyway," he
continued, "how can you resist that smile? Why the shape would
confound Euclid himself. I know you've been dreaming about
planting a big, wet kiss right on those crooked lips despite the odd
angle you'd have to hold your head."

"Okay, Jonesy. Let's not get carried away here." And so it
went. Jones teased me along these lines for a day or two until his
ever-fertile imagination moved on to fresh challenges.

~

I was surprised and unexpectedly pleased to see Lucy's face
framed in the window of the Model Clothing Company. Smiling
back, I returned the hat to the clerk, telling him I'd be back for it,
and headed out the door to greet her.

"Why Miss Gerin, what a pleasant surprise."

"Yes it is, Dr. Parker. You certainly were looking dapper in
your new derby." Her dark eyes twinkled up at me from beneath a
broad bonnet.

"Well, it's not mine until I go back in the store and
purchase it. In any event, it's Mr. Parker but I'd prefer that you call
me Jon."

"As you wish. But if we're to be on a first-name basis then
you will address me as Lucy, although I can't imagine what people
will think!" She fixed her eyes intently on my own. I smiled a bit
tensely. Over the past two weeks, I'd almost forgotten how
unnerved I could be by Lucy's teasing and barbed comments and
by my uncertainty of just what to make of her. She laughed and
punched me lightly in the arm. "You are a serious one!" she
exclaimed. "Please, try to relax!"

"Okay, very funny," I replied, recovering my composure,
"So, tell me, where are you off to on this beautiful fall day?"

"Perhaps you've noticed that it's lunch time. Some people
have more pressing priorities than inspecting the fall fashions."

"Such as lunch, I suppose. Yes, I'll need to eat as well.
Would you like to join me?"

"Hmmm," she paused for a moment in thought as if the
question was of great import. "Well, I was going home to dine with

mother but it just so happens that I told her this morning that I might get a bite in town. So, why not? What's your pleasure?"

"I like the Osborne Grill. And it's right around the corner."

"Everything is right around the corner in Auburn," she replied.

We turned to walk the short way down the block to the Osborne. The streets were crowded with a variety of horse-drawn vehicles from carriages to wagons, the dull thud of the horses' hooves echoing off the dusty roadway. The streetcar conductor clanged his bell insistently in hopes that the tracks would stay clear. Lucy waved to a young woman who passed by on the streetcar. She said it was a childhood friend of hers, who was now a school-teacher, a woman whose unusual name, Viroqua, stuck in my mind. A moment later, Lucy greeted a pair of middle-aged ladies by name as we walked past them.

"Now," she said, "all the gossips in town will be saying I have a new beau. As if it isn't perfectly ordinary for a lady to have lunch with a gentleman of her acquaintance."

"I've noticed you brace a bit at conventional expectations."

"As you know, it's different for a man. People aren't so quick to judge. A limited social life is just one of the many double standards we women have to put up with. What makes it all the more galling is that it's more often our own sex, like the two esteemed ladies we just encountered, who do the enforcing."

As we arrived outside the Osborne, our conversation was interrupted by the sound of several shrill whistle blasts from across the street. We looked over to see a police officer chasing down the sidewalk after a bicyclist. Auburn had recently enacted a strict rule against riding bicycles on the downtown sidewalks. Many of the bicyclists, preferring the generally clean sidewalks to the busy and often muddy streets, openly flaunted this regulation and quite a few citations had been issued. In the current case, the rider had a head start going downhill toward the north on State Street. He had no trouble evading his pursuer.

Lucy and I watched until the bicyclist disappeared around the bend. She commented that sooner or later such behavior would lead to a serious accident. I nodded in agreement and we turned to enter the Osborne, proceeding directly to its fine dining room. A high ceiling with ornate metalwork made the room seem spacious despite the closely set tables. The room was nearly filled with diners whose various conversations merged into a gentle hum in the background. Sunlight streamed in from a bank of windows facing the street. The host greeted us and, weaving his way past diners and wait staff, led us to an available table. But before we could sit down Lucy pointed across the room toward an elderly couple saying, "Oh, look. There's some people I'd like you to meet." Without waiting for a reply, she led the way across to the far corner of the crowded dining room. Nonplused by this turn of events, I followed reluctantly, if obediently, behind. The couple greeted Lucy with enthusiasm.

"Why, Lucy Gerin. What a nice surprise. How are you?" said the woman.

"Fine. Quite fine, Mrs. Fitch," she replied. "I'd like to introduce you to a friend. This is Mr. Jonathan Parker." She seemed to put extra emphasis on the word mister. "Mr. Parker is in Auburn for the fall working as an intern with my father. Jonathan, meet the Reverend and Mrs. Fitch of the First Methodist Church, which my family attends."

"Pleased to meet you," I said a bit uneasily. An introduction to Lucy's minister was not at all what I had expected this afternoon. "Lucy and I just ran into each other during our mid-day breaks and she graciously agreed to join me for lunch." I was perhaps a bit too eager to explain our presence there together, but Reverend Fitch did not seem to notice.

"Well, you couldn't have picked a more charming lunch companion." The Reverend extended his hand in greeting. "I am pleased to meet you as well and hope you'll come see us at church some time. I'm sure the Gerins would gladly make room in their pew." His wife smiled cheerfully and murmured her agreement. I just nodded and smiled in turn, hoping to avoid any discussion of my religious inclinations, such as they were.

We returned to our table which was in a warm, sunny spot by the window. The crisp, white tablecloth reflected the bright sunlight, giving the room a feeling of expansiveness despite the somewhat cramped table arrangement and the dull earth-tone wallpaper. As we took our seats, Lucy said "You know, of course, that ministers and their wives can be the biggest gossips of all. But it is a small town and I can't expect to go to far without running into someone I know."

"I envy you in a way," I replied. "In the city, once you leave your immediate neighborhood, you can wander for hours without encountering a familiar face."

Neither of us needed much time with the menu. The Osborne offered pretty typical fare, much as you would find in small town hotels around the country. As we looked over the selection, we discussed food preferences, hers for a light lunch, mine for more substantial fare. Accordingly, I ordered roast beef with mashed potatoes while Lucy chose the chicken fricassee with salad. Still feeling the strain from my morning at the clinic, I would have loved a beer but, since I would soon be returning to work, I settled for coffee. Lucy's drink of choice was buttermilk. Our business with the waiter settled, we turned our attention to one another.

"So, Jon," she asked, "how has your morning been?"

"Pretty tiring, I'd say. It seemed as if each patient had a worse attitude and a more difficult condition than the last. It can really wear me down. Does your father ever complain of it?"

"He does, but only in the most off-handed manner. And he'd never call it complaining, just reporting on the day's events. For him, it's all in a day's work, as it has been day in and day out for years."

"It's a way of life I'd just as soon never get used to." I replied, "But, what about you? How's your day going?"

"Oh, my job is easy. Mr. Holley, my boss, is no trouble at all. He's your typical banker. Even tempered, meek, and officious. Always speaks in a slightly hushed tone as if matters of high finance were at stake. If I get his papers and correspondence typed on time and remind him of his appointments, things go pretty well for me."

"Actually, I'm surprised that you work as a clerk. You seem ready to take on the world. Surely you studied more than typing at college. Where was it you attended, anyway?"

"Vassar, over in Poughkeepsie, in the Hudson valley. I was class of '01. We rang in the new century in style."

"Yes, I'm familiar with Vassar. A swell school. Top notch, really."

"Indeed. And I'm well-educated because of it. The best teachers taught me all the classics of literature and philosophy, the history of the world, and more Latin than the Pope himself. Oh, and more math than the dullest clerk at the Auburn Savings Bank. Not that in my position I get to use much of it."

"It's hard to imagine you as particularly bookish. You must have had a more outgoing side in school?"

"Oh, I surely did. I was an all-around girl, achieving competence on the basketball court and honing my skills in theatrics. I was popular in a certain set and gained acceptance into the Nine Nimble Nibblers, a selective assemblage with a long gustatory tradition. Did you have eating clubs at Cornell?"

"We did, but I never joined. You do nibble nimbly, by the way." Our meal had arrived and Lucy had made short work of her salad.

"Ha! I don't think so," she protested, gesturing with the indelicately large piece of chicken now dangling from her fork. "Of course, at Vassar food was quite the thing. It was always advantageous to surround oneself with girls whose parents sent regular packages of treats."

"You said you learned theatrics as if that was a skill I should have already recognized in you. I suppose, in a way, I have. What sort of theater was it?"

"Actually, I participated in several of Vassar's theater clubs. The zenith of my acting career took the form of serious melodrama performed with the Dickens Club. With all of these many activities, social experiences, and even some formal education, on graduation, I was ready to face the world."

"I think I detect a hint of sarcasm in that last statement, and I definitely understand what you're implying about a college education. It seems that college does as much to socialize young men and women as it does to educate them. Even my friend Jonesy, who loves to play the wiseacre, in the end still finds a way to conform."

"I met Mr. Jones when he came for dinner. He did put on quite the show of flippancy and irreverence, but I don't think it went very deep. Really, he was fairly sedate as compared to the uncomplimentary terms with which my father usually speaks of him. It's not that Dad expects him to be a bad physician but that he finds him to be an annoying student."

"As have many of our professors."

"I don't think your friend Jones liked me very much.."

"Oh, he's just not used to a woman with a mind of her own. But I'd rather talk about you than Jones. I get plenty of him as it is. So tell me, it's pretty unusual for a woman to go to college, was it your idea or your parents'?" I bit into a piece of succulent beef while I awaited her reply.

"It was my father's wish from the time I was a child. He believes that an educated woman is less likely to be easily stampeded in life, and that four years spent, as he put it, in trying to distinguish between what you know, don't know, and can never find out is time well spent. But I was his willing accomplice. By the time I was finishing high school, I was ready to get away from home."

"But now you're back in Auburn. How did that happen?"

"It's simply that I'm not quite ready to go head-to-head with my father over the question of my independence. My parents' goal for me has always been marriage and family, despite their desire to see me educated. Not that I'm opposed to marriage, in the right way and at the right time. But they don't approve of a single girl going off into the world on her own. So I came home to bide my time until I could figure out what I want to do and make a proper break. My goal is to find a way to apply my ideals to a professional life. My work at the bank is really just to save some money and to take on an air of respectability while I consider other pursuits."

"So, where is that thinking today? Have you found your higher calling?"

She laughed. "That's not the how my father would describe it." Lucy used her napkin to wipe away any hint of a buttermilk moustache and explained to me how her father was convinced that, while at Vassar, she fell under the sway of questionable influences. Dr. Gerin, while appreciative of the knowledge and experience his daughter gained at college, felt that the ideals she absorbed at Vassar unfitted her for reality in the world. Now, he tells her, she has the mind of a radical. I was not surprised to hear this, considering how father and daughter had butted heads that night at dinner. They would do well to avoid political topics altogether. As Lucy spoke, I looked nervously over at Reverend and Mrs. Fitch. It was with some relief that I discovered that they were paying no attention to us. I felt self-conscious about the appearance of this unplanned rendezvous with my mentor's daughter, particularly in a town that seemed rife with her acquaintances. These few chance encounters on the street and here in the restaurant had been strangely unsettling. Somehow, despite the fact that I barely knew her, I felt as if Lucy's world was quickly closing in around me.

"I think I was fortunate to attend a serious college and one that had only women," Lucy continued. "A couple of generations ago there were no colleges for women. The founding of schools like Vassar is one of the real achievements of the past half century. You might be surprised to learn that the administration at Vassar was against women's rights and sought to protect us from the world. But some of our teachers were well advanced in their political thinking. My own mentor, Professor Salmon, a historian, was a wonderful woman who really fought to introduce students to the important work that women leaders were undertaking on our behalf. By my last semester, I was constantly arguing with the swell girls who saw the world as their playground. Now I've got a hundred ideas. But I still haven't put together what I want to do with them."

"'A hundred ideas,'" I repeated the phrase slowly. "We might have time for you to tell me a few of them."

"I see you liked your potato," she teased, pointing to the corner of my plate where the mashed potatoes had reposed a few moments before. "The best way to explain is to start with the basics. Thanks to the influence of several of my professors, a few of my classmates, and even some of their mothers, I got involved in the great question of the day. No, I don't mean the new role of Imperial America. And I don't mean the speculation about TR's future in the White House. What I'm referring to is the place of women in society, our subordination if you will, and how to work effectively for change. I was fortunate enough to meet people who were committed, informed, and engaged in the struggle for equality for women. In fact, last year, our debating society, Qui Vive, addressed the proposition 'That women should have an equal voice with men in municipal government.' In debate you are supposed to be able to take either side dispassionately. I was relieved to be a member of the audience for that one."

"And what was the result of all of this nefarious influence at Vassar? Did you join the fearsome ranks of the suffragettes?" I hoped that she could tell from my tone that I was teasing.

"Suffragists, if you please." she chastised, giving me a severe look and taking on for a moment the stereotypic demeanor of the humorless women's rights proponent.

"Suffragist! Suffragette! What's the difference?"

"It's quite simple. One is what we call ourselves. The other is the derogatory term used by our enemies. I would hope to count you in the former group."

"All right," I grumbled, "I stand corrected. "

"To answer your question, I am indeed a suffragist, but you must understand that the right to vote is only the beginning, just one piece of the puzzle."

"The puzzle?" I asked uncertainly, caught between my desire to become better acquainted with my companion and my trepidation at continuing a discussion of women's rights with her. I had never really conversed with a self-identified suffragist before. In my circle at Cornel, the handful of girls who were strident proponents of women's suffrage were avoided like the plague. We considered them unlikely romantic partners and unpleasant prospects for even the most casual of conversations. We used to joke freely about the women's rights movement, referring to right movements we would like girls of our acquaintance to undertake. The newspapers typically derided their leaders as manly spinsters who had few problems that the proper attentions of a good husband wouldn't solve. Carrie Nation was currently the favorite target, maligned for her corpulence, met with hisses and catcalls, and lampooned as a hatchet-wielding joint-smasher. While I braced at Lucy's reprimands, I could not help but assume that she was cut from a different mold.

"The puzzle is one of how to place women on an equal footing with men in our society, what Susan B. Anthony called 'equal power in the making, shaping, and controlling of the circumstances of life'" she explained. "The vote is an important step since it will allow us to influence legislation that can bring about other goals. The vote has both practical and symbolic importance. But it's been a confounding problem to figure out how to get men to vote to share their power with women. A few states out West have extended the franchise to women but things have

not gone well elsewhere. Of course there are many other rights
that are important to women as well. The right to purchase, own,
and dispose of property. The right to work. The right to an
education. The right to marry and divorce as we see fit."

"I assume you would also include the right to get plastered
at the corner saloon?" I said, attempting a joke at the expense of
the notorious Women's Christian Temperance Union.

"That's right," Lucy replied, not missing a beat. "The
temperance movement to the contrary. And don't forget the right
to light up a big fat cigar. Whatever right a man has, women
should have as well, for good or ill. It's really pretty simple, isn't it?"

"But I thought the whole argument of the suffrage
movement was that women's better qualities would purify politics
and redeem it from the drunken excesses of the male, that under
women's rule saloons and perhaps even cigars would be outlawed."

"And so many will say and it might even come to pass
given trends in public moralizing. But, basically, I think that's a lot
of hogwash. If women seem pure it's because our options are so
limited. Think about the double standard in marriage. For a man
it's practically expected that he be unfaithful, but, if a woman
strays, she's marked for life with that big scarlet 'A.' There's also
that little matter called children. If the women went out carousing
in the evening along with the men, the little ones would have to
fend for themselves. Why shouldn't the man stay home on an
evening and let his wife get out on the town?"

"Aren't you overlooking the fact that it's the man who's
out working all day? The last thing he needs is to come home to
look after a brood of children and take care of a lot of housework,"
I was sure that I had caught Lucy at an extreme of
unreasonableness.

"And where is it written that a woman shouldn't hold a
job if she's so inclined? I know for a fact that a woman can do
pretty much any occupation as well as a man. Are you saying that a
man is of lesser capability and cannot look after a child? Or mend a
sock?" Lucy's voice hit a shrill note and I felt myself shrinking back
into my chair.

"Now hold on a minute!" My fork dangled helplessly over
a slice of roast beef that a moment earlier had been imminently
destined for my mouth. "I'm not saying anything. I'm just trying to
understand how you think and what you're looking for in life."

"So, you want to have it both ways. First you claim that men should be protected from child rearing and then, when questioned, you suddenly have no opinion whatsoever on the subject of women's rights?" She upbraided me with a fierce, reproachful look in her eyes. Her skewed lips were drawn tight into a frown I had not seen before.

"No, that's not it. Slow down a minute. Please realize that you've caught me a bit off guard here. It's only natural for me to defend my sex. I just haven't thought about these things as much as you have. I confess that I'm pretty ambivalent about women's suffrage. There definitely were a lot of smart girls in college who were as qualified to vote as any man. I might even lean towards supporting the vote for women except for one thing: the combination of suffrage and temperance. It bothers me to see such strong religious moralism brought into the affairs of state." I abandoned my fork and took a long sip from my coffee cup.

Lucy took a deep breath and smiled, appearing for the moment to have dropped her combative stance. Her eyes resumed their familiar, elfin quality. "Well, Jon Parker, we do seem to agree on some things. I believe that if women's suffrage arrives on the back of the temperance movement, it will be a Pyrrhic victory. We'll have won the vote but not our freedom. We'll still wear the shackles of a Puritan moralism that should have gone out in the seventeenth century."

"I'd never thought of it like that. The temperance folks have just always rubbed me the wrong way. It seemed that they were out to enforce a kind of conformity and discipline that was antithetical to the American spirit of democracy and to the freedoms our nation stands for. The label 'Puritan' suits them well. But it does seem that there are more women working for temperance these days than for suffrage, or at least that they're more outspoken."

"You're right about that. Quite a few women leaders think that the association with temperance is hurting the suffrage movement. Every time there's a key referendum for women's suffrage, the liquor industry pulls out all the stops to defeat it. They, at least, buy all that purity nonsense and are convinced that women voting will lead to legislation against their interests."

"You know, as men, we're raised to believe that we are beset by base instincts that we can barely control." I stabbed, finally, at my last piece of beef. "We're told that we must have a strong woman at home to keep us in line, first the mother, then the wife. Some medical textbooks make that point. The implication is that if women enter society, through such means as the vote, then there will be no one to guard the moral fabric. But what you're suggesting is that if women are allowed to take full responsibility for their lives, then men must do the same. Men could no longer shirk their responsibility to live morally. That sounds like a pretty common-sense prescription, but a pretty tough one to fill given the way most men think." I smiled sheepishly to myself as I imagined Lucy adding the phrase "present company included" to my last remark. Across the room, the Reverend and Mrs. Fitch got up from their table and headed toward the exit. Mrs. Fitch waved as she caught my eye and her husband smiled in turn. I waved back. Lucy smiled coyly. "Don't worry, Jon, you won't be expected for services quite yet."

"Not yet?" I replied, not pleased with the implications of her phrasing. "Not ever is more like it. Church attendance is not a high priority for me these days."

"Well," she answered with a slight frown, "there are some things one does for one's parents or just as part of the community. And some things one does with one's friends. Much as I think of myself as independent--at least for a young woman who still lives with her parents--I still see that church is a strong link to society here in Auburn pretty much irrespective of one's theology. Perhaps things are different in Brooklyn." As I wondered how to reply, she scanned my plate, empty now except for a sprig of parsley. "Your meal was satisfactory?" Lucy asked.

"It was," I was happy to put off the discussion of religion. "I am well satisfied and ready for a nap. Fortunately, there are plenty of beds at the prison."

She laughed. "I don't think you're qualified to occupy one."

"Not yet, anyway," I replied, squinting my eyes and thrusting out my jaw in what I imagined was a sinister expression. She laughed again.

"And, how was your chicken?" I asked.

"Good. Very tender."

"Will you be having dessert?"

"Oh, no thank you. I need to be getting back to the bank."

"Well, the Reverend was right. You are indeed a charming lunch companion. I hope we can do it again." Hearing my own words, I realized that I meant it. Once we'd started talking, with the exception of that one tense moment, Lucy had been less abrasive and very interesting. And she had certainly been exposed to a number of ideas that were new to me.

"Jon, I was wondering," she asked, "have you been up to the Logan Monument?"

"No, I've heard of it but I don't know where it is."

"Then it's settled. We'll have a picnic over in Fort Hill Cemetery."

"In the cemetery? That doesn't sound like a very pleasant place to eat."

"Actually I know a lovely little hillock, right across from the monument. How would lunch time next Tuesday be for you?"

"Now wait a minute here," I protested, "It's supposed to be my job to invite you!"

"Fine," she replied, "I'm all ears."

I rolled my eyes in frustration. "Lucy, how would you like to go with me on a picnic next Tuesday to see Logan Monument?"

"Why, I'd love to, Jon! What a sweet idea! And don't you worry about a thing. I'll pack my mother's basket and have everything we need."

With that agreed, I paid our bill and, leaving the Osborne, we turned our separate ways, she down Genesee Street to the bank and I up State Street toward the prison walls that somehow seemed much less gloomy than they had an hour earlier. I grumbled to myself about Lucy's forwardness but, in the end, I had to admit that I had accepted her invitation for the simple reason that I had enjoyed her company and wanted to do so again.

Chapter Seven

~

Tuesday, October 8, 1901

The clinic clock seemed to tick ever more loudly as 11
o'clock approached. I paced around the cramped examining room
in nervous anticipation of the arrival of the assassin. Despite my
sense of success in the first session, the gnawing self-doubt and
sense of being in over my head had returned. In my agitated state,
it might have appeared that I was the convict awaiting execution
rather than merely the medical student impatient for a meeting. At
last Czolgosz arrived. He sat down heavily into the chair, his eyes
closed wearily, and his head fell back as if he were too exhausted to
hold it erect.

"Tired?" I asked.

He struggled to sit up, opening his eyes.

"No, not really. It's just the sitting in that cell, day in, day
out. Nothing to do. Nothing changes. No daylight. It puts you in a
certain frame of mind so's you just want to flop back and close your
eyes."

"Don't they take you out in the yard?"

"Oh, yeah, I get a walk in the morning, real regular like the
warden's dog, but then it's right back to the cell all day. I see the
other prisoners on their way to the shops, all marching in a row in
their matching suits looking like a pack of miserable school kids
following the teacher to class. That's not for me and I'm glad I
don't have to do it. I wouldn't mind all that sitting if I had
something to read or someone to jaw with."

"It sounds tough. Are you feeling all right otherwise?" I
was pleased with Czolgosz' readiness to converse with me.

The prisoner smirked. "No complaints, Doc. The food's
better than in that Buffalo jail. And they let me smoke my pipe.
I'm just glad when the other inmates shut up and leave me be." I'd

heard that some of the others on death row were hostile to
Czolgosz, casting a variety of slurs and idle threats his way.

"I've been thinking about our last discussion," I said,
beginning my planned line of inquiry. I intended to follow the
threads of work and politics from the previous session hoping that
one or the other would eventually lead in a more personal
direction, hoping also that the assassin would begin to relax his
guard. "Last time, you told me about the strike at the wire mill. I
was wondering if you'd been involved in other strikes or labor
disputes over the years?"

He thought for a moment. "Not directly, no. But I guess
just about everyone in Cleveland was involved in the big streetcar
strike a couple of years back. One way or another they were." He
grew silent as if this were sufficient answer to my inquiry.

"I'd like to hear about it. Can you tell me more?"

"Lot of folks came out in support of the workers. Big
crowds would form and attack the scab streetcars and their scab
drivers. The mayor called in the state militia to help the police
arrest sympathizers. If you rode on those cars during the strike you
were in big trouble. Volunteers, women mostly, would follow you
wherever you went to do business and tell the owners that if they
served you they'd be boycotted. Then you'd get home and find a
stake in your yard, with a sign saying 'scab lives here.'" He smiled
grimly.

"But if you were a strike supporter," the assassin
continued, "you didn't need those scab streetcars to get around
town. Anyone who had a wagon or jitney put it in service taking
people wherever they needed to go. The immigrant neighborhoods,
Polish and others, were all out against the streetcar company. It
wasn't just that they supported the strikers either. Folks were
pretty ticked off at that company letting their cars speed through
busy neighborhoods, scaring people. They even ran down a few
children. Don't give a damn for human life, those bosses."

"That's terrible." I remembered similar incidents in New
York. It sounded like open warfare on the streets of Cleveland. At
the same time, I reminded myself that I could not take Czolgosz'
stories at face value. I was uncertain to what extent he might tend
to exaggerate such incidents or whether he might even be prone to
outright invention when it served his purpose. As an anarchist, he
belonged to a political movement that considered assassination to

be "propaganda of the deed." He would have few qualms about propaganda of the more conventional sort. "How did things work out in the end?" I asked.

"They settled it before too long but, as usual, the company tried to wriggle out of its promises. It's pretty frustrating for workers to suffer through a strike until they finally get a deal and then the bosses turn right around and ignore it once you're back on the job. You can't trust the capitalists for a minute!" Czolgosz' eyes glowed angrily for a moment as if he were still embroiled in the tense days of the streetcar strike.

"I guess you were in Cleveland at the time. Were you involved at all, personally, in that strike?"

"Not too much. In those days, I was still feeling pretty sick, but I went into town for a rally or two. Kicked in my two bits to the strikers' fund."

"Is that the closest you've been to a big strike other than at the wire mill?"

"I suppose it is, but I've heard about plenty, some of them pretty bad. We didn't get the worst of it at the mill, just losing our jobs. Others, like the men at the Lattimore mines, got themselves murdered. When the workers fight back, they call out the troops on 'em. That's why we say they've all got to go, the bosses and the rulers. They're all in cahoots to keep the working man down."

"Lattimore? I haven't heard about that incident."

"Oh, you wouldn't have, would you? That's the other problem, you see. The bosses own all the newspapers and they won't tell the workers' side of the story, not one bit. The Lattimore mines are somewhere over in eastern Pennsylvania. It was a few years ago, '97 maybe. Just like us, their wages got cut and they went out, these miners. Hundreds of 'em went marching to the mines, peaceful, wanting to protest the company rules and state laws that were keeping 'em down. Marching like they got a right to do. All of a sudden, the sheriff appears with a hundred deputies and they open fire on the workers, murderously shooting men in the back. A lot of men died that day, a lot more were wounded."

"Sounds horrible," I offered, despite my certainty that it must have been the workers who fired first.

"You're right on that point but I'll tell you what else. Afterwards, they tried the murderers and let 'em off scot free. Now you take a look at that trial and then take a look at mine and you'll learn something about how justice is doled out. I'm not saying I should've got off or nothin' but justice in this country is like everything else: them that's got gets." On the contrary, I thought. It was likely that if a trial had exonerated the sheriff and his men then they had probably acted within the law.

"So, how did you learn so much about Lattimore?"

"Well, you might be surprised how workers talk to each other. At the end of the day at the tavern it's not all baseball and horse races. There were a lot of Polish workers at Lattimore so we heard about it through the grapevine. Plus, we've got our own newspapers, in different languages for the immigrants. Not the kind of papers that you read but good, honest papers. So we heard all about it in Cleveland and everywhere else."

"I guess that's not all that unusual, for a strike to end in violence. The papers do seem to tend to put the blame on the workers." Perhaps by endorsing the prisoner's viewpoint I could encourage him to say more. As far as I knew or believed, the workers were the likely instigators in these various strikes. At the same time, the consistency of Czolgosz accounts was beginning to lend them a certain amount of credibility.

"They sure do. And it's such a lie. Look at the Homestead strike, back in '92. You're maybe a bit too young to remember it."

"Isn't that when the anarchist, Berkman, shot Carnegie's man Henry Frick?"

"You've made my point." Czolgosz' voice carried a note of triumph. He was now intently engaged in this discussion. I could imagine him similarly arguing politics with his brother or at some meeting in Cleveland. "Frick is remembered as the victim at Homestead. No one remembers that it was Carnegie who cut the wages on the steel-workers, driving them to strike. No one remembers that it was Frick himself who hired two hundred Pinkertons to fire into the crowd of workers and break the strike. That one was every bit as bloody as Lattimore!"

"Is that common, for Pinkertons to be called in?"

"You bet it is. And troops, too. You heard about the Pullman strike of '94?"

"A railway strike, I think." I tried not to show it in my tone of voice, but I was bristling at this common, uneducated worker taking it upon himself to be my teacher. It mattered not that I was the one requesting an education.

"Yup. It was at the same time as the wire mill strike and for the same reason, wage cuts and all. But, it involved a lot more workers and federal troops were called out to put a stop to it. President Cleveland it was. They're all alike. No one can tell me any ruler takes the side of the working man. Not ever. They jailed Eugene Debs in that strike. He came out a hero and a socialist. Paved the way for his presidential run. I've got a lot of respect for Debs, a great man, but I don't agree with this idea of running for president. How many votes did he get? Not many, I can tell you that. Trying to get in with the rulers, that's not gonna get workers anywhere." I noted the prisoner's praise for Debs in contrast to his condemnation of Carnegie and the other "bosses." As with his admiration of Edward Bellamy, Czolgosz seemed to idealize any critic of the status quo, all the while reviling those who were generally seen as its staunch pillars.

Things were going well now and I was ready to try to shift the topic a bit. I was unremittingly aware of the brief time available for completing my exploration of the assassin. I could almost feel my watch ticking away in my pocket, a constant maddening reminder, like Poe's *Tell-Tale Heart*. A voice of gnawing impatience chided me that Freud's methods would not work with this subject. There was too little time, too little trust. Patience, I reminded myself. Patience.

"You said last time that you'd spent a lot of time reading and talking about things with your brother Waldek. What about your other brothers and sisters, do they think about politics much?"

Czolgosz paused to consider this question. He scratched his left ear pensively. Concerned, no doubt, that I might be seeking information against his siblings. "I guess I don't mind telling you," he said at last. "Except for Waldek, they all pretty much go along with things, just trying to make a living, I suppose. Really, considering how we were brought up, it's surprising that even Waldek learned to think for himself."

"Or that you did?" I ventured.

Czolgosz curled his lips into the now familiar near-smile. "Well, I guess we learned together. Waldek's the only one who really remembers the trouble our Pa got into. I was just a baby at the time."

"What kind of trouble?"

The assassin was again silent for a while and then, looking me straight in the eye, dead serious, replied, "I just might tell you about that some time. Just might." For today, the subject was clearly off limits.

Now it was my turn to pause in thought. As I did, Czolgosz leaned back again and closed his eyes. If our conversation mattered to him, he wasn't about to let me know it. In the brief silence, I could hear one of the keepers let out a loud laugh in the next room. I was glad they were amusing themselves. Finally, I decided my only recourse was to return to the topic of politics and hope the prisoner would eventually relax his guard.

"You said last time we met that you stopped working at the wire mill in 1897. What made you quit?"

Czolgosz slowly leaned forward and opened his eyes. "I'd be lyin' to you if I said it was all fancy political thinking that made me stop working. Not that it wasn't a part of it but the main thing was, I got sick. The air in that mill was just plain nasty. Breathin' it twelve hours a day rots your lungs out. And those long shifts, day after day, month after month, they just wear you down. Most men would quit if they thought they had a way to get by. Anyway, after a while, I started coughing up a lot of phlegm. Waldek wanted me to go to the hospital, but I said there's no place there for poor people. If you have lots of money they'll take care of you, but otherwise, forget it. "

"How did you get by?"

"My family owns a farm near Cleveland. It's really my Pa's place but we've each got a share. Hunting was good and I could contribute rabbit or squirrel to the table. And there are plenty of little fish in the pond. Mostly I took it easy. Rested. Read a lot."

"Did you ever see a doctor for your illness?" I wondered if the assassin's aversion to authority had extended to the medical profession as well.

"I did. I was due some sick pay at first but needed a doctor's note to get it. They can't take a worker's word that he's too sick to do his job. I saw a couple of different doctors. I was short of breath, coughing all the time, catarrh they called it, and I ached all over. I spent an awful lot on medicine. Don't know if it did me any good, any more than a steady dose of tea and cod liver oil did."

"Not together, I hope."

This meager attempt at humor had no effect on Czolgosz. He seemed resolved to remain stoical to the end. "Nope. That would have been too much to swallow," he showed no awareness of his pun.

"Is that when you got involved with the anarchist groups?" Czolgosz stretched his arms back. He clasped his hands behind his neck and sat again for several minutes in thought. I worried that he would reject this line of questioning as well but, to my surprise, he replied frankly.

"At first I didn't hear much about the anarchists. They're not that easy to find. I'd been thinking of myself as a socialist for a long time, ever since the strike. Bandowski was big in the Polish Socialist Society, got to be secretary before they broke up. He helped me out, showed me the ropes, introduced me to folks. After that I belonged to the society and all, but mostly I stayed home and did a lot of reading like we talked about before. Working at the mill, I was usually too worn out to get involved in much else. I'll tell ya, I've got a lot of respect for workers who spend their little bit of free time organizing. Anyway, then I got sick. After a while, I got to feeling better and could get into Cleveland now and then. It was good to be able to pick up a paper or go to a meeting. I was sure there must be something big going on, but pretty soon I figured out that the socialists were mostly interested in a lot of talk and I didn't think too much of 'em."

"Did you make any friends at the Socialist Society?"

He regarded me with that distant, wary look. With Czolgosz' heavy lids, his gaze tended seemed more sleepy than inquiring. Again, he sat in silence, staring at me, not moving. I realized that I had asked just the sort of question that would provoke the assassin's suspicious nature. Although for me, the lack of friends could be one sign of a dementia with an anti-social component, Czolgosz would once again suspect that I was fishing for clues of a conspiracy.

"I'm thinking maybe it's time for you to tell me something," he said at last. "Why's a young fellow like yourself, says you're going to be a doctor and all, why are you so interested in my family and my friends?"

I stumbled for words at this unexpected turn of events. Unlike my interlocutor, I did not feel I had the luxury to sit idly for several minutes while I considered a reply. "It's as I said before. I'm hoping to gain some insight into your motivations and the psychological makeup that underlies them."

"I don't know nothin' about this psychological business. Tell me somethin' about how that works?" Czolgosz' attitude remained indifferent and the words fell unhurried from his lips. Nonetheless, this seemingly lazy question must be taken as a serious demand.

"I guess that's fair," I replied, recognizing that this could be a critical moment in the process. "Think about it this way. There are lots of working men but only so many of them become socialists, lots of socialists, but relatively few anarchists, and, even among the anarchists, the person who will risk his life for his beliefs is rare." I almost said "commit murder for his beliefs" but caught myself and selected the more positive portrayal. "My hope is that, in the few meetings that we have together, I can learn enough about both your thinking and your life experiences to begin to understand what makes you the unusual man that you are."

"I said in Buffalo and I know you read about it, I done my duty. That's all."

"Yes, but my question is: what made you, one among millions, able to rise up to your duty in such a fashion?" I stifled a grimace of distaste at putting his heinous act in such favorable terms.

"And, I guess my question is, what do you care? Why's it so important to you that you'd sit alone in a room with a convicted killer?"

Here, I did take a moment to think. It was essential that I provide a sincere answer to this question, as truthful an answer as possible. I was sure that Czolgosz would know if I was giving a half-cocked reply. But, how well had I even worked out my motivations for myself? My intended journal article seemed remote in the immediacy of the assassin's probing questions. At best it would be a by product of the work at hand. These sessions with Czolgosz had become a consuming preoccupation for me. I was caught up in these meetings as if they held the key not only to determining the course and success of my medical career but to justifying my choices to my father and perhaps even to myself. The prospect of failure again reared its ugly head. In the end, the best I could do was to convey my own uncertainty to the prisoner. Now it was my turn to lean forward, elbows on knees in much the posture

Czolgosz had taken earlier in the session, hoping to convey to him my sincerity.

"The best way I can explain it is that I've had this interest in psychiatry, not in the way you usually think of, working with crazy people and all, but more in a new direction. To me psychology is an aspect of everyone's life. My idea is that society can be improved by understanding it. Maybe that's something you and I have in common, an interest in improving society. It's just that the methods are different. So, here I am working in the prison, but I was pretty much just going through the motions, not really very motivated. I'd thought about trying to interview some of the prisoners but never seemed to get around to doing anything about it. But there was something that struck me about you that very first day. I felt that I could really gain some insight from working with you. I didn't know what it would be. I'm still not sure. All I know is that I want to see this through and that it's up to you. I want to go as far into this as you'll let me. And, believe me, I recognize that you have a right to be suspicious." I sighed with unexpected relief at completing this little speech.

Czolgosz did not reply. He stared into the distance through half-closed eyes, his unfocused gaze seeming to look right through me and far beyond the prison walls.

"Listen," I said. "Our time's about up. Why don't you think about what I've said and I'll think about it some more as well and we'll pick it up next time. That is, if you're willing."

He nodded his assent. His impassive expression said only that he had heard my words but offered nothing as to his thoughts or feelings.

"Okay. Let's go then." I got up and opened the door to the outer room. The two guards cut short their conversation and stood up from their slouched positions by the wall. The prisoner walked slowly out into the rough waiting grasp of the keepers.

~

Minutes later, the clinic clock struck noon. I headed quickly from the prison, eager for the change of pace that my rendezvous with Lucy Gerin would bring, hoping that she would turn my frantic thoughts away from the assassin. The sun shone

through high, white clouds. An occasionally blustery wind did little
to diminish its warmth. The fresh air invigorated my lungs but did
little to clear my head. I felt frustrated and distressed by the way
things had gone with Czolgosz. I had learned some valuable
information about his life but the tone of our conversation had not
progressed much beyond that of the previous week. He had
carefully limited the range of topics to events and ideas, subjects
that would no doubt enthrall a journalist but that did little to meet
the analytic needs of the aspiring alienist.

It was the question about friends, one that many would
consider innocuous, that had brought us to an impasse. But, if
Czolgosz carefully guarded even his friends from my inquiries, how
would I ever get to the emotional factors that rose out of his
upbringing? A feeling of helplessness and inadequacy overcame me
as I realized that I was utterly dependent on the uncertain interest
and cooperation of the prisoner. I had mustered all my sincerity in
answering his concerns, but surely that could not count for much
to a man in his position. I dreaded the humiliation that would
accompany failure and contemplated whether I might save face by
giving up the project at this juncture. Gerin, I thought, would be
disappointed but would accept my stipulation that the prisoner was
uncooperative, a conclusion that was not far from the truth. Facing
myself could be the greater challenge.

As I reached Genesee Street, I found Lucy already waiting
at the corner. She waved when she saw me in the distance. Under
her arm was a small picnic basket, which I took from her as I
reached her side. Her round cheeks were set off by a wide-brimmed
hat that curved down toward the high linen collar that topped her
sensible full-sleeved shirt-waist. We walked side by side to the west
on Genesee, past the imposing stone courthouse and the pink
sandstone of the new post office. The store awnings were mostly
rolled up this time of year to let the sun's warmth enter the shops.
Lucy was cheerful and chattered on about her morning and the
various noontime activities of downtown Auburn. In her company,
I perked up a bit and pushed my obsessive thinking about the
assassin to the back, but not entirely out, of my mind. I did not
view myself as a man consumed by his work, and was intent upon
enjoying my break.

After a few blocks, we turned up Fort Street and entered
through the granite archway into Fort Hill Cemetery. The small,

gothic chapel had a quaintness reminiscent of the ancient stone
sanctuary I had stumbled across on a jaunt through the English
countryside a few summers back. Beyond the chapel, steep slopes
rose up abruptly before us to the summits of several low hills. The
lawn was just turning from bright summer green to the dull brown
of autumn. Sections of the cemetery were edged with mature oak,
maple, and elm trees. The setting abounded in color. It would have
been a dream come true for a landscape painter. From where we
stood, we could just see the first few headstones poking up from
the top of the hill. The effect was somewhat magical, not at all like
the eerie silence that is characteristic of the typical graveyard. It
was very different from the crowded city cemeteries that I was
familiar with in New York.

"This really is lovely," I said to Lucy. "I'm glad you brought
me here. I don't think I would ever have thought to come this way
on my own."

"It gets better. C'mon." She placed her arm around mine
and led me toward a sandy path that began just ahead of us.

We followed the path as it wound its way upward between
two hillocks. As we neared the top, the two hills leveled out, the
path continuing through a slight depression that now ran between
them. The southern hill, to our left, was well-covered in
headstones. In the center, atop an earthen mound, an impressive
stone obelisk rose toward the treetops.

"That must be the Logan Monument," I exclaimed. I
scampered up the slight embankment to get a better look. "Do you
know how high it is?"

"Fifty-six feet, exactly," Lucy replied, "but that's not where
we're going just yet. The picnic spot is this way." I turned to see
that she was pointing toward the more northern of the two hills.
This one had no grave sites, just an expanse of lawn leading up to a
stately elm tree at the top.

I followed her lead toward the summit of this second hill
and discovered that it afforded an excellent view of the monument
and a bit of a panorama over the surrounding cemetery.
Concentric circles of gravestones surrounded the monument.
Smaller obelisks, no doubt memorials to Auburn's more prosperous
citizens, dotted the scene as if lesser chieftains had gathered in
perpetuity to honor a great leader.

Out of the basket Lucy took a thin blanket which we spread over the grass. The picnic contained simple but satisfying lunch fare: two smoked turkey sandwiches sweetened with cranberry relish, a couple of bright red apples, and two bottles of sarsparilla soda.

"These hills are really something," I said after swallowing my first bite of the sandwich. "I haven't seen anything like them in Auburn, rising so suddenly as they do."

"They're partly man-made, you know," Lucy replied.

"You're kidding!" It would not have occurred to me that such a natural-seeming part of the landscape could have been fabricated by human hands. "Were they put up as part of the cemetery?"

"Oh no. Indians made them, centuries ago, before Columbus. Supposedly they were an unknown tribe that preceded the Cayugas. The mounds are said to have served as a kind of fortification. Whoever built them was long gone when the first English settlers arrived in the seventeenth century. The Cayugas called this area Was Kaugh, from which we get the name Owasco. It means 'the crossing place.'"

"You're certainly a fount of local lore."

"They lay it on pretty thick in school, and you know how children love stories of mysterious, vanished Indian tribes."

"Even girl children?" I asked, immediately realizing that I might have opened a Pandora's box.

"And why not? Maybe in Brooklyn the girls are satisfied with tales of ladies and tea parties but here in rustic Auburn we thrill to the frontier history we take as our heritage, even if few of our ancestors actually lived here at the time."

"So, who is this fellow Logan?" I was happy to return to the original topic. "He must have been pretty important to merit such an impressive obelisk."

"Growing up in Auburn, you assume the whole world knows the story of Chief Logan and his famous speech. Do you like stories?"

"I do, especially if they come embellished with Vassar theatrics."

She laughed. "Well, I don't know about that. But why don't you relax and I will recount the tale of Logan as told in the grade schools of Auburn. Logan was the son of the chief of the

Cayuga or Mingo tribe and was born in this area. His given name was Tahgahjute. His father moved the family to central Pennsylvania where Logan grew up." While Lucy spoke, I picked up one of the apples and bit in. It's crisp flesh yielded with a loud crunching sound, at which I smiled sheepishly. She smiled and continued on unperturbed. "When he became chief in turn, he took the name Logan after a colonial official who was highly regarded by the Indians. Eventually, Logan moved his family to what was then the Ohio Territory, where the Virginia Colony was at war with the Indians. Logan considered himself a friend to the white man and believed in peace so he refused to fight. Then, in the spring of the year 1774, a robbery and murder were committed at a frontier settlement by two Indians of the Shawnee tribe. The neighboring whites, as was their custom, undertook to punish this outrage in a summary manner. A famous Indian fighter, Colonel Cresap, collected a party, and went in search of vengeance. Unfortunately, what he found was a canoe of women and children, with one man only, unarmed, and not suspecting a hostile attack from the whites."

While listening attentively to Lucy's tale, I imagined the hills around us alive with the affairs of an Indian village or perhaps the scene of a bloody battle. Fort Hill Cemetery definitely held its share of ghosts, and not just of those formally interred there over the past half century. Lucy recounted the story with a well developed stage presence. Her hands moved rhythmically, like those of an orchestra conductor as she wove the web of her tale. She had the air of a master story-teller, at one with the lyricism of her yarn.

"Cresap and his party concealed themselves on the bank of the river," she continued, "The moment the canoe reached the shore, they fired on the Indians, killing them all. Now, it so happened that this was the family of Logan. He couldn't believe that his friendship was returned in such a manner, and he accordingly joined in the war and fought quite fiercely. That fall, the Indians were defeated, and sued for peace. Logan disdained to be seen among the suppliants. But, lest the sincerity of a treaty should be distrusted because of the absence of so distinguished a chief, he sent by messenger the famous speech which is commemorated on the monument. They make us memorize it in school. Would you like to hear it?"

I nodded eagerly. A chunk of apple prevented a verbal reply.

"Okay. It went like this: 'I appeal to any white man to say, if ever he entered Logan's cabin hungry, and he gave him not meat; if ever he came cold and naked, and he clothed him not. During the course of the last long and bloody war, Logan remained idle in his cabin, an advocate for peace. Such was my love for the whites, that my countrymen pointed as they passed, and said, `Logan is the friend of white men.' I had even thought to have lived with you, but for the injuries of one man. Colonel Cresap, the last spring, in cold blood, and unprovoked, murdered all the relations of Logan, not sparing even my women and children. There runs not a drop of my blood in the veins of any living creature. This called on me for revenge. I have sought it: I have killed many: I have fully glutted my vengeance. For my country, I rejoice at the beams of peace. But do not harbor a thought that mine is the joy of fear. Logan never felt fear. He will not turn on his heel to save his life. Who is there to mourn for Logan? -- Not one.'" Lucy paused for a moment of dramatic affect before continuing. "It is those last words that are etched into the monument: 'Who is there to mourn for Logan?' A sad testimony to the fate of the Indian peoples."

Throughout our picnic, thoughts of the day's session with Czolgosz had jealously struggled to grab my attention away from Lucy Gerin. This story of Cresap and Logan, Ohioans like the assassin, brought inevitable comparisons to the fore. The vengeance against the Shawnee by the settlers seemed to share a common brutality with Czolgosz' recounting of the treatment of striking workers by their employers. Logan had held to high principles and struck out only when pushed to the limits of endurance. I was incredulous to realize that I entertained the possibility that Czolgosz had followed a similar trajectory. Perhaps it was Logan's dispassionate-sounding pronouncement 'this called on me for revenge' that evoked Czolgosz' matter-of-fact attitude and plain statement that "I done my duty."

"So, are you telling me that everyone who's been through the Auburn public schools can recite that?" I handed Lucy her apple, hoping that the wandering of my thoughts had not been apparent.

"Well, not everyone is such a devoted student of history, and probably not many can still recite it ten or more years later. In school we read the version of the story recorded by Thomas Jefferson in *Notes on Virginia*. Jefferson compared Logan to Demosthenes and Cicero and said that no European orator had produced a more eminent speech than Logan's. Jefferson maintained that the Indians had many great orators, but there was little record of it because their oratory was displayed chiefly in their own councils."

I looked across the field of grave stones at the obelisk rising high above. The red leaves still clinging to the half-barren maples seemed a fitting backdrop to this monument to the red man, Logan, who clung to a hope of peace in the autumn of his race. Lucy's eyes traced my gaze across to the monument.

"A penny for your thoughts, Jon," she said softly, as if not quite willing to impinge upon the somber stillness of the moment. I drained the last few drops from my bottle of sarsparilla.

"I've been thinking about these hills and the forgotten people who built them up. As much as I am a believer in the superiority of European and American civilization, sometimes I have to ask myself who is to judge one people against another. There's something about this setting and your history lesson that put me in a philosophical mood."

"And quite a philosophy it is. It seems to me that we might make a radical out of you yet," Lucy flashed her strange, beguiling smile at me and I laughed, wondering who the "we" was that she referred to, absurdly imagining her plotting with Leon Czolgosz to win me over to the causes of anarchism and women's rights.

"You must have put something in my drink," I protested. "You know, whoever decided to put the monument here made a wise choice. It would not have nearly the same effect if it were in front of city hall."

"I think you're on to something. Not about the location of the monument. About civilizations. Every story has a winner's version and a loser's version. We honor Logan because our history views him as a good Indian, one who refused to fight against us until his own family was harmed. It's easy for Americans today to praise the noble life of Chief Logan, but that nostalgia glosses over the fact that his people were virtually exterminated. They had many chieftains who fought valiantly against that fate but who we neither honor with monuments nor even remember."

"I suppose you're right," I replied. "If the Indians had prevailed against us then they might remember Logan about as fondly as we think of Benedict Arnold."

"Don't you think there is a parallel between the current war against the Filipinos and the Indian wars of colonial times? Emilio Aguinaldo could be much like Logan, an ordinary man who wants nothing more than peace but who will rise to heroic proportions to protect his people. Most Americans consider the Filipinos to be a bunch of savages in need of our civilizing Christian influence. No doubt Colonel Cresap would have said the same thing about Logan and his tribe."

"I'll bet he did. But I don't know about your analogy. After all, the US freed the Philippines from Spain. Now we're just trying to help them come into the twentieth century and join the world economy."

"And they don't seem to want our help. Aren't you the one who just said we can't judge another people's civilization?"

I sighed and frowned. Why did every conversation with Lucy have to turn to these exasperating political questions?

"All right. Forget I asked," she laughed at my obvious annoyance. "We'll talk about it another time. Anyway, we ought to get going, We bankers don't have the same flexible schedules as you physicians."

The sound of her laughter brought a smile back to my face. "Are you kidding?" I countered, knowing full well that she was. "You know the severe countenance with which your father will greet me if it's even one minute past the hour when I return."

We tossed the apple cores into the nearby brush and gathered up the remains of the picnic, returning them to the basket. We dusted a few brown leaves off the blanket, which I helped her to fold. When we reached the last fold, our hands met and, as they remained lightly touching, she paused, looking inquiringly up into my eyes.

"Why don't you kiss me, Jon?" Lucy asked at last. She leaned gently forward until her lips brushed faintly against my own. My own lips parted slightly and we kissed slowly, awkwardly, uncertainly. She rested her hands on my shoulders. I could feel her breasts pressed ever so lightly against my chest.

A sudden wave of confused self-consciousness rushed over me. I froze. It took a moment for Lucy to realize that my lips were still. She took a step back.

"Lucy, I..." Words eluded me.

She looked up at me, her brow wrinkling in an expression that bespoke both pain and bemusement. Whether the pain was for me or for herself, I could not say.

"Don't you like me, Jon?" she asked in a hushed tone, her lips curving into a tiny pout.

"Yes, it's not that. It's not you. Really. It's me. I guess I'm just not ready or not sure what I want. I really do like you. You're a real pretty girl. And sharp as a tack. It's just that..." And again, words seemed to fail me.

She lifted up her left hand and patted me softly, reassuringly on the cheek.

"It's all right," she said. "I like you too." And with a weak smile she took the blanket from my hands and stuffed it back into the basket.

As we walked back down the hill toward town I felt incredibly awkward and embarrassed, as if I had done her some terrible wrong. Finally, I gathered my wits about me and spoke.

"Lucy, I hope you're not angry with me. Could we have lunch again next week?"

She took my hand and squeezed it briefly. "Yes, Jon, that would be nice."

~

All afternoon I was distracted by thoughts of this encounter and the gnawing accusations of my nagging conscience. A turbulent self-doubt declared that I had behaved abominably with Lucy, that I had unnecessarily hurt a most decent person, and that I was a damned fool for not falling in love with her or at least mustering sufficient desire to fully explore a tender embrace. My self-recriminations brought forth the memory of Judith Cooper, my first adolescent "love interest." We were in the seventh grade together. Casting a pubescent eye her way, I embarked upon the various courting rituals of that age which amounted most often to finding pretexts to be in her proximity and, on rare occasions, daring to speak to her. This soon rose to the occasional carrying of her books, usually when none of my fellows were nearby to notice, to escorting her home from school, and to cinching her affections with the gift of an occasional sweet. She responded suitably for her age and sex, giggling at my jokes, approving of my physical strength and prowess, and passing me "secret" notes during class or recess. These tokens of intimacy amounted to little more in content than a commentary on our classmates or teachers--"Mr. Reilly looks like an old prune today" or "Isn't Cynthia Wallace a conceited little thing?" But the passing of such messages was tantamount to the suggestive flattering of later years. Finally, I seized the initiative to bring my most closely-guarded fantasy to life and, one afternoon as we reached the stoop leading up to her flat, I leaned forward and ventured a kiss, full on her young lips. She was appropriately surprised and hesitant at first, but then smiled and kissed me back, a quick peck on the cheek, before fleeing through the front door.

For a day I was aglow with happiness, confident that I had taken one of the giant strides required by my impending maturation. But my bubble was burst the following afternoon when, on our walk home, Judith informed me of her great delight in knowing that I was truly in love with her and of her joyous expectation that some day, after high school or perhaps college, we would at last be married. Unfortunately, I did not yet understand that such conceits were the necessary window dressing of puppy love. Suddenly I felt snared, as if the path of this idle courtship, and even of my life itself, were now wrenched from my control. The next day in class, Judith passed me a note suggesting that we might stop at the candy shop on the way home. Shamefully, I did not even turn to look back at her when receiving her message. After school, she stood waiting in the usual place, but, shunning her, I joined my pals in storming off toward the vacant lot that then served as our Sherwood Forest. Out of the corner of my eye, I saw the look of pain and dejection on her face before she turned to hurry off in the opposite direction.

At that age, one quickly moves on--yesterday's fancies losing out to the passions of tomorrow. Thus, I easily buried my guilt. Only years later did I at last feel the sting of rejection myself. I then thought back to Judith Cooper and regretted the pain I had brought to her young heart. Now, I remembered her again. The remorse of the child fanning the flames of confusion in the adult. I desperately wanted to view myself as a mature person, but I had to question whether my actions and insights today were any more responsible than those of my twelve-year-old self. I might or might not ever fall in love with Lucy Gerin. Or, perhaps in my own curious fashion I was in love with her already. But, one thing was for certain, I vowed to myself that night: I would not run away from her.

Chapter Eight

~

Thursday, October 10, 1901

"Parker!"

I was startled to hear my name called out as I strode along Genesee Street.

"Parker! Wait up!"

I turned around and peered through the fleeting daylight to find Joe Whelan walking quickly toward me. From his gait, it was clear that he had followed close on my heels from O'Malley's and had hurried to catch up.

"Hey, Joe, what's up?"

"I'd like to talk with you a minute, Doc. Can I walk with you a ways?"

"Sure." I could not imagine what he might want to talk to me about—some medical matter, no doubt--and we continued east, toward North Street. We walked in silence for a moment. I looked questioningly at Whelan. Catching my eye, he began to speak.

"I might as well talk plainly and get right to the point. Do you ever see him, talk to him?" Whelan spoke hesitantly, with an uncharacteristic nervousness. From his tone, he could only be referring to Czolgosz.

I demurred, knowing I could not reveal the extent of my conversations with the assassin. "I do. We examine all the prisoners." I wondered if rumors of my activities might have spread from the prison keepers to the townspeople.

"I was thinking that, if you had a chance, you could let him know that there are those of us out here who are heartened by his act, who think of him as a comrade. It might help his spirits to hear it." I could tell from Whelan's earnest tone that this was an important favor that he was asking.

"Joe, I'm surprised that you'd say this to me. Don't you think it's dangerous to express such views? It's tough times for anyone suspected of holding anarchist sympathies."

"Sure, we've got to be careful since they started rounding us up." This was the first I'd heard Whelan refer to himself as an anarchist. "Sure, they're breaking our presses and throwing us out of work. But, Doc, I'm pretty confident that it's safe speaking with you. Like yourself, see, I'm a student of human nature and, from the first day you showed up at O'Malley's, I pegged you for a fair-minded fellow. One who would not judge too harshly without all the facts."

"I'd like to think so. I didn't realize that there were anarchists in Auburn. Other than a few campus dilettantes and Leon, you're the first I've met, at least that I know of."

Joe looked me over as if sizing me up anew. "'Leon', is it? I didn't expect you'd be on a first name basis with him but I'm not surprised either."

"If that's all, I guess I'll be heading home now," I said, hoping to cut the conversation short. That one slip up was one too many as far as I was concerned. I started to turn toward North Street and Mrs. T's when Whelan grabbed me by the arm.

"Listen Parker, what do you say we walk down by the river and talk some more?"

Shocked by his action, I was about to pull away when I realized that an opportunity was at hand. "Happy to," I replied, trying to hide my discomfort. I was intrigued by Whelan's overture. He might give me some background on anarchism that would help hone my thinking for my next meeting with Czolgosz. I was frustrated with the impasse I had arrived at with the assassin. Hungry for any insight that might help me through my dilemma, I took a chance

"Ok," I said, and fell in step with Whelan as we turned back onto Genesee Street, heading east.

"There's a lot of misconceptions about anarchists," Whelan said. "Reading the papers you'd think that anarchists were only found in the big cities, like New York and Chicago. But you'll find us wherever working people are struggling under oppressive conditions. In other words, pretty much everywhere. It's just that we don't go out of our way to wear the anarchist label in public.

Easier to keep your job that way. Especially since the
assassination."
        "But that's just my point. They're making anarchists out to
be utter monsters. Since McKinley was shot there's been a kind of
hysteria about it. If there's a shred of truth to these fears, it's no
wonder they want to lock you all up."
        "Well, Parker, maybe after we talk awhile you'll come to
see there's not a word of truth in all those attacks. We anarchists
have always been vilified by those in power. But, you're right, this
is about the worst I've seen. The editor of one Washington paper
wrote that 'public vengeance should have full sway, unhampered
by legal interference, and every avowed anarchist should be taken
to the nearest tree.' That's pretty strong language for a nation that
prides itself on due process of law. If one of our papers had
published sentiments like those, it would be shut down in a
heartbeat, the editor jailed."
        "It's not just the papers. The President called anarchism a
kind of degenerate lunacy that must be stamped out by any means
necessary."
        "Yeah, that Roosevelt is quite a piece of work," Whelan
frowned at the thought of the young President. "He's calling for
special laws for anarchists that would reserve for us a unique justice
without the protections of the Constitution. Of course, Teddy has
the political need to make such an attack so he can stop the talk of
his own involvement in a plot to murder McKinley."
        I had read of such insinuations. Some of the newspapers,
those with Democratic sympathies, the Hearst papers in particular,
had hinted at just such a conspiracy. William Randolph Hearst had
his own problems since the assassination. The Republicans had
long resented his editorial attacks on McKinley, his strong support
of Bryan, and his use of his papers to build up the Democratic
Party. Now, newspapers with Republican sympathies were trying to
connect Hearst to Czolgosz as if the flamboyant publisher had in
some way incited his act. In particular, Hearst was in hot water
over an editorial from a few months before the assassination that
said "if bad institutions and bad men can be got rid of only by
killing, then killing must be done." A recent cartoon depicted the
publisher standing behind Czolgosz offering him a match to light a
bomb's fuse. As a result, Hearst was now among the loudest calling
for a crackdown on the anarchists and casting innuendos at

Roosevelt in turn. But most Americans saw TR as a war hero and took any suggestion of his malfeasance as partisan politicking which, no doubt, it was.

"This way," Whelan gestured to his right as we came to where the road crossed the river. I followed him down a grassy embankment and along the river until we found a couple of barrels in a vacant lot at the edge of the Osborne property. A few scraggly trees did little to obscure the hulking brick buildings of the main Osborne plant. The smoke billowing from the tall stacks indicated that the second shift was hard at work. Sitting on a barrel and motioning me to do the same, Whelan said "We sometimes have lunch out here, me and the boys from the factory. It's a good place to sit. Maybe a little too down-to earth for you, Doc?"

"No, this is fine. You'd be surprised at some of the places I've sat."

Whelan took off his brown coat and folded it over his lap as he took his seat. Underneath, he wore a tousled white shirt, much like any of the working men who frequented O'Malley's. I was beginning to recognize him as a familiar type. On first encountering him at the saloon, I'd taken him to be something of a blowhard. I'd braced at his speech-making and at his tendency to ensconce himself at the center of attention. Now I saw that Whelan was indeed a talker but of a respectable sort, perhaps even an orator. I'd seen his kind before. In college, there were those men who acted as if the attention of the entire lounge or dining room was their personal due, who had only to speak and others would gather around and listen. Living in New York, Jones and I occasionally took the opportunity to attend a rally to hear some prominent political figure speak. At those events, one dull speech seemed to follow another until at last a speaker appeared whose skill and personality drew the crowd to a pitch of excitement. Such an accomplished orator could turn the idle observer into an eager foot soldier of the campaign at hand. The past summer, I'd stopped in passing to observe a labor rally at Union Square. A short bespectacled, gravel-voiced man addressed the crowd in some East European tongue. Although I could not understand his words, I could feel the power with which by tone, exhortation, and sheer force of will he made the crowd his own. I could now readily imagine Joe Whelan atop that same platform bringing the masses to rapt attention. Leon Czolgosz I could only envision standing sullenly if steadfastly amidst the throng.

Whelan continued his earlier line of reasoning, "Now here's how I see it. If anarchism is what Roosevelt would have us believe it is, then it doesn't have a chance. He won't need to declare martial law to defeat anarchism. The common-sense people will dismiss it to the oblivion to which it rightfully belongs. If, on the contrary, it is what every clear-thinking investigator knows it to be--a criticism of the present unjust state of society, with its billionaires and paupers, and an effort to encourage the people toward a more civilized and just society--then the millionaire class who rule us are no more than tyrants in their efforts to interfere. We may as well give up prattling about our 'free country' and admit that it is despotism.

"Parker, you know the old warning that the price of liberty is eternal vigilance. Anarchists today are those who heed those celebrated words. Who else truly takes them to heart?"--I knew the quote well and was firm in my belief that the United States itself comprised that vigilant guardian. Whelan did not share my confidence--"Most Americans are content to blindly believe and follow the words of their rulers. They sit idly by while the power of the people is pushed aside by the power of the trusts. Things have gone so far that the President and Congress can prepare laws to punish those who speak and write about a social philosophy with which they do not agree. That's the way it is with rulers, whether elected presidents or divinely appointed kings. They rule in the manner best calculated to serve their own ends and those of their class. And they can thumb their noses at the Constitution, since the judges who interpret it are appointed by the rich from among the rich."

Whelan's words brought to mind Czolgosz' insistence that no ruler would take the side of the working man. Although the anarchist leaders may have disavowed the assassin, he most assuredly held to a common political philosophy with my evening companion.

"But, don't you fear such repression, especially if the system is as rigged against you as you say?"

"One takes care, of course. I can't say that I'm happy about the wholesale arrest of anarchists, sacking their homes without any warrant, holding them for days or even weeks in jail without any cause other than the fact of their being anarchists. And all of this based on one newspaper article found in Czolgosz' pocket! But, all this attention will do more for the spread of anarchism than years of agitation of our own. These new laws sound bad, but how, in the end, will they enforce them? Short of a man proclaiming himself an anarchist, who is to judge? Will a censor be stationed in every town with the power over what can be said and what can be printed? What then will have become of our boasted freedom of speech? Won't ours then be a country like Russia or worse, a despotism through and through?"

"That's ridiculous, comparing America to Russia," Russia was a backward nation under harsh rulers, the very antithesis of the United States. "Anyway, there was more than that one article. Czolgosz is known to have attended a speech of Emma Goldman's. He told me he's met her." I caught myself, realizing that I had let out more on my interaction with Leon than I had intended. Attempting to gloss over it, I quickly continued, "and, there's been speculation he's connected to the notorious Paterson, New Jersey, anarchists."

"You've kept up with the papers, Doc. But, think a minute." Whelan stood up and began to pace back and forth across the small clearing, apparently oblivious to my faux pas. "What sense does it make, even granting that Czolgosz is an anarchist, to hold all anarchists responsible for his act? When Guiteau, a Republican, killed President Garfield no one suggested the repression of the Republican Party."

"That's because the Republican Party does not advocate assassination."

Whelan, caught up in his own argument, ignored my point." And don't forget, Guiteau acted purely in his personal interest, avenging his own frustrated claim on political patronage. Czolgosz killed McKinley because he saw him as one of the chief instruments through which a cruel system of capitalism was exploiting himself and his fellows." Whelan's footsteps echoed dully on the hard ground. His hands moved forcefully to underscore his words. "Czolgosz, Leon as you call him, killed McKinley because he loves his fellow men more than his own life. No fair-minded person, even condemning the act itself, can fail to recognize the strength of character that will inspire a man to give up his own life to call attention to the wrongs being perpetrated upon humanity. Is his heroism any less than that of the Minutemen who fell at Concord Bridge?"

I was flabbergasted at this comparison. "That's a bit much for me to swallow, Whelan. A murderer can never be considered a hero. To do so would be to dispense with morality entirely. The Minutemen were at war with an armed foe, one that was oppressing the American citizenry on behalf of a tyrant."

"And in truth, Parker, Czolgosz' deed must be understood as an act of war. It rests on the same moral principle, the struggle for freedom and justice, as the uprisings at Lexington and Concord. McKinley reaped only what he himself had sown. When he makes war upon the working men at home and on the defenseless men, women and children of the Phillippines, and when an individual, exasperated by such tyranny, makes war upon him in turn, there is no just cause for complaint."

"How can you call a democratically elected President a tyrant?" I was getting fed up with Whelan's analogies. He was sounding less like a harmless "social philosopher," as he termed it, and more like a member of a dangerous political movement. Roosevelt had offered the phase "degenerate lunacy" as a possible category for anarchist thought. Surely, part of my project with Czolgosz was to determine if such a label could be applied generally to anarchists. Joe Whelan's maddeningly slick argumentation at times seemed diabolical. But degenerate? Not that I could see so far. "McKinley was no tyrant," I repeated.

"Wasn't he? Czolgosz saw first hand how so many of his fellow Americans struggled desperately with pangs of hunger. Meanwhile he read in the papers of the $50,000 feasts of their rulers and exploiters. Not that he would ever witness such a feast first hand! He saw the armed Pinkertons arrayed against strikers. He saw troops mustered to help the rich defeat the poor working men who struck against starvation wages, shooting them down like dogs. He could not bear to witness these wrongs without acting. Tortured to the limit of endurance by the sight of suffering humanity, he registered a final, valiant protest against a cruel system that starves men, women and children while food lies rotting in the storehouses. McKinley was the apparent leader of that vicious system, and for that Czolgosz slew him."

"But even granting such injustices, surely you must see McKinley as a fellow human. How can you fail to condemn Czolgosz' act?"

"What I'm trying to get across to you, Parker, is that the shooting was a social act, an incident in the great struggle between the oppressed and the oppressors, between those forces in society which are for progress and those which attempt to block the onward march of evolution. Czolgosz was an implement in the hands of evolution, and to condemn him for his act would be as absurd as condemning the flood for sweeping away a village built in the bed of the river."

My exasperation was mounting. I would not let Whelan overwhelm me with a rhetorical onslaught or bulldoze me into accepting his point of view. For all his yeoman's grandiloquence, Joe was evading my questions in a maze of polemic. "So, you anarchists will not condemn him, " my voice strained, practically a shout. "But, how can you simultaneously fail to accept responsibility for him? He read the anarchist literature and attended your meetings. Was Czolgosz not drawn to his task by the example of Bresci and the writings of American anarchists? Surely, the journals he read described the assassination of King Humbert in the same noble language you now use in reference to the murder of McKinley. Can you deny Czolgosz was influenced by such ideas?"

Whelan looked me over as if assaying the extent of my agitation. "To say that Czolgosz was inspired to commit his act by anarchist speeches and literature explains no more than to say he was inspired by reading the Declaration of Independence which taught him that all men are created free and equal, entitled to liberty and happiness. Looking around, where would he see that liberty or that happiness? Let's say he had studied anarchy and learned the truth that labor creates all wealth and that the plutocracy robs the working man of that wealth through such devices as taxes, rent, interest, and profit. Let's say he learned that newspapers and politicians serve to glorify this system of robbery and to keep the toilers ignorant, feeding their minds upon garbled news, perverted history, religious cant, and patriotic twaddle. If Czolgosz learned such unpleasant truths from us then of what crime can anarchists be charged other than that by studying their works the truth is learned?"

"You're side stepping the issue, Whelan." I could no longer keep to my seat and leaped up and strode across the clearing to the opposite side from my companion. His pacing came to an abrupt halt and he stared at me in surprise. Never before had he seen such a display of emotion from me. "Sure," I continued, "Czolgosz learned these so-called unpleasant truths from the anarchists, just as he learned violence from them."

"Parker, would you believe that many anarchists are vegetarians, so revolting to their moral senses is the taking of life?"

"And so what if they are? What kind of sophistry are you spinning here? Anyway, I do believe I've seen you down your share of O'Malley's pork chops."

Whelan chuckled. His laugh, a deep, slow growl, had over the weeks become quite familiar to me. "I may be more the exception than the rule here. The point is that anarchism is a deeply moral philosophy. Anarchist groups are not suicide clubs organized to kill rulers. We would be the last to entertain the delusion that a handful of intellectual weaklings called kings and presidents are so powerful that their removal will issue in the millennium. It is not the rulers, but the ideas existing in the minds of the people that enslave them. Who has ever seen a government? Many a working man sees the policeman's club. But the anarchist sees the idea behind it, and knows that once that idea is destroyed the club will fall harmlessly to the ground. The fight then is one of idea--the anarchist idea of freedom against the governmentalist's idea of authority."

"A war of ideas that happens to be fought with guns," I sputtered. I realized that I was beating fist against palm in rhythm with my words. I recognized this as an unfortunately aggressive gesture and took a deep breath to regain my composure. "Listen, Whelan, I'm really just trying to grasp what your movement is about. I've heard about anarchists touring and lecturing. I've heard of their involvement in labor unrest, supposedly provoking honest workers to violence. Everyone knows the story of Berkman's attempt to assassinate Henry Frick during the Homestead strike of '92. But, what does it all amount to? It's one thing to talk about change, but quite another to make change actually occur."

My conciliatory words had a calming effect on both of us. Whelan walked back over to the barrel and sat down. He held out his hand inviting me to do the same. Only when we were both seated again amicably face to face did he speak.

"Don't forget, Doc, that talk must precede and guide action. We anarchists seek out fertile soil in which to plant our ideas, battling with the forces of ignorance and authority. That alone, given the strength of our opponents, is an overwhelming task. Anarchists believe in evolution and know that only through ceaseless agitation will our ideas gradually take root. There is no elaborate program by which we plan to bring on some sort of reign of anarchy. We are too sensible for that. The world does not move according to programs. When the time comes for the transformation of society, the means will suggest themselves. Will those means be peaceful? Probably not, as long as government persists in preventing a peaceful and gradual application of new ideas as they develop.

"Please understand what this movement means to me and perhaps to Czolgosz as well. Anarchy infuses the human heart with feelings of comradeship and a love of liberty, justice and right-doing. That one word--anarchy--encompasses all the hopes and aspirations of the working class. Our goal is to wipe away the cobwebs of ignorance and superstition which ages of statecraft and priestcraft have woven across the path of progress." He delivered these words with a flourish and a feeling of sincere good-will that had a captivating and pacifying affect.

"You know, Whelan, speaking of priestcraft, you ought to have been a preacher. Or a politician. You've quite a way with words."

"Thanks for the compliment. I'd like to see a time when all people, men and women, are free to develop their faculties of expression and creativity. That, too, is part of the anarchist vision. It's important to me to know what I want to say so I work on it. I want to be able to get these ideas across to people, maybe light a spark here or there."

"Well, I'm unlikely to prove a fertile ground for such a spark. Still, you've given me plenty to think about. And I'll look at newspaper reports on anarchism in a new light thanks to our conversation. But that whistle from the six-thirty train told me that my dinner's getting cold. I'd better get going." I'd learned that the regular whistles of the passenger and freight trains were a reliable way to keep track of time in Auburn. "Going native" was

Jonesy's term for it. In any event, I was ready for a break from this conversation. I was not getting anywhere with Whelan and needed time to think, time to try to make sense of his wildly unacceptable philosophy. But his last heartfelt and personable declaration had answered any lingering question as to the sanity of this particular anarchist. Joe Whelan's arguments might be maddening but they were far from the ravings of a degenerate lunatic.

We retraced our steps along the riverbank back up to Genesee Street. I held out my hand to shake his. "I appreciate your candor, Whelan. It's helpful to me. And, of course, whatever you've told me is held in strict confidence."

"Thanks, Doc." His grip was firm and vigorous against my own. "And you'll deliver the message?"

"I'm pretty sure I'll have a chance to do that." We turned to part. "Oh, Whelan, one more question." He looked back and raised an eyebrow. "From what you know of him, do you consider Czolgosz to be a legitimate anarchist?"

Joe Whelan looked at me long and hard. "It's funny you should ask me that," he said, "I've been thinking that when all's said and done, that might be a question you'd answer for me." He pumped my hand again in his and patted me on the back, a smile spreading across his face. "Anyway, you know that no anarchist could claim him as one of our own. Not in times like these."

And with that he turned back down Genesee Street. I watched for a moment, stunned by this last remark, as he disappeared into the now darkened heart of Auburn. I trudged on in the opposite direction, my thoughts raging, my stomach growling.

Chapter Nine

~

Tuesday, October 15, 1901

A single white cloud crossed the morning sun, painting a long, gray shadow across the prison walls as I arrived for work. The street and nearby train platform were empty. The air was still; the only sounds distant echoes from downtown Auburn. I took a deep breath, steadying myself as I approached the gate.

"Parker!" Griffin, the front gate keeper, called to me, "the warden wants to see you. He said you're to go directly to his office."

"Thanks," I replied, "I'm on my way." In my mind, there was only one topic that the warden might call on me to discuss with so precipitous a summons

Warden J. Warren Mead was an imposing figure. Any man who rises to the top position in a major penitentiary must become accustomed to command. Although the prison did not seem to make its administrators cruel, it did impart to them a stern demeanor. In many ways, the prison environment was like the military, a clear hierarchy where the chief's word was law. Mead held to the philosophy that maintaining strict discipline with the staff would set the tone for their treatment of the prisoners and for the inmates' dealings with each other. He ran a tight ship. At the same time, he was not a callous or punitive man. Like Dr. Gerin, Mead was a pragmatist.

The warden's secretary showed me directly into his office-- a large room on the second floor of the administration building with windows looking out over the prison grounds. Mead's office was a Spartan affair with none of the clutter that typically filled Gerin's, and little in the way of decor or refinement. The most prominent adornment was a finely-antlered deer's head mounted on the side wall. If this were any indication of the fate of those who displeased Warden Mead, it did not serve to put me at ease. As I

entered, the warden waved his left hand directing me to the chair
on that side of his desk.

"Mr. Parker," he began immediately, removing an unlit
pipe from his lips, "I'd like to get right to the point here so that we
can both get on with our morning tasks. I have heard from Mr.
Tupper that you have been meeting with the assassin, Czolgosz, on
the pretext of his requiring medical examination. I have already
spoken with Dr. Gerin in regard to his authorization of this affair
behind my back. He maintains that your likelihood of success is
improved by minimizing official notice. I'm not sure about that but
am quite willing to give the doctor the benefit of the doubt." He
paused and tapped on the side of his pipe bowl. I was relieved to
learn that, once again, Dr. Gerin had proven to be a most effective
accomplice.

Mead continued, "Actually, I am pleased that these
discussions are taking place. The prisoner, as I'm sure you are
aware, has been tight-lipped ever since his arrest. It is widely
believed that he could not have carried out the assassination
without help, but all investigations so far have failed to turn up
clear evidence of a conspiracy. The Buffalo police who delivered
the prisoner asked that we take careful note of any comments he
may make in regard to his recent activities and associations. Now, I
don't understand your personal interest in the prisoner or what you
hope to gain from these interviews. I'm not sure that Gerin does
either, for that matter. But, nonetheless, if you can gain Czolgosz'
confidence, you may learn something useful for the investigation. If
he does reveal any as yet unknown factors concerning his crime,
his travels, or his associations, no matter how seemingly
insignificant, you are to report them immediately to Dr. Gerin who
will pass them along to me. Is that clear?"

"Yes sir, quite clear." Despite the nervous lump in my
throat, I tried to convey the officious tone that was common
among the prison administrators.

"Thank you then, Mr. Parker. You may go. And good luck
with your researches."

"Thank you, sir."

I rose and walked from the room having said only those
few words to the warden. I realized I was trembling, and paused in
the hallway to pull myself together and contemplate this
unexpected discussion. It was disconcerting, to say the least, to

find myself an object of the warden's scrutiny. I braced at having been ordered, in effect, to serve as a spy for the police. I was a medical student, almost a doctor, for Christ's sake, not one of his underlings. And I'd be damned if I'd comply. The relationship of trust that I was attempting to build with Czolgosz did not have room for even the hint of such a devious agenda. But, I reminded myself, at least the warden was allowing my project to continue. That was most unexpected.

As I trudged up the stairs toward the clinic, I was surprised to find Jones waiting for me on the landing. He leaned awkwardly against the wall as if he'd been standing there for a while. His arms were folded across his chest, his brow wrinkled in a pensive frown, and his lips drawn down reprovingly.

"What's up?" I asked.

"Parker, you've been holding out on me," he said, maintaining his serious expression. "I think it's time for you to come clean and fill me in on your little projects."

"Projects?" I asked, surprised to hear that there might be more than one.

"You certainly have become the man of mystery lately. I've counted two so far but that's only in the 'L' category. There's L.C. and then there's L.G. Both are serious pursuits for young Doctor Parker, projects his best buddy and steadfast pal ought to have been in on from the get go."

"Jonesy, you're right," Still unnerved by my encounter with the Warden, I needed Jones on my side. "Things have been moving so quickly that I've lost my bearings a bit. What do you say let's you and I talk this evening and I'll tell you all about it, ok?"

"I'll be counting the minutes, pal," he answered. "You go on and enjoy your secret meeting later this morning. I'm sure you're looking forward to it. But I'll be expecting a full disclosure tonight."

~

I was indeed eagerly anticipating this morning's session. My talk with Joe Whelan had produced a powerful effect. In the days since, I found myself increasingly intrigued by his expectation that I, not he, was the one who might finally divine the mystery of the assassin. It was not just his words that had affected me. The more I thought about our conversation, the more Whelan had gained my respect as a man of knowledge, strength, and conviction. As he looked steadfastly into my eyes, his gaze had spurred me to seek comparable qualities within myself and to embrace my role in this great drama of our time, come what may. With a bit of cooperation from Leon Czolgosz, I just might be up to the challenge.

A few hours later, right on schedule, the guards brought Czolgosz to the examining room. Tupper tried to catch my eye, seeking recognition that he and I shared a bond of secrecy. I avoided his gaze, not wanting to alarm the prisoner.

"So, Leon," I began when the guards had left us, "do you mind if I call you Leon?" I had decided that my project could be furthered by adopting a more personal tone, that Czolgosz' comfort might develop more quickly. Time was running out.

Czolgosz barely nodded his head providing only the most meager acknowledgment of my words.

"Very well then. Leon it is. Have you been holding up all right?"

The prisoner shrugged, "Not too bad, I s'pose."

"That's good. Last time we met, we agreed to each think more about the direction of our discussions and to talk about it again today. I'm wondering if you've had a chance to follow through on that."

"Well, Doc--you mind if I call you Doc?" Despite the blatant sarcasm, the question was delivered with a straight face.

"That's fine, if you like, although technically I'm not a doctor yet." It seemed as if I might as well start getting used to people calling me by the title that would soon by rights be mine.

"Okay, Doc, I've had plenty of time to think. About you and lots of other things. Plenty of time for thinkin'." Czolgosz regarded me warily, as if still uncertain how much of his ruminations he could safely reveal. "That first time, when that fellow Gerin said I might value having someone to talk to, I thought it was a lot of guff. But since then I've learned that it's not a real friendly place, down there among the murderers." He said this is if he was describing a lower class to which he himself did not belong. "I'm glad to get up here for these talks even if all I've got is a couple of weeks. So, the way I'm figurin' it is, if you want to hear about my family and my life and all, then what's the harm? I might as well give it a go. But, like I told you before, don't be thinking you can trick me into tellin' tales on nobody. That's not gonna happen."

"And it's not my goal, believe me."

"One more thing. What get's said in this room stays in this room. Between you and me. I want your word that you won't go writing a book or blabbing to some reporter or cop or even to your boss out there." Leon spoke with a rare assertiveness. He fixed his gaze on my eyes as if intent on measuring the veracity of my reply. I was definitely on the spot. Mead had charged me to disclose. Czolgosz was insisting that I maintain silence. Were I truly a physician, I could justifiably hold a patient's confidences, that is if Czolgosz were truly my patient. As it was, I had no real basis for withholding information if the warden pressed me for it. Yet, of all these considerations, it seemed that Leon's sensitivity to our own developing relationship was paramount. I must, above all else, be honest with him. It was with that view that I measured my words.

"I really have no interest in talking to reporters. And, if you don't want me to publish anything about our conversations, I will agree not to. The prison officials are another story. They will want to know if you say anything to incriminate others, but, since you assure me that you will tell me nothing of the sort, then I can in turn assure you that my answer will be as simple and direct as 'no he did not.' I hope that is a satisfactory reply."

"It'll do. I guess. Under the circumstances, it will have to do." Czolgosz' gaze drifted off, his voice returned to its usual monotone.

"So, what do you think?" I asked. "How shall we begin?"

Czolgosz quietly considered this question. Finally, he said, "I guess the beginning is as good a place as any. How's that strike you."

"Good," I replied, "very good." Czolgosz leaned back in his chair and stretched his legs out. His eyes drifted up toward the ceiling. Several minutes passed in silence.

"From the beginning. Yes, sir, that's how it will be told. From the beginning." The prisoner took on the detached air of the casual storyteller as if the tale he told was not his own, as if his days were not already numbered. "I was born on April 15, 1873. My folks are Polish. Paul Czolgosz and Mary Nowak. I have five

brothers -- Waldek, Frank, and Joseph are older, John and Jacob
are younger -- and two younger sisters, Ceceli and Victoria. We
were quite a brood when we was small. What my Ma would call a
handful. When I was twelve, Ma died, a few weeks after the birth
of another baby. That baby died as well. That was a pretty sad and
troubled time." Czolgosz hesitated for a moment perhaps recalling
that sadness.
	"That's a great loss," I said. "So, both of your parents were
born in Poland?"
	"Actually, my Pa was born in Prussia, on the Polish side, a
town called Gora. He came across the year I was born. My Ma
came over with my brothers a few months later. She was pregnant
at the time and I was born soon after they got to Detroit. We
moved around a lot when I was growing up, mostly in Michigan.
Detroit City when I was little, some other town, can't ever
remember the name, for just a few months, then when I was
around 15, we move to Alpena and then finally to Posen. After
that, we left Michigan and moved to Pennsylvania, a small town
called Natrona near Pittsburgh. When I was eighteen, we finally
arrived in Cleveland where we've been since."
	"Why did you move around so much?" I asked, although I
was hesitant to interrupt. I was surprised and pleased by his
readiness to tell his tale. I knew that his family had not yet visited
him and that the keepers and other prisoners gave him a rough
time. Perhaps it was his loneliness and basic human need for a
sympathetic ear that opened him to me.
	"Like any working man, my Pa was always looking for
somethin' better, a few pennies more. You hear about a better job
so you pack everything up and move on. Sometimes it pans out,
sometimes it don't. Of course, there was that one time, the time he
got into trouble. That's the story I wouldn't tell you last week. I'll
bet you'd like to hear it now." He looked at me for a moment and
crossed his legs. "I bet you would. So, I guess I'll tell ya. Back when
we were still living in Michigan - I was pretty small, so what I know
is what I heard from Waldek - that's when Pa got into trouble. The
worst kind of trouble--murder, that's what it was. We was living
near Detroit in some company town and the big boss man got
himself murdered. A lot of people thought Pa was involved, but
Waldek says Pa was out of town when it happened. Anyway, Pa, he
high-tailed it out of there after that, which is what anyone would

do if they were smart. Working men can't trust to the law for justice, that's for sure, and even Pa, he knew it."

"Do you think he did it?"

"Waldek's always been suspicious maybe Pa had a hand in it, but me, I look at Pa and don't see him as the type to make waves. I don't see him raising his hand against nobody tougher than his own children." Here was the first real indication of family dynamics. Finally, we were entering the terrain that interested me as a budding alienist. Leon's talkativeness encouraged me to abandon the conservative approach I'd taken during the earlier sessions. I pressed on with this opening.

"Did he raise his hand to you often when you were growing up?"

Czolgosz shrugged. "I guess about as much as any father would. If we'd mess up or sass him we'd get a beating, sure."

"How did that make you feel, being beaten as a child?"

He paused and looked at me with some surprise. "Well, I guess you don't know, do you? I guess the rewards of privilege start at a pretty young age." He stared at me intently through narrowed eyelids as if appraising the extent of my ignorance. I took note of his thorough disposition to see things in terms of class. It was not sufficient that I had a father who was not given to violent discipline, but it must be seen as an expression of my social class. Czolgosz continued, "I'll tell you how a kid feels to be beaten. You hate it and hates the hand that does it. But, as you get bigger, it hurts less and you start to look down at the man who can no longer control you, who's looking smaller every day. Then you get older still and you begin to see how sorry that man's life is and that it's no wonder he takes it out on his own family. But most men, by that time they're already working fourteen-hour days and about all they can do is go out and find a girl and start their own family to beat on. It's really somethin' when you think about it, beatin' on their wives and kids when they ought to be goin' after the bosses." It really was something, and so was the assassin's insight into the social origins of family violence.

"How was your Pa otherwise?"

"Oh, he's pretty rough overall. Quiet man, with a good little temper. Worked hard to make a home here. He never wanted to learn much English, though. That held him back but he kept us going pretty well anyway. He owned a bar once for a while, in

Cleveland, but mostly he's worked as a laborer like the rest of us. I didn't understand it when I was a kid, but lately I've thought of him as kind of brave, setting out across the ocean for a strange country and all. Maybe that's the bravery of desperation, but there's a lot more desperation than there is bravery in the world. My Pa's had a pretty tough life. And it's bound to get tougher now. He won't like hearing about what I've done. He never approved much of my reading or going to meetings."

I was struck by this expression, "the bravery of desperation." Might Czolgosz dare to characterize his own actions in such terms?

"I guess you weren't ever going to grow up to be like him?" I ventured.

"No, not now I'm not. But I figured someone's got to take a stand. If we all just work our whole lives and raise a bunch of kids nothing's ever going to change. With all my brothers there'll be plenty of Czolgoszes to carry on the name. That is, if they'll want to keep it after this." We sat quietly for a moment as I considered this hint of despondency. Leon thought he'd done his duty in Buffalo. How disheartening it must be to think that he might have tainted his family name, shamed his siblings and even their descendants.

"That must be sad for you, to think that they might react like that."

"Naw. They're just ignorant, 'cept for Waldek."

"Tell me more about your childhood. What were you like?"

"I guess I was pretty quiet as a kid. Not that you'd think so with all this gabbing. No one talked too much in our house. Pa could get pretty rough if the kids got too noisy when he was home. Ma had her hands full with all my brothers and sisters but she always seemed to have some time for me. She found a way to make me feel special even in that crowded house."

I recognized that need for a mother's favor and made a mental note to observe where it might crop up again. I scanned Leon's face for any hint of emotion as he recalled his mother's attention, but he only rubbed his fingers distractedly and continued on with the same placid expression. "Most places we lived there weren't too many Polish families around and my folks kept pretty much to themselves. So we didn't have many playmates apart from each other. Maybe that's why I've always been pretty shy and kind of quiet. It takes me a while to get to know people. Sometimes folks are suspicious of you if you don't say much. I was especially scared to talk to girls. To tell the truth, I still am. I'd even cross the street on Sunday mornings if I knew girls my age were coming from church. Oh, I wanted to talk to them all right. Just never figured out how to come right out and do it."

"Have you never had a girlfriend?"

"I had a girl one time, but not for long. She tired of me, I guess, and moved on to some other fella. My brothers were always on my back about it. Friends, like the Dryers, were too, always having some girl in mind for me to have a go at. But I was too shy, I guess, and didn't ever get the hang of it. Sometimes I'd watch my friend Hauser. He'd just say any old thing if some girl took his fancy. And then he'd keep after her like a bloodhound on the chase. Most of 'em seemed to go for it but that's just not my style. At the bar, Dryer's bar that is, the one they bought from my Pa, I'd sit by myself and read and have a drink. Never more than one though. The guys would say to me 'Come on, blow yourself off.' But I'd tell them I had use for my money. Never smoked cigarettes neither. Didn't care for it. I carried a cigar sometimes or a pipe, mostly just to impress people. But I did smoke one from time to time."

"That must have been hard spending so much time by yourself, just you and your books."

"Oh, it wasn't too bad. And there were other things I liked to do. One thing a boy learns when he's a loner is to hunt. I loved to track down those rabbits. When I was little, I could hardly catch one, but when I did I'd run straight to my Ma, proud as can be, and she'd add it to that day's supper. When I got older, I learned to use fire to drive 'em out of their burrows. They'll run right into a sack. Later, after I was sick, I might use my shotgun, a breech-loader, at a distance or my revolver at close range. I also helped out some around the farm. Mostly fixing machines and wagons. I've got pretty much of a knack for tinkering, taking things apart and getting them back together."

"Your stepmother must have appreciated those rabbits."

"Her? She never appreciated nothin' and I didn't give 'em to her anyway." A flicker of resentment burned in his eyes. "She never did believe I was sick. Thought I was just gold-brickin'. She would light into me sometimes pretty bad. Pa never said a word, just let her rail on. The old woman pretty much put me off. It was hard to feel at home when she was around. When I was sick I took to eating by myself. I'd just catch a fish from the pond or get some milk in the barn and have it in my room or under a tree, maybe with a piece of bread or cake, if I was lucky. Finally, I started to feel like I needed to get out, meet some comrades, maybe do some work. I was feeling better and I thought about getting my money out of the farm and heading West. All the brothers had equal shares in the farm. That $70 would take me far. I told the family I might go to Kansas City or California even. But I had other destinations in mind."

"Other destinations?"

"Well, Doc," Czolgosz replied, "I think that's another area we'd do best to skip over. Where I planned to go and where in fact I went, that'll have to stay my business for now and I guess that means forever." His expression held none of its earlier defiance but was matter of fact, as if he were merely reminding me of the stipulations of our 'gentlemen's agreement.'

Before I could reply, there was a tap on the door. I looked up to see Tupper's face through the small window. He gestured that we should come out.

"Look's like our time is up," I said with some disappointment. "I hope we'll be able to continue next week." I held open the door.

"I'll see you then, Doc." The assassin rose slowly from his chair and ambled out of the room.

As the guards led Leon from the examining room, I found that I was alone. Gerin, Jones, and the rest of the medical staff were apparently occupied elsewhere. I poured myself a cup of water and sat down to think over this morning's session. My emotions were mixed. I felt stymied and frustrated by the session's untimely interruption, yet I was pleased with how far we had come. The session had gone well, far beyond my expectations. Czolgosz was ready, even eager, to talk. A picture was now forming in my mind of a lonely child, lost amid a throng of siblings, ignored by his father except for the regular beatings, motherless at a pivotal age, his loving, idealized mother replaced by a harsh stepmother.

This last point seemed key. I knew full well that a beloved mother, lost at an early age, could never, in fact, be replaced, and, I presumed, any intended substitute might be fiercely resented. I had often wondered for myself what it would have been like to have had a stepmother, whether I would have enjoyed her motherly solicitude, resented sharing my father's precious attentions, or even have hated and resisted her for attempting to take my mother's place. Clearly the latter was the case for Leon. And that was what I had to get him talking about next time, hoping against hope that there would be a next time. Would the longing for the kind, idealized mother, the resentment toward the harsh stepmother, or the hatred of the tyrannical father help explain his turn to anarchism? And what of the anarchist leader, Emma Goldman? She was the one woman who was known to have figured in his political life and who perhaps had inspired his crime. If Leon was still feeling cooperative I might hope to discover exactly how she had affected him and how she was set off against mother and stepmother in his mind.

~

Dr. Gerin kept me late that afternoon and, when I finally got back to the boarding house, I found Jones waiting for me in the small room that served as our study. As I came in, he looked up from his magazine, the latest issue of Scribner's, and removed his deep-bowled meerschaum pipe from between his lips. He greeted me with a broad grin.

"So, buddy," he said amiably, "tonight's when you come clean, is it not?"

"That's what I said, so I suppose I'm bound by it."

"But reluctantly."

"I'm pretty tired this evening and generally kind of confused about things so if you'll promise to go easy on me we can have a talk."

"Then on go the kid gloves." Jones performed a quick pantomime of donning a pair of gloves. I sat down in the armchair opposite him and planted my feet alongside his on the single shared ottoman.

"Okay then," I said, "which of the two L's shall we start with, Leon or Lucy?"

"By all means, Leon." Jones tapped the ashes out of his pipe into a nearby ashtray.

"It's pretty straightforward, really. You remember the day Czolgosz arrived? We talked about the possibility of my interviewing him?"

"Yeah. And I said Gerin would never go for it, but apparently he did."

"Right. Even more surprising is that he seems to want to help me succeed to whatever extent might be possible."

"I got that impression. He warned me not to talk to anyone about this. He thinks that if Mead finds out he'll shut you down in a minute. But I don't understand why you didn't tell me about it earlier. I am your confidante, am I not?"

"You are. You are. But, I think that when I'm uncertain about something there's a tendency to want to wait to talk about it, to see how things pan out. That's all. Mead does know by the way. Tupper told him. The warden and I had a talk this morning, just before I ran into you. He agreed to allow me to act as a spy for the police."

"And you told him he's dreaming or rather, you didn't tell him, but you thought it. So, apart from the warden's interference, how's it going?" Jones tamped a wad of fresh tobacco into his pipe.

"Pretty well, I think. I'm not sure what the standard for success is here but Czolgosz has come back for three sessions so far. At first it was hard to get him to say much about himself or his family. A week ago, I was just about ready to give up, it was so frustrating, but things went a lot better today. He talked pretty freely. I get the feeling that he just needs someone to talk to and, given the circumstances, I'll have to do. What worries me, though, is having only one more week for this project."

"Yes, executions can be so inconvenient." He had gotten his pipe lit at last, and a sweet cherry aroma filled the room. Jonesy leaned back into the soft chair, the picture of contentment.

"I don't know if that's generally true," I replied. "Many of the men on death row don't even have families that care about whether they live or die. Czolgosz doesn't seem to have heard from his yet. Which leaves me with my personal interest in his case and, yes, for me the brief time is a real inconvenience."

"Which means you have to make the most of it. What have you learned so far?"

"Quite a bit, really. A lot about strikes and working conditions. Some information on his background, education, work experience, etcetera. And a bit of his family history, siblings, where they lived, that sort of thing. But, say, I have a proposition for you."

"Oh, do tell. I'm all ears." Jonesy, as interrogator, was truly in his element here.

"I'm wanting to read up some more on criminal psychology and on the various theories of dementia, see what I can find in some of the journals that are not available here. I've gathered a lot of pieces of the Czolgosz puzzle and would like to find some clues to help put them together. You and I are both off on Friday. What do you say we catch a train down to Ithaca together? You can enjoy an afternoon on campus while I busy myself in the medical library. Hopefully I'll be feeling much more rested and relaxed and, en route, we can talk this through at length. I'd like to hear your views on my strategy."

"That sounds fine. Cornell should beautiful this weekend. And, who knows, maybe I'll find some local lass to join me in a hike up the gorge."

"Great. Then it's agreed." I started to get up to head to my room.

"Not so fast," Jones tapped his pipe stem on the end table to command my attention. "There's still the matter of the other 'L'. That can't wait until Saturday."

"You can't blame a guy for trying. You might have forgotten."

"Not likely. Not with the scent of Parker in heat wafting over Auburn all day."

"Hey! You promised you'd take it easy and I'll hold you to it." I tried to sound forceful, but could hear the weariness underneath my words.

"You're right. I'll just listen." Jones took a long draught on his pipe as if to say that his mouth was now occupied.

"Thanks. It turns out that you were right. I am attracted to her, peculiar smile and all."

"It sounds like you've gotten over Abby Tolson, then." Jones had heard from Abby's sister Judith with the news that Abby was now indeed officially engaged.

"Yes, and you were right, Lucy took my mind off Abby. I really like her and she definitely likes me. The problem is that I'm not sure that I like liking her. Last week we had a picnic, in the cemetery of all places. I really had a great time. Lucy was very affectionate, but I just ran hot and cold. I couldn't help it. She was real sweet about it, but I could tell she was confused by my behavior and I'm afraid I've hurt her feelings. We're going to have lunch again tomorrow. Let me tell you, I'm feeling pretty uneasy about it." I paused, not certain what else to say, and noticed Jones pursing his lips as if holding his words back. "Okay. Okay. You can speak."

"Well, my son," he said in his most pious air, "I can see that it is time to change my role from goad to guide and give you the benefit of my wisdom and experience." He smiled beatifically. I understood my role and bowed my head in deference. "You see, my son, it is a universal law in such matters that the stronger the feelings the greater your resistance to them must be. For that which is desired so ardently will provoke a commensurate fear, whether that be the great fear of losing or the equally powerful fear of having. Young Parker, as you navigate the rocky shoals of adulthood, you will thirst for the experience of profound love, but will at first stand uncertain whether the promised love be true and, if so, whether it can be attained, and finally, once attained, whether it will not prove ultimately to be ephemeral." With that, he returned his pipe to his mouth with a smile of satisfaction.

I sat for a moment in stunned silence, taking in the meaning of my friend's words. "Jonesy," I said at last, "you truly are a fount of wisdom. But now I think I must take my leave to ponder your great words in solitude."

"Go, my son. But remember, for this wisdom to flow freely it must be fed and it can only feed by hearing the tale of your love, fully, as it unfolds."

"Of course," I said. "I'll see you at dinner." And for the moment, we left it at that.

Chapter Ten
~
Thursday, October 17, 1901

Jones and I emerged together from the prison, both late for our lunch break. "Give her a kiss for me," my friend said with a grin as he turned to cut across the railroad tracks toward Seminary Street and the boarding house. Somehow, Jones had surmised that I had a lunch date with Lucy Gerin. Given the way he harped on my love life, he was bound to get it right eventually. I continued up State Street toward downtown, watching Jones' lanky form striding across the tracks to my left. On the platform outside the station, a half-dozen travelers in heavy coats stood restlessly clutching their hats against the wind while waiting for the 12:30 westbound train. A few minutes later, I sat in the plaza in front of Auburn City Hall waiting for Lucy. We had initially planned to meet at noon for lunch but Dr. Gerin had returned to the clinic just as I was about to depart and asked Jones and me to look in on a patient. I telephoned Lucy at the bank and we agreed to meet for a few minutes by City Hall to talk. I was eager to speak with her about our last encounter, which had been the subject of much rumination and agitation on my part over the past week.

It was a cold day for October. As I sat, I watched men and women hurry by holding their coats tightly around them for warmth. I was wearing my heavy woolen overcoat with my recently acquired derby pulled down over the tops of my ears. The blustery wind nipped with icy teeth at my earlobes. Soon, I saw Lucy coming down Market Street. She also was cloaked in a heavy coat, but wore only a thin lace bonnet to protect her head. The wind had blown stray strands of hair loose from the bun into which they hand been carefully gathered. I stood up to greet her as she approached.

"Hi, Lucy. It's nice to see you. I'm sorry about having to cancel lunch."

"Hello, Jonathan. It's no problem, really. I know my father can be a harsh and unpredictable task master."

"Were you able to get something to eat?"

"I picked up a sandwich, and, knowing you wouldn't have time to eat, I bought one for you as well." She reached into her pocket and pulled out the small package, which I took from her hands and pocketed for later. Despite a demanding mid-day appetite, I did not want to spend the few minutes we had together thinking about food.

"Thanks! That was very thoughtful."

"Well," she replied, "we can't have our prize inmates being treated by an undernourished physician. We wouldn't want the scalpel to slip from fatigue."

"You know I don't use a scalpel in the prison. But, if I did, I'd probably cut myself sooner than the patient."

"It's just a metaphor, Johnny." A gust of wind blew a strand of hair into her mouth as she spoke.

"Are you warm enough," I asked, "with just that meager head covering? Do you want to go inside?"

"And are you warm enough, Jon?" she countered in a slightly harsh tone though still smiling. "Or is your concern that I am a frail woman unable to cope with the weather?"

"Not everything is a question of sex, Lucy." Although a disagreement was the last thing I wanted today, I did not like the feeling that I had to continually monitor my words so as not to offend her. "Look around. You're the only person in sight, male or female, who's practically bare headed. I was just expressing a natural concern."

"That may well be, but I suspect I'm not doing a proper job of educating you on changing sex roles. Perhaps some reading assignments will be in order." She paused for a moment in thought and then, ignoring my nettled tone, continued gaily, "Anyway, I'm actually enjoying the weather today. It's a nice change from the Indian Summer we've been having. I like to feel the wind blowing through my hair. And the cool air will wake me up for the afternoon." She brushed a lock of hair back off her face as she said this. "So, tell me, Jon, are you looking forward to seeing your father?"

My father was expected for an overnight visit on Saturday. He had asked me to invite the Gerin family to join us for dinner that evening.

"I suppose so. We get along pretty well, as long as we don't get into an argument about my specializing in psychiatry. He's pleased I'm in medical school and that I'm doing well but he'd like me to go in what he would consider a more serious direction. Neurology rather than psychiatry."

"What's the difference?"

"On the level of practice, there really isn't any. You're more likely to find a neurologist in a clinical setting and a psychiatrist in an asylum, but both are engaged by and large in the treatment of nervous disorders. But there's a big difference in terms of theory. Neurologists take a somatic approach. They view mental illness as symptomatic of specific disorders of the nervous system. They used to be very critical of psychiatrists, belittling their profession as unscientific. The two fields have gotten a lot closer together lately. I'm interested in more of a psychological approach that emphasizes the mind and the emotions. I think that's best suited for psychiatry. Unfortunately, Father still holds to the belief that neurology is the preferable course."

"Then we'll just have to set him straight on that, won't we?" Lucy flashed an impish grin, emphasizing her inclusion of herself in this project.

"Oh, I've tried, believe me. I just don't think he'll be satisfied I'm on the right course until I've proven myself in the field."

"I don't know about that. You haven't had Lucy Gerin on hand to put in a good word for you before." I couldn't tell for sure if she was serious. I feared she was.

"That will be swell! Between you and Jones on the one hand and our fathers on the other, I'll be lucky to make it through Saturday evening in one piece."

"Don't forget mummy."

"Don't worry about that. I'm counting on your mother to keep things civil."

"And she won't let you down."

"Lucy, we need to talk," I began awkwardly, feeling ridiculous at my own words. "About last week, I mean."

"Yes, Jon. What is it?" Lucy fixed her gaze on mine in an effort at earnestness. She struggled to suppress a slight smile so as to provide the serious attention demanded by my plaintive fumbling.

"Lucy, I feel as if I rebuffed you in a way I never really intended. I'm afraid I've hurt your feelings and maybe confused you." I paused. Lucy sat quietly, attentive. She was not going to help me out here, at least not yet. "What I want to say is that last week caught me by surprise. I wasn't ready for it and I acted like a cad. The way I behaved then does not truly reflect how I feel toward you, how much I like you. I guess what I really want to say is that I hope that we will soon have another private moment together and that you will allow me to kiss you properly."

She looked up at me sweetly, almost pityingly, as a smile slowly spread across her face. "What about right now, Jon?"

"I don't think this is the proper place, right in the middle of town. It wouldn't be right." I pulled back from her almost reflexively, tensing my neck and shoulders.

"Really, Jon! You are such a stickler for convention. I'll just have to take matters into my own hands, won't I? So, I want you to close your eyes."

"Lucy, I don't think we should," I objected. I looked anxiously up and down the street at the passing Auburnites. "Not here."

"Jon, if we're going to get anywhere, you'll have to start doing as you are told. Now close your eyes."

Feeling flustered but unwilling to press my case after last week's clumsy performance, I meekly obeyed.

"Good. Now, I want you to keep them closed until I tell you to open them."

"Okay," I agreed uncertainly.

A few seconds passed and I felt the warmth of her breath on the cold skin of my cheek. Clothed in the enigma of her unknown intentions, the sensation was exhilarating. Then, for a brief moment, I felt her moist lips press softly against my own, more of a caress than a kiss and the most intoxicating sensation I had ever known. Ready now to return her kiss, it was suddenly too late. As mysteriously as her lips had played across mine, and as quickly, they were gone.

"Don't open your eyes yet," she said in a hushed but commanding tone. "I want you to count out loud slowly to fifteen and then open them."

I started to object but, realizing that it would be futile, began to count. "One. Two. Three..." When I reached fifteen, I opened my eyes. Lucy was gone. Not pausing to register potential embarrassment at having sat eyes closed in public counting for all to hear, I ran to the corner and strained to look far down both Market and Franklin Streets but could not pick her out among the swiftly moving lunchtime crowd. As I turned to walk back toward the prison, I touched a finger to my lips. They were still damp from her kiss. The sense of her warmth, whether real or remembered, lingered through the afternoon.

~

When I got back to the boarding house that evening, I sat for a few minutes on the porch just to enjoy the fresh air. I realized that I was happy. And excited by Lucy's enticing little game. There was no question that her brief kiss held the promise of more. I was thrilled by the expectation of our next encounter, for the moment forgetting that it would take place in the company of our parents.

As I entered the house, Mrs. T, wearing her favorite apron, came out of the kitchen to greet me. She carried a small package in her hands.

"A young lady dropped this by for you earlier this afternoon. A very lovely young lady."

"Thank you." I took the parcel from her as she smiled knowingly. I was sure that, given the small population of Auburn, she knew full well the identity of the young lady in question. Wrapped in plain brown paper with only my name written on it, the package clearly contained a book. I walked across the hall to open it in the study.

"What have you got there?" asked Jones. He was seated in one of the easy chairs reading the afternoon paper. I sat down in the chair opposite him.

"It seems to be a gift from Miss Gerin. A book, apparently." I removed the brown wrapping. A small sheet of paper slipped out and fell to the floor. I bent over to pick it up but Jones was too fast for me. Grabbing the note, he read, "'For your edification. L.'" Jones regarded me with a raised eyebrow. "So," he asked, "what is the title? If it's not too intimate to share with your best buddy."

I opened the book to the title page and read out loud for Jones. "*Women and Economics. A Study of the Economic Relation Between Men and Women as a Factor in Social Evolution.* By Charlotte Perkins Gilman. Ever hear of it?"

"I have. It's your basic women's rights claptrap. If you ask me, Miss Gerin is looking for a convert. Let me know if you learn anything." He handed me the note and turned his attention back to his paper.

I briefly examined the note, searching its few words desperately for any sign of the afternoon's intimacy. Stymied, I started thumbing through the book, wanting to take it for a love token, baffled that such a serious tome could hardly be one. Chapter after chapter yielded no clue as to the particular message from Lucy that might lay hidden in the book. I stopped to peruse a page with the vague title "A Coincidence."

"Uh oh, Jonesy," I nudged his foot with my own. "You're not going to like this. Gilman writes that the deepest forces of nature have tended to evolve pure, lasting, monogamous marriage in the human race. What do you think of that?" Perhaps, I thought optimistically, this was the passage Lucy had intended for me.

Jones shook his head. "I think that if human idiocy is a deep force of nature, which it appears to be, then I agree with the author. But, even though most marriages may be lasting, they are by no means pure or monogamous."

"You're such a cynic," I scolded, continuing to skim the page. "But listen to this. She goes on to postulate that in no other animal species is the female economically dependent on the male."

"Wait a minute there. I don't think that's correct. What about bees and other insects? The queen sits on her duff in the middle of the hive while the workers bring her food."

"Maybe she means mammal rather than animal. But you'll like her conclusion. Gilman writes that an economic imbalance results. Men have all the power materially and women must obtain their bread through the sale of sex functions.'

"Hence that exalted profession, prostitution."

"Not only that. According to Gilman, it is also hence that exalted state of matrimony. She says 'we justify and approve the economic dependence of women in the sex-relation in marriage. We condemn it unsparingly out of marriage.'" I read now from the page titled "A Sin Against Nature."

"So, what's her point?"

"She seems to be implying that a host of social ills will be cured by the economic emancipation of women."

"Then what will they need us for?" Jones seemed irritated by this line of thought.

"I guess the same things we need them for."

"In other words, sex."

"Yes, sex. But also friendship, and intellectual and artistic stimulation." My scant few hours with Lucy were happily brought to mind by this list of qualities.

Jones wrinkled his nose. "Parker, Lucy Gerin is playing you for a sap and you're too smitten to realize it." This appeared to be his last word on the subject as he turned his attention back to the newspaper. Smitten or not, I felt compelled to delve further into the meaning of this gift. Part of me rebelled at the thought that Lucy took it upon herself to educate me, indeed, that she had honed in on an area in which I was particularly ignorant. Jones interrupted my reading.

"Here's a good one for you. Did you know that bad grammar is a disease?" he asked, looking up from the paper.

"Let's hear it."

"A Dr. Ernst Liebmann of Germany has invented the disease grammicitis. People who suffer from a tendency to say 'he done it' or 'they was' can be cured by three tablespoons daily of a pale brown mixture."

"A mixture of what, precisely?"

"It doesn't say or, perhaps, it doesn't matter. But listen. It gets better." He read now directly from the newspaper article, "'Dr. Liebmann's use of the Greek suffix in his definition of the ailment shows that an inflamation exists, which is of course the province of the physician.' I tell you, buddy, we've gone into the right profession. Any time we run out of patients we'll just add a Greek suffix to a common problem and invent a new disease. Coming up with a cure will be no more trouble than concocting a brown paste."

"Jonesy, you are sure to be an inspiration as a doctor. I can see you in a few years engaged in a competition with this German to see who can come up with the most far-fetched new illness." Jones laughed and we returned to our reading. Before long I found another point that I felt compelled to bring to Jones' attention.

"I've got a big disappointment for you, Jonesy. It turns out that women are not the root of all evil after all."

He sighed. "Okay. Let's hear her reasoning."

I read out loud, "'Not woman, but the condition of woman, has always been a doorway of evil. The sexuo-economic relation has debarred her from the social activities in which, and in which alone, are developed the social virtues.'"

"You know what I think of that. She has it backwards. The so-called sexuo-economic relations put women in just the activities that develop her virtues, at least the ones I care about."

"I don't know. What she says next makes sense to me. Half of humanity is at the starting post while the other half runs ahead. Since we each have two parents, she says, it is not surprising that we are a little mixed up. Certainly, from a psychological standpoint, her argument has some merit. What if both parents were allowed full economic and social competence? They might well breed a better stock of human."

Jones just shook his head in resignation. "On that note," he said, "I think I'll get myself a cigar." He stood up and stretched his arms high up toward the ceiling with a loud groan. "Do you want one?"

"No thanks. You know you'll get a lecture from Mrs. T about it."

"But, fortunately, I have her at a sexuo-economic disadvantage." With a smirk, he left the room.

I stretched my legs out on the now unoccupied ottoman. This discussion of Gilman highlighted much of the difference between Jones and me on the subject of women. He was direct and unapologetic about wanting women for one thing only. And, he was quite happy with a social system that gave him an advantage in that regard. Jones' opinion was that marriage, like death and taxes, was pretty much inescapable. But he was committed to avoiding it for as long as possible. I, on the other hand, wanted something more, or at least something different. Although I thought of myself as a romantic by inclination, I had been hampered by an awkward

ambivalence whenever love appeared on the horizon, unable to
make its promised fruits my own. It made sense to me when
Gilman argued that "there is no natural, simple medium of social
intercourse between men and women." It made sense because it
matched my experience.

   But why had Lucy given me this particular book? On the
face of it, she was merely wanting to educate me on the tenets of
women's rights, following up on our several discussions. I had told
her earlier that "not everything is a question of sex." Gilman's book
was a manifesto to the contrary, and it frustrated me the extent to
which her ideas made sense. A stronger interpretation might be
that the book was intended to directly inform me of Lucy's
intention of maintaining economic independence throughout her
life with or without a marriage. But it seemed that there was
something more fundamentally important, something that spoke to
her philosophy of life, to her very raison d'etre. Was I taking things
for granted which were very important for her to question? I
remembered our earlier discussion in which my choice of term--
suffragist or suffragette--was tantamount to choosing sides in an
epochal struggle. Was I with her or against her? If understanding
and supporting the cause of women's rights was required to place
me in the former camp, then, perhaps a bit begrudgingly, I
welcomed the writings of Charlotte Gilman.

   I returned to the book and skimmed through sections on
the organization of the household, motherhood, child-rearing, old
age, and youth. Gilman's title of "Women and Economics" seemed
to belie a focus on the whole spectrum of human affairs. But one
passage caused me to stop and read it slowly, not just twice but a
third time.

> In the course of social evolution there are
> developed individuals so constituted as not to fit
> existing conditions, but to be organically adapted
> to more advanced conditions. These advanced
> individuals respond in sharp and painful
> consciousness to existing conditions and cry out
> against them according to their lights. The history
> of religion, of political and social reform, is full of
> familiar instances of this. The heretic, the
> reformer, the agitator, these feel what their

compeers do not, see what they do not, and,
naturally, say what they do not. The mass of the
people are invariably displeased by the outcry of
these uneasy spirits. In simple primitive periods
they were promptly put to death.

As I read these words, I could not help but seek to apply them to
Leon Czolgosz and his anarchist compatriots. I recalled Joe
Whelan's idea that Czolgosz was little more than an implement for
the furtherance of evolution. Much as my respect had grown for
Whelan and even, to an extent, for Czolgosz, I was just not ready
to lump them among the great reformers of history. Still, there was
no question that these anarchists left "the mass of people"
displeased. The recent public call to imprison and even lynch all
anarchists seemed evocative of Gilman's "primitive periods." We
might not be so far removed from the primitive as she seemed to
believe. So absorbed was I by this passage that I did not even hear
Jones return. Only when his cigar smoke began to tickle my nostrils
did I look up to see him smiling at me and shaking his head.

"Buddy," he said, "you've got it bad." I knew he was
referring to my putative feelings for Lucy Gerin. How surprised he
would have been to learn that, while absorbed in the gift from the
young lady in question, I had been lost in thought contemplating
whether Leon Czolgosz fit Charlotte Perkins Gilman's definition of
an "advanced individual." I decided that it would be best to keep
such speculations to myself.

~

Jones had not gotten very far with his cigar when Mrs. T
called to announce that dinner was ready. As we entered the
dining room, we found a strange man already at the table enjoying
his meal. He looked to be about thirty-years old, with a heavy five
o'clock shadow covering a fleshy jaw. He had removed his jacket
and was seated at the table in an unbuttoned vest and shirt-
sleeves. Seeing us enter, he wiped his mouth quickly with his
napkin and, still chewing, stood up to extend his hand in greeting.

"Archibald Baxter, New York Telegram," he said. "That's
Archie to you. I'm up from the city to cover the Czolgosz

execution. I'll be your newest, best friend from now until the switch is thrown."

Jones and I looked at each other quizzically and, after shaking his hand and introducing ourselves, took our seats at the table.

"I'm afraid I'll have to disappoint you," Jones said. "Parker here is already my best friend. The position is just not available at the present time."

"Oh, it's just a manner of speaking," Baxter replied. "When you're in the news business, you've got to be everyone's best friend. That's the way you get a story." He somewhat indelicately stabbed a thick slice of his pork chop and chewed it eagerly. This, however, did not diminish his enthusiasm for conversation, his words only slightly garbled by his simultaneous chewing. "So, Mrs. Thomas tells me you fellows are working over at the prison. You might be just the kind of friends I'm looking for."

Jones, unlike Baxter, swallowed before speaking. "Well, Baxter, you're in luck! Parker here just happens to be planning an in-depth psychological study of the assassin." He caught my eye and winked before I could choke on my meat.

"Yup. That's right," I agreed. "We figure we'll be the country's most famous medical students once we write up our findings. I know that since you are accustomed to dealing with confidential sources we can trust you not to speak about this to anyone. The last thing we would want is a flock of reporters hounding us for information."

"You fellows are a barrel of laughs," Baxter replied, shaking his head. Jones and I mugged at each other with expressions of mock consternation, as if we could not imagine to what he referred. "Mrs. Thomas told me that you are students working in the prison hospital so I can figure out that you won't have much contact with the assassin. Still, you never know if you might hear something you could pass my way."

"Unfortunately, we're pretty much viewed as outsiders in the prison," Jones said, dropping his previous affectation. "The administrative and medical staff whom we deal with are all pretty tight lipped. And the keepers, frankly, would be more likely to talk to you over a pint of beer in a saloon than they would to us. But, like you say, you never know."

"That's right," I agreed. "You never know. And I'm sure you will have plenty of scoops to share with us. I look forward to your providing many pleasant diversions from the humdrum existence of a medical intern. But, tell me, the execution isn't scheduled for two more weeks. What will you be doing in the meanwhile?"

"Are you kidding?" Baxter replied. "This is the biggest story in America. People are hungry for any scrap of information about Czolgosz. Did he stub his toe? Did he eat all his peas? You name it. That's why you fellows ought not consider anything you stumble upon too insignificant. I'll tell you a well-known secret. The news business runs on the magnification of the trivial. And don't forget the human interest angle. How do Auburnites feel about having the nation's most notorious criminal in their midst? What does Keeper so-and-so think about soiling his hands with such scum? And, how do America's two most famous medical students like being thrust into the limelight?" He stared at me pointedly with an expression that said he was all business.

"Now, wait a minute," I said. "We're not looking for any limelight."

Baxter let out a guffaw.

"Ha! Well there's one on you. I got you going all right. The thing is, you're correct. You two are outsiders. You're on the margins. No one cares what you think."

"Hey!" This time it was Jones who objected. "We're not quite as insignificant as all that. After all, Parker here cleans the stethoscope of the prison doctor."

"I think you've caught my point exactly," Baxter replied. He was looking down at his plate, which allowed Jones to cast a quick smile in my direction, knowing the relief I felt at our having successfully dissuaded the reporter from any potential interest in our activities.

Archie Baxter proved to be a fine addition to the household. His well-honed reporter's personality could readily draw you out or chew your ear off. I had no doubt that he would soon make the many "new best friends" in Auburn who would help him get his scoops. And, as it turned out, within a week he knew more local gossip than Mrs. T. As the scheduled execution date drew near, he kept us abreast of the many notables arriving in Auburn, mostly his fellow journalists but also a variety of

government officials. But most entertaining were his lessons in
newspaper appreciation. Baxter loved to go over the daily papers,
carefully instructing us in the fine distinctions between "lies,"
"bald-faced lies," and "outright fabrications." Although I found his
criticisms to be exaggerated and unduly cynical, after two weeks
under his tutelage, I would never again take a newspaper at face
value.

Chapter Eleven

~

Friday, October 18, 1901

It was a rare morning that found Jones and me together at the breakfast table. We sat, side by side, grappling with Mrs. T's sweet chewy oatmeal--'the cereal that separates the men from the horses', Jonesy had dubbed it. I washed mine down with our landlady's thick, over-cooked coffee. Jones refused to drink it. He preferred the equally unpalatable version available at the prison, a transparent brew that tasted more like stale water than a refreshing beverage.

"I had an interesting dream last night," I told Jones. Over the past year I had developed a keen interest in dreams, ever since learning of the publication of Sigmund Freud's *Interpretation of Dreams*. Unfortunately, the book was only available in the original German and was hard to come by. I was eager to read about Freud's latest theories and was frustrated that even the medical school library had not yet obtained a copy. Although we did not study the psychology of dreams in medical school, I was aware that many alienists considered dreams to be meaningless or primitive expressions of the psyche. But I was of another mind, and was intrigued by the German F.W. Hildebrandt's description of "the workings and weavings of the genius of dreams."

"Let's hear it," Jones replied between mouthfuls.

Like others I'd had recently, this dream had been vivid, and I could recount it in some detail. Strangely, I dreamed that I was sleeping, rocked back and forth by a gentle rhythmic motion. The loud screech of railroad brakes startled me into wakefulness. I looked out the train window to see only my reflection staring back. Peering more closely, I discovered that the train was speeding past stone walls and understood that I was on a subterranean railroad perhaps like the one then under construction in Manhattan. The train came to a jerking stop at a station which was oddly now above ground. Straining my eyes to overcome the contrast between the brightly lit train car and its dark surroundings, I saw that I was at the New York Central Depot in Auburn. I emerged from the empty car, crossed State Street and entered the prison, hardly noticing that the gates were wide open and unguarded. Empty hallways echoed with my footsteps as I walked through an unfamiliar part of the prison. Reaching a darkened stairway, I descended down two long flights guided only by a murky light below. Moving steadfastly forward, I emerged into a dimly lit corridor, at the end of which a single doorway opened onto a well-lighted room. An indeterminate fear struck my heart as I looked down the long hallway, but I felt compelled to continue onward. As I approached the room, I recognized it was the execution chamber. Entering, I saw Warden Mead poised stiffly like an automaton, ready to throw the electric switch that would send the deadly current to the chair. In that dread device, an unrecognizable figure sat, clothed in generic prison garb. A leather mask bound the convict's head to the chair obscuring all facial features. I cried out "Stop!" to the warden and stumbled forward. Frantically, I grappled with the straps of the mask and pulled it loose. I shrunk back in horror at the sight of a single slab of flesh devoid of eyes, nose, mouth, or any feature that would make it recognizably the face of a man. I had woken, trembling, in the first light of dawn.

"So, buddy," I concluded, "what do you think?"

"First, let's hear what you make of it."

"Okay. I have given it some thought. Clearly this dream supports the argument that dreams are little more than a continuation of the day's thought processes but without the structures and restrictions of the conscious, rational mind. But it's an expression of anxiety as well. In the dream, I am embarking alone on a journey that will take me through strange, dark territory, much like my project with the assassin. If the man in the chair is Czolgosz, which makes sense, then it would seem that I am concerned about how little I've been able to glean of his psychology and how difficult it has been to put features on his face. In other words, just what I've been worrying about while awake."

"That's certainly a plausible, if somewhat superficial, reading," Jones replied. "But let's try another approach, a different theoretical framework. Let's say, hypothetically, that all significant images in dreams represent facets of ourselves, of our own personalities or psychological makeup. In that case, the person in the chair might not be Czolgosz at all. It could be you. What if your anxiety derives from the hidden, faceless aspects of your own life, buried, as it were, deep underground, facets that may be influenced, shaped, or revealed, or even in some way endangered, by your work with the assassin?"

"Are you serious?" I set my spoon down in the empty bowl. "Completely."

"So, you're saying that I'm looking at my own face and cringing from it? That sounds a bit farfetched." Despite my protest, I found Jonesy's theory to be intriguingly credible.

"It's my professional opinion, buddy," he replied, eyeing a thick lump of gruel that stuck to his spoon. "It's worth exactly what you paid for it."

"Which is nothing?"

"Which is nothing."

~

Breakfast finished, Jones and I walked out of the boarding house to find a crystal clear day awaiting us. The sun cast pink halos behind the small clouds that dotted the eastern horizon. A slight chill still hung tenaciously over the city, left behind by the cool Autumn night. We walked quickly across town toward the Lehigh Valley Railroad Station. The crowds that flocked to downtown Auburn on Saturdays had yet to arrive, but the scene was nonetheless enlivened by the many shopkeepers setting out their wares, cranking out an awning, or sweeping the night's accumulation of debris from the sidewalk. It was not long past shift change and we passed a number of laborers plodding wearily home from their toils, their empty dinner satchels clutched close. When we arrived at the station, only a few people were waiting, pacing around the narrow platform or staring impatiently down the track. I roused the sleepy station-master long enough to purchase two round-trip tickets to Ithaca at $1.22 each.

The 8:30 train finally arrived and we found two seats together midway back in the second of three passenger cars. Jones insisted on the aisle seat, claiming, with a wink, that he preferred the view. If it was a view of females he had in mind, there were indeed a number of women, from schoolgirls to grandmothers, scattered around the car. But from his seat or mine, all that could be seen was a variety of hats and bonnets. I thought that the vivid foliage on the hills rolling toward Lake Cayuga would provide a more suitable backdrop for my ruminations on the short trip.

As the train pulled out of the station, Jones turned to me. "So, buddy, tell me, have you come up with a diagnosis of Mr. Czolgosz yet? Tired nerves, I'd guess. Nothing, I'm sure, that can't be remedied by an extended stay at a health spa. I've heard that pine-needle baths can be very effective for a variety of conditions. They're said to cure just about anything."

"Yes, yes," I replied waving my arms with feigned enthusiasm, "It will be my first great medical discovery. Assassination as a symptom of neurasthenia! But I was thinking more along the lines of a water cure. A few weeks of regular regimen of mineral baths should have him feeling better in no time."

"He'll certainly be feeling a lot worse in no time as things stand. But then, of course, he soon won't be feeling at all."

"You're right about that. It's hard for me to imagine that he'll really be dead in a few weeks. It's pretty unusual just beginning to know a person when they're getting ready to die. I guess as doctors we'll wind up doing it a lot, but this is a first for me. The surprising thing is that, in an odd way, I'm growing to like the fellow. He's a strange one, that's for sure, but there's something compelling about his personality."

"It's too bad then that he won't be available to serve as best man at your wedding to Lucy," Jones grinned, pleased to have stuck me with two barbs at once. "I'd gathered from Gerin's comments that you'd been getting familiar with Czolgosz. But he wouldn't, or couldn't, tell me anything about your methods. Just what have you been up to with the notorious assassin?"

"Talking. That's about all. Do you remember me telling you about a lecture in my psychiatry class last semester on the cathartic therapy of Sigmund Freud and Josef Breuer?"

"I think so. Aren't they those Austrians who are obsessed with sex? It's disgusting, really!" Jones raised his voice and frowned in his best imitation of the moralistic society matron. "My own theory is that the *gutte doktors*"--Jones put on his best German accent--"are not getting enough at home."

"You may be right, but their work is really interesting. The idea of cathartic therapy is that there is a traumatic event underlying the mental illness. Most of their work has entailed the study of hysteria."

"Right, which, as I recall, was the title of their book."

"Exactly. In their most famous case study, a woman, Anna O. they call her, experienced hysterical paralysis in her right arm. Dr. Breuer hypnotized her and she remembered an incident when her arm fell asleep while she was caring for her dying father. In other words, the link between the illness and death of her father on the one hand, and the physical discomfort on the other continued to manifest as a hysterical symptom. When she came out of the trance, presto! The paralysis was gone."

"So, is Czolgosz' arm paralyzed? And, if so, how did he pull the trigger?" A man on the bench in front of us looked back inquisitively on hearing the assassin's name. Jones gave me a look of mock alarm.

"Very funny!" I replied, lowering my voice but otherwise ignoring our neighbor. "That's obviously just an example. My point is that Freud and Breuer maintain there is a link between psychological symptoms and the repression of traumatic life experiences, particularly sexual ones. Czolgosz is quite reluctant to talk about his family, but I do know that he lost his mother at an early age. That loss or some event connected to it could provide the trauma that led to his adoption of anarchism and his willingness or even desire to serve as an assassin."

"What else? Have you been hypnotizing him?"

"No, you know I don't have that kind of training. And I don't know if Czolgosz even could be hypnotized. But Freud himself has abandoned hypnosis in favor of an approach that leads the patient to insight through a dialogue with the physician. He believes it is not enough for patients to remember the traumatic event. They must search for its hidden meaning as well."

"I suppose that when you're done with Czolgosz you can work on the hidden meaning of your own forgotten trauma." I frowned at this suggestion. Jones laughed and punched me playfully in the arm. "Take it easy, pal. I'll stick to the subject at hand. Promise. Anyway, how do you know so much about this Dr.

Freud? Certainly not from medical school. And definitely not from Gerin. He'd be the last person to have an interest in such matters."

"You'd be surprised. Did you know that Gerin got his start as assistant physician at the State Hospital for the Criminally Insane? That was years ago, of course, but I believe his interest has been piqued by my project. I don't think he'd admit it, though. Still, you are correct that he wouldn't know much about Freud and Breuer. Gerin is pretty conservative in outlook and no longer keeps up with the latest in psychology, if he ever did. But Jonesy, I'm sure that not even you could have progressed this far without discovering the library. They've got books and articles by Breuer and Freud. Fortunately, my German is still pretty good. Few people keep up their language skills after college or take the time to read articles that haven't been translated."

"Or have such empty lives that they would choose to."

I ignored Jones' insult. "The problem I'm facing is that the cases reported by Freud and Breuer involved many months of regular sessions with the patient. I have only four meetings with a very sharp man who's not likely to disclose anything he doesn't want to."

"Sharp? He struck me as kind of dull."

"Superficially, yes. That's how he appeared when we processed him into the prison. But I saw something else as well. He's much more clever than he lets on. He's read a lot and thought about what he's read, more so than many of our schoolmates."

"That may be, but what about the alienists in Buffalo? Several of the most distinguished in the nation gave him a clean bill of health."

"Yes, but they were just determining his fitness for trial, if he understood right from wrong and if he could comprehend the meaning of the charges. There are other levels of psychological dysfunction that are far afield from their concerns. Plus, they spent even less time with him than I will."

"So," Jones pressed on with his inquiry, "let's say you're successful in your remaining--how many is it--are you down to your last session already?" I nodded. "Let's say you get him to open up and talk about his feelings for his lost mother or his hatred of his father. What of it? You're not going to help Czolgosz since he'll be dead. What will you learn that's of value to yourself or to your training?"

"I guess I'm not entirely sure. But, what I do know is that I haven't been this excited about a project since we started medical school. Think about it, Jonesy. Anarchism and regicide are two of the biggest political problems of our time. Hardly a nation has been spared. You know I want to make my mark as an alienist. If I could gain some insight into the psychological factors that lead a man down that path. I could make an immense contribution."

"And a year from now you'll be serving the inmates at some asylum. What difference will the killing of kings and princes make to you then?"

"Maybe I won't take a position at an asylum or at any institution. Maybe I'll work with individual patients as Freud and Breuer do. Who knows, I might even find another anarchist patient down the road. Perhaps I'll make a breakthrough in understanding the psychology of the working class."

"Anarchists don't strike me as the sort of people who are likely to be looking for the care of a good alienist." He paused, staring attentively toward the front of the train. "Buddy, I'm going to have to excuse myself. Duty calls." As Jones stood up, I saw the object of his attentions. An attractive young woman had entered the car and was struggling to carry a heavy valise down the aisle. Jones strode quickly to her and, after a few words, took the leather burden from her hands and led her to the empty seat across the aisle from his own.

Jones had a way with women. His tactical repertoire was broad. He moved with grace and ease from teasing to cajolery to flattery to disdain and back again. And Jones had a knack for honing in on which approach might appeal to a particular woman. With little at stake in any single encounter, he could pursue a woman with aggressive persistence one day only to drop her completely the next as he moved on to a fresh object of desire. I was in awe of his style and success, which stood in sharp contrast to the mawkish uncertainty with which I stumbled from woman to woman, often with a long hiatus in between.

"Miss Newhart," Jones said before taking his seat, "allow me to introduce Jon Parker, soon to be a renowned alienist. Parker, this is Jenny Newhart." She smiled demurely.

"Very pleased to meet you," I said, somewhat miffed at Jones' abrupt interruption of our discussion. "Are you also going to Ithaca?"

"I am," she replied. "I have a position there starting Monday morning."

After a few more pleasantries, I let Jones pick up the conversation with Miss Newhart. I gazed out the window at the green pastures that rushed past. One particularly large cow seemed to be staring back at me, sleepily chewing its cud. Its vacant expression reminded me of "volunteers" from the side-show audience that, as a boy, I'd seen "mesmerized" by some carnival mountebank. It had looked so easy! Once again, I lamented the lack of either time or technique that might allow me to effectively complete my project with Czolgosz. Thoughts like these still furrowed my brow as the train pulled into Ithaca Station.

Jones and I agreed that he might find me in the Cornell medical library in the afternoon or, at the latest, meet me for the 6:15 train back to Auburn. He turned his attention to Jenny Newhart and her hefty luggage. I watched them for a moment with some amusement and then headed over to catch the streetcar. As the trolley lumbered up the steep hill toward campus, I looked back over the panorama of Lake Cayuga. Even in mid-October, from this vantage point, its waters looked clear and inviting. Several sails could be seen in the distance while closer to the lake's southern terminus a crew team powered their vessel smoothly across the waters.

The first time I had ascended this hill had been years earlier, when I had first arrived at Cornell to begin my studies. Gazing out at the lake and wooded hillsides, I had felt that I was truly in the wilds, that I had left the familiar comforts of civilization behind. As a child, I had stood by the bay in Brooklyn Heights and, looking over the boat-filled harbor toward the crowded shores of Manhattan, had imagined that I was Henry Hudson first encountering a virgin land. The sight of Lake Cayuga gave substance to such youthful fantasies, and drew out that yearning to step into the pages of the Leatherstocking Tales that lies in the heart of the American schoolboy.

To my freshman's eyes, the town of Ithaca had seemed so small and so quaint as compared to the hustle and bustle of the busy streets of New York City. Like many an urbanite, I arrived with a strong prejudice that, when it came to cities, bigger and more were inevitably better. Although little had transpired to change that perspective, I now had an appreciation for the charms of small-town life as found in an Ithaca or an Auburn. To commonly encounter a familiar face on the street, to feel a kind of intimacy with an entire community, and to be able to walk a few miles in any direction to lose oneself in field or forest, these were all qualities I came to value despite the fact that I would remain a city-dweller.

Soon, the streetcar reached campus, passing by old Cascadilla Hall. I got off at the Quad and headed over to White Hall, home of Cornell's nascent medical college. Jones and I could have joined the first class of the medical school, but had decided that we would be better off with a more established program. Our professors had urged us to stay but we were ready for a change of scenery. Jonesy, in particular, had been eager to get back to the city after four years of college in remote, provincial Ithaca.

~

As I climbed the stairs toward the fourth-floor quarters of the medical college, I encountered a familiar face heading in the opposite direction. It was Dr. Lewis Stimson, a surgeon and the most distinguished member of the school's new faculty. Dr. Stimson was also a friend of my father's.

"Why if it isn't young Parker," Stimson exclaimed as he stopped on the third-floor landing and held out his hand in greeting. "What brings you to Cornell? I thought you were busy in medical school."

"Dr. Stimson, it's good to see you," I replied, shaking his hand vigorously. "Yes, I am in medical school. And pretty busy. Fourth year. I'm doing an internship this semester with Dr. John Gerin over at Auburn State Prison. I'm here for the day to do some research. You can help me out by directing me to the medical library."

"I would be happy to do so except that the library is closed for the mid-semester holiday. But, I suppose I can let you in. Our fairly small collection is in the far corner of the top floor, the northeast corner." Stimson turned back in the direction he had come, beckoning me to follow. "What is it that you are looking for?"

"You may have heard I'm planning to go into psychiatry." Stimson nodded. "So you can imagine there's not much material of interest to me at the prison. I'm looking for various books and articles on psychiatry, particularly those relating to criminal behavior. Mercier, Régis, a few others. I'm hopeful that you'll have some of the journals I need that Dr. Gerin does not receive."

"Criminal psychiatry, is it? You haven't by any chance taken an interest in the Czolgosz matter? I know that young minds drift naturally toward the notorious."

"Czolgosz, among others. We have a number of infamous cases at the prison." It seemed that I could safely acknowledge an interest in Czolgosz without revealing the exact nature of my project.

"Well, I do hope you find what you're looking for." We had reached the library door which Stimson unlocked for me. "Be sure to lock this door when you are done. And let me know of anything you can't find. We are trying to build up our collection. Oh, and do send my regards to your father."

"I will. I'll be seeing him tomorrow, in fact. And thanks so much for letting me into the library. I'll be careful to lock up when I leave."

As Dr. Stimson departed, I entered an L-shaped room, crammed with medical books and journals, that wrapped around the corner of the top floor. The library had the familiar, musty odor of old books. Except for the handful of tables and chairs near the door, bookshelves filled the room, from wall to wall set so close that it was hard to maneuver between them. The library had a temporary feel to it with its mismatched and worn furniture. I was pleased to have the place to myself.

It did not take long to find the first volume I sought, *Regicides in History and the Present* by the great French alienist whose name oddly suggested his subject matter, Emmanuel Régis. I hoped his work would help answer my first question: did Czolgosz fit a particular psychological type associated with assassins? Régis identified several characteristics which he believed were indicative of the madness of regicides. First of these was an inclination toward mysticism, a trait I could not find in Czolgosz. Even his expressed interest in the Bible was of a critical nature. Second was a tendency to cogitation and solitude. Czolgosz had reported several years of illness during which he kept to himself, read a great deal, and contemplated the political questions that had aroused his interest. Finally, Régis pointed out that assassins "are always restless and dissatisfied and searching for a change." Here, I found that I must disagree with the learned Frenchman. How could restlessness and dissatisfaction be considered a sign of madness? After all, did not all human progress depend on these two elements? Nonetheless, Czolgosz' departure from Cleveland and his mysterious movements over the summer gave some relevance to Régis' description. I jotted this point down in my notebook. Throughout the day, I wrote down ideas and citations at a furious pace, as if the sheer volume of my notes could compensate for a dearth of relevant insights.

In his description of the pursuit of the crime, Régis' analysis proved particularly compelling. The regicide, he claims, is a "*solitaire*," conceiving, preparing, and accomplishing his deed alone. Despite official efforts to uncover a conspiracy, as far as anyone could determine Czolgosz had acted entirely according to his own devices. I placed a question mark next to this point in my notes. This was an item that warranted further reflection after my sessions with the assassin were completed. Régis' description of the act itself might have been drawn directly from a newspaper account of Czolgosz' movements in Buffalo. Once the act has been decided upon, he wrote, the assassin is grimly determined and he "hesitates no more, but goes straight to the end; proud of his mission and his part, he strikes at his victim in broad daylight, in public in an ostentatious and theatrical manner; and, far from fleeing after the crime, he puts himself in evidence as if he had performed some great deed."

Even here, Czolgosz refused to conform exactly to Régis' model. Unlike John Wilkes Booth, for example, he had shown no theatrics when committing his crime and his subsequent attitude was more matter-of-fact than proud. But, like Régis' typical assassin, he had struck in daylight and disdained to flee the scene. This was a matter that had so far confounded me in regard to Czolgosz. His failure to attempt escape or evade punishment for his crime seemed to indicate a desire for his own death. But in our discussions thus far, although he did seem resigned to his fate, I had detected neither moroseness nor an inclination to reach the end of his life. If anything, he seemed to have a sort of unnatural detachment from either life or death.

Before returning to the stacks, I struggled to push a heavy window open a few inches. Cool raw air rushed in but could not dispel the room's stuffy mustiness. Taking a deep, refreshing breath by the window, I decided to move on to a more general analysis of dementia and was pleased to find a copy of *Psychology, Normal and Morbid* by Charles A. Mercier. Just published, it promised to incorporate the latest thinking. Mercier had been praised in particular for his study of delusions. It was a fundamental question: whether or not Czolgosz was the subject of an insane delusion which led him to commit his crime. Mercier defined delusions as "beliefs which may or may not have some foundation in experience, in authority, or in ordinary testimony, but which however formed are entirely indestructible by any or all of these agents." That Czolgosz held firmly to his beliefs was certain.

I was interrupted by the sound of a throat being cleared and looked up to see a grey-bearded man, presumably another professor, standing in the doorway.

"I regret to inform you that the library is closed today," he said.

"Oh, I know. Dr. Stimson let me in with instructions to lock up carefully when I'm done."

He nodded, apparently satisfied, and disappeared down the hall. I was sure that, with my head buried in the books, I had not looked at all out of place. The brief interruption brought to awareness a growing numbness in my right leg that had pressed so long against the hard wooden chair. Reaching down to my calf, I massaged away the tingly sensation before returning to the volume at hand.

Mercier outlined five categories of belief for normal individuals: the Inconceivable, the Conceivable, the Credible, the Relatively Certain of Fact, and the Absolutely Certain or True. I mulled over this taxonomy and decided I would have included a category for the ambiguous, which has elements of both truth and falsehood. In Mercier's view, delusion was constituted by the "unaided operation of the mind itself" in transferring a concept from one category to another. Here again, I was not sure I agreed. Could not the unaided mind move from certainty to uncertainty, or vice versa, merely by the application of its own deductive powers?

It was clear that Czolgosz held his anarchist beliefs on a level of absolute truth but I could not see that this constituted a delusion under Mercier's definition. The alienists in Buffalo had looked at several criteria in determining that Czolgosz was not delusional. Was there evidence of hallucination? Did he believe he had been specially chosen to do the deed? Did he claim that the idea of killing the President was original with him? Answering each of these questions in the negative, they had declared him sane. Many, alienists and laymen alike, would point to McKinley's popularity to argue that Czolgosz' conviction that the President had been an enemy of the people was most assuredly delusional. But already the assassin had revealed to me a number of experiences which could have "aided the operation of his mind," accurately or not, in reaching such a conclusion, one that he seemed to share with a not insignificant number of compatriots.

Before going back to the stacks, I unpacked my lunch--a beef sandwich on thick white bread and my usual apple. Biting into the tart, crisp fruit, I took care that its juices not land on the nearby books or drip onto my fingers. Still chewing as I scanned the bookshelves, I soon found the next title on my list, Dr. William A. White's *Outlines of Psychiatry*, a standard text. Although I found that White was pretty much in agreement with Mercier, one point in his discussion of dementia stood out: "The origin of simple dementia is insidious... At first the patient begins to show a lack of interest in things, ceases going out and associates less and less with others. There is a general listless, apparently lazy and tired-out attitude toward life assumed."

That last phrase could have been written for Czolgosz. Listless and tired-out. Yes, that was his attitude. But still, the overall description did not fit. A superficial observer might agree that Czolgosz showed a lack of interest and had, reportedly, kept to himself in recent years. But, from the standpoint of my analysis, that was contradicted by his own reports of his reading, his attendance at meetings, and his keen interest in political questions. And, if his initial withdrawal from society was a legitimate result of his illness of several years back, then the explanation seemed more complicated than White's description of simple dementia could allow. Intently, I began skimming through the book in search of additional insights.

"Mr. Parker, I have something that may be of interest to you." I looked up to find Dr. Stimson standing at my side. In his hand was a sheaf of paper. "I received this article to review for one of the journals. It is by Dr. Sanderson Christieson. I thought you might like to take a look at it." I returned my sandwich to its wrapper as Stimson handed the document to me. I believe my jaw dropped as I read the title: *Epilepsy and Responsibility in the Czolgosz Case: Was the Assassin Sane or Insane?*

"Wow!," I blurted out. "This looks really interesting. Thanks a lot!"

Stimson smiled at my youthful enthusiasm. "I'll need it back before you leave, if you'll just drop it off in my office down the hall. And, of course, since it's an unpublished work, you must not make any reference to it as yet."

"No, of course not. I really appreciate your showing it to me."

"Happy to be of help." Stimson patted me on the shoulder and walked out of the library.

I just stared at the title page for a moment, not believing my good luck at being in the right place at the right time. Forgetting my lunch, I eagerly read through the short paper. Christieson was fully convinced of Czolgosz' insanity, albeit he had not met nor particularly studied his subject. His conclusion was dramatic: "Such a monstrous conception and impulse as the wanton murder of the President of the United States arising in the mind of so insignificant a citizen without his being either insane or degenerate, could be nothing short of a miracle. To assume that he was sane is to assume that he did a sane act, i.e. one based upon facts and having a rational purpose." I wondered what Christieson would have thought if he knew the "facts" as reported by Czolgosz, his description of the stark working conditions in the factory, the various strikes of the 1890s, or the violence done to laborers by agents of their employers and of the government. Even if the assassin exaggerated, there was some weight in the totality of these accounts.

I realized that I was painting Christieson with the same brush used by Joe Whelan that day at O'Malley's when he accused Jones and me of class prejudice. Yet, as far as "rational purposes" were concerned, those of the working class seemed to follow their own logic, quite distinct from that of their employers, and perhaps equally as valid when set in the context of the workers' lives. I was annoyed at Christieson's concept of Czolgosz as "so insignificant a citizen." It seemed to be a sneering sort of comment not fit for a scholarly article. Sure, I believed that education and opportunity made for differences among citizens, but Dr. Christieson was presuming a great deal with this statement. Then again, perhaps I was feeling an inappropriate attachment to my patient.

After reflecting at length on Christieson's particularly relevant article, I found that it was difficult to keep my energy up during the rest of the afternoon. I plowed my way through a number of recent journals, at times discovering half way through an article that my thoughts were wandering even as my eyes obediently went through the motions of reading. This was not a great way to learn. Finally, surrendering to my fatigue, I leaned back on the stiff wooden chair, folded my hands behind my head, and allowed my eyes to fall shut. My mind drifted easily into that uncertain state that lies somewhere between wakefulness and sleep.

Some minutes later, rubbing my tired eyes with my fists, I stood up and walked over to the open window hoping to rouse myself. After a vigorous stretch, I sat on the broad sill, letting the crisp breeze blow over me, and looked out over campus and the fall scene that spread out below. A few students, some with the big red "C" stitched onto their sweaters, tossed a football across the green. Others ambled along the paths, intent on their various pursuits, whether leisurely or academic. Such a panorama could not fail to raise a sense of nostalgia for my college days, even as recent as they were.

I pondered how my early interests had led me along the path that today found me immersed in the great theories of psychiatry and the most sinister crime of our era. From my first days at college, I had pursued an understanding of the human condition in its physical, intellectual, and spiritual forms. Thus, my studies had turned toward philosophy and religion, more so the former as I was not personally given over to religious convictions. As undergraduates, Jones and I had loved to argue philosophy. He, never more than a dabbler, was taken with the pessimism of Schopenhauer and loved to grumble about the wretchedness of the

world and the nastiness of human nature. Then, as now, I was
more of an idealist. I was fascinated and inspired by Hegel's famous
dictum that "the history of the world is none other than the
progress of the consciousness of freedom," an idea, I now realized,
that dovetailed neatly with the less prominent philosophy of Joe
Whelan.

As far as religion was concerned, as an adolescent, I'd
decided that if there was a God, he was ill-served by the ponderous
systems of worship that man had invented, and that he should
have more important things on his mind than my activities. As an
agnostic, I was indifferent at best. Nonetheless, I was enamored
with what I considered to be the bizarre twists and turns of the
history of religious thought and particularly with the study of
comparative religion as taught by Professor Barron, one of Cornell
students' favorite teachers. Barron's popularity rested in part on his
long, curling moustache, which had the effect of transforming a
wry smile into a maniacal grin. He loved to play the devil's
advocate, accenting an extreme position with his zany facial
contortions. This, coupled with his fervent interest in his subject
matter and his genuine solicitation of his students' views, made his
classes among the most sought after. A deep impression was made
by Barron's final lecture, in which he at last revealed his own
religious inclinations. These he claimed were derived from a
melding of his own Christian heritage with an infusion of Jewish
mysticism, known as the Cabala, and a touch of Darwin for good
measure.

"God," Professor Barron had said, "and the creation are not
two separate entities. The conventional notion of a supreme being
looking down from the heavens represents a limited tribal
perspective, the patriarch watching over his people. What is not
generally understood is that, when we say that God is omnipresent,
this includes the dimension of time as well as space. Thus, the
divine act of creation is simultaneous with God's own being.
Within the mind of God, each of us is contemporaneous with
Adam." Although most final lectures could not overcome the
students' eager yearning to be free from class, Barron's swan song
held the class in rapt attention.

"But the important question for mankind," he continued,
"is not how God creates, but why. God, in the beginning, as
Genesis instructs us, is looking out over a void. It is probably not

much fun. So, the way God enjoys his existence is by differentiating himself through the myriad forms of creation as they evolve through all of time and space, a matrix of infinite infinities. As an expression of God's own unfathomable potential, our responsibility as humans is not to repeat some dull cant or monotonous ritual but to live our lives in the most stimulating and rich manner possible, to make our contribution to furthering evolution through the highest fulfillment of our own nature.

"Now, I will leave you with a mental image that will give a sense of what you individually mean to God. First, though, a word of caution. If this exercise seems to have erotic implications, please understand that it is the Lord's doing, not my own." A few students laughed uncomfortably or cast questioning glances and raised eyebrows toward their friends. "Now, close your eyes and imagine, if you will, a most beautiful sight." The Professor's voice took on a sing-song quality as he paused briefly between each phrase. "You see a fabulous garden, rich with flowers and fruit trees, Eden perhaps... Through this garden walks a most beautiful woman, a feast for your eyes... You pluck a fruit from a nearby tree... As you bite into it, your taste buds are transported by its exquisite flavor, and all the while a bouquet of delicious aromas delight your nostrils... Finally, a thousand gentle fingers caress every inch of your flesh, and I do mean every inch." Again, a few of the students laughed nervously. Barron lowered his voice almost to a whisper. "Now, you must make a last change of perspective because the thousand fingers are in fact your own and the flesh that they experience is the most soft and smooth and sensuous. Linger a bit in that moment: the beautiful sight... the delicious flavors... the delectable aromas... the sensuous feeling all over your body... your fingers enthralled..." As his voice drifted off, the classroom was completely silent.

A loud clap from Barron's hands brought our eyes open and we found the Professor smiling radiantly before us. "Multiply that experience a billion billion times and you will understand the why of creation. If I have taught you well this semester, you will understand that this is no mere hedonism, but the deepest possible grounding of evolution, life, and consciousness. Anything further will await your more advanced studies. Class dismissed."

Now, as I remembered Dr. Barron's clap, I was jarred alert again by the sound of two hands striking together. I looked up and found Jones standing in the doorway, a bemused smile on his face.

"Wake up, little Johnny," he called out. "Nap time is over."

I stretched my arms out to my sides and stifled a yawn. "Look at all this." I gestured at the many books and journals strewn around my place at the table. "I'd say I've done a good day's work. But what are you doing here so early? What happened to your lady friend?"

"Oh, Jenny? She's gone and almost forgotten. I gallantly helped her to her boarding house, downtown on Albany Street. Then I took her out to lunch. But by the time the meal was half through, we had run out of things to say, and I'd discovered that I must excuse myself to seek out my friend Parker. Poor lass. I so hated to let her down. She did encourage me to look her up when I am next in Ithaca."

"Jonesy, you cad," I kidded him. "After all your bravado about women, to think that, when the conversation runs down, you of all people would lose interest. Why, if anyone found out, you might have to give up your membership in the Don Juan Society."

"Hey! Maybe I'm just having a bad day. After all, you didn't really want me to abandon you all afternoon, did you?" He looked at me sheepishly, an unusual expression for my friend.

My only reply was a steady smile, pleased as I was to have gotten the better of him for once.

"So, buddy," he said, "it does look like you've made your way through the stacks. I hope you found what you were looking for. Why don't we clear out of here and get a drink before our train."

I found this suggestion quite agreeable. I closed the window and locked the library door behind us. After returning the Christieson article to Dr. Stimson's office, we left the confines of the Cornell medical school and headed back down the hill in search of a tavern. Jones listened with interest as I recounted the various descriptions of dementia and delusion I'd encountered in my day's research, generally agreeing with my conclusions as to their applicability to the assassin. The fact that stood out was the ambiguous nature of Czolgosz' personality. Each of the theories of dementia seemed to apply to him in certain regards and to miss the mark in others. And none of them took into account the difficult conditions of the laboring class or acknowledged a role for political principle as a factor in criminal psychology. This seemed to me a glaring error, apparent blinders on my intended profession. But the obstacle I kept stumbling over was a simple one: not enough was yet known about Czolgosz to determine clearly whether or not any of these psychiatric theories fit his case. Nor was it likely that enough ever would be known. Through it all, my thoughts kept returning to Professor Barron. The beloved educator had passed away the previous summer. I could have used his counsel today, but somehow I felt I knew what he might advise. He would encourage me to plumb my present opportunity for all that I could get from it. "Carpe diem, my boy," I could imagine him saying, his eyes aglow at the pleasure of passing on his own lifelong philosophy. Barron would not have me hold back merely because the great alienists had failed to adequately address the conundrum embodied in Leon Czolgosz. Find my own way, he would urge, perhaps then quoting the poet's call "to strive, to seek, to find, and not to yield."

Later, as the sunlight faded across the hills to the west, Jones and I trudged wearily over to the train station. We got back to Auburn to find Mrs. Thomas grumbling that we were late for dinner, which she had left waiting for us, cold, on the dining room table.

"Jonesy, my man," I said after assaying the cold roast and Mrs. T's even chillier reception, "for this you gave up the chance to dine with Jenny Newhart and all of the possibilities that might have accompanied it."

"Parker," he replied, "what can I say? I guess I've just gotten too accustomed to staring at your mug across the dinner table." But I was already struggling to chew up the toughened meat, and could only raise my glass in acknowledgment of his friendship.

Chapter Twelve

~

Saturday, October 19, 1901

At 2:05 p.m., I stood on the platform of the Garden Street Depot watching the train from New York City ease into Auburn. With the familiar sigh that accompanies a respite from hard work, whether by man or machine, the engine let out a last gasp of steam as it reached full stop. I could faintly hear the conductor's voice from within the train calling out "Auburn! Aauuburn!" just before opening the passenger car doors. Only a handful of people disembarked, among them my father.

For a moment, I felt like a spectator at a play. The hustle and bustle of the small town train station provided a suitable backdrop for a dramatic entrance. Yet, Father was an unlikely candidate for the hero's role. An unassuming man of average height and build, his brown tweed suit and woolen overcoat added little to distinguish him from the crowd. Still, in that moment when he emerged onto the platform and looked slowly around the station, in that instant before our eyes met, he could have been Cortez stepping out among the Aztecs, appearing before me as he did with the strength and power that fathers command well into their sons' adulthood.

I waved and walked across the short platform.

"Welcome to Auburn, Father," I said. "I'm so happy to see you." I extended my hand in greeting.

My father and I were close, but it was an intimacy in large measure forced by circumstance--which is not to say it was not genuine. In the absence of my mother, he had held a certain anxiety about me, as if unsure whether I would receive my requisite emotional nurturing. As a consequence, he had sought to provide some of that tenderness and understanding which he thought a growing boy needed in life. It did not come easily to him. He could happily join me for a game of catch or take me on a hike or out to the beach, but a man must look to action first and feeling second, not always the order in which a child needs them.

This disjunction could have painful repercussions as on one occasion when, on my way home from school, I had been roughed up by some Irish street toughs from a nearby neighborhood. I can still see their gaunt dirty faces, still remember the typical Irish names they called each other–Mick, Paddy, Sean. It was Mick, apparently the leader, and named in taunting defiance of the common ethnic slur, who first accosted me. "Where do you think you're going?" "Home. I'm not bothering anyone," was my timid response. "Well yer botherin' me!" he replied with a sneer, his comrades closing in around me. After a few minutes of taunts and shoves, I broke free and ran like the dickens. I took advantage of my greater familiarity with the area to elude their pursuit, making sure they could not follow me and identify where I lived. Returning home, I held back my tears and nervously approached my father for needed comfort. The interrogation, with which so many boys are familiar, came apace: Why were you on that street? (it's the way home from school) What did you do to provoke them? (merely exist) Did you stand up for yourself? (it was five to one, they were bigger, I ran) Chastened as well as battered, I took refuge in whatever novel I was reading at the time, something of Dumas' as I recall; a tale in which five to one odds were no obstacle to heroism.

My mother's slow decline, her increasingly erratic behavior, did not quite beat him down but seemed to leave Father with a lasting sense of fatigue. When he came upstairs from his office after a long day with patients, I could tell he just wanted to retreat within himself, to be served in his home as most men believe is their due. Still, he would transcend his lethargy to ask about my studies, advise me about some schoolboy's uncertainty, or, rising occasionally to the heights of paternal wisdom, speak of my noble future should I follow in his footsteps, and of the valuable service a physician provides to society. Into my early teens, I was thrilled when he would reach out to give me a hug or let me sit on his lap. Greta, our tough-hewn German housekeeper, provided occasional mirth but little real warmth to our household. Father's relief was palpable on those occasions when his sister would come by, babying me at whatever age, showering me with treats. My cousins Emily and Susan, respectively three years and one year older than I, would tease me mercilessly, despite my protests, giving me the attention I craved.

Father was, in the end, fundamentally a man's man, raised to value strength, competency, and a certain degree of stoicism. He lived in an era that defined manhood through its roles as husband and father, breadwinner and citizen, and through its corresponding qualities of industry and honesty, of duty and the proper habits of respectability. Much as he loved me, he had difficulty breaking free from the mold of authoritative guide and stern disciplinarian. But, as often as Father lectured me about the ideal of manhood, it could never unequivocally be mine. I was too much influenced by his own uncertainties about fatherhood and too driven by the demands of my own still unmet needs for a sanctuary of ready nurturing and intimacy.

He grasped my hand firmly in his own. "I'm glad I was able to make it up. For a while there, I wasn't sure it would work out." Father had been planning to take this trip in September but was unable to get away from his practice. Auburn, for him, was just a one-night stopover en route to the Exposition in Buffalo. He had urged me to accompany him to see the great fair, much as we had gone together to various carnivals and festivals in my childhood. Unfortunately, my work as a medical student was even more demanding than his as a physician.

I took his bag and led the way toward State Street. A strong wind chafed at our cheeks and blew our small talk down the street, its gusts assaulting our easy familiarity. I asked about Aunt Ruth and my cousins. All were well. Emily, I knew, was expecting her first child, the first of its generation, in a couple of months. I would be back in New York in time to assist father with the delivery. We walked the few blocks to the Empire State Hotel on Genesee Street, and father checked into his room. He splashed some cold water on his face to refresh himself after the long train ride, complaining idly about the latest corruption of Brooklyn politics.

~

I had arranged for a tour of the prison that afternoon, and we now left the hotel to walk the few blocks back up State Street to Auburn's best known edifice. Despite the wind, the business district was swarming with Saturday afternoon traffic. A life-long New Yorker, Father felt nowhere more at home than on a crowded street.

As we approached the prison, Father paused to assess the high, imposing walls.

"Not the most uplifting place to report to work, is it?" he asked.

"No. It can be pretty gloomy. Just wait 'til you see the inside. In some respects, I'll be glad when this internship is over."

Father frowned. "I still don't really understand why you chose to come here in the first place. You could be training at any of the finest medical facilities."

I sighed.

"For good or ill, what's done is done. Let's just try to enjoy your brief visit."

"That is a good suggestion," he replied. "Lead on."

I pointed up at the roof of the Administration Building indicating to Father the statue of "Copper John" perched on top. The likeness of a colonial soldier had been fashioned by a local coppersmith in the early days of the prison, back in the 1820s. The rifle alone was said to weigh 100 pounds. We agreed that the statue added a touch of artistry that one did not usually associate with prisons.

At the prison gates, Frank Winegar, the chief clerk, was waiting. Dr. Gerin had asked him to give my father the prison tour. After brief introductions--I'd only met Winegar once previously myself--he led us into the Administration Building.

As we walked through the building, Winegar outlined a brief history of the prison, one he'd clearly delivered on many other occasions.

"Auburn is the oldest operating correctional facility in New York State," the clerk told us. "It was originally built to relieve overcrowding at the old Newgate Prison in New York City. The first inmates arrived in 1817. You've probably heard of the 'Auburn system' for prisons. It was developed here and placed into wide use in the last century-- first at Sing Sing and eventually at numerous prisons in other states and countries." Indeed, any newspaper article on prison conditions or construction was likely to mention the system first instituted here in Auburn.

"It is certainly a famous prison you have," Father replied. "Between the Auburn system and the Kemmler affair, it is quite well known." I was too young to remember the controversy that swirled around the execution of William Kemmler when the world's first electrocution was conducted here in 1890.

"Don't get me ahead of myself," Winegar said. "We'll see where Mr. Kemmler met his maker in a bit." He continued with his prepared presentation. "As you may know, the Auburn system was the first to put each inmate in his own cell. It also instituted congregate work during the day, enforced silence, lockstep walking, and striped uniforms, the same uniforms you'll see on the prisoners today. At one time, the yoke, ball and chain, and lash were common punishments, but many of the harsher elements in the Auburn system have been phased out in recent years."

We emerged from the Administration Building into the main courtyard. Wide walkways angled before us to the far ends of the yard. The grass had turned a dull greenish-brown in preparation for the winter. At one side, under the watchful eyes of the blue-coated keepers, a few prisoners raked the crisp leaves which had fallen from the yard's several large elm trees. Across the way, another group walked in lockstep toward the shops, eyes down, submitting to the enforced silence. All wore the gray and white horizontally striped vests and pants with white shirts and flat-topped brimmed caps. The effect was dismal.

"It looks like a hard life," Father commented.

"For hard men," Winegar replied. He pointed out the various buildings that could be seen from the courtyard, finally indicating the high wall to the west. "Over there is the State Prison for Women, which opened in 1893. Previously, that facility served as an asylum for insane male convicts. When the asylum closed, its inmates were transferred to Matteawan."

"Which would be a more sensible place for an aspiring alienist to intern," Father muttered. This was an old tiff between Father and me. When I first announced my intention to do an internship that would allow me proximity to criminals, he argued forcefully that Matteawan was more appropriate than Auburn. I attempted to explain my interest in the psychology of those criminals who were considered sane. Try as I might, I was not able to overcome his objections. He held very conventional views, both of psychiatry and of his son's career.

"Where were the women held before 1893?" I asked
Winegar. The last thing I wanted was to rehash my choice of
internship with my father.

Winegar was oblivious to the subtle tensions between
father and son. "Women were confined here at Auburn when it
first opened. Then, in 1838, they were transferred to Sing Sing.
This new Prison for Women is the first prison exclusively for
female felons in New York. It mainly houses older women who are
second-term felons. Other than that one wall, the only thing it
shares with the men's prison is the administration. Both are under
the charge of Warden Mead."

The clerk now led us through the north cell block. Father
marveled at the precipitous wrought iron stairs and balconies,
hardly more than cat-walks, and at the four levels of tightly fitted
narrow cells. The dark stone walls and the meager light let in by
the high, thickly barred windows contributed to the bleak
atmosphere of the cell-house. The cells themselves were barely
large enough for a grown man to stand up and stretch.

"I guess these quarters might drive a man crazy if he wasn't
to begin with," Father said. I cringed at the dig that was scarcely
concealed between the lines of this seemingly offhanded comment.

"Oh, you'd be surprised," Winegar replied, not realizing
that the remark was meant for me. "Most of the inmates have had
pretty rough lives. The prison is not so bad for them. But for some,
it's like you say. They develop a kind of madness. Two kinds we see
mostly. Men in the first few months who kind of go crazy for a few
days before they adjust. Then there's the long-timers. Some of
them get just plain loony."

Winegar then took us to the chair shop and the weaving
room. The piles of wooden chair parts in the former, and the bolts
of cloth stacked ceiling high in the latter, spoke clearly of the
productive capacity of the prison labor force. Warden Mead, for all
that he was a professional disciplinarian and an agent of the state,
was nonetheless an accomplished industrialist.

Emerging from the workshops, we found ourselves by a
stone-faced building at the end of the south wing. Although I had
not been in this building, I knew it contained the death house and
the prison jail where inmates were confined for offenses against
prison discipline. I tried to imagine Czolgosz within his cell. Would
he be pacing frenetically, sitting quietly in that dreamy state I'd

often seen, or perhaps engaged in political debate with one of the keepers? The latter seemed the least likely. Opening a solid iron door, Winegar indicated the direction of the condemned cells. "Off limits to visitors," he explained as he led us in the other direction, down a passage at the end of which were two more heavy iron doors, to the right leading into the death chamber and to the left the jail. The execution chamber was a sterile, brightly lit, but otherwise unimpressive room. Except for the wires and leather straps hanging from it, the heavy wooden chair was not much more imposing than that of a barber or dentist. Winegar was of little use here. He had not attended an execution and was not yet at the prison at the time of the Kemmler affair. Father's questions on these matters went unanswered.

I had seen prisoners brought to the hospital directly from the jail and had some sense of its unpleasantness. As we entered the room, our ears were assaulted by a loud humming sound coming from the prison dynamo which was housed beyond the far wall. This dull rhythmic vibration would be the jailed prisoners' constant companion, twenty-four hours a day. The jail itself was a vaulted, stone dungeon with two small windows at the far ends and eight cells running along one wall. Those confined to the jail, Winegar told us, were fed only bread and water, and not much of that. The cells were constructed of solid sheet iron on all sides, with exposed rivets even on the cold, hard flooring that must serve as the inmates' bed. There were no furnishings or provisions except for a small bucket, which would serve in the absence of a proper toilet. Peering into the dank, darkness of the first cell, I shuddered to imagine what confinement here might do to the mind of a man- -no light, no ventilation, little sustenance, and no distraction-- locked away for days at a time. Winegar informed us that an inmate had committed suicide in the very cell in which I stood. I shrank back, ready to move on to the remainder of the tour.

Our last stop was the prison hospital. William Patterson, the hospital steward, greeted us but deferred to me to show Father around. I explained to him the organization of the clinic, the kinds of cases we saw, and the responsibilities assigned to Jones and myself. Father frowned at what he judged to be an ill-equipped facility but, in the end, he conceded that the prison environment seemed to provide a powerful initiation into the world of medicine. Though not necessarily for an alienist, he made sure to add.

I thanked Winegar for the tour and led Father back out onto State Street. We walked over to North Street and down Seminary to Mrs. Thomas' boarding house. No one appeared to be home (Jones, I think, was napping). I showed him my room and the shared study which he acknowledged were quite satisfactory. Afterward, I directed him back up North Street toward downtown. We would meet again later at the hotel for dinner. When he'd heard that Father was coming, Dr. Gerin had invited us to dinner at his home but Father had insisted that the Gerins and Jones be his guests at the hotel dining room. I nervously anticipated dining under the watchful eyes of both father and mentor, especially considering the disarming presence of Lucy Gerin, but overall I was pleased with Father's Gesture.

~

The dining room of the Empire State Hotel was fancier and more formal than anything I'd yet encountered in Auburn. Its decor clung to the fine line that separates the ornate from the ostentatious. A deep red wallpaper was embossed with golden lily-shaped designs. Carefully placed mirrors in highly buffed gilt frames imparted a sense of greater spaciousness and afforded the well-positioned diner a view of companions seated to his right or left. The room's overarching sense of grandeur stemmed from the large hemispherical chandelier hanging from the center of the ceiling, its many small incandescent bulbs illuminating a mass of crystal tendrils that hung from gold fixtures.

Jones and I asked for the Parker party and were led to a corner table where my father was already seated with the Gerins.

Father stood up to greet us, extending a welcoming hand to Jones. "Thaddeus, how good to see you!"

Lucy struggled to suppress a giggle. She was not accustomed to hearing Jonesy's prissy first name, which ran so counter to his flamboyant personality.

"Good evening, Father," I said. "Sorry we're late. I take it you've met the Gerins."

"That I have, although we've only been here for a few minutes. By the way, it's a very nice hotel that you've arranged for me. With a dining room to match."

"Nothing but the best for my old man," I replied.

"Dr. Gerin was just telling me a bit about the life of a prison doctor. It sounds quite challenging, working day in and day out with men and women arriving from conditions of squalor, people who in many cases have had no previous contact with physicians and who hold little respect for our profession."

"Challenging is a positive term for it, as I'm sure your son and Mr. Jones will agree," Gerin replied. "If we were not gathered for dinner, I could tell you stories that would pique your professional interest but that might turn the stomachs of the ladies."

"Now father," Lucy said, "you know that mother and I have heard all your stories. We're not the least bit squeamish."

"Nonetheless," her father replied, "there is a time and a place for everything." He picked up his menu and again addressed Father. "The food here, you'll find, is excellent."

The Empire State's bill of fare was extensive, offering a wide range of fish and meat entrees with a variety of fruits and vegetables as side dishes or appetizers. A waiter approached and stood stiffly by Father's side. He explained a few of the menu items and then took our orders in turn. After deferring to the possibility of an objection from Mrs. Gerin, Father ordered a bottle of French wine for the table.

"Dr. Parker," Lucy said, "I see you've not yet jumped on the temperance bandwagon."

"No, Miss Gerin. I believe that a sip of wine is good for the body as well as the soul. After all, did our Lord Jesus not only partake of wine but multiply it for the wedding guests?"

"Yes, he did," she replied. "It makes you wonder why so many seemingly ardent Christians are for its prohibition."

"Some prohibitionists distinguish between wine and hard liquor but, unfortunately, the movement as a whole does seem to be driven by zealots. In any event, I hope you will all join me in a toast this evening." The wine had arrived and the steward had filled our glasses--all except that of Mrs. Gerin, who graciously declined. Lucy modestly asked for "only an inch."

Father now raised his glass and, catching the eye of his counterpart, offered "To health!"

"To health!" Dr. Gerin replied, "but not so much of it as to put us out of business." We laughed and sipped the wine.

"Dr. Parker," Mrs. Gerin asked, "have you always practiced in Brooklyn?"

"I have. In fact, except for my college days, I've lived my whole life there. I took over the practice from my father who passed away a few years ago."

"Oh, I'm sorry," she said. "Do you enjoy being in practice for yourself?"

"I enjoy getting to know families, seeing children grow. Watching the changes in people's lives over many years. What I don't enjoy is always being on call and never knowing when dinner or sleep will be interrupted by the needs of a patient. And certain patients or conditions demand house calls, which can be quite taxing. I envy Dr. Gerin his staff and interns and his fixed place of practice."

Gerin shook his head, smiling. "Not so fast, there. You'll find that there are as many problems caused by subordinates and especially interns"--he added some emphasis here for Jones' and my benefit--"as are relieved by them. My philosophy is that all vocations involve trade offs. The key is to follow your interests and learn to balance the good with the bad."

"Spoken like a true philosopher." Father raised his wineglass in salute.

"But I should add that when I hear of my colleagues in Auburn spending half the day traversing muddy roads to visit patients at remote farm houses, the life of a prison doctor does not seem too bad. No, not too bad at all."

As they conversed, I looked back and forth from my father to Dr. Gerin. They were of comparable age, training, and position in life but quite different in temperament. Gerin's strongest facial features were the deeply carved arcs in his forehead above the eyes. The line over the right eye was low and close, this being the eye through which he peered intently during examinations. The opposite wrinkle lay high on his brow, resulting from his raised-eyebrow expression of imperious interrogation or command. By contrast, Father's wrinkles lay gently around the corners of his eyes, his thick brows hanging heavily over his soft, blue-grey eyes, all weighted down by years of fatigue. Where Gerin's posture was forcibly erect, in the military style, Father allowed his shoulders to slope forward slightly, as if hoping his burdens might thereby slip away. In speech, both tended toward formality, but, while Gerin displayed the same crisp, commanding style whether in clinic or restaurant, Father allowed a softer tone to reveal itself around the edges of his diction.

Mrs. Gerin continued to probe Father's life in her innocuous, easy-going manner, "It must have been hard running a medical practice on your own and raising a child, especially after your wife passed away."

At this, Father's brow gathered in a dark humor. He glared at me intensely, causing some evident discomfort around the table. He did not like me to tell people that mother was dead. It was an issue that had caused friction between us ever since I was in high school and had first sought the safety of subterfuge against the teasing of my peers. I knew I'd hear about it later. His sense of propriety would not allow him to upbraid me or even to correct me in public. Catching himself, he turned a milder gaze toward Mrs. Gerin.

"It's not as hard as you might think for a man to raise a child on his own, especially a man in my position. I've always had dedicated help, both in the office and in the home. And, for the first few years of his retirement, my father was quite willing to help out in a pinch." Mrs. Gerin was satisfied by this reply and, as the first course arrived, conversation turned to food and the weather. Only Lucy continued to stare at me a moment longer, her eyes narrowed into a brooding frown.

As we ate, the topics ranged from the sights and sounds of upstate New York to some friendly debate over city versus small town life. Everyone was quite ready to agree that each had its charms. When dessert was served, Father spoke.

"There is one thing that I've been most curious about, which has made Auburn the center of national attention this month. I refer, of course, to the assassin Czolgosz. Have you had much contact with him? Has his presence had much impact on things in Auburn or in the prison?"

At these words, all eyes reflexively turned my way. In an instant, I realized that even Lucy and Mrs. Gerin had some knowledge of my work with Czolgosz.

"Why is everyone looking at you, Jonathan?" Father asked.

I attempted to clear my throat, stalling in effort to decide how to handle this turn of events. Once again, Dr. Gerin came to my rescue.

"Certainly, Dr. Parker," he said, "you are aware of your son's interest in criminal psychology. Why, since the arrival of the assassin, he's been regaling us with great enthusiasm with his ideas about Czolgosz' sanity and on the mental health of anarchists and assassins in general."

"He sure has!" said Jones. "Why Parker and I will be opening a clinic for the cure of anarchism as soon as we're out of medical school. We expect a booming business."

Father chuckled. "You know, Thaddeus, I've always said you'll make my son a wealthy man some day." My friend and my father had always gotten along well. Jones' own father was a distant man, both important and self-important, who had sent his children to boarding school at an early age. From his first of many holiday visits to our home in Brooklyn, Jonesy had enjoyed the more relaxed atmosphere and my father's friendly, if paternal, interest. I had visited the Jones family only once in their spacious, Manhattan home. Husband and wife had sat at far ends of a long dining table with Jones and me in between. The conversation had been polite, formulaic, and mirthless. The wine was excellent, the food bland.

Father turned his attention back to me. "So, Jonathan, tell me about these theories of yours. Have you contradicted the conclusion of the esteemed alienists in Buffalo that Czolgosz is sane?"

"Well, Father, you know that sane for the purposes of trial and sane from the standpoint of psychiatry are not necessarily one and the same. There are alienists who insist that the belief in anarchy is in itself a form of dementia. I find that a little far-fetched. But, at the same time, targeting the President for assassination is so extreme as to automatically bring into question the sanity of the perpetrator. I've been reading up on theories of regicide and dementia but I'll have to disappoint you for the time being since I haven't really drawn any conclusions."

"I have to say that I've been struck by the seemingly frenzied nature of anarchist activity," Father replied. "Now I won't go so far as to say that all those who believe in the teachings of anarchism are insane. But they are certainly enthusiasts and fanatics, led and controlled by frenzy. That is why I doubt that the execution of Czolgosz will be much of a deterrence for others. When persuaded to take life, anarchists do not think of the consequent punishment, nor would it make a difference to them if they did."

"Have you met many anarchists, Dr. Parker?" The question was Lucy's. Her mother regarded her anxiously, and began unconsciously stirring her pudding with her spoon.

"No, Miss Gerin, not that I know of. I can not recall meeting a single one."

"In that case, I would respectfully like to observe how easily even those with scientific training will leap to conclusions sharing the public prejudice."

Dr. Gerin started to speak, but Father held up a hand indicating that he would reply for himself. His initially severe expression changed slowly to one of good-hearted amusement. "I must say I appreciate the reminder, Miss Gerin. Your point is truly well taken. My ideas on anarchists come from the newspapers on which I am forced to rely for much information. Nonetheless, you are correct that one must take care not to quickly condemn an entire class of people based on the actions of only a few. Not even when, as in this case, the actions are quite notorious and extreme."

"In any event," Mrs. Gerin saw her opening, "the unfortunate Mr. Czolgosz will soon be little more than a memory. We can only pray that no others of his kind will be tempted to such bold action. And speaking of prayer, Dr. Parker, would you like to join us in church tomorrow? It's a very nice Methodist service and Reverend Fitch gives an inspiring sermon."

"Thank you, but unfortunately, I will be on the morning train. Perhaps on another occasion."

After a few more pleasantries, we left the dining room and in the hotel lobby thanked my father and bid him good night. Jones and I walked up North Street with the Gerins. After we left them at their house, Jones said what had been on his mind since dinner.

"Your father seemed pretty peeved about that business about your mother. You know you're going to have to deal with it one of these days."

"I'm sure some day I will. Just not today. By the way, thanks for helping to deflect the question about Czolgosz. Did you notice Lucy and Mrs. Gerin's reaction? They definitely know what's up."

"I'm sure they do. Even Doc Gerin needs someone to talk to, you know. And I'm sure Lucy picks up on anything discussed by her parents."

"Well, I guess I'll find out soon enough."

~

In the morning, I met Father at the hotel in time to walk with him to the train depot. He did not waste any time in informing me of his ire.

"I was not very happy that you told the Gerins that your mother had died. I had hoped you would have outgrown the need for that sort of childishness by now." We were walking down State Street, side by side. As he spoke, Father kept his gaze fixed stonily ahead.

"I am sorry, Father. I didn't expect it to come back to you in this way. I'm still not reconciled about how to explain about Mother. It's natural for people to inquire as I make their acquaintance, but it seems the question catches me unprepared each time and I make my habitual reply. The last thing I want to do is to cause you discomfort, but I really must come to terms with things in my own time and in my own way."

"You are twenty-four years old, Jon. You've had half your life to accept the reality of your mother's condition. What kind of an alienist do you think you'll be if you can not accept the truth about your own mother? I do believe that the time and the way should have come to you by now."

"I agree with you. Really. You are correct," I said, hoping to placate him. "I'm just asking that you have some patience with me."

He let out a sigh of resignation and shook his head, his body visibly relaxing with the release of tension. With an unspoken agreement, we let it go and turned our discussion to my planned return to New York at Christmas time, to my good fortune at working with a fine physician like Dr. Gerin, to the anticipated weather in Buffalo, to anything except for our thoughts and feelings about my mother. At the train station, we shook hands warmly--I was sad to see him go after such a short visit--and Father was off to the great Pan-American Exposition.

As I walked back from the Garden Street Depot, I found Lucy Gerin sitting on her porch engrossed in a book.

I stopped to lean on the white picket fence that surrounded the Gerins' yard.

"What's that you're reading, Lucy?" I called out.

She looked up from the book. "Something up your alley, Jon. *From India to Planet Mars* by Flournoy. Do you know it?"

"I've heard of it, of course, but I haven't read it." Flournoy's book described and analyzed the experiences of a clairvoyant who could remember previous lives as a fifteenth century queen of India, as Marie Antoinette, and as a denizen of Mars. The subject supposedly spoke Martian fluently. "I must say that I am surprised to find you reading it, rather than some treatise on the rights of women. I didn't know your interests ran in the direction of psychology or esoteric mysticism."

"They don't," she replied, "and, judging by public reaction, Flournoy is not particularly esoteric. Or mystical for that matter." Despite its scientific tone, the book had become widely popular with a general public that could never seem to get enough of the metaphysical. The work had been criticized from many quarters and widely lampooned, but among serious critics Flournoy's monograph was celebrated as a tour de force of psychological analysis. Even William James had given it high praise. "Anyway, you know I strive to be a well-rounded girl. I thought I'd give it a try considering what a fun read people say it is. I'm enjoying it, but I think the comparisons to the novels of Jules Verne are a bit overblown. So tell me, where are you off to?"

"Home," I said. "I just left my father at the depot. He's gone on to Buffalo."

"Jon," she said, "I'm bored. Why don't you come and sit with me for a while."

I happily agreed and, reaching around to unlatch the gate, walked over to join her on the porch swing. Lucy was wrapped in a wool blanket against the cool fall temperature. I was quite comfortable in my coat. I took my hat off in hopes that a few rays of warm sunshine might penetrate the autumn air.

"I enjoyed meeting your father," she said. "He seems like a very nice man."

"Oh, that he is. Very nice. It pretty much comes naturally to him. When I was younger, there was a point when I thought I was idealizing him, but I've since realized that, in many ways, he is the ideal physician. Caring, knowledgeable, thorough. Care, of course, is quite contrary to the virtues they teach us in medical school. We are gravely warned against familiarity. Conviviality, we are told, has a leveling effect. Only by maintaining our distance can we secure our proper authority."

"I think my father took that lesson to heart." Lucy laughed and I smiled thinking of Dr. Gerin's ever-serious demeanor. "Not that he is not a fine physician as well. But with your father, it's more than that. I think you hit the nail on the head with the word caring. He seems like such a caring and thoughtful person. Like you, Jon." She smiled coyly as she delivered the compliment.

"Thanks," I replied. "Unlike a lot of men my age, I can see my father's virtues as well as his faults and don't mind being compared to him. Although my own ambitions are to do something more noteworthy, I suppose I could do worse than to follow in his footsteps as a competent pediatrician."

"He certainly rises to the occasion when challenged, much more gracefully than my father does."

"I take it you are referring to your comments on Czolgosz." I said. "You were definitely at your most brazen and, yes, Father demonstrated that he is the consummate gentleman."

She laughed. "He most certainly did! But I was surprised that he didn't seem to know that you were meeting with the assassin. Haven't you told him anything?"

"It is a bit of a secret, you know. In fact, I was just as surprised to discover that you and your mother know about it. Just what did Dr. Gerin tell you?" I was very curious to know how my mentor had portrayed my controversial activities.

"He didn't say much, just that you had been having private sessions with the assassin, that you were trying out some psychological theories or some such. But you shouldn't worry. He cautioned us most severely not to mention it to anyone." A puffy white cloud began to pass across the sun. Lucy gathered the blanket more closely around her shoulders.

"That's a relief. I was worried that word might be spreading all over Auburn."

"Worried?" she replied. "You would be famous. A hundred reporters would descend upon you and hang on your every word. As it is, only Czolgosz is hanging, so to speak."

"Very funny, Lucy. I didn't know you would stoop to punning. Anyway, notoriety is the last thing I'm interested in."

"So, tell me Jon, do you get along with the assassin?"

"Well, get along is an odd way to put it. I wouldn't really think of it in those terms. Yet there does seem to be some rapport growing. He is by nature or by circumstance quite suspicious, but he seemed to be more willing to talk with me at our last meeting."

"I guess I was wondering if you might have some strange sort of affinity toward him. I read in the paper how he lost his mother at around the same age you lost yours." She looked at me pensively as if gauging my reaction.

"What an odd idea," I said. "There are so many differences. An only child versus one of a large brood. A middle class versus a working class upbringing. The presence of a stepmother. The huge difference in education. I suppose I could go on."

She smiled. "No need. It just seemed to me that the loss of a mother is so fundamental. And then your comment a moment ago, about wanting to surpass your father, I'm sure many boys do, but I wonder if that's also a trait you share with Czolgosz. Oh, I suppose you're right. There are so many other factors."

"Another of which, in fact, is my father. The difference in the two fathers is staggering, one involved and attentive, the other distant, violent, and crude."

"I wonder what he was like at your age. Your father, I mean," Lucy said with a far-off look in her eyes. "You seem so different from him. It could just be your youth but you seem more complicated, more troubled. Oh, I really shouldn't comment. He is a fine man. From first impressions, I would say you are pretty fortunate to have him as a father."

"I am," I agreed, "but, you know, he was in some ways shaped by raising me on his own. I think that had a softening effect on him. And, if anyone has had trouble in life, it's my father. He went through a lot with my mother." Lucy did not immediately reply, her brow wrinkling in contemplation. "What is it?" I asked. "What are you thinking?"

"I don't know how to say this, Jon, or even if I should." She hesitated again, looking into my eyes as if trying to fathom some deep mystery. "It's about your parents. There was that moment of tension between you and your father at dinner last night. The way he glared at you at the mention of your mother's death. Everyone could feel it. Everyone could tell that it was both deeply private and terribly important. So, I don't know if I should even ask. It's really not proper..." Her words drifted off into increasing uncertainty. My own impulse was a certain one. I wanted to bolt from that seat and run as far from this conversation as I could, to run until I could run no further, and to collapse, a furor of emotion spent into exhaustion. Somehow, I restrained myself, aided by Lucy's compassionate expression. Her eyes held a message that her awkward words could not articulate. I was like the single starved survivor of a shipwreck, having been tossed for days on a makeshift raft, at last sighting the distant shore, and ready to leap into unknown waters. I didn't know if I could swim.

"L-L-Lucy," I was stammering, "let me try to explain." I felt compelled to give this young woman the answer to the question she could not bring herself to ask. But I could not find the words to express the straightforward truth that was demanding to be revealed. "I'm not sure how to say it, how to explain. It's just that, well," I struggled to find a beginning. "There is a reason my father doesn't like me to suggest that mother is dead... " My words came suddenly to a halt, my jaw immobilized by fear. Lucy's concerned demeanor took on a grave cast. Finally, I drew up my courage in a supreme effort of will. "The reason is, Lucy, that my mother is not dead." Somehow I witnessed myself saying these words as if from a great distance, as if this deep betrayal were not my own. "She's alive. She's been in an asylum on Long Island for the past twelve years." I choked on my words, trying to hold back a flood of tears. "Please don't tell anyone." My long-standing humiliation and grief now held the floor. "I'm sorry," I whimpered pathetically, "I have to go." And before she could say a word, I leapt up from the porch swing and fled from her presence.

Chapter Thirteen

~

Monday, October 21 to
Wednesday, October 23, 1901

Francis Bacon to the contrary, not all of the fruits of
friendship are noble. We use people throughout our lives to meet
the needs of our unfolding circumstances and evolving character.
This is by no means a cynical proposition. Though some may take
advantage of others, feigning interest or affection, it remains a
basic truism that the dictates of our personalities and of the
changing conditions of our lives determine our friends and
associates, our enemies and competitors. Thus, Jones had appeared
at a time when I was ready for a close and steady friendship, one
that would accept me in my then guise of shy but serious college
freshman and grow with me from there, a friendship that would
salute me at the helm of the ship of my life and not rock the boat.
If Jones did not exist, then, like Voltaire's god, it would have been
necessary to invent him.

So it was with Lucy. To reflect on our various encounters,
culminating with Sunday's discomfiting conversation, was to
recognize that my attraction to her was not merely physical or
intellectual. It was emotional and in a most unexpected way. I
understood the nervous anticipation, the persistent excitement,
and the pervading obsession that in sum bear the name "falling in
love." I felt all of that with Lucy and something more. In some
unspoken manner, she offered a different kind of closeness, one
that required that I confront the demons of my past and that
offered me safe harbor in which to do so. As we sat together

Sunday on her porch, it was my knowledge of that requirement, without the corresponding confidence in the proffered safety, that had been terrifying. Over the ensuing days, I mulled over that brief conversation and was able to place it in the context of our previous meetings. Although I could not entirely escape the fear of a previously avoided intimacy, it began to dawn on me that perhaps the desperately needed refuge was at hand.

It was with these thoughts in mind that, on Monday morning, I had written her a short note apologizing for my behavior. I thanked her for her patience as well as for her interest, and expressed the desire that we could continue our last discussion now that I was in a calmer frame of mind. It was the most difficult letter I had ever written. I labored over each phrase, every word, and even the careful composition of my handwriting. Sealing up the envelope at last, my heart-beat quickened and, with a volatile mixture of hope and trepidation, I posted the missive to her office at the bank. Throughout the day, I felt the familiar anxiety with which I had once awaited news of my admission to college or to medical school. The issue was fundamentally the same: would my application, that meant so much to me, be judged as worthy, would it be accepted? That night, I lay awake, seemingly for hours. I played out in my mind a hundred scenarios of Lucy's response. My imagination ranged wildly between the fear of utter rejection and the hope for sympathy and affection. Clinging desperately to the latter, I finally fell into a deep sleep.

Tuesday, when I arrived at work, truly distressing news was waiting for me. There were a number of new prisoners arriving and we would be busy all day with examinations. According to Dr. Gerin, it was unlikely that either I or the examining room would be available for my 11 a.m. session with Czolgosz.

I was disheartened by this turn of events. Last week, I had made a definite breakthrough with Leon. He had embraced our discussion and was speaking much more freely. The week had been charged with a thrill of anticipation that he would today begin to reveal to me those key aspects of his life that had set him on the

path toward his notorious deed. I had been eagerly looking forward
to today's meeting, thinking and rethinking my line of inquiry.
Now, the anxieties of the previous weeks returned. I worried that
my project might lose its moorings. Would there be another time
in the coming week when the interview could be rescheduled?
Would Leon view today's missed session as a betrayal and retreat
to his former reticence? Questions like these ran through my mind
as I mechanically went about my duties through the long morning.

Sure enough, at eleven o'clock, it was not Czolgosz but a
young prisoner named Lavinsky who arrived. Lavinsky had been in
the hospital a week earlier for surgery on his ear. Since then, he
had been discharged and, with his wound still unhealed, assigned
to the coal shoveling detail. The prisoner had complained about
his infected ear and was sent as punishment to the grim confines of
the prison jail where he was held for two days with no clean cloth
or water to tend to his wound. His moaning apparently grew too
much even for the thick-skinned keepers, who finally brought him
back to us. Dr. Gerin and I worked gingerly to clean and bandage
his nasty, oozing ear sore. As Lavinsky was sent off to one of the
adjoining rooms to rest, I saw that the time was now approaching
noon and understood that Leon would not appear this day.

Finally, late in the afternoon, Gerin informed me that
Wednesday would be less busy and that he was sure my session
with Czolgosz could be rescheduled, probably for its usual time slot.
He only had to confirm that the prisoner would be available and
cooperative. Despite a sense of relief, I left the prison that evening
with some uncertainty as to what the morrow would bring.
Somewhat aimlessly, I headed over to O'Malley's to see what was
going on. Jones was not there and I drifted around the edges of
several conversations without really joining any of them.
Eventually, it dawned on me that I was not in a particularly
sociable mood and I headed out the door and back toward the
boarding house.

Entering Mrs. T's foyer, I rifled eagerly through the mail.
Nothing. No letter from Lucy. Nothing at all. You've blown your

chance with her, I cursed myself. What a fool! I tried to tell myself that it was too soon to think that she would not respond, that surely I could have confidence that I would receive her reply the next day, but I could not escape a sinking feeling of disappointment.

~

The next morning, as 11 o'clock approached, I paced anxiously around the examining room, not quite believing that Czolgosz would show up. A thin bead of perspiration dripped down my forehead. My worries, it turned out, were for nought. The keepers brought the prisoner in right on schedule, leaving him and me, once again and perhaps for the final time, alone in the smaller room.

Czolgosz looked wretched. His still careful attention to his grooming could not overcome the cumulative effect of weeks of imprisonment. His skin had a deathly pallor from lack of sun. His eyes were encircled with lines of fatigue. His ill-fitting prison uniform completed a picture of despair. As he tumbled roughly into the cane-backed chair, he seemed a beaten man.

He saw the look of concern in my eyes. "Don't worry, Doc. It ain't so bad."

"You don't look too well," I replied.

"I'm sure it looks worse than it feels," he smiled wryly. "Anyway, it'll soon be over." He relaxed back into his chair.

"You say that so casually. Surely, Leon, you must be afraid?"

"Sometimes I am. Sometimes I lie awake at night and imagine a big chair with lots of wires and hate-filled faces all around me. That makes me sweat, I'll tell ya. But mostly, you don't think about it. Days in prison are a lot like days in the wire mill. You just try to get through them, one at a time, hour by hour. Anyway, maybe that's not what we're here to talk about this morning."

I took this as a none-too-subtle directive to change the subject. Hopefully, we could return to it later. I wondered what he thought we *were* there to discuss in this our final session. I had decided not to mention the significance of today's meeting to him. He was probably as aware of it as I was and there was no need to explicitly add the tension of this being the last of our weekly sessions. It seemed so long ago, the mere three weeks since we had first sat in this small room together. So much had happened in my life in that time. I wondered how time moved for Czolgosz as his unvarying days in the condemned block ran one into another and the moment of his execution drew inexorably nearer. Did time run quickly past or did it expand, the hours getting ever longer as the end approached? And hanging over this session like the heavy sword of Damocles was my sense of our own time running out. An hour, probably less, was all that remained to solve the enigma of Leon Czolgosz.

But, more so than in the preceding weeks, I felt that I was ready for today's session. My resolve, already braced by my encounter with Joe Whelan, had intensified that day at Ithaca. Although I had gone looking for some grand theory to lead me out of a dilemma, my failure to find one had firmed up my conviction that, doing the best I could, I would come to a worthwhile conclusion based on my own endeavors. As much as my readings, it had been reflection on the personality and teachings of Professor Barron that had shored up my self-confidence. Over the past week I had thought through several approaches which I hoped would keep the interview with Czolgosz moving toward ever greater disclosure. The key was to get him to talk about his feelings, about his mother, about his father, about Emma Goldman and about anarchism. But discussing their emotional lives is something few men, particularly those of east European extraction, are accustomed to doing. It was with this in mind that I offered my opening gambit.

"At our last meeting, you were telling me about your shyness. Never talking to girls, spending a lot of time by yourself.

But you said there was one girl you went with for a while. I'm
wondering what that was like. What happened with her?"
    Czolgosz braced physically at this question. I could see his
shoulders tense up as he replied "She wasn't worth much. I'm sorry
I ever spent any time with her."
    "Did she treat you badly?"
    "At the end she did, taking up with another fella and
laughing at me like I was just a fool, some kind of plaything for her.
Even before that, she was always putting me down, like I wasn't
good enough for her. I wanted to talk serious about all that's going
on in the world but all she cared about was to go dancing which I
couldn't do or on a picnic or some such nonsense. So I don't really
know who's not good enough for who as far as that goes."
    "But you liked her?" I asked.
    "Yeah. I did. And I thought she did me at first. It was kind
of frustrating for me. I just couldn't figure a way to make it work. It
was a pretty bad time for me all around, kind of soured me on
women, at least for the last few years."
    "What was it like with other girls?"
    "Like I said, I was never too comfortable with them.
Sometimes, I'd see someone who looked like maybe she was my
kind of gal but I never had the gumption for much more than
stealing a look every now and then. The shy ones, they'd notice my
gaze, especially if I forgot myself and stared too long. They'd look
quickly away, casting down their eyes all embarrassed. I felt
ashamed to humiliate them so. Some girls, the brazen type, they'd
stare right back, their eyes burning into mine, taunting me. Then it
was my turn to look away, feeling all wretched and small. Either
way, they seemed beyond approach. Talking to them was out of
the question."
    "I wonder if you were more outgoing in other contexts. I
remember our earlier discussion when you were talking about how
you first started going to the socialist meetings. Was your shyness a
problem for you there as well?"

"I do think of myself as a pretty bashful sort of fellow and mostly I am. But, you're right, it depends on the circumstances." Czolgosz reached both hands up to gently rub his temples. His facial expression relaxed a bit. "I guess when I'm around people for awhile, I get more comfortable, more at ease to strike up a conversation and even pick up a friend here and there. Back at the mill, I'd gotten to know some of the guys pretty well. They elected me to the Knights of the Golden Eagle. Quite an honor, especially for a Catholic. I liked their motto: 'fidelity, valor, humanity.' To belong, you've got to be of good moral character and a champion and advocate for the best interest of the people. It was very patriotic but that was before I learned what I know now.

"I kept up with Golden Eagle meetings after I got sick. Pretty soon, I started to go to socialist meetings as well. They weren't hard to find. Pretty much anywhere there's working people, there's discussion groups, newsletters, party organizations. Some of them really mean business. Some are kind of lazy. I got involved in the Polish Socialist Society. That's where I met my friend Hauser. It was just one of those things. Something gets discussed in a meeting and a few fellows get to talking about it after and before you know it you're chumming around with some guy you hardly knew before. Hauser was a pretty good friend to me. He knew what was going on and helped me get moving in the right direction."

I made a mental note of this name, Hauser. It might prove to be an acceptable revelation to placate Warden Mead. I had decided to take my agreement with Czolgosz seriously. If I intended to betray him to the authorities, I was sure that he would pick up on it. Thus, I had set as my goal merely to acquire some relatively harmless information that might please the warden while not breaking confidence with Leon.

"The right direction?" I asked. "Do you mean the direction of anarchism?" This was the kind of question that would have caused Czolgosz to shut down a couple of weeks earlier. Now, he just shook his head.

"Naw. He knew all the anarchists, knew everyone, really.
But they won't pin nuthin' on Hauser. He's a smart man and a
good friend but he's what I'd call a dabbler, went to meetings,
talked a good game, but never one to do too much."

"So what did get you interested in anarchism."

"Really, it was Emma Goldman. I guess I can tell you about
that since the Buffalo coppers found that article on her talk in my
coat pocket. Of course, if they'd have troubled themselves to read
it they'd have seen that she spoke against violence that day. But I
won't say nothin' more about seeing her except for that one time. I
ain't saying I saw her again and I ain't saying I didn't. That first
time, she was speaking at the Franklin Club. I'd been going there
pretty regular. I liked that they let anyone in and didn't charge no
dues. Their motto was 'truth combats error.' I heard some good
talks there on economics, free love, ethics, politics. None of them
was a match for Emma Goldman. She's surely the best speaker I've
ever heard, and not just for a woman neither. "

Unlike the previous sessions, Leon was now speaking freely
with little encouragement from me. It was as if our discussion was a
refuge from his grim existence as a condemned man. As a Catholic,
Czolgosz might unconsciously long for the comforting sacraments
of last rites and confession. True to his anarchist convictions, he
had so far steadfastly refused to see a priest, not even the man who
Warden Mead had brought in from the Polish congregation in
Buffalo. I wondered if I might unwittingly be an unintended stand-
in for his father confessor. As Leon continued, his voice was
increasingly animated, revealing the excitement of an earlier
period in his life, a time only a few months earlier that must have
seemed to him long past.

"I'll always remember the date. May 5th. She talked about
how Vanderbilt wants his own freedom, the rest of us be damned,
but the anarchists want freedom for all. She talked about how
some men could not stand idly by and see wrongs done to others.
That day, I pretty much vowed to be such a man. I was all stirred

up by her speech and wanted nothing more than to spend hours talking with her, learning about anarchism and revolution.

"After the talk, I went up to her and asked if she could suggest some books to read. She looked at me so hard as if she could see right into my soul. You know, she's not a real good-looking woman, kind of bookish and all, but there's something about her that just sort of grabs you. The more time I spent around her, the more I felt like she was the kind of woman who could straighten me out. In the end, I could hardly stop thinking about her. And I tell you, I would have followed her right out of that room that first evening and gone along just about anywhere she'd have let me. As it was, I just stood there real nervous, surrounded by folks, and all I could do was to ask about books and clam up." He shook his head as if regretting a lost opportunity. As much as he ascribed his reticence to his innate shyness, his tone was the familiar one of many a young man who has frozen up and lost the chance to ask out his dream girl.

"Anyway," Czolgosz continued, "she was real busy, but took a few minutes to pass on some titles. I think she might have talked with me longer if there hadn't been such a crowd of people gathered around, asking her so many questions and all."

"The papers have written you were with Goldman in Chicago. Would you be comfortable telling me about that encounter?" I asked hopefully.

"Naw, Doc, I think I'd better not say anything about that one way or another. I've caused her enough trouble as it is."

"Okay, then." I paused for a moment to decide on a course of inquiry. I wanted desperately to peak at my watch, but dared not remind the assassin of the fast fleeting hour. "I didn't realize that it had been only a few months since you were first exposed to anarchism. I guess you gave yourself a pretty quick education."

"I guess I did." Leon leaned back again in his chair, the fervor of a few moments earlier gone now from his expression. "After the Goldman talk, I told Hauser I wanted to get more involved with the anarchists and he sent me to the Liberty Club and to see Emil Schilling. I don't mind telling you about him since everybody in Cleveland knows what he's up to--which is nothing. Schilling gave me a book on the Haymarket martyrs and some copies of *Free Society*. I'd seen *Free Society* before, and knew some about Haymarket, but this was a lot of information all at once. I particularly liked the different points of view, the debates, that appeared in *Free Society*. But Schilling only wanted to talk and read. I saw him a few times, even had dinner at his house once, but he wouldn't help me much. He put on these airs like he was so much smarter than me. Acted like I was hardly fit for him to talk to. I didn't take to that at all. Anyway, I didn't like him much either. So I told him I hadn't read his books." Czolgosz sneered and shook his head.

"Schilling was a suspicious sort. He wouldn't tell me about any secret societies and wouldn't tell me if there would be an American Bresci. I'd thought Bresci's assassination of King Humbert over in Italy was good revolutionary practice, something anarchists ought to be talking about. After Emma's talk, I was of a mind to take some action. But, if the Cleveland anarchists were up to anything, I wasn't going to learn about it from Schilling, or about anything else for that matter. He wouldn't even give me a letter of introduction to Emma, which I thought at the time I might need. That was before I knew just how friendly she is. My hope was that, if I could meet her and show her that I was committed to the cause, she might accept me into her group. Schilling told me I could just go to Chicago and meet her myself. He was right about that, but that was about the only useful thing I got out of him. He reminds me of something I heard Mother Jones say. She's that tough woman who organizes the mine workers over in West Virginia. She gave a talk in Cleveland last February. I memorized this one line I liked. You want to hear it?"

"Sure." I replied. Czolgosz had unwittingly let slip that he had met with Goldman in Chicago. The more he talked, the more I hoped to learn.

"It went like this, 'I have no use for teapot socialists who are satisfied to put in their time sitting around a parlor and discussing abstract ideas.' Teapot socialist--that fits Schilling all right and a lot of others I've met as well."

"But not Emma Goldman?"

"No, not her. She gives her whole life over to traveling around, giving speeches, helping strikers, getting folks organized. And she's smart as a whip as well. There's no topic I wouldn't seek her advice on. She's a nurse too, you know. She'd work just as hard to heal one person or to heal the whole country." I remembered Joe Whelan's comment on Goldman's offer to nurse McKinley to health. It had struck me as bravado at the time, but she had clearly impressed Leon with her sincerity.

"So, I take it you did see her again, in Chicago?" I might as well venture the direct question. Czolgosz seemed comfortable with his sense of the limits of our conversation.

He stared hard at me in reply. "Doc, I told you I'm not going to talk about that and I meant it. Like I said, I've put her in enough danger as it is. She's so prominent and so hated by the rulers that anything that happens comes back to her whether she was involved or not. So, the official story is I didn't see her 'cept for that one time. That's it. She didn't know nothing about my plans nor did anybody else."

"All right," I resigned myself that we would not get past this impasse. The implication was clear that Leon had indeed met with Goldman and perhaps others in Chicago. But the specifics of those meetings seemed destined to go with him to the grave. I took a minute to consider where we might go from here. Time was running out. I decided to strike forward with a bold approach, hoping to link his embrace of anarchism fundamentally to the loss of his mother.

"So, tell me," I said, trying to sound as if I was making just another casual comment. "Is there anything about Emma Goldman that reminds you of your mother?"

Czolgosz' eyes grew wide at this question. I was prepared for an abrupt disavowal but that was not at all the nature of his response.

"I don't know what could have given you that idea." Leon's ignorance of the field of psychology was complete. "You see, my secret idea has been that there is a likeness, not that I would ever have told anyone so. How can you compare the quiet life of a mother of eight with a national leader, a revolutionary? And Emma Goldman is close to my age. How can she remind me of my mother? So, I don't know what made you think of it, but, for me, they're the only two people who cared about me in my life, really truly cared. Oh, there's Waldek. He cared some in his way, and some others too. But to make me truly feel that I could be important, that I might do something worthwhile in my life, only two people gave me that kind of feeling." I remembered Leon's earlier mention of his mother making him feel special.

"I suppose it was just a natural question to wonder about the two women who influenced your life. Can you tell me specifically what it is about your mother that Goldman reminds you of?"

"It's nothing physical. Not her voice or her looks or anything she did. Like I said, it's a feeling, how she felt about me and made me feel about myself. There's one thing my Ma said just before she died that I've always remembered."

"What was that?"

"She said, to all of us, but maybe most especially to me, 'My children, the time will come when you will have greater understanding and be more learned.' When I met Emma, I saw that she had those qualities that my mother valued, that I'd been aiming for myself. That's partly why I looked up to her so. I guess I thought that maybe she would understand me in the way that Ma had done, that she would appreciate the road my Ma had laid out for me."

"And did she? Understand, I mean."

"Oh, I don't know. Some, I think. Maybe if we'd had more time, if she'd gotten to know me better, seen what I meant to do." As Leon's words drifted off, his mouth hung open as if awaiting the intercession of some oracular being to speak through him as to what his future might have been.

"And, what about your mother? Do you think you've lived up to her message?"

"I don't know," he said in a low voice. "I always took those words to mean two things, her notion of what was to come and her advice to me on how to live my life. It always seemed that I owed her that, to gain understanding and learning. Sometimes, I think I've done all right by her. I'd hate to think I'd let her down." Leon's voice was strained. His shoulders heaved with a muffled sigh. I half expected to see a tear run down his cheek, but his eyes, with that far-away look, remained dry.

"And now," I said softly, "you must lose your life, never being sure, at best having faith that you've lived up to her hopes for you."

Czolgosz looked up at me, his eyes red, his expression subdued.

"I'm not one for faith," he said gruffly, his voice cracking from a sudden parching of his throat. "At least not the way folks speak of it. But I had a dream the other night. I'll put some stock in that dream."

"Do you want to tell me about it?" I asked, realizing with some amazement that I had attained my goal. In this final session, as he faced his death, Leon was reaching out to me. It was no longer even a question of whether he would respond to my inquiries. Now, in these last moments, he was leading the way.

"I might as well." He sighed out loud. The anarchist bravado was gone. Here was only the sadness of loss, the dolor of defeat, a solitary man facing his imminent demise. "In a way, it's all that's left." He closed his eyes as if to summon the memory of the dream.

"It went like this," he said after a few moments. "I'm in the mill, pulling out a long line of wire. It's real hot. Men are all around me hard at work. There's a lot of noise from the machinery, always is, but it starts to get louder and louder until finally I can't take it any more. I drop the wire and start walking toward the door. The foreman, Mr. Page, calls after me but I just keep going. I walk out the door into this blazing sunshine, so bright I'm nearly blinded by it. When my eyes adjust to the light, I can see that I'm back in Buffalo at the Exposition. There's a huge crowd of people milling around, this way and that. I start to walk along, not really knowing where I'm going and then I realize that Emma Goldman is there at my side. 'Walk with me a ways, Leon,' she says and she takes my hand in hers.

"We're walking through the center of the fair, down the Esplanade, not paying any attention to the crowds. We pass the Temple of Music. The colors are so bright and lifelike, the yellow building, the gold and red trim. Somehow, I know that McKinley's inside. There's a long line waiting to get in, but Emma says 'Don't you worry about him. He's just a puppet.' So we walk on by and continue along until we finally come to the Electric Tower. If you'd have been to the Exposition, you'd know it. It's the one site you can't miss--a tall building, surrounded by columns and fountains, rising high above the fair grounds.

"Emma and I walk inside and over to the long spiral staircase that leads hundreds of feet above to the dome. She gestures for me to walk up those stairs. I look up and can see the statue they call the Goddess of Light atop the tower way up in the distance. Then all at once it seems I've been climbing those stairs awhile and that I am by myself. I look back down and see Emma far below talking to a man. It might be that friend of hers, Hippolyte. I can't really tell for sure. She doesn't seem to notice me and I continue climbing the stairs, except now I'm rising quickly as if the stairs themselves are lifting me up. As I get close to the top, the goddess seems bigger and bigger, except that suddenly it's no goddess but only my mother, lying on her death bed, smiling weakly at me like she did that day. She says to me only the same five words she said to me in the end. 'It's time, Leon. It's time.' And, even though I woke up weeping, a grown man bawling like a baby, that dream is why mostly I'm not afraid to die. Mostly, I'm not afraid."

I sat quietly for a few minutes, not sure what to say. Certain somber sentiments allow only a respectful silence in reply. I did not need the theories of Sigmund Freud to understand Leon's dream. He and I both recognized its meaning. Although from day to day, dreams may hide their significance in an enigmatic language whose Rosetta Stone has not yet been found, at times of crisis they tend to speak plainly. Leon stared down at the floor, his hands clasped together in his lap, his shoulders hunched forward. His fate seemed to weigh heavily upon him. Finally, as if remembering my presence, he spoke again.

"You know, Doc, when they first brought me up here I was pretty sure it was a way to trick me into talking. I had you pegged for a cop despite what that Gerin had to say. And, who knows, maybe you've got me fooled. But if you're a cop, you didn't get nothing out of me after all. And, if you're really some kind of alienist, which I think maybe you are, then you might have got some of what you're looking for. I don't know. But I think I got something out of you. It's been good for me to have a chance to talk about my life, to think about the people I've known and the things I've done, the thing I did. It's been good for me. It has."

I smiled at this admission. "Leon, I am truly happy to hear you say that. Whether you believe it or not, I am, or rather will soon be, an alienist. I've learned a great deal from you, but I think it will be some time before I fully understand it all."

We sat silently together for another moment. Then I spoke again.

"I guess this will be our last meeting. We've probably said all that we can, for now." I stood up and held out my hand. "I want to wish you well, whatever that may mean for you in your final few days. I doubt that we will meet again."

He rose stiffly from the hard-backed chair, shook my hand firmly and, with a slight smile, looked intently for a moment into my eyes. "So long," he said. Then, he blinked once, his eyes glazing over, and, without a word, walked slowly out of the room.

I sat back down to contemplate what had just transpired. I was dazed by the impact of Czolgosz' revelation and the unmistakable air of finality in his departure. In truth, I could not imagine how I might see him again. In the remaining days leading up to the execution, his activities would come under ever closer scrutiny by administrators, visiting dignitaries, and the growing army of reporters covering the story . But even if we could meet again I was not sure if the discussion could go any further. It was clear that he would not speak of his mysterious summer travels, of his days in Buffalo, or of his contact with various anarchists. And to delve further into the subjects we had already discussed would take more trust and more time, time that he just did not have. Whatever conclusions I might draw from the case of Leon Czolgosz would have to be based on what I now knew.

The door to the examining room swung open and Dr. Gerin appeared before me, a concerned expression on his face.

"Is everything all right?" he asked.

"Oh, fine really," I replied. "I was just taking a few minutes to gather my thoughts."

"Did the session go well?"

"Yes, I think it did, as well as it could. He spoke of his conversion to anarchism and of his feelings for Emma Goldman. But he was always very careful not to give any information that might incriminate anyone else. I did get one name for Warden Mead. There's a fellow named Emil Schilling in Cleveland. He's apparently a well-known anarchist there who met with Czolgosz on several occasions." I hoped the "teapot socialist" would have little reason to fear some attention from the police.

"The Warden will be pleased, I'm sure," Gerin replied.

I stood up and we walked out into the main examination room. There was no sign of Czolgosz or his guards. Another prisoner had arrived and now sat uncomfortably on the examining table--an old man, grey and wrinkled, who I had not encountered before. It appeared some men did achieve old age in Auburn prison. I walked over to the side table to retrieve Dr. Gerin's stethoscope and we began the examination.

~

When I walked into the foyer of the boarding house, I reached down mechanically for the small stack of mail on Mrs. T's little table. As my eyes fell on the one small envelope that bore my name, I realized I had completely forgotten my expected missive from Lucy Gerin, so wrapped up had I been in the rescheduled session with Czolgosz. I stared mindlessly at the envelope. A feeling of dread and humiliation froze me in my tracks. Shaking my head, as if I could physically cast such emotions aside, I raced up the stairs two at a time seeking the privacy of my bedroom. Not pausing even to sit myself down or remove my coat, I tore the envelope roughly open, giving this potential love token none of the tenderness it deserved. Inside, I found a small sheet of stationery which bore, in the crisp penmanship of a well-practiced hand, the following note:

> _Dear Jon,_
> _Thank you for your frankness and for your willingness to share your thoughts with me. I apologize if I was too forward in my questioning on Sunday._
> _Yes, I would love to get together again soon. My suggestion is that we go for an outing to the lake._
> _If you find that agreeable, you could meet me at the bank when I_

get off work on Saturday at 12:30. I
look forward to your reply.
              Yours truly,
              Lucy Gerin

I reread Lucy's letter several times. The anxiety of the night before once more engulfed me--the certainly that, as a man, I was a failure. I knew I had not achieved the personal mastery that marked the success of men like Dr. Gerin and my father. How could any woman truly respect me, let alone love me? But Lucy's note insisted by its plain, direct language that she cared for me nonetheless. I probed those few lines for any hint of rejection. What a relief to conclude that there were none. This brief message conveyed an acceptance of the bitter truths that I had revealed to her--the embarrassing truth about my mother, the sad truth about my failure to come to terms with Mother's illness, and the disconcerting truth that I was not the dispassionate man that our times called for. Her message was an invitation to more than an outing. Unbeknown to herself, she was beckoning me to face my past, to risk revealing my closely-guarded secrets to another, and to take the chance that I might be worthy of a woman's love. At the not-so-tender age of twenty-four, I was being offered the opportunity to grow up.

Chapter Fourteen

~

Friday, October 25, 1901 to

Saturday, October 26, 1901

Each Friday, Jones and I met for an hour or so with Dr. Gerin to review the past week's cases. Gerin would also take time to answer any questions we might have in regard to our readings or on medicine in general. Although this meeting took place at the end of the long work week, Dr. Gerin was always patient and showed interest in our questions and ideas. He seemed to enjoy the break from his administrative duties and from treating uncongenial patients. For me, this was the most pleasant aspect of the internship. Part of my inclination toward psychiatry was based on the fact that I relished the theory and ideas of medicine more so than its practice. I missed my classes, the regular contact with professors, and the continual stimulation from my peers that had characterized the previous three years of medical school. I looked forward to a career in which the contents of the mind would be my daily preoccupation. Perhaps, among physicians, I was equivalent to Czolgosz' teapot socialist. I would have welcomed these discussions with Dr. Gerin on a daily basis.

But an hour a week was all we got. This time, we talked at some length about the skin condition of the embezzler, Whitfield, and the difference between eczema and psoriasis. Finally, the allotted time was up and Jones and I got up to leave.

"Mr. Parker, please stay a moment," Dr. Gerin said off-handedly. "You and I have one more matter to discuss."

Jones hesitated and looked back.

"Go on, Mr. Jones," Gerin insisted. "Your friend will be along in a few minutes."

As the office door closed behind Jonesy, Dr. Gerin turned his attention back to me and said "It's about my daughter." I gulped and sat up a bit straighter in the chair. He continued, "Lucy, as I'm sure you know, is a bright, head-strong, energetic, and independent young woman. She fancies herself a free thinker, an emancipated woman, and a risk taker. By Auburn's standards, she probably is all of those things. Some of these are traits which she shares with you and I am not surprised that an attraction has formed. And it is not just with a father's blind adoration that I note that she is most decidedly a lovely young woman."

He paused for a moment and I shifted uncomfortably in my seat, uncertain whether it was my turn to speak or just what I would say if it was. To my relief, the doctor continued, "My goal in speaking with you today is to convey to you that her mother and I do not necessarily agree with certain aspects of our daughter's thinking, and that in many ways we are somewhat traditional. Should your interest in our daughter continue to develop, we would anticipate, as her parents, that you would proceed in the proper manner. We don't expect Lucy to accede to a chaperone, but we do expect matters to be above board.

"I want to be clear with you as well that I do not think that our brief professional association should preclude your courting my daughter, if you so choose. Or, perhaps, I should say, if she so chooses." Only a crinkling around the corner of his eyes betrayed the slightest hint of a smile at this conclusion.

I was thrilled at this turn of events, my nervousness transformed, but I still was not sure what to say. Gerin had, in effect, given me his seal of approval without my even having to ask for it. By implication, he knew that I had already spent time with Lucy. No doubt she had told him. Or, more likely, she had spoken with her mother, using the more accessible parent as a conduit. This discussion also meant that the mother approved, which was not surprising. All my life, other people's mothers have liked me and wanted to take me under their wings.

"Dr. Gerin," I said, "I appreciate your having this conversation with me, which I otherwise would have had to initiate myself before too long. I have hesitated because of the awkwardness, for me, of bringing up such subjects with you, my mentor and supervisor. I appreciate your wanting to make the situation more comfortable for me." He nodded in understanding.

I went on, "Your daughter is a kind, fascinating, and beautiful woman. I am enjoying getting to know her and look forward to continuing to do so. I want to assure you I will treat her with all the respect and consideration that you, Mrs. Gerin, and Lucy deserve."

He stood up and offered me his hand, apparently satisfied that this discussion had come to its proper conclusion. Shaking my hand warmly, but still maintaining his ever serious countenance, Dr. Gerin said, "I think you are a fine young man, Parker. Well brought up and well educated. I don't think you have quite found yourself in regard to medicine, but I have every confidence you will. I will see you on Monday."

Walking from his office, I felt elated. These were the first words Dr. Gerin had spoken to me of a personal nature, and the first real indication of how he thought about me as his student and as a budding physician. How exhilarating to think that I might be on the threshold of joining the world of medicine not as his subordinate but as his peer! I was surprised to realize that I wanted nothing more than to tell Lucy how thrilled I was by her father's approval.

～

When I got up the next morning, the early sun was bright, bringing an unseasonable warmth to the autumn air that a slight breeze did little to diminish. Happily, I donned my light cotton pants and jacket, looking forward to the extra mobility that came with their loose fit. After Mrs T's standard breakfast fare, I took my coffee to the study and spent a couple of hours ostensibly at the books, but mostly, in fact, playing with the cat. At noon, I put on my walking shoes and headed downtown. Genesee Street on Saturday was bustling with people. It seemed that most of the women of Auburn were out shopping, many with children in tow. The stores were busy and a buzz of conversation enlivened the familiar scene. I ambled down the street, smiling at a person here or greeting another there, complete strangers all. After two months in Auburn, I was beginning to feel like a citizen.

I waited only a minute or two at the bank before Lucy appeared. She had found attire that looked proper for work, yet comfortable enough for an outing: a simple green dress cut loose to allow easy movement. A touch of femininity was maintained through an ornate lace bodice closed with a row of emerald-green buttons that matched the dress. Greeting her with a tip of the hat, I held out my arm which she grasped with both hands. "Off we go," she said gaily as we headed down Genesee Street to catch the street car that would take us the scant few miles to the lake.

The mid-day trolley was about half full. I hopped aboard as it stopped and reached out a hand to Lucy. To my relief, she accepted my assistance and, with the ease of an accomplished trolley rider, swung up on to the car. We found two seats together near the back. A number of passengers were returning from a morning downtown and got off as the south-bound trolley neared their homes. They were quickly replaced by others heading out for an afternoon on Lake Owasco. Lucy chattered away, pointing out the various sights along the route: factories, churches, and schools, or the street where some friend of hers or of her parents might reside. Particularly impressive were the smokestacks rising from the big D.M. Osborne plant that stood along the west bank of the Owasco River. Although Joe Whelan and I had sat much closer to them a couple of weeks earlier, their height had been obscured by the nearer buildings. White plumes of smoke drifted off to the east.

Even on Saturday afternoon, workers were busy building Osborne's highly regarded farm equipment.

Soon Owasco Road left the denser in-town neighborhoods and headed out through the outlying farm land that marked the last stretch down to the lake. The street car was full of weekend revelers. Lucy explained that, although the beach was closed, the other attractions of Lakeside Park were open until the end of the month, and that, given the fine weather, we should expect a crowd. We rode in silence the last few miles, listening to the voices around us and looking out over the surrounding fields. The harvest was not long past and piles of corn stalks lay waiting to be plowed under before the first freeze.

When we reached the park, a couple of children nearly overran us in their eagerness to disembark. We stepped down onto the macadam pathway and walked toward the lake. Our ears were assaulted by the screams of people careening around the roller coaster that dominated the view. It was one of the largest I'd seen, rivaling those at Coney Island I had enjoyed the previous summer. Turning to Lucy, I asked if she'd care to take a ride.

"Not now," she replied. "I'm famished. I haven't eaten since breakfast early this morning. Let's just walk around for a while and get a bite to eat."

Arm in arm, we continued on toward the lake. On the far side of the roller coaster, a small steamboat with "Lady of the Lake" painted across her bow was just setting out with a festive crowd for a trip around the lake. We walked along the boardwalk by the pavilion. Lucy explained that young and old came out for the fine dances held there on summer evenings. At the moment, it was occupied by only a few matronly women seeking shelter from the midday sun. We strolled along the water's edge. Tiny waves gently lapped the shore. A few picnickers sat by the sandy beach watching a toddler splash in the shallow tide. Passing by the carousel, we encountered a mother firmly instructing her son that three rides were enough for the day. He insisted, quite as firmly, that just one more would satisfy him. We did not wait to find out who would prevail but, I had a sense that the little boy was used to getting his way.

To one who'd grown up in the hustle and bustle of Brooklyn, the goings-on around the lake had a quaint, countrified air to them. I thought I might impress Lucy with a description of the wonders of the amusement parks at Coney Island, but was surprised to learn that she had been there on an excursion while at Vassar. We agreed that each area was well-suited to its particular locale. They shared the virtue of providing a pleasant escape for the local citizenry from their day-to-day concerns.

Near the carousel, a vendor delivered candied apples into the eager, soon to be sticky, fingers of small children. Nearby was a lunch cart offering hotdogs, sarsparilla, and roasted nuts. I bought a couple of hotdogs and drinks. Lucy delved liberally into the mustard jar and we made our way to a wooden bench overlooking the lake.

"So," I asked, after swallowing my first bite, "could your mother limit your carousel rides?"

"She wouldn't even have tried. My father had the job of setting limits and, as you can imagine, he was pretty good at it."

"Speaking of limits, I suppose you know he spoke to me yesterday,"

"Really? I would have thought he spoke to you pretty much every day."

Her dissembling might have annoyed me a week or two earlier. Today, I took it in stride. "It seems that he and your mother would not be opposed to my courting you. That is, if the proper etiquette were followed. I believe that means I am to speak to him again should the occasion arise."

"Why, Mr. Parker! I don't know what to say!"

I smiled at her feigned shock. "So, what did you tell them to set me up for this. I was pretty nervous, as I'm sure you can imagine, when your father sent Jones on his way and kept me behind after our Friday afternoon meeting."

"Well, actually, I didn't speak to my father at all. He can be so difficult about certain things. I did mention to my mother that I had been enjoying making your acquaintance. I can't imagine why father felt the need to speak to you. Really, who would think of such a thing?"

"I can't imagine!" I could not help laughing as I shook my head in acknowledgment of her relentlessly demure posturing. "Yesterday's talk really took me by surprise. Your father is not a man I would want to displease, at least not before his evaluation of my internship is on file. But it would have been a lot harder for me to have taken the initiative with him in such a discussion." It was my turn to bat my eyelashes coyly. I could tell by the satisfied look on Lucy's face that this was exactly what she had been thinking and precisely the direction in which she had wanted things to proceed.

Around the curve of the lake, I had been watching two boys carefully guide a kite high in the air over the water. I envied their skill as they kept it on course. Their concentration and focus were complete, as was their happiness. For them, in all the world, there could only be the lake, the kite, and themselves. Somehow, adulthood could never be that simple. Much as I would like to have this one afternoon just for Lucy and myself, others—her parents, my parents, Czolgosz, Jonesy—seemed inevitably to intrude.

"There was one aspect of the conversation I was very pleased with." I continued. "Your father, who is usually a fairly reticent fellow, indicated he has some genuine respect for my intellect and for my work. I really appreciated hearing that. On the other hand, he seems to think I am a bit adrift in the medical field."

Lucy wiped a mustard smudge from her lips before speaking. "Father works with different medical students every year and I would expect that he's become a pretty keen judge of their capabilities and potential as physicians. Despite his gruff demeanor, most of them seem to develop a genuine affection for him during the course of the semester and many have stayed in touch over the years. I expect that praise from him is something to feel good about. But, what does he mean that you are adrift?"

"I am not sure myself," I recognized that my answer was paradoxically emblematic of the very condition in question. Over the lake, the kite lurched perilously close to the water. I could hear the excited voices of the boys shouting to each other, but could not make out their words. "It could be that he senses my own lack of conviction or certainty about my future as a physician, or it could just be that he isn't very happy with my interest in the assassin. Don't get me wrong, he has supported me one-hundred percent. Dr. Gerin--your father--is not like a lot of doctors, some of my professors even, who have trouble viewing psychiatry as a legitimate part of medicine. He understands criminal psychology as a potentially important field both for rehabilitation and for prevention. It's just that the assassin is so repugnant to him. He doesn't think Czolgosz is worth any more energy than the electricity it will take to execute him."

"Many people would see it as a bit bizarre," she said. "After all, you have sought to develop an association with the most reviled man in America."

"Yes, and it's fascinating. Whether you look at Czolgosz in terms of his family background, his social experiences, or his political philosophy, such as it is, he makes for a compelling case study. I would think that any alienist would jump at the chance to examine him in depth. Really, it's surprising that Dr. MacDonald and the others in Buffalo spent so little time with him in determining that he was sane for trial, as if he were just your run-of-the-mill criminal." I paused in thought for a moment, considering an idea. "You know, Lucy, I don't have anyone I can talk to about Czolgosz with except for Jones, and he doesn't take it very seriously. I wonder if you'd be willing to discuss it with me."

"I would love to but I'm not sure what perspective I can offer."

"Oh, you are wiser than you know," I said truthfully. "It's just that last Wednesday was in all likelihood my final meeting with Czolgosz. I find that I feel sorry for him. His life has been so hard and now, at such a young age, it's over. It troubles me that I could do so little for him. A real alienist, one experienced with psychological analysis or what Sigmund Freud is calling psychoanalysis, might really be able to help him, to make him fit for society."

"But, Jon," she replied, "isn't it too late for that? After the assassination, society owes him nothing. You owe him nothing."

"No, of course I don't. No one does. But I can't help thinking that perhaps someday we might come to an understanding that, when crime results from mental illness, cure rather than punishment is called for."

"And have you decided that he is mentally ill? As your father pointed out last week, the several well-qualified alienists in Buffalo did not seem to think so."

"Yes and no. It's really very complicated," I struggled to organize my thinking which, although mostly chaotic over the past month of meetings with Czolgosz, had recently started to come to a kind of resolution. "You see, he was sick, physically ill, for several years. That's why he left his job. As I put the pieces together, it seems his illness, coupled with the resulting idleness, fed an emotional trauma that stemmed from his childhood. Had he gotten the medical treatment he needed in the first place, his life might have proceeded along a very different course. It seems to me that, with all the wealth in this country, there ought to be a way to provide for the health needs of workers. A good doctor ought to be able to identify when a patient seeking treatment for a physical condition also shows symptoms of emotional distress. That's not really part of our medical training today but I think the treatment of that aspect of health should be a routine part of medicine. If I do go on to become an alienist, I think I'd like to work toward that end."

"You are certainly right on one point. Both medicine and society have a long way to go before the kind of care you are describing is available to factory workers."

"And there's something else in regards to Czolgosz' sanity. The more I learn about working conditions in the factories and about the treatment of strikers, the more I question whether a failure to adapt to such an environment should be considered insane or whether it might in fact be a properly healthy response. It strikes me that those who demand change, who refuse to accept such harsh treatment might be the sane ones. In a way, they are not so different from the patriots we celebrate in history class." I was astonished to realize I was quoting Joe Whelan practically verbatim.

"Why Jon! You are becoming a socialist. It seems that Czolgosz is curing you while you are busy curing him."

"I don't know about that. I am thinking about a lot of things I took for granted before. But, as you can see, I'm of two minds. Looking at his life history, Czolgosz is undeniably a troubled man, perhaps on the borders of sanity. Yet, seen in the context of society, his actions might not be at all crazy. I think what I'm saying is that I disagree with the common view that it is his adherence to anarchism that makes him a madman. He suffers from a nervous disorder of another sort."

"But you are overlooking something. Even if you are correct about workers and the factories, it still does not explain or condone murder, especially not cold-blooded murder like the premeditated assassination of the President."

"You are right about that. And so, Czolgosz will die. I just wish there could be another way. You know, you were on to something the other day in your suggestion about the importance of his mother. It seems that, after her death, he had little else left to lose. Overshadowed in the middle of that pack of kids, with a hostile step-mother and a harsh but indifferent father, he must have yearned for attention and been willing to go to almost any lengths to receive it."

"And what about the importance of your mother, Jon?" Lucy asked softly. "How has her loss effected your life?"

I was momentarily startled by this question. The whole to-do surrounding my mother had been tucked away in the back of my mind. Although the fear of the previous Sunday was gone, I was still not comfortable pursuing this long-avoided topic. It was just too new to me.

"Lucy," I said, "I'm really sorry about what happened last weekend. I've always been embarrassed by my mother's condition."

She interrupted me here. "It must have been so hard for you, Jon. Children can be so cruel. If you told the truth, who knows what a rough time they might have shown you."

"But it's more than that. You can't imagine what it was like for me." Suddenly, I was eager to tell all and my words, bottled up for so long, came pouring out. "Before Father sent her away, for the last year or so, she was increasingly irrational. It was really scary for me. There was one time when we went to the market together, just the two of us. After shopping, she headed off in the opposite direction from home. I told her to go the other way. I pulled at her arm. I screamed at her. And she just stared at me with that uncomprehending expression she would get, as if nothing was the matter. She just insisted on going the wrong way. Finally, I sat down on the curb and started to cry. Luckily for me, a neighbor came along and was somehow able to get her going in the right direction. I was accustomed to look to my mother for stability and care, but she began to behave so erratically. In the end, she might not even recognize me or might be oblivious to my presence. She could be busy in the kitchen, singing to herself cheerfully, and turn to me saying 'Could you tell Johnny that his lunch is ready?' How is an eleven-year-old boy supposed to respond to that? But even since then, I can hardly bear to visit her at the sanitarium. I know she is ill, that her state has no bearing on her feelings toward me but to face her blank stare, the lack of acknowledgment, it still makes me feel like an abandoned child. I feel so ashamed." I stared down at the grey stone, unable to face her.

Lucy took my hand and squeezed it gently. It took a moment for her touch to penetrate the emotional cloud that hung over me. I let out a sigh and raised my downcast eyes. My head could have weighed a ton.

"How terrible for you," she said. "And for your father. And for your mother, too, of course." She held my eyes in a long, earnest look. "Don't worry, Jon, your secret is safe with me. We can talk about it as much or as little as you like."

I took another deep breath and managed an appreciative, if pained, smile. "What I really want to know is how you felt when I ran off last Sunday. You must have been mortified."

"I was stunned at first. I surely did not anticipate so much emotion. Nor did I expect you to disappear so suddenly. But, if you've been holding these feelings inside for so long, it's not surprising they would cause some disruption when finally revealed. And I hope you won't take it as too vain to add that I fully expected you to show up again." She flashed her mischievous little smile at this suggestion that she might be anything other than a properly modest young lady.

"Thank you," I was in awe of Lucy's compassion and understanding. "I'm so glad to have finally confided in you."

"You should understand, Jon, that it's a relief for me as well. For a couple of weeks, you had been acting as if you weren't sure if you liked me. But, I couldn't help believing that you did and that, for some reason, you were uncomfortable with it. Frankly, I was rather perplexed by you. Last Sunday, you told me the source of your discomfort. At least that offered the possibility that we could talk about it and find some resolution together." She paused, looking far out into the blue sky.

"You know," I said, looking up as if I might find some distant object of her gaze, "for years I was sure that anyone knowing the truth would want nothing to do with me. I spun such an elaborate web of deceit. Last week, I was driven by the sense that the only way to forestall your rejection of me was to make a precipitous departure myself. It is no small comfort to have spoken freely and to find that you are still here."

"What about Jones? At dinner with your father, he seemed to understand what was going on."

"Jones is different. He and I have spent so much time together that it would be impossible for him not to know the truth. He loves to tease but is never too hard on me when it comes to my mother. But at the same time, he's not the sort of person who would be sympathetic about my childhood trauma. Like my father, he thinks I should have gotten over it by now. So we've had a tacit agreement to avoid the topic."

Lucy did not immediately reply and, after a moment, reached up and stroked my forehead as if she could brush away the furrows of agitated thought. "Anyway," she said, "maybe that's enough for today. I think we'll have lots of time in the weeks ahead for you to tell me more, if that's what you decide to do. Besides, your hot dog is getting cold."

I looked down at my half-eaten lunch. "Well there's nothing like a cold hot dog," I replied, lifting it to my mouth. Lucy had finished hers while we talked and now sipped on her sarsparilla.

"I hope you'll get to come down here sometime in the summer." Lucy demonstrated the same conversation-directing skill that her mother had employed so ably at dinner. "The water is so nice on a hot day. Always a bit cool. And crystal clear. The only problem really is that about half the town can be out here on a Sunday afternoon."

"Well, I'll look forward to the opportunity to come back for a swim, preferably in your company." I finished off the last of the hot dog. In the distance, two boys dragged a soggy kite from the lake. I could not hear their voices, but their posture showed that they were no longer very happy.

Lucy saw me watching them and laughed. "Boys. Their pleasures are so simple and can be so simply dashed. But, don't worry, your afternoon is just beginning." Her smile was at its most beguiling.

"Oh? And what do you mean by that?" I looked around, back toward the amusement park and trolley, across to the ball fields, out over the lake and the surrounding woods. I held up my hands in a questioning shrug.

She laughed again. Standing up, she said, "Come on. I want to show you one of my favorite places around the lake."

I followed as she led the way toward the southwestern end of the park. As we approached the woods at the park's edge, I saw a narrow track continuing on. Lucy led the way since the path was mostly obscured by a cover of red and yellow maple leaves which soon crunched and crackled under our footsteps. Although the woods were thick, the lack of foliage gave a clear view down to the edge of the lake. Bright sunlight reflected up from its ripples and through the branches. At one point, as the path curved closer to the lake, Lucy stopped and said, "the going gets a tad rougher for the next little bit," and, hoisting her wide-flaring skirt a couple of inches off the ground, she struck out toward the west, uphill and away from the shore. Grasping the hem with one hand, she avoided branches with the other, never allowing one to snap back on me but holding each until I had taken it in turn. The lords of fashion have long decreed that men, unlike women, should be able to move about unencumbered by their clothing. With both hands free, I felt I was better equipped to take the lead but, considering Lucy's political views as well as her easy familiarity with the terrain, I did not dare suggest it. My companion moved like an experienced hiker. Lucy nimbly skirted the edge of a muddy area along the way. She skipped effortlessly over a rotting tree trunk that crossed the path. A ridge of soft orange fungus crumpled under her footsteps. Finally, we came to a small hillock, which we climbed, finding at the top a rocky escarpment left, no doubt, by the same glacier that eons ago had dug out the lake. Lucy now let go of her skirt and bounded easily up the rocks. I followed less certainly behind.

"You never told me you were part frontiers woman, part mountain goat," I said as we reached the top. She took my hand and led me a few steps further to a smooth hollow that millennia of wind and rain had worn into the rock.

"This is where I like to sit," she said.

The view here was fabulous. The climb up the hillside and rocks had taken us almost to the top of the trees which sloped down toward the lake below us. Enough leaves had fallen so we could see across the width of the lake to the brightly colored hills on the other side. The water glistened and we watched a few small boats with white sails bobbing in the distance. Far off, a trail of thick, grey steam followed the Lady of the Lake to the south.

"What a spot!" I exclaimed. "I'm surprised there aren't more people up here enjoying this view."

"Well," she said, "as you noticed, we're a bit off the beaten track, even the unbeaten track. Occasionally some children find their way up here, but rarely their parents. It is beautiful. I am always reminded of the lines from P. Hamilton Myers' poem *Ensenore*: 'And where, in many a shaded dell, the viewless echoes love to dwell.' They made us all memorize it in grade school."

Lucy took my hand and we sat down atop the crisp leaves that lined the hollow. They crumbled under our weight, giving off a dank, musty odor.

"And is there an echo?" I asked.

"No, not really. You can find out for yourself if you like."

"I think I'd prefer to enjoy the quiet. So, tell me, is this where you take all the boys?"

"It sure is! As schoolgirls, Eleanor Grant and I would come up here often, and in our bold imaginations we would be joined by Lancelot or Ivanhoe and later on by Mr. Rochester or Mr. Darcy. Ah, the affairs we had in this place. They were truly scandalous."

We sat for a moment in silence, enjoying the tranquillity, the gentle breeze, the beauty all around us. I looked at Lucy and found her eyes smiling sweetly into mine. The brilliant autumn sunshine glistened upon the lighter strands of her hair, brightly framing her radiant smile. I felt compelled to speak.

"Lucy, I'm really having such a great day. I--" but before I could finish, she interrupted.

"You really talk too much, Jon. I must find a way to shut you up on occasion," and leaning toward me she placed her lips gently over my own.

Thrilled, this time I was ready to receive and return her affections. Still, I moved cautiously at first, kissing her so softly that our lips barely touched, as if any more deliberate movement might break the spell. We held that tender kiss for a while until, with a barely audible murmur, she reached around my back to pull me toward her. We kissed more ardently now and I moved closer, taking her in my arms.

Holding her firmly with my left hand, I lifted up my right and caressed her hair, as soft and exciting to my touch as for weeks it had been to my eyes. Her hands reached up to my shoulders, clutching me in turn. Gently, my lips moved from hers across her face, resting and nibbling at that tender spot where cheek and neck converge. Following the length of her hair, my hand moved slowly across her shoulder and down her side, barely brushing against the exquisite curve of her breast.

"Oh, Jon," her voice came softly as if a part of our embrace, "don't be so shy." She took my hand in hers and placed it over her breast, pressing her lips more strongly against my own. As we kissed, I fumbled with the buttons of her lace bodice, finally getting the top three open, just enough to reveal the arc of her bosom curving down to her small pink nipples. I bent over and buried my head in the shadowy softness between her breasts. She sighed languorously, tightening her grip on my shoulders. I nuzzled around her bosom, my tongue darting here and there, my lips closing from time to time on her now hardened nipples. Her hands gently but insistently explored my body, running over my chest and stomach, lingering over my thighs, and glancing, as if in passing, over the swelling concealed in my pants. It was now my turn to emit a sigh, deeper than hers, almost a moan. With this encouragement, Lucy's fingers skipped tantalizingly again over my inner thighs and played with the buttons of my pants. Practically overcome, I reached up, drawing her lips once again to mine, kissing her more deeply and with a passion I had not known before. Then she pulled her lips away and whispered in my ear "I love you, Jon Parker," her sweet voice as much as her delicate touch a source of delight. In dreamy ecstasy, I cradled her head on my shoulder and once again softly caressed her hair. "And I love you, Lucy Gerin," was my earnest reply.

We lay there quietly for a time, gently holding each other, cooling off under the autumn breeze, feeling as if the rock beneath us was love's softest mattress. Finally, she pulled her head up from my shoulder and looked into my eyes, her smile, once so strange, now most familiar. I opened my mouth to speak but she held her index finger up to her lips for a moment and then leaned forward to tenderly kiss me again. Faintly, in the distance, we heard the high whistle of the Lady of the Lake as if it too were celebrating our happiness.

Chapter Fifteen

~

Sunday, October 27, 1901

"A word with you, Parker," was all Joe Whelan had said, beckoning me to follow him to a table in the far corner of O'Malley's.

"What's on your mind?" I asked as we sat down.

Whelan leaned toward me in a classic conspiratorial posture and spoke in a low voice. "We're having a meeting. Sunday night. It's to reflect on and commemorate the life of Czolgosz. I thought you might be interested."

I pondered the implication of these words. What did it mean that Whelan thought I "might be interested" in such a meeting? Was he recruiting me to the cause?

"I have to be frank with you, Whelan," I said. "I'm not looking to join any political movements. That's just not where my interests lie at this time."

A soft laugh rumbled in his throat. "No one's looking to sign you up, Parker. Folks are pretty uneasy about newcomers showing up these days. If you want to come along, it will be as my guest and you will only be admitted because I vouch for you. I just figured that, given your interest in Czolgosz, you might want to hear what his comrades are saying. It could be an eye-opener for you since there's by no means unanimity of opinion among us."

"I appreciate your invitation," I replied. "Is it ok if I think about it?"

"Sure, Parker. How about if I give you the address. If you decide you'd like to come, you can just show up."

"Okay," I said. Whelan pulled a stubby pencil and a scrap of paper from his pocket and scrawled out an address. As he got up to leave, I looked around and was relieved to see that no one seemed to have taken note of our private conversation.

I was surprised by Whelan's invitation. Joe had not spoken directly to me of Czolgosz since our tense debate in the scruffy field by the Osborne factory. In the saloon, he had treated me with greater respect and more seriously, an attitude that had rubbed off on O'Malley's other patrons. The jabs and teasing that so rankled Jones and me were a thing of the past. Thanks to Whelan, a new discomfort loomed ahead. I shook my head uneasily as I contemplated the prospect that he placed before me.

~

On the night in question, a cold, hard rain made for a particularly unpleasant evening. I walked up North Street away from downtown, pulling my coat close around me. Whelan's easygoing and engaging character encouraged trust in his seemingly innocuous invitation. Yet I could not help but worry about entering into the forbidding realm of secret anarchist meetings. My greatest fear was that, like Alice stepping through the looking glass, I would arrive at tonight's meeting to find myself in a world turned upside down, a chaotic universe in which familiar values and conventions did not hold.

I considered heading back to the boarding house, using the nasty weather as an excuse to myself or others. But, as was so often the case, it was inertia, aided now by a healthy dose of curiosity, that compelled me forward and I trudged on, doing my best to avoid the puddles that filled the hollows of Auburn's uneven sidewalks. I was drawn on by the hope that I might learn something from these anarchists which would resolve my questions about Czolgosz once and for all. My overcoat, unable to shed the rainwater quickly enough, grew heavy on my shoulders. I regretted my decision to leave my umbrella in the stand in Mrs. T's foyer. It was Sunday evening and most people could stay indoors, sheltered from the relentless downpour. Only a few unfortunates were making their way through town. Their forms were like dark specters, walking huddled up against the sides of buildings, taking respite in recessed doorways, and finding the occasional relief that an extended awning might bring.

Walking west now down Seymour Street, increasingly appreciative of my sturdy boots, I turned north again onto Washington and entered an unfamiliar neighborhood. The houses here were two or three stories tall, built close together with little more than narrow alleyways running between them. Most seemed to be divided into flats or apartments. Only a faint glow of gaslight emerged from behind thin curtains drawn across the windows against the cool autumn night. This was a different world than the familiar neighborhood of bright middle-class homes that lined North Street. It was nearly impossible to make out the house numbers in the blurry, wet night, but I soon found the address that Whelan had indicated. Walking around to the back, I descended a short stairway leading down to a basement entrance. Now in utter darkness, I knocked uncertainly at the door before me.

"What do you seek?" demanded a low voice from within.

"Liberty," I felt a bit silly providing the secret password that Whelan had said would serve to open the door tonight and this night only. I heard a bolt turn. The door swung open on squeaky hinges. A short, wiry man with a gray beard squinted at me in the darkness and gestured for me to come in. I followed him through a narrow hallway to a well-lit room in which eight or ten people were already seated, talking in twos or threes.

"You can hang your coat over there." The man gestured toward some pegs protruding from the far wall. "Then take any seat you like. We go by first names only here. Mine is James." He did not offer me his hand.

"Jon," I replied attempting a friendly smile. I shook the surface water off my coat and hung it up, keeping my hat with me. Looking around the room, I found an empty seat next to two women who conversed almost inaudibly. To my left, beyond the women, a coal-burning stove blasted out heat. Several small gas lamps were mounted on the walls casting their yellow light across the room.

"Feel free to warm yourself by the stove," the woman to my left said. "We're still waiting on one more. I'm Kate, by the way." She was a young woman, probably not much older than I, but in these few words displayed the serene and confident demeanor of someone of far greater age.

"Thank you. I think I will." After introducing myself to Kate and her companion, I walked over and crouched low to take in the warmth of the hot iron. When the heat had penetrated my damp clothing, I stood up and returned to my seat. One man watched me carefully as I went by. I don't think it was my imagination that detected a look of dark suspicion in his eyes.

"That feels a lot better," I said as I sat down again next to Kate. "It sure is a nasty night out there."

"We working folk don't take much mind of the weather," the women to Kate's left said sharply. "The rich can wait for the weather to change and think about which coat or hat to wear and enjoy the comfort of their fancy carriages. We just have to go where necessity sends us, no delay permitted, and hope we can dry off when we get there."

"Oh, hush, Helen. Leave him be," Kate said to her companion. She turned to me with a conciliatory smile. "The heat feels good now, but in half an hour it will be stifling in here. You'll be wishing you were back out in the rain."

"Oh, I can't imagine that," I brushed a few droplets from the brim of my hat.

"Wait and see. At the least you'll be wanting to take off that nice jacket. You should know that you are at a bit of a disadvantage here. Pretty much everyone knows who you are. We had to approve of Joe's extending the invitation. You, in turn, probably know few, if any, of us. Your presence here is not uncontroversial. As you can see, your attire alone marks you as a different sort." I looked around the room and realized that she was right. For the most part, the others wore the garb of working men and women, plain clothes, often rumpled looking, frayed, or soiled. My clean white cuffs and collar and my dark, wool suit, even disheveled as they were from the rain, marked me as a denizen of a different class. Only Kate and one other woman wore crisp, fresh-looking clothing of the sort that most laboring women would don only for Sunday services, if at all. Of course, it was Sunday, and for this group, many atheists no doubt among them, tonight's meeting might be the closest thing they had to a formal occasion.

I heard the outer door open again and recognized the voice of Joe Whelan in the hallway speaking to James. Joe appeared in the room already shucking off his sopping wet coat. He looked around the room smiling and nodding at one person or another. With the appearance of a familiar face I recognized how uncomfortable I had felt before. As hard as it was to arrive alone at a meeting of complete strangers, that difficulty was compounded by the realization of the chasm that separated me from my companions. I had never before sat among a group of individuals whose life experiences were likely so different from my own. I could almost hear Jones' voice telling me that in my obsession with evaluating Czolgosz' sanity I had lost my own. After all, who could say I was really safe among these people? In the popular imagination, at least, I had just walked into a den of assassins. More realistically, I wondered, what would be the damage to my reputation and to my career if Dr. Gerin or Warden Mead learned that I was attending secret anarchist meetings in the dead of night?

I never thought I'd be happy to see Whelan's face, but I felt genuine relief when he crossed the room and, placing his left hand on my shoulder, offered his right in greeting.

"Sorry I'm late," he said. "I hope this pack of ne'er-do-wells is treating you all right," Whelan grinned.

"I'm doing just fine now that I'm drying off," I said. "Kate here has been very friendly." Whelan said hello to Kate. He was about to take the seat to my right when the suspicious looking man appeared by his side.

"Whelan, we need to talk," he said gruffly in an unmistakable Italian accent. "And you too." His hand jabbed roughly toward Kate who rose and, shrugging her shoulders in resignation, followed the two men to the hallway. A chorus of whispered conversations around the room marked their departure.

I could hear the tense tones of muffled argument from the hall, but could not make out the words. One phrase only, "I don't like it, I tell ya, I don't like it," came clear as a bell in the Italian's unmistakable accent. Finally, the three of them returned, the Italian casting a scowl in my direction as he stalked over to the stove. He crouched down, opened the heavy iron doors, and rubbed his hands before the flames, his thick knuckles glowing red in the firelight. Joe and Kate took their seats on either side of me. I tried to imagine they were my personal bodyguard, but I did not feel very safe.

"I believe everyone is here so we can get underway." To my surprise, the voice came from my left, from Kate. For some reason, I had assumed that Whelan would be the leader of this group, as self-assured and articulate as he was, but the meeting was in Kate's hands.

"Vincent, please take your seat," Kate addressed the Italian in a soft but commanding tone. He glared at her for a moment before trudging over to his chair. She then turned her attention to the rest of the group. "Although some wanted to meet on Tuesday, we agreed that we could all more readily manage it tonight. No one can predict what conditions will be like in the aftermath of the execution. In recognition of the somberness of the occasion, we are departing from our usual practice. We have agreed that we will have no debate tonight. We will have plenty of time for that in the future. Tonight we will, each in turn, make our own statement, whether praising or defaming, on the life and legacy of Leon Czolgosz. Let's start with Helen and move around the circle to my left."

Helen, seated next to Kate, was the woman I had already met. She was older, probably in her late 30s, her hair just starting to gray. Lines around her lips and near the corners of her eyes hinted at the approach of middle age. A plump woman, her figure was concealed in a shapeless maroon dress and heavy brown sweater.

"Good evening." Helen's voice cracked with nervous tension. "I'm a little uncomfortable being the first to speak." She cleared her throat once, and again. "No matter how you look at it, our assembly tonight has been called to honor Leon Czolgosz. I have trouble agreeing with that purpose since I just don't think he is deserving of any praise. I thought about staying home this evening but want to stand in solidarity with you all. And here I am." She smiled weakly at her compatriots. "So here's my question: can it be for a moment entertained by any rational mind that Czolgosz' act was helpful to the cause of progress? McKinley was no bloody tyrant; he was a tool. It was in the interest of capital to bamboozle the people into accepting him as their representative, but the fact remains that the people viewed McKinley as their leader, and they supported the atrocious acts of his administration.

"They are the ones with whom a Czolgosz must reckon, and it is folly to imagine they will ever see any point in murder. And now, McKinley has become a saint. He exerts a more insidious influence than if he had been allowed to live and continue his puppet rule. The forces of government have profited from Czolgosz' deed and have in every way increased their strength to oppress the good working people of this land. No good has come of it." She smiled grimly at this conclusion and looked down at her lap. None returned her smile. I was shocked by her summary condemnation of Leon. I had fully expected these anarchists to applaud his deed.

The circle continued on the far side of the coal-burner with a young man, hardly more than a teenager, dressed in workman's overalls. His fingertips were a dull, orange color, reflecting no doubt his daily contact with some wood stain or leather treatment that left a mark no amount of scrubbing could remove. His tousled blond hair and peach-fuzz side burns exaggerated his youthfulness. "I don't really have much to say except that, like Helen, I can't bring myself to approve of his act--I don't believe in violence except in defense of human life and liberty, and I don't think the death of McKinley has served that purpose. The way I see it, we're the ones who denounce the murderous acts of government. We can't just close our eyes when violence is done by individuals in the name of anarchy. But, at the same time, I don't see that anyone can call Czolgosz a criminal. If his deed was a crime, the cause of it was ten times more a crime. That's it, I guess." He rubbed his hands on his thighs and looked around as if not quite sure how to relinquish the floor.

"Well put, Ross." These words of approval came, not surprisingly, from Joe Whelan on my right.

The next man to speak was James. He had taken a seat opposite me, and I could now see he was somewhat older than I had perceived in the darkness of the hallway. His hands were scarred from a lifetime of labor, his face creased and worn looking.

"There's been this question bandied about as to whether this Czolgosz is an anarchist or not. And there's a lot of confusion about just what makes a man an anarchist in the first place. The way I see it, a warm-blooded being who can comprehend the passions which are vented occasionally in a violent, desperate deed, may be an anarchist. And a person who philosophically sits back in a chair and demonstrates that human life is sacred and that even a king has a life which should be respected may be an anarchist. A person may celebrate or denounce the act of an assassin and be an anarchist or not an anarchist. The only thing that makes you an anarchist is if you believe in and work toward the abolition of the state and of the trusts. Does Leon Czolgosz hold to those beliefs? We may never know for sure, but from his few words reported by the newspapers it seems to me that he does."

The next woman was young and nicely dressed. As she spoke, I had that gnawing feeling that comes when someone looks familiar but you can't quite figure out why.

"Is Czolgosz an anarchist?" she asked rhetorically. "What does it matter? If he was a conscious slave rising in revolt against a master, the act gratifies me. His reported words signify that he knows what his position in society has been. And why is there such a to do by the slaves in all quarters about the death of a master? Do they not realize their condition? Why should the lives of our masters be of more importance to us than ours are to them? They treat us like animals, kill us off as if we were flies. And we seem to take them at their word that we are no more than vermin. A rebellious working man who deliberately gives his life in exchange for that of a worthless hulk of a ruler has such a very modest estimate of his own value. Despite this, I recognize and accept the act as the supreme protest of a brave and generous heart against the curse of government." How Czolgosz would have thrilled to make the acquaintance of such a sympathetic young woman.

As she finished, I realized where I had seen her before. This was the young woman of whom I'd had only a fleeting glimpse--Viroqua was her name--who Lucy had waved to on the street car on the day of our first luncheon together. Lucy's childhood friend, no common laborer but a school teacher, was an anarchist!

I felt a drop of perspiration run down my forehead and realized that Kate was correct: the room had gotten uncomfortably hot. Others had already loosened their vests or collars. The next speaker was the man who had glared at me earlier. Whelan leaned over and whispered that this was Vincent Maggio, recently arrived in Auburn from that hotbed of anarchism, Paterson, New Jersey. Maggio's voice had the same gruff quality as his gaze. The beads of sweat dotting his brow only accentuated his rough appearance.

"I've been traveling around some since the assassination and I can tell you, this is the worst crisis we anarchists have faced. We won't soon forget the massacre that threatened us the night of

McKinley's death. Across the country, hundreds of us were imprisoned or put under the watchful eye of blue-bellied hang dogs. Half the Bible-bangers and all the bourgeois pencil pushers in America busied themselves inflaming the passions of the people against us. All along, the millionaire thieves were pulling the strings. They could count on the faithful cooperation of the police and the militia. The ass who was becoming President had not yet brayed, as he did before Congress a few weeks later, but there was little doubt that he too would do as his masters required. But, even though government's vice tightens around us, in the end we will be the stronger, our ranks swelled by those who have seen how much the actions of just one man can accomplish." Maggio paused, his fierce, glowering gaze surveyed the room. His words and bearing would convince any politician that the fear of the anarchists was justified. Maggio spoke as powerfully as Joe Whelan but without the smooth delivery.

"But mark my words, Czolgosz is not an anarchist. If there are comrades who still dislike hearing that said, I must remind them of the facts. I've been to Cleveland and Buffalo and talked to others who've traveled around. No one has ever acknowledged Czolgosz to be associated with any anarchist group. Don't forget that an anarchist society will never be built from solitary efforts. From the get go, it depends utterly on the self-organization of the people."

I listened to these speeches with great interest. I was surprised and a bit confounded by the range of opinions expressed by these anarchists. Like most Americans I had believed, ignorantly, I now realized, that anarchism was a uniform philosophy and that its adherents would have a high level of agreement on its basic points. Something as profoundly important as a Presidential assassination would surely be an expression of the fundamental tenets of anarchism. Those gathered this evening, while somewhat perplexed by the mystery of Leon Czolgosz, expressed divergent views on anarchist methodology, various interpretations of assassination as a tactic, and even differed on the very definition of an anarchist.

The anarchist perspective on the relative value of Czolgosz' life versus McKinley's was particularly unsettling. Although America claimed to equalize the worth of its citizens through the promise that any one of them might "grow up to be president," by the time they reached adulthood class division ruled supreme. Who ever looked at a factory worker straining with a heavy load or at a farmhand stooped over from a long day in the field and declared optimistically that this laborer might someday attain our highest political office? The fact remained that society viewed William McKinley as the great man and that Leon Czolgosz, prior to his deed, was no one. For the earth-shaking blow he had struck, he was now generally reviled. Yet, these anarchists managed to turn all that on its head, deploring McKinley and holding Czolgosz in esteem. In the society envisioned by those assembled, no one would need the hope of growing up to be president for inspiration. All would be equal political and economic actors. My companions this evening viewed Czolgosz, in his presumed adherence to that vision of equality, as McKinley's superior.

I watched the wall-mounted gas lamps cast our shadows before us in the dimly lit room--a strange reversal of Plato's cave-- as if accentuating the uncertainty of these theories on Czolgosz that each anarchist in turn laid out before the conclave. A small man whose hunched up posture and ink-stained fingers gave him the look of a clerk rather than a laborer was next. He turned slightly to his right and spoke almost directly to Maggio. "It makes no difference to me whether Czolgosz was an anarchist or not, but we ought to hold only one opinion among us about his deed. It was an act of protest and rebellion inspired by high motives and manly courage. Despite your calculations and protests, these facts remain."

The woman on his left seemed lost in thought. When at last she spoke her voice choked up with emotion, her words barely audible. "We see in Czolgosz a man who took the sorrows and sufferings of the great mass of working people to heart. He carried his burden silently until he could no longer endure it, and he offered up his life. It is easier for him to face death than to live in the midst of slaves and tyrants. Not being either, he is alone in the world. Who can conceive of greater suffering?" There was such a tone of sorrow in her voice, her sympathy and respect for Czolgosz unmistakable.

Now, it was Joe Whelan's turn to speak.

He reached into his back pocket and pulled out a rumpled newspaper. His heavy coat had protected it from the downpour. "I thought it would be worthwhile to reflect on the inspiration for Leon Czolgosz' act. Our detractors have seized upon the article about Emma Goldman that was found in Czolgosz' pocket and declared that we anarchists are responsible for his deed. We in turn have been quick to deny this association, our instinct for self-preservation rising to the fore. We have contended convincingly and truthfully that Goldman's speech that night argued against acts of violence. But you don't need to look very far for evidence to substantiate our enemies' case. At times like these, it is fortunate they do not pay much attention to our literature. I've been rummaging through my stack of old papers and came upon an issue of _Free Society_ dated June 2 of this year. It is very likely an issue that was read by Czolgosz. In it, you will find an interesting article by Miss Goldman on the Bresci matter."

He spread the paper open on his lap, lifted it up and began to read. "'Bresci has paid the penalty of his crime. And a crime indeed it was to have loved one's kind, to have felt the existing wrongs in the world, and to have dared to strike a blow at organized authority. He has lived and died true to himself and the world will have to learn that while one Bresci is killed, hundreds are born ready to lay down their lives to free mankind from tyranny, power, ignorance, and poverty.'"

"I remember that article," Kate murmured. Others nodded, sharing her recollection.

"Yes, I'm sure we all read it," Whelan replied. "Who can say how such words might impress a young man like Leon Czolgosz, a man who was already inspired by hearing Emma in person." I alone could appreciate the accuracy of Joe's assessment. Such evidence of Goldman's respect for Bresci could easily have encouraged Leon along his path in hopes of garnering her admiration in his turn.

As Joe finished, all eyes turned to his left, to me. Whelan had explained to me the nature of the event and that I did not have to speak if I preferred not to. I cleared my throat nervously.

"It's awkward for me to come here tonight as a stranger, particularly as someone who does not share your beliefs. I'm not really sure what I have to offer. Mostly, I came just to listen. And to learn. I am aware of the risk you take in inviting an unknown person here, especially these days, just as I am sure you understand the risk I take in joining you. I appreciate being given the opportunity to attend this evening's meeting." I looked around the room at the serious faces surrounding me. Maggio's frown was particularly severe, as if more than agreeing that my presence was inappropriate. The look in his eyes made me glad that my prepared statement followed a conservative approach. I did not want to say anything that might arouse any antipathy or even stir too much interest. The information I had about Czolgosz, if revealed, would earn me the complete respect and attention of those assembled. But, I reminded myself, neither their respect nor their attention had brought me here. It was bold enough for me to speak at all. I must remain circumspect. Prior to my last session with Leon, I might not even have attended this meeting. If I had, I would not have opened my mouth. It was strange to realize that I had in the end formed some kind of bond with him, one that made me want to hear what his comrades had to say about him, a bond that emboldened me to add my own words to the mix.

Kate smiled at me, encouraging me to go on. I smiled back appreciatively and continued. "Since I wouldn't feel right adding my opinion to yours, I have decided to recite the final stanza from

the popular poem 'The Man With the Hoe' by Edwin Markham. I
am sure that most of you are familiar with it." Markham's poem
was inspired by viewing the famous painting of the French artist
Millet. A great sensation a couple of years earlier, it had been
reprinted in newspapers across the country, hailed as a harsh
indictment of conditions in American society. I took the small
piece of paper from my pocket on which I had written down
Markham's verse, never quite believing that I would dare to read
it. Adopting a somewhat somber tone, I delivered the lines to the
awaiting anarchists.

> O masters, lords and rulers in all lands,
> How will the Future reckon with this Man?
> How answer his brute question in that hour
> When whirlwinds and rebellion shake the world?
> How will it be with kingdoms and with kings--
> With those who shaped him to the thing he is--
> When this dumb Terror shall reply to God
> After the silence of the centuries?

The assembled men and women listened in respectful
silence. Several nodded in recognition of Markham's words. Even
Maggio's expression had noticeably softened by the time I finished.

Now we had come full circle and Kate took the floor. She
stood up--none of the others had left their seats when speaking--
and looked slowly around the room. As she rose up beside me, my
attention was drawn at once to her strong voice and confident
bearing. "You have each spoken well for yourself," she said.
"Although we are not all in agreement on the matter at hand, I am
sure that our shared commitment to the philosophy of our
movement is not diminished. As the convener of tonight's
assembly, I have taken the liberty of giving myself the final word,
and of preparing my remarks with that in mind. In so doing, I
recognize that in keeping with the anarchist emphasis on
individual autonomy I can speak for no one but myself." She

paused and looked slowly around the room. All eyes were fixed
upon her as she began her speech.

"We who are drawn together by a common ideal can not
permit the impending execution of Leon Czolgosz to pass in
silence. Silence would shame the great cause whose first seeds were
sown in the red blood of its advocates and martyrs. Rebellion is
thought in action. Thought that does not produce action is like a
tree that puts forth blossoms but bears no fruit." There could be no
teapot socialists in Kate's movement.

Kate went on to describe Czolgosz in terms much like
those Joe Whelan had used two weeks earlier. She was an
impressive young woman, confident and well-spoken. Whether or
not she was self-educated as Joe Whelan professed to be, she was
clearly well-educated. Her elocution and her bearing contradicted
all of the expectations associated with working-class figures.
Though, for all I knew, she might be the product of an upper-class
household drawn to the idealistic proclamations of anarchism. Her
demeanor was that of the classic rebel, a Spartacus or Patrick
Henry, whose pride rose up nobly against the severity of
oppression. Listening to her, even more so than with Whelan, I
could no longer believe that anarchists were by definition
deranged. Misguided, perhaps. Extreme in their beliefs to the point
of fanaticism, maybe. But I could not give credence to the notion
that the woman standing beside me was any more delusional than I
was.

Slight in build, Kate nonetheless exuded a certain force.
She held herself erect, shoulders back, head high, in an almost
stately manner--an ironic term to associate with a professed enemy
of the state. Her eyes flashed with conviction as they moved from
face to face, ensuring the full attention of her audience. I
wondered what it would be like to befriend such a woman. If I were
not already in love with Lucy Gerin, might I succumb to the
evident charms of this ardent anarchist who I had only just met? I
smiled to myself as I considered the upheaval such a liaison would
cause.

"All hail Leon Czolgosz," Kate concluded, raising her arms dramatically, "Know this: though they may soon take his life, the spirit that spoke at Buffalo will not die. That spirit kindled new fires that now smolder in the minds of a multitude. Government is doomed. On the far hills of our vision gleam the lights of social revolution. We do not weep for its dead, we only learn a lesson from their fortitude that drives more nails into the coffin of authority.

"Liberty's martyrs are crowned with the flowers of hope. Tyrants are crowned with despair: they are dead for all time. But our dead speak the language of the living and are resurrected in each generation, to live in new beauty and strength."

There was no sound either of approval or disavowal as Kate completed her eulogy–it could be described as nothing less-- only a respectful hush in character oddly like the moment of silence a minister might call for at church, or at a funeral. Kate lowered her eyes to the floor and returned to her seat.

"This is a weighty moment for us and for all of our comrades around the country," she said as she looked up again. "Perhaps we may have some cause for rejoicing before too long. In any event, we agreed that we would conduct no other business this evening, so let us bid one another a good night." As the others fell back to their separate conversations and prepared to depart, Kate turned to me.

"Thank you for your contribution," she said. "I know it could not have been very comfortable for you to be here tonight."

"Thanks. I confess that at first I could think only of how long it would be until the meeting was over. But I have to say it was an educational experience. Your words were quite eloquent. It never occurred to me someone might look at Czolgosz in such a light."

In fact, I was troubled by my reaction to the anarchists' testimonials. Far from the sense of danger and uncertainty that had accompanied me into the meeting, I now found myself questioning how comfortable I had finally felt among these people. Other than for the glare of Vincent Maggio, this group had been unthreatening and congenial, no more menacing than the evening crowd at O'Malley's. And they were engaged with questions that had become deeply important to me. I remembered Dr. Gerin's words when I had first broached the subject of interviewing Czolgosz. He expressed concern that I might be "infected" by exposure to the anarchist. What would he think of me now, exchanging friendly words with a radical like Kate. Much as Gerin chided his daughter for her political views, Lucy would be well out of her depth in this gathering. But I, a political novice at best, had fit in and made my contribution. I did not feel infected, only more open in my thinking. Yet somehow that very openness was worrisome, as if it might comprise a first step on a slippery slope toward an ignominious future.

One thing had been established for a certainty that night. Joe Whelan had been correct. Unless there was someone with a detailed knowledge of Leon's activities last summer, there could be no one better qualified to judge his standing as an anarchist than me. These committed radicals had been fishing, seeking to apply a shifting definition of anarchist to their scant knowledge of the assassin. I alone knew in some detail how Leon viewed his deed and understood something of the philosophy, principles, and life experiences that had set him down his chosen path.

Kate accepted my compliment graciously. "Oh, there will be a long debate ahead among the anarchist faithful as to whether he was a hero or a madman. I am sure you would be welcome to continue to participate." She looked intently into my eyes conveying the sincerity of her words. There was no hint of feminine charm in her gaze, only the power of her convictions.

"Doc here is kind of shy, Kate," Whelan had been listening by my side and knew when to butt in. "Give him plenty of room for reflection and he'll do the right thing. I guarantee you. He may not join the movement but he'll serve the cause of justice all right." Whelan patted me on the back.

Kate smiled at Joe's testimonial to my character. "I don't mean to push you, Jon," she said. "Really, I don't. I hope you haven't taken it that way."

"No," I replied. "I am happy to receive both your invitation and your encouragement. After all, that's how Joe got me here tonight."

"I have enjoyed meeting you," she said, "and I do hope our paths cross again." And she turned to look for her coat.

"C'mon, Doc. Let's get out of here." Whelan and I fetched our damp overcoats and, bidding a few brief farewells, went out into the October evening.

Fortunately, the rain had departed, leaving behind a clear night sky and a monotonous chorus of droplets falling from rooftops and tree limbs. Joe walked with me as far as North Street. He explained to me that Vincent Maggio was the brother of Antonio Maggio, who was being held in New Mexico for allegedly conspiring with Czolgosz. Someone had accused Antonio, an itinerant musician, of predicting that McKinley would be assassinated before October 1 of this year. There were supposed to be a number of corroborating witnesses. Maggio had told Whelan that although his brother was a serious anarchist he was also a loudmouth given to exaggeration. He may have shot off his mouth about McKinley, but it was unlikely he was acquainted with Czolgosz. Vincent Maggio was one of a number of anarchists who'd fled Paterson in recent weeks. Things had gotten pretty hot for them there with government agents looking for links to both Bresci and Czolgosz.

"He argued pretty strongly against your presence here this evening," Joe concluded.

"And, I suppose, with good reason," I replied. Given his concern for both his brother's well-being and his own, Vincent Maggio had plenty of reason for his simmering anger and suspicious attitude.

We continued to talk for a few minutes at the corner of North and Seymour. Whelan was concerned to hear about the

testing of the electric chair and how much pain Czolgosz might
experience. For all of the bravado about electrocution being a
humane method of killing, it was well-known that if not done right
it could be horribly painful for the convict and gruesome to behold.
Joe thought the designated means of execution made a mockery of
McKinley's much celebrated words at the time he was shot: "Go
easy on him, boys" he was reported to have said of Czolgosz. I
assured Whelan that the equipment was being thoroughly tested.
As to the reliability of those tests, I had no knowledge. Whelan
and I shook our heads, lamenting Leon's unfortunate fate, and,
with that, went our separate ways.

~

Arriving home, I ascended the few steps to the front porch
and found Archie Baxter sitting in one of the maple rockers,
smoking his pipe. Despite the dampness in the air, it was not too
cold and Baxter sat bareheaded in his shirt sleeves. The dim light
emerging from the house cast a pale glow on his high forehead,
exaggerating the early signs of a receding hairline.

"Take a load off, Parker." He pointed to the empty rocker
opposite his. "It's a lovely evening for porch sitting."

"Thanks," I said, "I think I will join you. Have you been
out here long?" I eased down into the rocking chair, lifting my feet
up against the porch's wooden railing, and leaned back. Stretching
out, I allowed my fingers to relax across the curve of the smoothly
finished arms of the chair.

"I just got home a few minutes ago and plopped myself
down. It's such a beautiful evening. I figured my dinner was already
cold and could wait a little longer." He tamped a fresh wad of
tobacco down into his pipe. "How's your day been?"

"Not too bad. I got some reading done. Took a Sunday
afternoon nap." I dared not tell him of the meeting with the
anarchists.

"Any news of the assassin?"

"Not really. I haven't been to the prison today." I was not about to give the reporter the slightest indication that I'd had any contact with Czolgosz. "They say he eats his three squares daily, jaws it up with the keepers from time to time, and sleeps a lot. Not a particularly interesting prisoner, really. What about you, what have you been thinking about, sitting out here by your lonesome?"

"Actually, I'm doing a bit of star-gazing and brushing up on my mythology. See that constellation up there?" He pointed to the right of the porch, toward the northeast. I looked up and saw that, as was often the case after a storm, the stars were shining with an unusual brilliance. It was a clear night and the moon had not yet risen. The leafless tree branches did little to obscure the constellations. The sky had the glossy depth of the blackest obsidian, through which the stars blazed brightly.

"Which one do you mean? Perseus? Cassiopeia?"

"I should have figured you'd know your stuff. Perseus is the one I've had my sights on. I've been thinking about the constellations and how the Greeks could put their heroes up in the sky thousands of years ago and we still recognize them today. Perseus slew a king, just like Czolgosz did, and he's immortalized for it. A hundred years from now, Czolgosz, Bresci, and that whole sordid pack of anarchist assassins will be long forgotten. Regicide just ain't what it used to be."

"No, I don't suppose it is." I smiled to myself, realizing the implications of Baxter's analogy, the full significance of which he could not possibly understand. After all, Perseus had slain King Polydectes to free his mother Danae and be reunited with her after his many adventures. Baxter would never know the extent to which Czolgosz' longing for his own lost mother had shaped the course of his life.

"But there's more," Baxter went on. "So the sky's all filled up with all of the Greek heroes and the monsters they fought. That leaves us the earth for our monuments, like those you'll find to Washington or Lincoln. Now few people in Greece will ever see the Washington Monument, but, while I've never been across the

Atlantic, I've seen their monument to Perseus up there in the sky.
That's some powerful memorializing they did all those centuries
ago."

"Archie, I didn't know you were such a philosopher. But
let me stretch your analogy a bit. We've got two slain monarchs,
Polydectes and McKinley. Polydectes is pretty well forgotten. In
fact, he's only remembered as part of the story of his slayer. In the
case of Czolgosz, it could well be the opposite. He may only be
remembered in the context of the life of McKinley. After all, few
today know many details about the acting career of John Wilkes
Booth or much at all about Guiteau." I was enjoying this abstract
discussion, a pleasant palliative to the intense thoughts and
emotions of the evening's earlier event. "And here's another irony
connecting back to your thoughts on monuments. Perseus used the
Medusa's head to turn the king to stone, stone that is long since
crumbled away and forgotten. Czolgosz' deed will result in
memorials to McKinley in the form of stone statues that could
keep the President's memory alive for centuries. Of course, it
would strengthen the recollection of future generations if his face
also winds up on the hundred-dollar bill." I smiled at making this
suggestion.

"Aw, with all of McKinley's pals on Wall Street, it'll have
to be the five-hundred." Archie laughed out loud at his hyperbole.
"But here's another thing I've been thinking about," he adopted a
more serious air while taking a slow pull on his freshly lit pipe. The
sweet aroma of the tobacco was soothing. "The Greeks have the
sky for their heroes. We have the earth for ours. So what's left for
the Indians who we took the land from in the first place? Where's
their memorial? Only in names, like Lake Owasco here or Lake
Cayuga to the west or Manhattan for that matter."

"There are the occasional memorials, like the obelisk to
Chief Logan here in Auburn." I offered.

"But that's built by the white man, not the red."

"Well, if you put it that way, the names are given by the white man as well. The places are named for who was here before." I was puzzled by this odd turn in the discussion.

"Yeah, there seems to be an inclination when it comes to naming things for trying to recapture what we drove out or killed off." He stabbed at the air with his pipe stem for emphasis. "Of course, Indian names are not the only ones we've got around here. It's kind of ironic, isn't it? We're looking up at the sky for evidence of the ancient Greeks when in fact we're sitting halfway between towns called Syracuse and Ithaca."

"Or, if you look a little bit more to the east in New York geography, you could say we are between Troy and Ithaca, like Odysseus, searching to find the way home." I rocked back lazily, fully enjoying this now utterly nonsensical conversation.

"Parker," Baxter said with a grin, "I think I've met my match. From now on I'll stick to constellations and leave such arcane musings to those more educated than myself." He raised his pipe in salute to my supposed erudition.

"In that case," I doffed my hat in return, "I think I'll follow Odysseus' example and head for the bath. If only, like him, I had my old nursemaid here to scrub my back."

Baxter shook his head and chuckled. "Buddy, at your age you should be wanting someone a bit more interesting than a nursemaid to do that kind of scrubbing. And I'm not thinking of Mrs. Thomas either!"

"I suppose you are right," I replied, "although you don't really know the capabilities of my nursemaid and I don't imagine that you have fully explored Mrs. Thomas' charms either." I made a vain attempt to muster up a provocative leer appropriate to my insinuations. Then, I raised my hat to him again, and, like old Odysseus bidding farewell to the ghost of the seer Tiresias, I left the reporter to his pipe and to the stars.

My bath and the odd conversation with Baxter were relaxing, but that night I slept fitfully, waking often. My unconscious mind offered no images to accompany those awakenings, only a vague feeling of unease. Neither the comfort of sleep nor the diversion of dreams would shelter me from the grim anticipation of coming events.

Chapter Sixteen

~

October 29, 1901

Dr. Gerin and I were the first to arrive. We stood by the door and surveyed the execution chamber. On my previous, more casual visit, the chair had seemed innocuous enough. In today's context, it took on frightful proportions. The rows of seats set out along the far wall for the witnesses insistently forced our attention back to the execution device. The electric chair is not a pretty sight, nor is its application. Some, Doctors MacDonald and Spitzka for instance, praise it as a great step forward in modern methods. To me, it is more like an implement for medieval torture or an instrument of the Spanish Inquisition. "The throne," the keepers called it. In Hell, it might well have served as one. The heavy wooden legs were bolted firmly to the floor. Thick leather straps would bind the arms, chest, waist, and calves of the victim. A mask-like strap would wrap around his face, securing the head to which a demonic looking electric coil was adhered to deliver the lethal current. A thick black wire to the leg completed the loop. Although of short duration, the execution itself could seem endless as 1800 volts were released for seven seconds, reduced to 300 volts for 23 seconds, raised again to 1800 for four seconds, and finally reduced to 300 volts for the remainder of a minute. That conscious life was obliterated in those first few seconds was undeniable to anyone who had the misfortune to witness such an event. Yet, uncannily, some survived to require a second dose.

Gerin had told me how electrocution was established as New York State's official means of execution as an outgrowth of the intense rivalry between electricity pioneers Thomas Edison and

George Westinghouse. In the 1880s, Edison was pushing for direct current while Westinghouse was committed to the more powerful alternating current. Aware of a growing public concern about the suffering caused by hanging, Edison promoted electrocution as a more humane replacement. But his real agenda was to cause the public to fear the alternating current that it used. Edison's associates traveled around New York demonstrating the power of the electric chair on various animals. Crowds would gather to watch in fascination and horror as a stray dog or old nag was sacrificed on the device, crude re-enactments of some primitive religious rite. Meanwhile, Edison's operatives in the State Legislature succeeded in getting electrocution adopted by New York for all executions. In defense of his preferred power system, Westinghouse refused to sell the needed generators to the state. Edison gladly provided them. Then, continuing this strange battle, Westinghouse began funding the appeals of convicts sentenced to the chair, spending the staggering sum of two-hundred thousand dollars toward that end.

Although Edison won the battle for establishing electrocution, Westinghouse ultimately won the war over electricity generation. It was his system that came into general use. Surely this was one of the few times that Edison has lost such a struggle. The first electrocution was that of William Kemmler, the notorious Buffalo axe murderer. Amid great public fanfare and after several delays, the execution took place right here in Auburn Prison in this very room back in 1890. In the decade since, dozens of convicts had been subject to this grisly new form of capital punishment. For some, today's execution would be just one more number added to the list, but for most Americans it would bring the electric chair even greater notoriety.

My thoughts were interrupted by the arrival of Superintendent of Prison Cornelius Collins. Gerin introduced us and asked Collins how his night had gone.

"I had a bit of sleep," he replied, "but the prisoner kept me busy. It turns out he had quite a lot to say in the end. First he told me some story about meeting a boy in Chicago who gave him money for his trip to Buffalo. I sensed he might at last let something slip out about his co-conspirators and asked him to tell me more about the money. He said 'what money?' and denied he'd ever mentioned it. He's a strange one, playing with me like that as if it didn't matter that he was going to die in a few hours. I can't decide if he's got a fiendishly bright mind or if he's just blundering from one idea to another."

"I don't think anyone will ever know," Gerin answered, carefully avoiding my gaze.

"He sounded delusional." Collins replied.

"I don't think so," Gerin said. "Doctor Fowler and his associates in Buffalo found him sane enough for trial. I've seen a draft of Fowler's report. They found no sign of degeneracy. I haven't seen anything here to contradict that. Nothing that can't be explained by his confinement and his knowledge of the impending execution."

"Well, be that as it may," Collins continued, "after that, I tried to trip him up so he would incriminate Emma Goldman. Then, I brought up the name of this woman Amy, who was mentioned in one of the letters sent to him at the prison. But he denied having any association with either of them. Then, I asked him why he killed McKinley and he said it was because he'd asked the President for a job and was not given one. That's certainly the first anyone's heard of that. What a ridiculous story! Finally, he even denied having wrapped his hand in a handkerchief at the Exposition despite the witnesses who'd seen it and the evidence of the handkerchief itself. He's a tough nut all right." Collins shook his head. "Anyway, it's time for me to get going and make sure the guards have him ready. The witnesses are pretty much all gathered in the administration building with the warden and should be down in a few minutes."

As Collins turned and left the execution chamber, Gerin raised an eyebrow at me quizzically. But before either of us could say anything, we were interrupted by the arrival of Davis, the prison electrician, and Thayer, the former warden of Dannaemora prison who was serving as assistant electrician for the execution. After a perfunctory greeting, they set about making a final check on the equipment.

The electricians were followed moments later by the ceremonious arrival of Carlos MacDonald and Anthony Spitzka, both prominent doctors affiliated with New York hospitals and medical schools. They entered the room as if they owned it and, in some ways, they did. MacDonald, former President of the State Commission on Lunacy, was considered a top expert on crime and insanity. He was a fierce proponent of electrocution. He shared with Dr. Gerin the status of official physician for this as for prior executions. While MacDonald conferred with Dr. Gerin, Spitzka stood nearby, checking and rechecking his pocket watch. Jonesy slipped in, hoping Gerin would not notice his late arrival, and installed himself quietly by my side. Several other physicians and state officials entered, greeting each other in hushed tones. Reverend Herrick, the prison chaplain, arrived next. Head down, he avoided the others and stood to one side mumbling prayers. Father Fudzinski, the Polish priest who had come all the way from Buffalo's Corpus Christi Church in the hope that Czolgosz would take the sacrament, was conspicuously absent.

Something about the somber mood of the execution chamber drew my thoughts back to the atmosphere that had filled our house on the day my mother was taken away to the asylum. What a sad and confusing day that was. I had tried hard to swallow my fear as I watched Father trudge up the stairs to fetch Mother for her departure. I sat on the divan by myself with the uncertain knowledge that she was going away. No moment in my life has felt more lonely, despite the presence of my grandfather and my Aunt Ruth who waited with me in the living room. I could see the worry in their eyes, feel the tension in the room, their whispered conversation reminding me of my grandmother's funeral a few years earlier. Two big men, bigger than my father and thus large indeed from my twelve year-old's perspective, were waiting to take

Mother to a "special home." There, she would be cared for in hopes that she would get well and return someday. "When will she come home?" I had asked. Someday, probably not too soon was Father's uneasy reply. We'll have to see. But don't worry, we will visit her often. He could provide neither the reassurance nor the comfort I craved. My anxiety was stoked by the sense that he knew little more of my mother's future than I did. Grandpa and Aunt Ruth cast worried looks my way. Ruth came over and sat by my side. She patted my hand reassuringly. I managed a weak smile in return.

Finally, Father appeared at the top of the stairs, leading Mother by the hand. She wore her emerald-green velvet dress and matching hat, as if she might be going to a church function. We all stood up as she descended the stairway. My eyes searched hers for any hint of recognition, in vain hope of a parting smile. But she stared fixedly ahead, eyes slightly downcast as if not quite ready to meet those of the two men waiting in the foyer. Did she understand where she was going? Was she capable of understanding? Later, Father said he thought that, somewhere deep within the fog that had descended over her conscious mind, she was aware of her destination and perhaps even happy about it.

I yearned to run forward and throw my arms around her waist, to plead with her not to leave. I held myself back. The recent months of her increasing unresponsiveness were too familiar, too painful. The attendants each took one of her arms, firmly but gently it appeared, and escorted her out the door to the waiting carriage. Father followed carrying Mother's small valise. He returned a few moments later, his face impassive, his hands empty. Grandfather approached him and took Father's hands within both of his own. "It's for the best, Jon," was all he said. "It's for the best." Aunt Ruth nodded in agreement. She sat down beside me and I collapsed into her arms. She could feel the sob shudder through me as I silently struggled to hold back my tears.

My thoughts were brought back to the present by Dr. Gerin beckoning Jones and me to meet the several physicians in

attendance. They were Dr. Ely of Binghamton, Dr. Howe of
Phelps, Dr. Trowbridge of Buffalo, Dr. Wolff of Rochester and Dr.
Huntley of Buffalo. All veterans, no doubt, of many a death watch.

Looking around at the assembled men, I realized that I
could not truly divine their inner feelings. Were they distressed to
be called to such an event? Only the prison staff and the official
physicians--Gerin, MacDonald, and Spitzka--seemed fully at their
ease. Was I the only one whose stomach churned? Were other
shoulders tense with nervous anticipation? Was mine the common
reaction of one called to witness a fellow human's death? Or was it
the impending demise of a man who had so unexpectedly become
almost a friend that made my hands tremble? The room, large
enough really, felt small with all these men crowded in. I took a
deep breath. The air seemed stale and thin. I longed for fresh air,
and sunshine. If only I could slip, unseen, from this chamber of
death.

Everyone seemed relieved when Warden Mead finally
arrived, followed by Collins. The Superintendent addressed the
group of us.

"You are here to witness the legal death of Leon F.
Czolgosz. I desire that you keep your seats and absolute silence in
the death chamber no matter what may transpire. There are plenty
of guards and prison officials to maintain order and to attend to
the proper details." We were all seated now except for Gerin and
MacDonald and Warden Mead. Also at the ready were the
electricians. Davis entered the small control room containing the
switchboard and, at a signal from Thayer, closed the circuit.
Current coursed through a panel of electric lights, flooding the
chamber with brilliant illumination and dramatically
demonstrating the power of the device. I cringed at the sight.

It was Warden Mead's turn to give a signal and Principal
Keeper Tupper swung open the heavy steel door leading to the
outer corridor. Two guards marched Czolgosz into the room with
two other guards behind as Tupper led the way. Leon's eyes were
blank, his shoulders slumped. He seemed oblivious, at first, to the

people gathered to witness his execution. The guards led the prisoner to the chair, set him down, and secured the straps around him. They jerked him roughly this way and that, binding him tight. Leon sat upright. Now, his eyes slowly scanned the execution chamber, pausing for only the briefest moment as they passed my own. A shiver ran up my spine. I nodded, imperceptibly I hoped, acknowledging the strange bond that had formed between us. Then I cringed again as Superintendent Collins approached Czolgosz, now bound firmly into the electric chair. Collins had a reputation for toughness, for not mincing words whether with prisoners, guards, or state legislators. He bent slightly, attempting to fix his eyes on the prisoner's.

Leon maintained an expression of stoic indifference, calm and self-possessed. He was masking, I was sure, a variety of feelings within--anger, insolence, fear. Only the whiteness appearing at the edge of his knuckles as he tightly gripped the wooden arms of the chair revealed his underlying tenseness. As the guards attached the head and leg electrodes, Collins asked solemnly "Do you have anything else to say for yourself?"

Leon's tone was more matter-of-fact than defiant as he answered. "I killed the President because he was the enemy of the good people--the good working people. I am not sorry for my crime." Then he fell silent and the guards began to adjust the face strap. His voice came once more through the leather mask, "I am awfully sorry I could not see my father." These were his last words. Despite a lifetime of distance and brutality, it was a boy's abiding love for his father that was expressed in the end. Feeling dizzy and still sick to my stomach, I glanced over Spitzka's shoulder at his again open pocket watch. It read 7:12, the second hand moving silently yet inexorably around the watch face. I looked nervously about the room. All eyes were on Collins. I struggled against an urge to rush over to Leon in desperate hope of comforting him in his final moment.

The Superintendent stepped back. Warden Mead signaled to Davis through the window of the little control room. The

electrician immediately turned the lever. The circuit was closed
and the deadly current coursed through Leon's body. His eyes
opened wide but suddenly empty. His entire body was wracked
with spasms exploding through every muscle. As the technician
moderated the flow of electricity over the long minute,
consciousness and sensation were absolutely abolished. The only
motion was that forced on Leon's lifeless form by the powerful
current. A nauseating smell of burnt flesh and a thin wisp of gray
smoke drifted through the air toward the assembled witnesses.
Leon Czolgosz was gone.

My own stomach was in upheaval, my head spinning. Just
then Carlos MacDonald, great expert on electrocutions, after
momentarily examining Leon's inert cadaver, insisted that another
contact be made, this time of 1800 volts for an additional 5
seconds. As the electrician moved back toward the switch, I knew
I could not take any more. Heedless of the distinguished men
around me, I fled from the room. I ran down the dimly lit corridors
like a man possessed. A keeper or two looked at me in wonder as I
flew past. In the morning's quiet, the sound of my gasping breath
pounded against my ears. Finally, I arrived at the clinic privy just in
time to lean over and lose the remainder of last night's dinner
within. Panting from the shock and exertion, I splashed cool water
over my face and sat for a moment to catch my breath. Try as I
might, I could not tear my thoughts away from the execution
chamber and the vision of Leon's agonizing death convulsion.
Gathering myself up, I walked quickly through the Administration
Building and out the front gate of the prison. I would deal with Dr.
Gerin and the consequences of my flight later.

~

Outside the prison a throng of reporters and curiosity
seekers were gathered. The buzz of dozens of conversations filled
the air, like the chatter of morning songbirds. As I emerged, several
reporters turned in my direction, hungry for any news from within

the prison. They struggled to place my face as that of a prison official or guard. Fortunately, Archie Baxter was there.

"He don't know nothing," he called out to his fellows. "He's just a kid medical student up from New York."

His word evidently carried some weight with his colleagues--the New York Telegram, after all, was a big paper--and they turned back to their chitchat. Relieved to be safe from the eager reporters, I pulled my coat collar up around my neck and began walking down State Street, reflexively heading away from the prison and its attendants. As I passed the southern guard tower, the noise of the crowd began to fall away into the distance. With the prison receding behind me, the world seemed to open up in my path.

It was just dawn and a gray haze hung over Auburn. I stopped for a moment and stared back at the grim walls of the prison, uncertain where to go or what to do with myself. I looked up at the statue of Copper John that rose from the top of the Administration Building, the early morning sunlight giving it a bright, ethereal sheen. Supposedly representing a colonial soldier in the fight for justice and freedom, in my mind's eye it now took the form of Leon Czolgosz striding forward as he never would again. I reminded myself that no one would build a statue of Czolgosz and that Copper John, whoever he may have been in reality, represented those who had fought to allow us to elect presidents, not to assassinate them.

In the distance, the shrill whistle of a departing train broke the morning stillness. And then, out of the ensuing silence, a soft voice called out my own name, "Jon, Jon Parker!" Turning, I saw Lucy Gerin walking up State Street toward me.

"Lucy!" I called out in reply. I ran to her, collapsing into her arms, and burst into tears. "It was so horrible."

"I know," was all she said, stroking my cheek and rocking me gently.

After a moment, I came to my senses a bit. "But what are you doing here? Why are you out at such an early hour?" Her work day did not start until 9, and usually, I knew, she would first be rising at this hour.

"I had a feeling that someone might need me this morning. Come on. Let's get away from this place." Taking me by the elbow, she led me toward downtown and away from the prison. I did not look back.

Arm in arm, we walked on in silence. A muffled sob occasionally broke from my lips and she would squeeze my arm more firmly, leading me east toward the sunrise and south across town. We passed only a few workmen trudging on reluctant legs toward their morning shifts. I paid no attention to our path until finally I realized we were entering Fort Hill Cemetery.

"I don't know if we should be here," I protested. "They'll be coming with the body."

"Not where we're going," she said, "and not for hours anyway. Don't forget they have an autopsy to perform." Sullenly, I reflected on my very conspicuous absence from that event, which was possibly already underway.

She led me up the path toward the Logan Monument and then to the hill opposite where the lawn was broken not by grave stones but only by a few large elm trees. The grass was still damp, it's sheen removed by our encroaching footsteps. Supposedly, we were now atop the ancient Indian fortification from which the Cayugas might have defended themselves from attack. But if such a fort had ever existed, no sign of it remained except for the hill itself. Nonetheless, in the still morning, surrounded by only the dead, it seemed like the safest place on earth.

Finding a relatively dry spot, Lucy drew me down beside her onto the dewy turf. "No one will bother us here," she said putting her arms around me. We sat there quietly for a while as the sky grew bright, holding each other gently, tenderly, far different from the passion that had gripped us on our last encounter.

I turned my head slightly, brushed a stray hair behind her ear, and kissed her cheek. "Thank you," was all I could say. She just smiled back at me.

Eventually, my body calmed and my thoughts returned to the reality that I was, effectively, a working man shirking his job.

"Your father will kill me," I said.

"And me too, if he knew. But you'll get off easy. Sure, he'll lecture you and instruct you that you can't be a good physician until you can casually watch a man fried to a crisp. He'll fault you for getting emotionally involved with Leon, but underneath he'll understand that you are not actually preparing to be a prison doctor, and that an alienist might do well to have a heart."

We sat for a few moments again in silence. I rested my head on her shoulder. In the distance I could hear the clang of the streetcar bell on Genesee Street. The red and yellow leaves around us glistened brightly in the now fully risen sun. The cemetery remained still. The headstones marching out into the distance did so without the accompaniment of human sound or movement. Only the occasional note of a robin or the rustle of a squirrel brought a sense of life to the scene.

I looked across the way at the monument to Chief Logan rising above the small hills. "Who is there to mourn for Logan?" I murmured, surprised to hear my own voice. I thought about the contrast between Logan and Czolgosz. Logan had killed many men and was honored with this huge monument. Czolgosz had killed only one. His grave would be barely marked, his body devoured by the strong sulfuric acid the Superintendent had ordered poured over the casket to stave off souvenir hunting grave robbers. Logan was esteemed by the victorious invaders of his land because he did not take up arms to resist their encroachments. Only when his own family was killed did he respond. But was Leon so different? Did he not take up arms only when he saw government and business combining to take the lives of working men? I wondered if future generations might look at him differently, might even raise an obelisk to his memory. Somehow, I doubted it.

Lucy gently stroked my hair. "Logan thought he would have no mourners yet they built him a monument," she said. "Leon too will have many to grieve for him. You are not the only one."

I looked up at her reassuring smile and nodded in agreement. She was right. Today, Leon might be reviled, misunderstood. Yet, ultimately, he would not be forgotten. Collins had said he would destroy the many letters and packages sent to Leon at the prison. But that would not be enough. The electric chair had burnt the life out of his body. The sulfuric acid would complete the task of obliterating his lifeless corpse. But neither could erase Leon's legacy. Leon was a murderer, that much was for sure. And for that, after the current fashion, justice had today been served. Whether he was more than a murderer, history would decide.

Chapter Seventeen

~

Epilog: A Sunday in Auburn

I sat impatiently through the church service, unable to fend off my boredom and restlessness. Although it was the same sequence of liturgy, hymn, and psalm as other Sundays, this time Reverend Rosengrant seemed to drone on endlessly. Ministers often stretched their imagery, but the Reverend's comparison of our raking up the fall leaves to Christ's gathering of souls was a bit much to take. I stretched and stifled a yawn. The hard, stiff back of the pew reminded me of my old friend Thaddeus Jones' comment that Jesus had invented Christianity to serve the interests of his fellow carpenters. "There's been plenty of work building pews over the past two millennia," Jones had said.

As I drummed my fingers rhythmically on my thighs, Lucy looked at me with an expression that was a mixture of curiosity and annoyance. She knew I was less than happy with her insistence on more frequent church attendance in recent years, especially as the children got older. Weekends like this one, when we were visiting her parents, necessitated the Sunday morning ritual. It's not so much that I don't believe in God, although I have remained pretty much of an agnostic. It's just that I have long felt that one's own religious practice is best done in the privacy of inner thought and through service to mankind. My twist on the phrase "practice what you preach" has been to emphasize the practice and dispense entirely with the preaching. But, theological considerations aside, with my busy work schedule I've preferred to treat Sunday as the day to sleep in.

But this morning felt no more like a time for sleeping than it did for sitting. I felt energized and tense and could readily have spent my time splitting fire wood, hiking around the shores of Lake Owasco, or playing tag until the kids ran out of steam. Anything but sitting on a hard bench mumbling prayers. The only time I'd fully enjoyed a church service had been on our wedding day the summer after I was graduated from medical school. Held in this same building, the service as conducted by Reverend Fitch, Rosengrant's predecessor, had seemed positively uplifting. In fact, its actual content was little different from today's, but was transformed by the emotional significance of the occasion.

At last, the seemingly interminable service came to a close, and we walked outside into the brisk autumn morning. My nervous energy had not subsided, and I grabbed the children up into my arms as we emerged from the church. After swinging them around to ensure they would retain none of the peaceful feeling of the service, I asked Lucy if she would mind taking them back to her parents' house so I could go for a walk. She was intimately aware of my various moods and their requisite remedies and immediately agreed. The Gerins were too absorbed in enjoying the children to give much thought to my departure. They did not see their two grandchildren nearly as often as they would have liked despite the convenient train schedule from Auburn to New York City. This unusual weekend visit--not even a holiday--was a great treat for them.

Taking their leave, I walked at a quick pace through the familiar byways of downtown Auburn. My spirit was renewed as I focused my energy in rapid strides and let my eyes roam from the cloud-streaked sky to the leaf-strewn yards to the various homes and businesses. Most of these had not changed since my original sojourn there a decade ago. I was not aware of my steps leading me toward Fort Hill Cemetery. Only when its grassy meadow and large stone entryway loomed ahead did it finally sink in. This very day, October 29, 1911, was the tenth anniversary of the execution of Leon Czolgosz. No doubt unconscious awareness of that fact and the knowledge of all that Leon had meant to me was, in some manner, the source of this morning's unease.

Entering the cemetery, I headed first to the hilltop where Lucy had taken me for refuge after the execution. Oddly, I had not been back since. Standing on the leaf-covered sward, I scanned the surrounding hillsides. The cemetery did not seem to have changed, embodying as it ought the permanence of death. Surely there were a few more graves, perhaps many more, but they neither added to nor detracted from the abiding tranquility. Logan Monument still reached skyward past leafless limbs as if mocking the aspirations of those interred around it. The refrain from Ecclesiastes--all is vanity--came to mind, ironically in contemplation of this memorial to the heathen chieftain. I thought back to the vanity of my own youth, the belief that at a tender age I might resolve great mysteries that had challenged generations, a conceit that had met its demise along with Leon Czolgosz ten years ago this day.

For something had changed in me after the execution, after I fell in love. My work with Czolgosz revealed to me the complexity of human affairs, the limits of what one person can accomplish, and the sad hubris of those who would take it upon themselves to change the world. As 1901 drew to a close, I had found myself a humbler, more focused man, with less grandiose ambition, and thereby better able to face the challenges ahead. This transformation could be detected that very day of the execution when I returned to my room at Mrs. Thomas' boarding house and once more opened the abridged edition of William James' *Principles of Psychology*, the "Jimmy" as it was called. No longer did it appear as an unwelcome obstacle to my happiness or as a bothersome chore. I picked up the book as one would a hammer, a saw, or any tool necessary to get a job done. I applied myself to it as I would to the remainder of medical school, reaching past my lingering adolescence to understand that the tasks of life are not necessarily synonymous with life itself. Thus it was that I became a doctor, and, I believe, a good one.

Criminal psychology turned out to be a passing fancy. I still sought to apply psychiatric insight to the lives of so-called normal, well-adjusted people, perhaps helping some avoid the path to madness or at least, I hoped, reducing their emotional distress. Although I have not sought training in psychoanalysis, I did travel to Clark University to attend Sigmund Freud's 1909 lectures. Freud's methods and theories have remained important to me, and I have incorporated free association and dream analysis into my work. I came to understand that my sessions with Czolgosz had been a rudimentary form of psychotherapy in Bernheim's sense of the therapeutic use of the doctor-patient relationship applied in an intimate and informal context. As I began my practice, I was able increasingly to separate my own childhood trauma and my concern for the fate of my mother from my day-to-day role as an alienist. As I came to outgrow the resentment and hurt that stemmed from the twelve year-old's sense of abandonment, I began to visit my mother more often, at times taking Lucy with me. Eventually, a warm commingling of sympathy and sorrow arose for Mother, her tragic decline, and her pitiable existence.

But the events of 1901 had their greatest impact on the course of my researches and writing. Setting criminal psychology aside, I pursued an investigation of the social dimensions of mental health, examining the differing tensions, opportunities, and expectations that articulated themselves across class lines, paying particular attention to the psychological condition of the laboring masses. In doing so, I made the acquaintance of a number of the reformers and muckraking journalists who came to define the era, many of whom shared my outspoken opposition to the death penalty. Eventually, I achieved my small place among them with the publication of my still controversial monograph, *Society and Sanity*, which argued in part that the achievement of many of the goals of the labor movement would ease the psychological pressures on the working class, thereby diminishing a variety of deviant maladjustments and improving social conditions. Unemployment, overwork, congestion of population, child labor, and a hundred economic factors exacerbate the problems of living for the poor and are often contributing factors in mental illness. Reforms are needed which make for the betterment of those upon whom the stress of living falls heaviest. This will save many from mental illness, I'd maintained.

Pulling myself back to the reality of 1911 Auburn, I cast a slight salute toward Chief Logan, and walked west toward the prison section of the cemetery. Over the years, my many visits to Auburn were absorbed by family concerns. It had never before occurred to me to visit Leon's grave. Only ten years later, few of Auburn's citizens would have considered the burial site of the once infamous assassin to be among their town's attractions. And indeed, it hardly could have been, since Leon's grave, like those surrounding it, was simple and barely marked. It was questionable the extent to which it could fairly be called his "final resting place," considering the harsh treatment given to his lifeless corpse at burial. I still shuddered to imagine that moment.

Standing at the grave side, I thought about the impact of the assassination over the past decade. I wondered about the dreams of the anarchists of 1901 and whether they still held so idealistically to them today. Despite the desperate hopes of Czolgosz and the bravado of Joe Whelan, little had changed politically. President Taft was more like McKinley than Roosevelt. Anarchism, which had achieved a height of notoriety in 1901, was today given much less thought. The anarchists were still regularly reviled whenever there was serious labor unrest. But given the lack of additional high-profile assassinations over the years, the specter of terror, once so vivid in people's minds, was no longer prominent.

I reflected on my lack of ease at church and Leon's own distaste for religion. "If any priest comes to my execution, I'll swear at him, you see if I don't," he had said, his voice still fresh in my memory. His rejection of the idea that a divinity or priesthood might bring justice to the working class haunts me to this day. Rarely could I find a plausible rationale to disagree with him. During the Sunday church service, my own thoughts would occasionally turn to that wonderful passage from Micah: "What does the Lord require of you but to do justly, love mercy, and walk humbly with thy God?" How many of our Senators and Captains of Industry, ardent church-goers all, had ever contemplated these words, ever taken them to heart? Precious few, I was sure.

As I turned finally to depart, I noticed a woman standing quite still under a leafless oak tree not far away. She wore a long, dark dress, common enough in those days to not necessarily signify a mourner. As still as the graven cherubim nearby, she gazed across the grassy field dotted with headstones. Paying her no mind, I started on my way home. But, as I turned my back to her, a flash of recognition froze me in my tracks. I did a quick about face and walked across the prison graveyard toward her.

Seeing me approach, she began to walk at a fast pace in the opposite direction.

"Miss Goldman," I called after her, "he was somewhat infatuated with you, you know,"

"I beg your pardon?" She stopped and turned to face me with a quizzical expression. Her air was calm if cautious.

"Leon... Czolgosz, I mean. I guess he only met you on those few occasions, but you were his hero and the object of his deep admiration and affection."

Emma Goldman's eyes narrowed and she surveyed me even more carefully. Her thick eyeglasses did little to diminish the power of her gaze. "So, you are telling me not only that you knew him, he who was such a mystery to so many, but that, in addition, you feel compelled to visit his grave site and claim to speak of his innermost feelings?" Her tone was intense, challenging.

I realized I had better slow down. "I'm sorry. Let me introduce myself. I am Doctor Jonathan Parker of Brooklyn. In the fall of 1901 I was serving as a medical intern here at Auburn State Prison preparing for my studies in psychiatry. At that time I was able to become acquainted with Leon Czolgosz and, to an extent, gain his confidence. I met with him only briefly on several occasions. In agreeing to those meetings, he required a pledge of

silence from me, a pledge that I have only broken this very
moment in my enthusiasm at finding you here. Of course, I have
seen your picture in the newspaper and recognized you. I assume
that, like myself, you are here to mark the tenth anniversary of
Leon's passing."

Emma Goldman stared at me intently. "No one calls him
that. Leon. None were so familiar. The anarchists all knew him, at
first, as Nieman. To everyone else, he was Czolgosz, subject to its
many awkward pronunciations." She paused for a moment in
thought. "No, I can not believe that now, ten years later, they
would attempt to entrap me into self-incrimination in the
McKinley assassination. But such an effort would surely fail, since
my acquaintance with Czolgosz was no more than I have publicly
described on repeated occasions. Doctor Parker, I will take you at
your word and happily make your acquaintance."

"Miss Goldman, I would be very pleased to discuss our
common acquaintance with the man whose life was taken this day
ten years ago. May I buy you lunch?"

"No, thank you. I'm not really hungry. But a cup of tea
would be nice."

"All right. Let's walk over to the Osborne House. They
have a pleasant dining room. It should be quiet this time of day."

We began walking down Fort Street in the direction of
downtown. As we turned up Genesee Street, passing the imposing
post office and courthouse buildings, we talked about our medical
experiences, mine as a physician, hers as a nurse. We discovered a
few mutual acquaintances such as Lincoln Steffens and Jane
Addams. We laughed to acknowledge that neither of us were
familiar with the other's writings. Goldman was interested to hear
how Lucy had moved to New York in 1902 to work at a settlement
house, not far from where I volunteered at an immigrant health
clinic. She nodded in agreement when I spoke of meeting Slavic
immigrants with the same reticent manner as Czolgosz, clearly a
cultural rather than a psychiatric condition. Goldman smiled on
learning that Lucy had completed her training in nursing and now

volunteered at Lillian Wald's settlement house on Henry Street. I myself could only take a few days a month to volunteer in general practice at a health clinic on Manhattan's Lower East Side. Goldman remarked that she had encountered few doctors who held any sense of obligation to society. She herself had spent countless hours tending to the needs of injured strikers and ailing comrades who had little access to medical treatment. We agreed on the great need for medical care for the working class and how small our own efforts seemed in comparison.

Emma Goldman was not a beautiful woman. She was, however, one of those rare women with whom a certain brilliancy of the intellect takes the place of mere prettiness. That is not to say her face was not attractive and charming. Her features were regular, and her eyes, which were large and fine, had the curious combination of brilliancy and softness rarely found in eyes of blue and gray. Her eyes displayed both those colors as she changed from one emotion to another. To call her pretty, though she really is a woman of charm, would be as much out of place as it would be to have called Daniel Webster handsome instead of brilliant.

As we neared the South Street intersection and the heart of town, I was aware of the scandal that might arise if we encountered any of my or the Gerins' acquaintances. It would be quite enough to be seen out with a woman other than my wife, even if my companion were not recognized as the infamous "High Priestess of the Anarchists" as the tabloids were wont to call her. Fortunately, we passed no one I knew and found the dining room of the Osborne to be all but empty at this odd hour. In a corner table, a lone fellow, most likely an out-of-town businessman, quietly enjoyed his lunch. Emma Goldman ordered her tea. I asked for a ham sandwich and a cup of coffee. Only now did it seem right to turn our conversation to the topic foremost on our minds, that which had brought us together in that unlikely corner of Fort Hill Cemetery that Sunday morning: Leon Czolgosz. Ten years had passed and I had discussed Leon's case, as I thought of it, with no one except Lucy. Though I respected his wish that I remain silent,

I had no doubt that Emma Goldman was the exception to this restriction. Still, I was uncertain.

"I want you to know at the outset," I told her, "that Leon asked me to hold all he revealed to me in strictest confidence, and to seal any record of our conversations until after my own death. But I am sure he would want me to talk to you. Still, I must ask that you, too, respect his wishes."

"Of course," she replied without hesitation. "I could offer Leon no protection or comfort while he was alive. At the least, I will do what I can for him now."

At those words, the sluice-gates of a decade of self-censorship were flung open, and I recounted in some detail the events of the fall of 1901. I described to her my initial awkward meeting with Czolgosz and my painstaking efforts to gain his trust, a trust which, under the circumstances, could never be fully granted. She nodded in understanding as I spoke of the difficulty in maintaining a view of Leon as a criminal or even as a patient when something in his manner called out for compassion and friendship. She seemed pleased by the tale of my encounters with anarchism, especially that one meeting that I had with such great trepidation attended at Joe Whelan's urging. She remarked that similar meetings were held across the country at the time. Goldman laughed to hear of my discomfort at being in a room surrounded by unfamiliar factory workers. Finally, a serious mood overtook us as I described the execution of Czolgosz and how I was moved by his words, his life, and his sacrifice. Therein, I explained, lay the foundation for the path my medical career had taken over the years. I had felt compelled to dedicate some portion of my own life to helping those who struggled against harsh conditions, those less fortunate than I, although more fortunate certainly than Leon.

I came to the end of my discourse, realizing I had monopolized the conversation. Chagrined, I apologized for not letting her get a word in edgewise.

"Not at all," Emma Goldman replied. "I am a great talker myself. You've held a lot within you for many years. The great adventure of discovery, which few have known so well, has had a lasting impact on your life. You are a fortunate man, Dr. Parker."

"Yes, I believe I am. Other than Teddy Roosevelt, I am probably the only man in America who could be said in some way to have benefitted from the McKinley assassination."

"Ah, but you exclude women from that benefit and thereby myself. Czolgosz' act caused me to reflect on the limits of my own courage and commitment. I know what you are about to say but you are wrong." She cut me off before I could reply. "People who stand on the plain cheer for one who has climbed the hillock. But from the hilltop you can see the mountain that remains to be climbed. Czolgosz sacrificed his life for his beliefs. As a result of his deed, I saw that the qualities I had admired most in the heroes of the past--the strength to stand and die alone--were lacking in myself. His act led me to a period of serious introspection followed by a renewed determination to steel my will to meet the exigencies of life, whatever they might be. After all, ultimately one may need more courage to live than to die. Dying is of the moment, but the claims of life are endless--a thousand petty things which tax one's strength and leave one too spent to meet the testing hour."

"Believe me," I replied, "for someone on death row as Leon was, dying is far more than a momentary affair."

Emma Goldman nodded, "Yes, I suppose it must be. All those weeks of waiting, of anticipation. That makes his act all the more courageous given that, in his premeditation, he must have considered the repercussions to himself. This is why Czolgosz has haunted my life over the past decade. In the early years, he would appear in my dreams, sometimes approaching me through a crowd, his eyes gleaming into mine. What would your Dr. Freud say to that?" I was not entirely surprised at her reference to the celebrated psychiatrist but she did not wait for a reply.

"At first, I could not overcome my sadness at his plight, my anger at the way my comrades deserted him. I could not decide which was more abhorrent to me: the capitalists' move to crack down on anarchists, which I expected, or the anarchists' rush to

disavow Leon's deed, which was a complete shock and
disillusionment to me. I felt that, compared to his courage, their
abandonment was an act of extreme cowardice. I rebuked and
consequently alienated many of my friends. I was outraged by the
notice in *Free Society* that warned against him. That he should be so
cruelly misjudged by the very people to whom he had come for
inspiration! Isaak, the editor at the time, felt that Nieman, as we
then knew him, was untrustworthy because of his talk about acts of
violence. After I challenged his decision to print the notice, he
agreed to put a retraction in the next issue. Unfortunately, it was
already too late. I've often wondered whether that eleventh-hour
rejection by those whom he'd hoped would be his comrades in
some way steeled Czolgosz' resolve to take such extreme action."

"You don't know how shocked most people would be by
your words," I replied. "it is not expected that anarchists might
disagree about such matters. The press paints you as holding to a
unified dogma of violence and terror. Of course, I have learned
differently. But what I am really most curious about are your direct
encounters with Czolgosz. Meeting you was, in his view, the pivotal
day of his life. Did you have any idea you had such an effect on
him?"

She slowly sipped her tea while considering this question.
"You would think that Emma Goldman meets so many people.
How can she take notice of one more so than another? And in
most cases you would be correct. But, with Czolgosz it was
different. The first time I met him was at one of my lectures. In
Cleveland. It was the spring of that fateful year, 1901. He asked me
for recommendations of books to read. He seemed so young, and so
ardent in his sincerity. I was surprised later to learn that he was 28,
only a few years younger than I was at the time, and that he'd
labored since childhood. His face impressed me with its odd
beauty, its sensitivity, the delicate pink complexion. Handsome
with his curly golden hair and large blue eyes. From that first
encounter, his remarkable face remained in my memory. It was
unforgettable, really.

"I met him again some weeks later when I was visiting the Isaaks in Chicago. Their house was the center of anarchist activities in the Midwest. I was getting ready to leave for the Rock Island station when this Nieman showed up at their door looking for me. He'd gone to the offices of *Free Society* and met Hippolyte Havel who brought him to see me. Nieman said he wanted to meet some of the radical leaders. I invited him to accompany me to the station. He rode with me on the el to the depot which gave us a little while to talk. He described his dissatisfaction with socialist groups in Cleveland and expressed his interest in joining the anarchists. At the station, I left him again with Hippolyte. That was the last I saw of him until I saw his picture in the newspaper after the assassination. I recognized him immediately. Although I only met him on those two brief occasions, he made a great impression upon me, both in his physical aspect and in his ardent interest in learning about anarchism."

"You impressed him just as much, if not more. He described you in truly glowing terms. They tried repeatedly to get him to incriminate you, both the District Attorney in Buffalo and the prison Superintendent in Auburn, but he maintained resolutely that he acted alone. Another man might have given in under the pressure, sought to sacrifice you to save himself."

"Yes, I know. The papers reported he broke down when brought to the prison and before his execution, but I never believed it. I fully appreciate the pains he took not to associate himself with me."

"You can rest assured he was thoroughly vigilant in that regard. Even after he had spoken quite frankly with me about most details of his life, he refused to acknowledge whether he had met with you or any other anarchists after that May lecture. He said he'd caused you enough trouble. I guess you did have your share of troubles after the assassination," I hoped to elicit something more from my unexpected companion.

"I certainly did. Right away, as you may know, I was jailed and interrogated. Given quite the third degree actually. The truth, as is usual in such cases, would not satisfy my interlocutors. Of course, there was no tangible evidence and, eventually, they had to let me go. Then, as soon as I was done with the police, the falling out began with some of the people who'd been most dear to me over the years. Even my good friend Sasha, Alexander Berkman, who himself was still in prison for shooting Henry Frick, criticized Czolgosz' deed. Reading his letter really shook me up. Given his own history, Sasha was the person who should have been the most sympathetic to Czolgosz. His condemnation of the assassination truly made me feel alone. Once the immediate commotion over the assassination died down, I found I was still unable to find work. The public attitude toward anarchists was quite severe at the time. Perhaps you recall Senator Hawley's offer to pay a thousand dollars for the chance to take a shot at an anarchist. So I had to take on an assumed name to find employment in nursing--E.G. Smith--not very creative but it worked."

She hesitated for a moment staring thoughtfully into the depths of her teacup. "But, really, how can I complain, considering the fate suffered by Czolgosz even before his execution? Sometime afterwards, a reporter came to see me. She had worked for one of the Buffalo papers in 1901. She was at the exposition grounds at the time of the assassination and saw the brutal treatment Leon received. Later, she covered the trial and saw him enter the courtroom, pale and emaciated, head bandaged, face swollen. He clearly had been treated very badly. But even she was taken by his brilliant gaze, what she described as large, wistful eyes roaming the courtroom. She felt a great sympathy for him."

"He did look a little bruised when he arrived at the prison. Including a few fresh ones from the mob that met him at the Auburn train station."

"Did you have any contact with his family?"

"No, I never had the chance nor, finally, the interest. His brother Waldek and his brother-in-law Bandowski were in Auburn at the time, but only briefly, and they met only with the Warden and the Superintendent. After the execution, my interest in Leon as a psychological subject was drastically diminished. I did read Doctor Channing's report in the *Journal of Insanity*. Channing concluded that Leon should not have been considered sane at the time of his trial. He seems to have spent a fair amount of time with the family. Have you read his article?"

"No, I never saw it. Channing wrote to me, asking my opinion as to whether Czolgosz was an anarchist. I replied, explaining the anarchist theory of self-defense, but I didn't hear from him again. I visited the family in 1902 when I had occasion to be in Cleveland. Czolgosz' parents were a dark people, the father hardened by toil, the stepmother with a dull, vacant look. They said Leon was a silent youth. They considered him aloof and absorbed in his books, referring to him as 'daft' and 'stuck-up.' The only one who appeared to have been kind to him was his sister. She had visited him in Buffalo, but he told her not to come again. She thought he was concerned about her ability to afford to travel. It must have been a very lonely life for him, coming out of that family and losing his mother at such an early age."

"Yes, I observed an underlying melancholia that seemed to run deeper than his stay in prison and treatment since the assassination would have caused." I realized this was an oddly clinical reply under the circumstances. Goldman did not seem to notice.

"This talk of his family reminds me of one thing that has always irked me." She paused while the waiter retrieved the empty plate that had held my sandwich. "That is the efforts by the ruling class to paint Czolgosz as other than an American. True, his father was an immigrant and spoke very poor English. But Leon and his siblings, the younger ones at least, were American born and bred. The newspapers and the politicians denounced him as a foreigner when in reality he grew up celebrating the 4th of July, taught that he too should fight for his country and die for liberty. The sad irony is that, if anything, he took those lessons too literally."

As she spoke, I understood how Emma Goldman so ably aroused the masses and struck fear into the hearts of the guardians of the status quo. Even in casual conversation, her voice took on the lofty notes of one whose words could stir men's souls. Her expression had the air of a well-practiced polemic, yet with a freshness that left me hanging on every word.

Goldman continued, "Now, you are the psychiatrist here and the expert on human motivation, but I believe firmly that it was Leon's sensitive nature that led him to see the hypocrisy and to feel the wrongs in American society more keenly than others. It is not cruelty or thirst for blood, as you well know, that induced him to strike a blow at organized power. On the contrary, it was because of his strong social instinct, because of an abundance of love and an overflow of sympathy with the pain and sorrow around us, a love which seeks refuge in the embrace of mankind, a love so strong that it shrinks before no consequence, a love so broad that it can never be wrapped up in one object as long as thousands perish, a love so all-absorbing that it can neither calculate, reason, nor investigate, but only dare at all costs."

"This sounds like a speech you've given before," I suggested, feeling a bit uncomfortable with her fervor.

She smiled. "I suppose I have. When I care deeply about something--or someone--it seems to bring out the orator in me."

"And it is a fine oration. But I think perhaps you are describing yourself more than Czolgosz,"

"Well, you don't know me very well. Do I say for certain that he is made of that material? No. Neither can I say that he was not. Clearly he impressed you that he was more than a mad assassin."

"Yes, he most assuredly did. But no one has ever been able to say for sure whether he was genuinely an anarchist."

"That's true. No one, as far as I am aware, really knew him, certainly none better than you yourself."

"Yes, and for my own purposes I concluded that he fit a vague definition of anarchist well enough. But no one who knew him understands anarchism better than you. What is your evaluation? Was Leon Czolgosz a legitimate anarchist?"

She laughed and shook her head at this question. "You must know that even Emma Goldman has no authority to say who is an anarchist and who is not. Even so, I can give you my opinion. From Czolgosz' attitude and behavior, I feel that he was a soul in pain, a soul that could find no home in this cruel world of ours. Whether or not Czolgosz belonged to an anarchist organization, it is souls like his that will one day make up the mass of men who will usher in the society of true liberty and justice.

"My work is the work of the social revolution. I embrace as comrades all those courageous enough to give their lives in a blow against tyrany. I am on the side of every rebel, whether his act has been beneficial or detrimental to our movement. I do not judge an act by its result, but by its cause; and the cause of Czolgosz' rebellious deed was the organized despotism, robbery, and exploitation of the rulers, and his innate sense of justice. His was the true anarchist spirit."

At that, she pulled a watch from her coat pocket and, checking the time, announced that she had a train to Rochester to catch.

"But first," she said, "I have answered you from my expertise as to whether Czolgosz was an anarchist. Now, you must now tell me from your standpoint as an alienist, was Leon Czolgosz sane?"

"If you mean, could he have benefitted from psychiatric treatment? He most definitely could have, as could many others who are regarded as decidedly sane by conventional standards. In our society, we often consider those who are burdened by the pain of a stark existence to be mad. And, in that sense, Leon was not sane. But, if it is insane for the downtrodden to rise up against those seen as their oppressors, then you and Joe Whelan are correct, Czolgosz was no more insane than Thomas Jefferson or Patrick Henry were in their day. Indeed, no more so than you yourself."

Emma Goldman laughed "And no doubt many do consider me mad." She smiled broadly and stood up. "Dr. Parker, I am most pleased to have made your acquaintance. I wish you continued health and prosperity and that you may, in your turn, leave your mark on mankind for the better."

Offering my hand, I wished her well in her own endeavors. And with that, she rose and took her leave from the Osborne House dining room. I never saw her again, nor any professed anarchist that I know of. But sometimes, late at night when Lucy and the children lie fast in slumber, a troubling sleeplessness lifts me from our bed to walk restlessly about the house. On such occasions, I may find myself looking a little more closely than usual into the mirror and, imagining the keen eyes of Leon Czolgosz staring back, I wonder just what kind of man I myself have become.

Author's Note
&
Acknowledgments

With the exception of Leon Czolgosz and Emma Goldman, all of the characters in this book are fictional. Although many share the names of the actual historical figures whose roles they play (e.g. Dr. Gerin, Warden Mead, Mrs. Thomas, Keeper Tupper, Dr. Stimson), they are entirely fictional and are in no way intended to represent those personages.

Little is known about Leon Czolgosz. The only person who met him and wrote about him at any length was Emma Goldman, who described two encounters with him in her autobiography. Goldman's friend and fellow-anarchist, Hippolyte Havel, wrote a short article about his encounter with Czolgosz which provides no additional information. The only serious attempt to gather information about Czolgosz' life was undertaken in 1902 by Doctor Walter Channing and his associate Doctor L. Vernon Briggs, each of whom published lengthy descriptions of their findings, Channing in his 1902 article "The Mental Status of Czolgosz, the Assassin of President McKinley," and Briggs in his 1921 book *The Manner of Man That Kills*. Neither Channing nor Briggs ever met Czolgosz during his life. All subsequent work has drawn on that of Channing and Briggs, both as to fact and as to interpretation (i.e. that Czolgosz was not a genuine anarchist but suffered from mental illness). A major departure from that trend is that of James W. Clark who, in his book *American Assassins*, attempts to situate Czolgosz in the socio-political context of his life. I found his work particularly helpful in my own project.

Despite the sparseness of detail about Czolgosz and his life, I have attempted to stick fairly closely to the available facts. Most of what is known about Czolgosz' life is recounted herein and, except for his sessions with Jonathan Parker, no fact of his life has been invented. Where I have introduced thoughts and feelings, I have endeavored to extrapolate from his known words, activities, and beliefs. There is no actual record of any of Czolgosz' dreams, of his opinions on literature (though some of the books he read are known), or of his feelings about his mother, Emma Goldman, or any of the other individuals discussed herein.

The tone of the various characters' discussion of the assassination is generally drawn from records of the time. In particular, I have endeavored to let the anarchists of the turn of the century speak in their own voice. The words of Joe Whelan in Chapter 8 are based on anarchist Jay Fox's little known 1905 pamphlet *Roosevelt, Czolgosz, and Anarchism*. The conversation among the anarchists in Chapter 15 is drawn from letters and articles which appeared in the anarchist journals of the time, many of which were reprinted by Dr. Briggs. The closing speech by "Kate," for example, is derived from an article by anarchist Kate Austin. Finally, the sentiments of Emma Goldman expressed in Chapter 17 are drawn from her often-published article *The Tragedy in Buffalo*, a variety of other articles, and her autobiography.

Among the dozens of works consulted in an effort to develop accurate portrayals of the many topics covered in this novel, the following stand out: *Alma Mater* by Helen Lefkowitz Horowitz, *Discovery of the Unconscious* by Henri F. Ellenberger, *Social Transformation of American Medicine* by Paul Starr, *Herstory* by June Sochen, *Up from the Pedestal* by Aileen S. Kraditor (editor), *Him/Her Self* by Peter Filene, *The Story of Psychology* by Morton Hunt, *Treating the Mentally Ill* by Leland V. Bell, *Vassar Women* by Agnes Rogers, *200 Years of Auburn History* by Stephanie Przybylek, and *Inside Prison Walls* by Thomas Mott Osborne (source of the Lavinsky incident described in Chapter 13).

Early readers were confused by my use of the turn-of-the-century term "woman rights". Hence, I changed it to the more modern phrase "women's rights." Similarly, although _Women and Economics_ was published when Charlotte Perkins Gilman was still married to her first husband, Charles Stetson, the name Charlotte Perkins Stetson was unfamiliar to some readers and I chose to refer to her as Gilman.

I would like to thank the following people who provided important assistance to my research: John Miskell for his knowledge of the history of Auburn Prison, Stephanie Przybylek of the Cayuga Museum, the staff of the Emma Goldman Papers at UC-Berkeley, and staff members at the Seymour Library, the Cayuga County Historian's Office, and, in particular, the Massachusetts Historical Society, where the papers of Dr. Briggs are held.

A number of friends lent their expertise to this project: special thanks to Susan Suchman Simone, Lewis Lipsitz, Claire Kirch, Peter Filene, and Sara Levine for reading and offering valuable insight on the manuscript, and to Shelton Stromquist for his knowledge of Cleveland labor history. Lastly, I can not overstate my appreciation for the help provided by my wife, Paula A. Michaels as editor, research advisor, and sounding board. Her constant support and encouragement were invaluable to the success of this project.

Daniel A. Coleman is a long-time political columnist and activist. He is the author of *Ecopolitics: Building a Green Society* (Rutgers University Press, 1994) which is being published in Chinese and Indonesian (Malay) in 2001. Coleman was invited to be the featured speaker at the McKinley Memorial Library for the centennial of the assassination of President William McKinley on September 6, 2001.